Driving Home for Christmas

EMMA HANNIGAN

HACHETTE
BOOKS
IRELAND

First published in 2012 by Hachette Books Ireland
Copyright © 2012 Emma Hannigan

1

A CIP catalogue record for this title is available from the British Library.

ISBN 978 1444 74324 1

Typeset in Book Antiqua by Bookends Publishing Services.

Printed and bound in Great Britain by Clays Ltd, St Ives plc.

Hachette Books Ireland policy is to use papers that are natural,
renewable and recyclable products and made from wood grown
in sustainable forests. The logging and manufacturing processes
are expected to conform to the environmental regulations of
the country of origin.

Hachette Books Ireland
8 Castlecourt Centre
Castleknock
Dublin 15, Ireland

A division of Hachette UK Ltd
338 Euston Road
London NW1 3BH

www.hachette.ie

For Sacha and Kim with love.
The most precious gifts I'll ever receive.

Acknowledgements

I absolutely adore Christmas time, so writing this book was a true treat.

Massive thanks must go to my lovely editor Ciara Doorley who continues to teach me so much. Thanks also to Hazel Orme for further editing, help and encouragement. Big Christmas hugs to all the lovely people at Hachette Books Ireland, especially Breda, Joanna, Ruth, Margaret and Jim. I love working with you all and am honoured to be part of the gang.

Tinsel and huge thanks for my wonderful agent Sheila Crowley of Curtis Brown who is always on my side. Thank you, lovely lady.

I am of the personal opinion that the world can never contain too much glitter. If I ruled the world everything from lampposts to shopping baskets would be encrusted in Swarovski crystals. So needless to say, Christmas is a wonderful time for unleashing that inner tackiness that I'm forced to quash in everyday existence.

My husband Cian is my polar opposite when it comes to naff decorations. As far as he's concerned one Christmas tree in the world is too many. So my sincere thanks must go to him for putting up with my decoration obsession. Last year we had six trees in total at home. I'm hoping to up that this year – even if it means erecting one in the bathroom. I admire Cian's lack of violence toward my many dancing, singing and jingling animals. Admittedly they can be terrifying, especially late at night after a couple of drinks when the dark silence is broken by the tuneless noise of a yuletide-themed creature. He doesn't share my delight in my personal favourite, a penguin that shuffles while singing 'All I want for Christmas is my two front teeth,' as it clangs tiny symbols attached to his flippers. Cian, you're quite right to point out that penguins don't have teeth nor should they wear 'creepy knitted scarves' and play percussion instruments, badly. But I guess at this point in our lives you've resigned yourself to the fact that grumbling about my decoration obsession only encourages me to buy more. Thank you for sticking by me over the years through sickness and health, in good times and bad, in spite of my unabashedly hideous taste in Christmas decorations.

Massive thanks to our son Sacha and daughter Kim for being the coolest kids on the planet. You give me so many reasons to keep going each and every day. More than that, you take the blame for some of the gaudy garlands and share my love of all things tacky.

Thanks to Mum and Dad for making each and every Christmas magical and memorable. You've passed on a love of togetherness and taught me what it means to be part of a caring family. Timmy and I are so lucky to have you both as parents. Family is the greatest gift of all.

Thanks to my brother Tim and his partner Hilary, who always buy extremely noisy presents for the kids at Christmas – the glockenspiel and electronic drum machine were particularly noteworthy last year. Believe me, it's all chalked down for future reference.

Christmas kisses to all my incredible extended family and ever-present friends who bolster and support me all the time, with a special mention to our au pair Camila.

Cathy Kelly is always there and my angel on earth, thank you from the bottom of my heart.

I've had the unexpected privilege of getting to know Katie Taylor this year. She's my hero – an inspiration to women and living proof that dreams come true. I am humbled to call her a friend. Thank you for lifting the hearts of the nation by winning gold at the Olympics and showing the world what can be achieved.

Thank you most sincerely to all my amazing readers who contact me and send me heartfelt letters and messages each and every day. Without you all I wouldn't be in a position to write. I'm holding out a cracker for you to pull with me!

In my mind Christmas is about showing the people around you how much you care. It's about making the effort to invite family and friends over for a drink or a bite of food. It's about looking back over the year you've just come through. And most of all it's about looking forward with positive excitement to all the surprises that lie ahead during the next twelve months.

I hope your home is dripping in decorations. I call on you all to embrace your inner glitter. Please, wear that silly paper hat, read aloud those terrible jokes. Spread the Christmas cheer!

I hope you enjoy *Driving Home for Christmas*. I've adored writing it – I was able to continue to languish in that wonderful yuletide zone for longer than usual this year! How great is that? If you could possibly read *Driving Home for Christmas* in front of the fire with a group of mechanical bears dressed in stripy knitted hats and scarves, preferably singing and dancing at the same time, I'd be so proud. If not I'll just imagine that you are, if that's okay with you?

Merry Christmas one and all and I hope your dreams come true in the months ahead.

Love and Christmas light to you all!

Emma

Prologue

✳✳✳

Dear Maggie

I know it's been a few days since I last wrote but it's all been a bit busy here at Huntersbrook. Your grandchildren all made a recent appearance so at least I can fill you in there. Young Joey was here with that madam of a girlfriend again. I know I'm the housekeeper and my job is to keep the place tidy, but that one seems to think I'm her personal slave.

If you were still here she wouldn't be swanning around doing the Lady Muck act, I can tell you. Your Holly might be able to crack the whip when she has to, but even she seems to be no match for this Sophia one.

Lainey was home for the hunt at the weekend. I popped over to have a bit of a chinwag and help Holly and Paddy with the teas and coffees. I never get tired of the spectacle of the hounds sniffing around as the horses and ponies dance and stamp in excitement as they wait for the Master to sound the horn. They'd a fine big crowd, which was great. At least this recession isn't stopping people enjoying the outdoors.

Lainey tells me she has a new friend at the office, who sounds like a bit of craic. It's about time that girl got out and had some fun while she's still young. I know she's a great horsewoman but that mare won't help with the loneliness when she's too old to fling herself around the fields.

Old Mr Cromwell was here lashing into the refreshments as usual. I'd swear he inhales the tea and sandwiches, they disappear so fast. He still asks after you every time I see him. God bless him, it's more than fifty years since your Stanley passed away and the poor old divil still seems to hold a torch for you. I told him you're having a wonderful time in Australia with Sid and how much you enjoy living in a vineyard, but he goes selectively deaf when I mention that. No fool like an old fool, eh, Maggie?

Pippa's still Pippa. What more can I say? Lives the high life, that one. Maybe she took all the fun and left her poor older sister with none. Do you think that's the way it works in families? She's off to New York now. Christmas shopping with the girls, she says. I don't know what's wrong with the shops in Wicklow but, as she'd be quick enough to point out, I haven't a clue! Holly asked her how she was funding it all and she did her usual flick of the hair and said, 'You worry too much, Mum.' You can't help but love her all the same. I'm probably just jealous because I'm still here doing the same thing I've done for nearly half a century.

I'd better press on – those stairs won't Hoover themselves. It takes me a lot longer now. I'm not as young as I used to be!

Mind yourself, Maggie, and don't forget to write back. I know it's been eleven months since I started this email lark with you, but I'm still terrified of hitting the wrong button and sending my letter to outer space.

Thank you for saying you enjoy my turn of phrase when I write. I suppose I'm using our little exchanges to put that writing course I did to some use. I never did manage to sit and write that novel! But at least I feel it wasn't totally wasted now.

I've remembered to do that spell-check thing you mentioned this time. I still laugh when I think of that error in my last email – what a difference one vowel can make in a word.

Bye for now, Maggie,

Your trusty friend,

Sadie

1

It's Beginning to Look a Lot Like Christmas

❄❄❄

Lainey could just about recognise a mutilated rendition of Wham's 'Last Christmas' as she stepped into the lift. She had to put up with it until the doors slid open to reveal over-the-top decorations with fuzzy polar bears in an array of stripy knitted accessories and more glittery baubles than you could shake a sparkly wand at. She had never been a shopping fan, and immersing herself in the pre-Christmas madness was possibly a step too far. This had been a spur-of-the-moment idea, which had evolved just before she and Jules had come out for lunch.

Lainey had grown up in the Wicklow countryside and was more comfortable in the family home, Huntersbrook House, than she was in the bustle at House of Fraser.

'Lainz! Isn't this magical?' Jules rushed over and linked her arm.

'Our ideas of magic are poles apart, Jules. Give me a frosty field just begging to be cantered across any day,' Lainey said, as the in-store music and warmth engulfed them.

'You're so funny! You sound like something from that film about the talking pig! There's to be no Mrs Farmer Brown with me at the office party this year,' Jules insisted. 'You're going to rock up in *the* most sexy gear.'

'That sounds great,' Lainey said, beginning to quiver.

'This is the best place to start,' Jules assured her. 'It's a bit like a selection box for clothes. A little taster of a whole pile of shops.'

As Jules snatched up garments and held them aloft, Lainey watched awestruck. This girl was a purchase-pro. Not only was she totally in her own comfort zone, but she was precise and speedy with it, moving with the stealth of a panther zoning in on her prey. Lainey could almost hear Sir David Attenborough's excited whispering: 'As she assesses the rails, engaging with her Yuletide instincts, she adapts immediately, clicking into outfit-for-the-office-party mode. The straight males of the species shy away from the fashion outlet, knowing their presence is superfluous. After they've been snapped at in this situation, they know to leave the female to her task, instead congregating at a nearby electrical or music store until she has secured an item that isn't that-old-thing. When possible, the male takes their young with him, as the normally protective and nurturing female can become irrational and mildly violent.'

'You haven't picked up a single thing. Don't you like the stuff in here?' Jules asked, breaking her reverie.

'Eh, yeah. Well, it's not really that,' Lainey felt pressurised, like a fawn confronted by a pack of coyotes. 'I'm just not great in shops. I tend to feel as if my throat is closing and I'm going to fall down in a big messy heap to be left for dead under a pile of hangers. I really meant it when I told you in work that I don't do the clothes thing.'

'Gosh!' Jules was astonished. 'You really weren't joking when you said you've worn the same black dress to the office party for the last three years running.'

'Pretty much,' Lainey said, flushing. 'I don't mind coming shopping with you, but please just do what you usually do. I'll watch.'

'Poor Lainz,' Jules said, stroking her arm and looking at her as if she'd just divulged a terminal cancer diagnosis. 'I'll help you. I mightn't be as good as you in the office but I certainly know how to shop! Come on!'

Lainey was catapulted into a cramped dressing room with an opaque glass door and instructed to take off her work suit. She wasn't sure about stripping in the company of a colleague but she hadn't the foggiest idea how to say no without offending her. But Seth had told her a million times how awful she was at picking clothes so she probably needed any help she could get.

'What size are you, Lainz?' Jules called.

'My suit is a twelve,' she said. With a dry mouth, Lainey wondered if she should've said sixteen. If Jules tried to dress her in her own style, things might get sticky. To say the girls were polar opposites was putting it mildly: Jules went for the least amount of clothing possible in every situation while Lainey was practicality's demonstration model.

'I have two dresses which I think would be über-stunning on you,' Jules said, reappearing. 'But I'm leaning towards the red.'

'Really?' Lainey said, hoping that she didn't look as uncomfortable as she felt. 'I don't think I've worn red since I was a teenager. Seth, he's my ex-boyfriend, hated that colour. Said it made me look like a tomato.'

'When did you break up?'

'Just over a year ago.'

'Are you still in contact? Do you meet for the odd shag, coffee or beer?'

'No! We didn't end on good terms,' Lainey confessed. 'I haven't seen him at all, but I'm still friends with him on Facebook.' She dropped her eyes, regretting that Jules now knew she still cared what he thought. 'It means I can keep tabs on him and avoid him.'

'Totally,' Jules said. As she held the tight red satin bandeau-style dress against her, Lainey swallowed. 'Give it a shot and if you hate it we'll find something else, yeah?'

She pulled the cubicle door shut as Lainey yanked on the dress.

'Well?' Jules asked, through the glass. 'Like it or hate it?'

'Um, I honestly don't know if I'd have the nerve to wear it.'

'Can I see?'

Lainey opened the door, walked out and stared at herself in the long wall mirror.

'Wowzers, you look amazing! Step into these shoes,' Jules said, grabbing the pair that belonged to the changing room. 'If you had a nice necklace, some dramatic, smoky eye makeup and bright red lipstick, you'd stop traffic in it!'

'Ah, go on out of that! I'm hardly wolf-whistle material!' she said uncertainly.

'Says who?'

'I'm either in jodhpurs, my biking leathers or a work suit. So this kind of thing is totally not me.'

'But you can so wear it!' Jules said. 'Look at how toned you are! Most girls would kill for your legs. All that throwing yourself around the hedges and ditches has certainly banished any chance of cellulite! I'm loving the red against your dark hair. Ooh, yeah, I'm seeing you as a young Demi Moore in this look. Work it. Walk it. Believe it,' Jules instructed.

Lainey burst out laughing. 'You're like a model and I'm like the Hunchback of Notre Dame's estranged twin sister shambling along behind you!' she said, as they strutted down the aisle between the cubicles towards the full-length mirror.

'It's all in here,' Jules said, tapping her head. 'Think sexy and you will be.'

'I wish I had your confidence.' Lainey bit her lip.

'Listen, I don't know what that Seth bloke did to you. Clearly you had an awful time with him. But don't you feel good about the Lainz in that mirror right now?'

'You're like Gok Wan.' Lainey smiled. 'I suppose if I had some makeup on and downed half a bottle of wine I might be able to get through an evening in this.'

'That's good enough for me. Now take that dress off, pay for it and we'll go for a bit of food before you change your mind. I think you should buy the shoes too, actually. They always put current bestsellers in these changing rooms, so ask at the till and the girls will get you a fresh pair.'

'Right so.' Lainey took a deep breath. 'Thanks, Jules. I appreciate your advice. I'm not sure I'll be able to walk in these all evening, though. I have some at home with a lower heel and they'd be more comfortable.'

'This, my darling girl,' Jules said, with an exaggerated sweep of her arm, 'is not about comfort. It's about being a siren! Sirens don't think about comfort. Anyway, all you need are those gel party insoles. Put them in the shoes and take two paracetamol washed down with half a bottle of schnapps! When you can't feel your feet, they don't hurt! Simple!'

'Okay so,' Lainey said, grinning sheepishly. 'I'll do as I'm told! Thanks.'

'Pleasure, doll! See you in a sec.' Jules shot off to look at more glittery clothes.

Lainey shut the cubicle door and scrutinised herself. This dress would never have graced her hips in a million years without Jules's insistence. But maybe this was the push she needed to come out of herself. It had been kind of Jules to compare her to Demi Moore, but all Lainey could see was an uneasy blocky-looking woman, with a sensible short haircut and about as much confidence as a mouse.

By the time she was back in her suit, Jules was in front of the mirror again. 'I have to have this! Isn't the colour just electric?' she bubbled.

'Certainly is,' Lainey said, trying not to stare like a goldfish. The kelly green shiny thing must have been manufactured as a belt, she thought, but on Jules it had turned into a revealing tube dress. 'If you love it, you should buy it,' she said. 'And it's nearly half past. We should pay, grab a sandwich and get back to the office. I'm going to take the red dress.'

'Good for you,' Jules called from inside a cubicle, where she was hurrying back into her work clothes. 'I wouldn't tell you to buy it if I didn't think you'd look brilliant. Okay, I'm coming!'

As they left the shop, Jules linked Lainey's arm. 'I'm so excited you took the dress. But I hope I didn't force it on you? There's no point in having it if you're not going to wear it. It's one thing my telling you it's gorgeous, but you have to feel good in it.'

'I know – and I suppose I need to push myself out of my usual plain black.'

'Not at all! I'm impressed that you're willing to try a new look.'

They went into a sandwich bar, where they ordered bagels and coffee. It was so packed they were lucky to find two high stools where they could perch and eat.

'My younger sister Pippa is more like you,' Lainey resumed. 'She's mad into her fashion and can't understand why I don't spend every cent I earn on shoes like she does.'

'It takes all sorts, Lainz,' Jules said, through a mouthful. 'Do the rest of your family like horses and motorbikes too?'

'Pippa hasn't ridden for years, and my brother Joey is a triathlon freak. He runs, cycles and swims his way through the week.'

'Cool! I'd be dead after five minutes doing any kind of exercise. My only nod towards anything healthy involves a dance floor.'

'Well, it seems to work for you – you're tiny.' Lainey giggled. Jules was probably most men's dream girl: with her petite frame, long straight hair and ample bosom, she had curves in all the right places.

'I thought you were a real rock chick when I met you dressed in full leathers on my first morning in the council office last month.'

'And now you're getting to know me you've worked out that I'm really just a sensible old maid,' Lainey said, smiling.

'Oh, I didn't mean it like that. How old are you anyway?'

'I was only kidding you. I'm thirty. My motorbike suits me because I live halfway between work, here in Dublin, and my family home in Wicklow. I can zip up the motorway and I don't have to worry about the traffic.'

'Do you go home a lot at weekends, then?'

'Yeah, I still hunt and I've a mare that needs exercising so I usually head back to Wicklow after work on Friday. What about yourself?'

'I moved out of home about a year ago. I rent a place near the city centre so I take the Luas to the office. I don't get on with my mum and I've no other family.' Suddenly Jules looked sad.

'That's tough. Huntersbrook House, my family home, is like a B&B at times, always people coming and going. My folks have a livery yard so they look after horses, and the hunt meets there during the season. I've grown up with a whirl of activity going on around me. So I can't imagine anything else.'

'That sounds wonderful,' Jules said wistfully. 'Still, I've great friends, and things had become so stressful with Mum that it seemed better we steer clear of one another for a while.'

Lainey finished her bagel, drained her coffee and wondered what Jules's mother was like that she could shun such a sweet daughter. Especially when they had only each other. 'We'd better head back to the office,' she said. 'Drake-ula will be hovering like the snake he is, dying to catch us being late back.'

'Is he always so mean?' Jules asked, as she tottered along beside Lainey in her high heels.

'He's in a permanent bad mood. Try not to take it personally. He hates everyone with equal intensity,' Lainey told her.

'Did you hear what he said to me this morning?'

'Yeah, the git.'

'I was so grateful when you came over to rescue me – I honestly thought I was going to start blubbing in front of the whole office,' Jules confided. 'Who would have thought buying him an iced finger instead of a Danish pastry would make him so angry? It's a tad boring going to Spar every morning for the same thing, so I thought I'd go wild and get something different!' She giggled. 'I won't bother in future. He really loses his rag when he gets going, doesn't he?'

'Don't mind him,' Lainey murmured, as they entered the office building once more. 'His real name is Dougal and he puts on that accent. He's from a dodgy part of town. Mike in Accounts went to school with him.'

'Seriously? It's amazing how some people can be so scary on the outside yet they're really unsure underneath,' Jules said, as they went into their office. They grinned at each other, then made their way to their respective cubicles.

With only a few weeks to Christmas the council offices were humming. As far as Lainey could make out the entire county wanted the world put to rights in time for the holiday season. She barely looked up from her desk for the next hour until Drake strolled over.

'You might want to give your new best friend a few pointers,' he said, with a lopsided grin.

'Pardon?' Lainey tried not to glower at him.

'Barbie over there is in charge of our leg of the Christmas party this year. It's an Abba night in the Regency Hotel, according to the email,' Drake said, tucking his nylon shirt into his high-waisted trousers, then smoothing his comb-over. 'Seeing as she can't even go to the Spar and find the right pastry, it might be a plan to tell her what's involved with the Kris Kindle thing and make damn sure she has the right numbers for our table. I don't want to look like a gobshite in front of the other managers.'

Lainey would've loved to say he'd do a fantastic job of being a gobshite without any outside help, but experience had taught her to smile and suck it up. Drake was her boss and at the end of the day she didn't really give a toss what he did as long as he kept off her back. She'd never given him any reason to dislike her and preferred to keep it that way.

'Still, Barbie is my idea of the perfect woman,' Drake sneered, as he licked a pocket of spit from the corner of his mouth. 'A body by Mattel and brains by Captain Birdseye.'

'What on earth do you mean?' Lainey asked.

'Mattel – the people who make Barbie dolls?'

'Yeah, I get that bit.'

'And the brain of a pea – Captain Birdseye!'

'That's just nasty.' Lainey was annoyed with herself for falling into his trap. She picked up her desk phone, making clear that she had finished talking to him. She rang Jules and filled her in on her party duties.

'It sounds like it could be a good laugh!' Jules said enthusiastically. 'I live literally across the road from the Regency Hotel too, so you can stay at mine afterwards if you want,' she offered.

'Thanks a million. I might take you up on that,' Lainey said.

'We can get ready together and have a couple of drinks before we go.'

'Good plan,' Lainey agreed, suddenly feeling less stressed about it all. 'If you've any questions about organising it or the Kris Kindle thing, let me know. I did it for a few years. The main thing is to give everyone a date to respond by. I'll send you the email I used before, if you like.'

'Thanks, Lainz! The Kris Kindle is where I put all our department's names in a hat, we pick one each and buy a present for that person, yes? It's like Secret Santa, isn't it?'

'Yeah, you've got it. The gift mustn't cost more than twenty euro and we're not meant to know who gave which present.'

'Love it!' Jules shrilled. 'That means you can get something naughty if your person's annoyed you all year – or, even better, a rattlesnake for Drake-ula!'

'You're wicked.' Lainey laughed. 'It's meant to create goodwill and a lovely warm feeling between us colleagues.'

'Yeah, right.' Jules snorted. 'It's revenge in Christmas wrapping, if you ask me.'

By four o'clock Lainey had a headache and decided to take her cup of tea outside. 'Want to get a breath of air?' she asked Jules.

'I'd love to.'

'That office gets so stuffy and smells of crisps mixed with *eau de* sandwich,' Lainey said as they perched on the low wall outside the office.

'Are you bringing anyone to the Christmas party?' Jules asked.

'No,' Lainey said. 'What about you? Do you have a boyfriend at the moment?'

'Well, it's kind of messy. My love life's gone a bit Pete Tong lately so I'll be on my own.'

'We can keep each other company, then,' Lainey said. 'The party's one of those things that's a real chore but has to be done.'

'I felt like a weight had been lifted off my shoulders when my last relationship ended. The idea of going out with someone just brings me out in a rash at the moment.

I'm sure if and when I meet the right person I'll change my mind, but until then I'm happy to be single.'

'I love being able to get on my bike and go wherever the mood takes me.' She paused. 'Can I make a confession?'

'What?' Jules leaned in closer.

'The staff Christmas party frightens the bejesus out of me. There. I've said it. I'd rather turn up disguised as a Christmas tree so I can blend into the background and nobody will expect me to entertain them with gas anecdotes from the office or the mad plans I have for Christmas. The very idea of having to banter with people I hardly know makes me want to crawl into a corner and rock.'

'This year will be great,' Jules told her firmly. 'We'll have a few bevvies while we're getting ready and if you wear that red dress you'll be beating the men off with a stick.'

'I don't know about that,' Lainey said, with a giggle. 'Still, thanks to you, I won't be dreading it as much as I usually do.'

'I'm looking forward to it, actually. I'll be on my own for Christmas – the girls I share my flat with are Slovakian and going home for the festive season, so I'll be glad to go anywhere I'm asked. Even a party with Drake-ula! How sad am I?'

'Listen, my family always has a big Christmas vibe. We've a ton of spare rooms and Mum loves to entertain. Why don't you think about joining us? You'd be so welcome,' Lainey offered.

'Seriously?' Jules was astonished.

'Totally. My sister Pippa and brother Joey will be there too and I'd be surprised if they don't have at least one friend each. The more the merrier in our house.'

'That's so kind of you, Lainz, and I'm really tempted . . .'

'Think it over, no pressure.'

But, as they moved back inside, Lainey really hoped Jules would come to Huntersbrook House. She was going to find Christmas without Grandma really strange, but her friend's presence might make up a bit for her absence.

2

Deck the Halls With Boughs of Holly!

❋❋❋

Dear Maggie,

It was great to hear all your news. I can't say I know what you mean about the difference between those grapes. I'd take a glass of wine if someone offered me one but outside of it being red or white I'd be a bit stumped. Now, I've had both, of course, but I'm no expert.

I'm not being a tell-tale but I'm sure you'd prefer to know that it looks like Jacob from next door won't be able to rent the four acres any longer. He dropped in yesterday and asked to speak to Holly and Paddy. I offered to make the tea and a few ham sandwiches with that French mustard Paddy adores. It seems he's not able to keep up with the lambing on account of his age. Said it's not worth the hassle. Cynthia has been diagnosed with dementia – the straw that broke the camel's back. She's very confused and can't be left on her own for long. Poor Jacob is taking it very badly. They're a lovely couple and my heart goes out to them. He's very bitter about their lad Matt. They never saw eye-to-eye, especially since he went to England to do an office job.

The good thing is that Matt's coming home to help mind his mam. He's obviously a decent lad if he's coming back when he's needed, but Jacob didn't want to hear that so I kept my opinion to myself.

The other exciting news is that Jacob's new helper arrived. He's from Australia and is called Scott. I asked him if he knows your fella Sid but he drew a blank. All I can tell you, Maggie, is that he's given me a whole new reason to make soup. Your granddaughters could do worse in my humble opinion.

Lainey's birthday is only a week away. I can't believe it's the start of December tomorrow. Christmas will be upon us before we know it. What'll you do down there, Maggie? Do they make it feel like Christmas even though the sun is shining? I can't begin to imagine it.

You did indeed jog my memory when you mentioned Holly and Paddy's wedding. No, I can't get over the fact it's thirty-one years ago this New Year's Eve. Indeed we did almost lose our rag altogether over Holly's dress. No other bride would insist on eating toast with raspberry jam on the way out the door to the church, but that stubborn streak you like to grumble about wasn't licked off the stones, Maggie.

Do you think your Stanley, Lord rest him, sent Paddy to balance out his two fiery women? I've said it before and I'll say it again, Paddy fell from his horse on the hunt that day so Holly could scoop him up, ferry him back to your kitchen and fall in love with him. He's still as mild-mannered and steady as he ever was, a darling man. When Holly had that episode after Lainey was born, a lesser man would've been gone.

Lainey's doing well, to answer your question. She's not as

haunted-looking. I know I didn't tell you that before, but that's the way she was when you went last December. An orphaned lamb up the back field would've been less upset. She's finally stopped mentioning Seth. I didn't keep my feelings about him a secret when they were dating and I still don't. He was a nasty piece of work, and Lainey's a gentle soul. She needs a man more like her father. But that's another day's email, Maggie! I'll be sure to give her that hug you sent her. Your parcel arrived and I have it kept aside in the pantry. I'll make sure she gets it the second she arrives home for her birthday at the weekend.

I'm all about stews in the oven at the moment. Unlike you with your barbecue and outdoor eating, we're trying to stay warm and cosy here! It's very cold this winter: you picked a good one to avoid, I can assure you. If I'm not wrong we're in for snow in the next couple of weeks. Who knows? Maybe we'll have a white Christmas.

I think I'll be putting extra herbs in casseroles to ensure they're especially tasty. I think Scott will like that. He's a fine-looking fella. I know I'm over the hill but I can still appreciate, can't I?

Mind yourself, Maggie,

Your friend,

Sadie

Each year once December dawned Holly came into her own. Huntersbrook House – her stone-built, double-fronted Georgian home – lent itself so beautifully to being decorated. It could be made to look like a scene on a Christmas card, and each year she enjoyed every minute of the build-up to the great day. As she cuddled into Paddy in their ancient iron bed she murmured, 'I'll be getting the Christmas patchwork quilt cover out today. I know it's countdown time once that's in place.'

'When we got married, I thought if I humoured you for a year or two about the whole Christmas obsession you'd lose interest,' he joked. 'In fact you've got worse.'

Holly threw back the quilt and got out of bed.

'Take it easy, woman, it's cold in here!' he complained, but he was smiling.

'I'm so excited!' She shot off to root in the hot press. Soon she was back with the red, white and green cover. She'd made it while she was pregnant with Lainey. Each evening as her tummy had grown bigger, so too had the quilt. Now, thirty-one years later, as she spread it lovingly on their bed, she took a step back and admired it. The white brought out the moulding in the ceiling above. It never ceased to amaze her how something as simple as changing the bed linen could alter the mood of the room. Their usual saffron quilt cover gave off a calming warmth, which she'd enjoy again in the new year. For now, though, she thrilled to the Christmas atmosphere.

'I think I'd like to get two red shades for our bedside lamps,' she mused.

'Holly, we don't need any more Christmas stuff. You should've married Santa Claus!'

But Holly didn't hear him: she had already charged out of their room and down the sweeping staircase. In a few days' time she'd have the whole place twinkling and sparkling. The wide wooden stairway was crying out for swags and tiny lights, and this year she'd picked up yards of thick, luxurious red velvet ribbon: she planned to tie it into huge plump bows, adding an Edwardian edge to the decorations.

Last year she'd been obsessed with white. She'd bought a box of plain white baubles and pristine white satin ribbon. She'd loved its crisp effect against the green foliage – and she'd been able to use her white napkins and tablecloths, no need to buy anything else. But from the moment she'd allowed herself to contemplate Christmas, straight after Hallowe'en this year, she'd known red would be this year's colour.

Sadie hadn't arrived yet so Holly put the kettle on the Aga and popped a couple of rashers into a pan. She'd make some toast and a big pot of tea to ease them into the day. Finding her notebook and pen, she made a list of jobs to be done. It was only Thursday but she knew the weekend would be upon them in jig time and she wanted to be organised.

But instead of her usually steady scrawl, the page filled with tears, smudging the pale blue lines. Holly's hands shook. She dabbed her eyes with a tissue she'd tucked up her sleeve, and willed herself to stop crying.

Gazing around her beloved kitchen, she couldn't imagine waking up in any other house. It had been her home for ever, her mother's and grandmother's before hers. The reality of what might be about to happen was almost unbearable.

At the sound of Paddy's footsteps descending the stairs she caught her breath and rushed to the sink where she splashed her face with cold water. She patted it dry on her apron and positioned herself at the Aga just as her husband entered the kitchen.

'That toast smells good,' Paddy said, as he joined her.

'Will you get a chance to gloss the front door today?' Holly asked, hoping Paddy wouldn't sense her upset.

He grinned. She'd be like a cat on a griddle now until she got at least some of her decorating under way. 'When I've had breakfast I'll sand it and try to do the first coat. I think I'll go for a duck-egg blue this time,' he said. He picked up the paper and began to leaf through it.

'You most certainly will not!' Holly exploded. 'If it's not cherry red it's not home.'

They had the same discussion every year. It was almost as traditional as Christmas itself.

'Quite apart from the fact that Huntersbrook House has always had a red door, I'm all about red velvet this year,' she went on.

'Great,' Paddy said, distracted now.

'Are you listening to me?' Holly swatted his arm.

'Huh? Of course I am,' Paddy said. He put the paper aside and filled the mugs with tea. Holly buttered the thick toast and piled the rashers on top. Paddy sat down in his customary chair which offered a view of the garden. 'Nothing quite like hot buttered toast as you're looking out at the frost, is there?' he observed.

'Indeed there isn't,' Sadie called from the side door. 'Morning, all.'

'Morning, Sadie,' Holly said. 'Sit you down and I'll get you a mug.'

'It's a sharp one out there today. You'll need a woolly hat,' she said, blowing on her hands.

'I'm headed for the back field to gather holly and ivy for my wreath,' Holly announced.

'Thought you might,' Sadie said, smiling.

'I wonder if there'll be many berries this year.' Paddy refilled his mug.

'We'll soon see,' Holly said, wriggling her shoulders.

After breakfast she went to find a pair of sharp scissors to cut the greenery, then pulled on a thick sweater and her coat.

She thought of her mother in Australia, lolling about in the sun totally unaware of the bubbling pool of bother that was threatening to hit Huntersbrook House.

Her meeting with Jacob had kept Holly awake for hours last night. She understood where he was coming from: he was too old to continue with the amount of livestock he currently owned. But the loss of the money he contributed was catastrophic. Things had been balanced on a knife edge as it was. But this latest blow meant Holly might be forced to make a decision she'd never previously contemplated.

She fought back fresh tears angrily. She'd never been one for crying. In fact, people who made a habit of it annoyed her. But the prospect of losing Huntersbrook House was overwhelming. Holly felt sorry for Paddy, the children, the animals – it would affect them all profoundly. More than that, though, she was ashamed. This house had been in her family for generations and she was about to lose it – unless some miracle occurred.

'I'll see you both in a while,' she called, injecting as much cheer as she could into her voice. As she whistled for Jess and Millie to follow her, the sight of their eager faces and wagging tails added to her sadness. The dogs adored running across the land and lazing in front of the Aga on cold days . . .

The low winter sun cast a soft buttery glow over the glistening grass. Holly bumped the jeep to the thickest hedges at the boundary of their land, then got out and stood where she was, enjoying the vista, despite her anxiety. She never tired of the rolling fields and welcoming sturdiness of Huntersbrook House. Many people moved several times in their lives and thought of home as a place to put furniture, but to her, Huntersbrook was so much more than that. It represented who she was. Its stature and grandeur made her feel secure and safe. She was proud to be the third generation of her family to inhabit the beautiful Georgian house.

Feeling the damp chilly air penetrating the many layers of her clothes, she knew she needed to get on with her task. She snipped away until she had a large, tangled pile of holly and ivy, then stooped to pick it up and toss into the car boot. Now she had to dig out the moss in the garden, and then she'd be ready to make the wreath. She got in, started the engine, and did her best to assume a cheery expression. The last thing Paddy needed was someone moping around as if the world was ending.

The sound of Sadie's singing mixed with the hum of the Hoover emanated from the living room. She'd the voice of a strangled cat, Holly mused, as she unloaded her moss and then the foliage into the kitchen, glad to have the warmth of the Aga engulf her. She went into the pantry where she found several wire coat hangers. She pulled them apart, then fashioned them into a large wide hoop, the base for her wreath, to be covered with moss first, then layers of holly and ivy . . .

When Holly stepped back to look at her handiwork, the lurking dread she was determined to bury taunted her. This might be the last time she'd hang a wreath on the front door. It might even be the last time she'd have the materials to make one. This time next year, she and Paddy might be living in a tiny apartment. If they were lucky . . .

'Hi, love. That looks great.' Holly started as Paddy came

up behind her. 'What's with the glum face? Aren't you happy with it?'

'Don't creep up on me like that, for goodness' sake,' she snapped.

'Sorry! I didn't creep – I was putting the paint away and I thought you saw me coming towards you from the shed,' he said, looking stung.

'Sorry, I was miles away.' Holly shook herself. 'Let's just get on with making the place look special, and we mustn't forget Lainey's birthday is on Saturday and then we'll be on the countdown to Christmas. There's lots to be thankful for,' she said, to bolster her own mood as much as Paddy's.

'Well, you're off to a winning start, love. That's going to be the best wreath ever,' he said.

'You say that every year,' Holly said, 'but it's pretty impressive, I have to admit. Just wait till I add the red ribbon. How's the front door coming along?'

'It's done. This stunning creation can take its place on the hook tomorrow. What time is the hunt leaving on Sunday morning?'

Huntersbrook was one of the favourite venues in the locality for the Wicklow Hunt. With more than a hundred members it was one of the longest-established ones around, and Maggie had been Master for many years. As well as supplying them with lots of great social opportunities, it was a steady form of revenue for Huntersbrook. Even now when people were cutting back on most things, local horsemen and -women continued to pay their cap and gallop across the land each week.

'Nine thirty, so I want it up before then. Joey's coming at the weekend so I'll get him to do the pillars on either side of the front door with you.'

'Is he bringing Sophia?' Paddy asked.

'Apparently. If she'll come,' Holly said, with a flicker of irritation.

'I didn't think she'd last as long as she has.'

'Me neither, but Joey seems smitten so who are we to argue? He's the one living with her. We only see her the odd time.'

'She's so different from us,' Paddy mused. 'She looks on the fields as a running track. She doesn't understand country ways because she's a city girl. And when she met our Joey on that training course she wasn't on the lookout for a fella.'

'I know, but I find it hard to bite my tongue at times. She makes no effort to meet us halfway. It's like she's right and we're wrong and there's no wriggle room,' Holly said. 'It's Joey I feel sorry for. She puts him in such an awkward position.'

'As long as he's happy . . .'

Holly squeezed her eyes shut in frustration. It bothered her that Sophia looked down her nose at Huntersbrook. She hadn't said it to Paddy and she certainly wouldn't let Joey know how she felt, but she took it as a personal insult that Sophia had so little respect for their family home. 'I'll make sure we have all the food we need for the weekend. Jacob gave us a gorgeous lamb for the freezer to soften the blow of him pulling out of his rental agreement,' she said. 'I've asked Sadie to put a stew together for Lainey's birthday meal. We've enough veggies in the greenhouse to keep us going for now.'

'I meant to tell you Mrs Healy gave me the nod that she has a turkey for us for Christmas. I didn't want to take money from her last week – I was only an hour moving the two horses for her – so she insisted on giving us one of her birds.'

'That's generous of her and most welcome,' Holly said. 'I can barter with Jim for a ham too. His three grandchildren want to hunt on St Stephen's Day so I'll waive their cap.'

'Good plan,' Paddy agreed. 'I've spoken to our kids and we're all agreed on doing a small token gift to open on Christmas morning. I can't bear the prospect of wasting a lot of money on stuff no one wants.'

'Neither can I,' Holly said. 'Everyone's feeling the pinch of this recession.'

'Is Pippa coming down for Lainey's birthday too?' Paddy asked.

'No, she's going to New York tomorrow, remember? She's back late on Saturday night but she won't make it down here, needless to say.'

'Fair play to Pippa,' he said, with a shake of his head. 'She's opting out of the recession, isn't she?'

'So it seems.'

Sadie came into the kitchen from the pantry, carrying a leg of lamb studded with rosemary and garlic.

'That looks divine, Sadie.' Holly moved across the kitchen to wash her hands in the sink. 'There's rather a lot of meat for us, though. Are we expecting a crowd?'

'Well, I bumped into young Scott on my way over and I told him we'd a fine lump of meat on offer, so I think he's coming. Lord only knows who else might show up,' Sadie replied.

'You've certainly been very generous with the herbs there.' Paddy smirked.

'I'm all about all things tasty at the moment.' Sadie winked.

Holly dried her hands as she watched Sadie tossing piles of vegetables into a huge pot for soup. She could probably fit into it herself – she'd the physique of a sparrow, with fluffy white hair and wiry little arms and legs. She ate a big dinner in the middle of the day and rarely more than that. Otherwise it was mere pecking at a scone or a biscuit plus copious cups of tea. Still, Holly mused, appearances could be deceiving. She'd enough spirit and will to contend with anyone, from stubborn children to Maggie, who was easily roused to fury.

When the children were small Sadie had effortlessly balanced them on one hip as she'd manoeuvred the old upright Hoover with the other. Her position as housekeeper had evolved naturally. She and Maggie had been friends for years. When Maggie's husband Stanley had died after a short illness, she'd been the first person in the back door to make her a cup of tea, then bring Holly into the living room and read her a story.

Maggie had come to depend on her and look forward to her frequent visits. With the running of Huntersbrook House, the land and the yard dumped in her lap, she had known she needed help so she'd offered Sadie a wage to continue doing what she'd naturally begun. Now, all these years later, Sadie was as much a part of the Huntersbrook House family as the Craigs themselves. She had no family of her own.

'Would you not prefer to move in?' Maggie had asked her, a long time ago.

'Thank you, Maggie, but I like my cottage. I know I only dip in and out of it, and the entire building would fit easily in the hallway here, but it's still home.'

'I didn't mean it like that,' Maggie had said, blushing.

'I know you didn't, lovey,' Sadie said mildly. 'But the fact of the matter is that there's no place like home, no matter where that may be.'

Over the years the ladies in the village had often questioned her about the Craigs. People loved to know the ins and outs of other folks' lives. But it became apparent rather quickly that Sadie would never broadcast the goings-on at Huntersbrook so they stopped probing.

'Maggie showed me how to roast lamb with rosemary and garlic. I was useless in the kitchen when I first came here,' Sadie told Holly.

'I can't image you ever being useless, Sadie,' she said fondly. 'I know I'd be lost without you. You're my angel.'

'Ah, bless you, dear,' Sadie said. 'I'm a poor substitute for your mum but I appreciate the sentiment.'

'You're certainly not a poor substitute,' Holly shot back. 'You're wonderful and you're still here, which is more than can be said for her. She's swilling wine with that old codger on the far side of the world.'

'Indeed she is, and sure fair play to her,' Sadie said. 'Now where is this wreath you were working on? Is it finished yet?'

'It is.' Holly brightened. 'The door's had its lick of paint too, so I'll hang it first thing in the morning.'

'Ah, sure we're flying along here,' Sadie said cheerfully. 'Give me a lift with the pot like a good girl. Once it's up on the stove it can bubble away and we'll have enough soup for the weekend as well.'

'Judging from the weight, you've made enough to feed the whole town,' Holly said, gasping as she lowered the pan on to the hob.

'Now show me the wreath,' Sadie said, with a twinkle in her eye. Holly picked it up and held it aloft. 'Oh! You've outdone yourself on this one, my girl. It's stunning!'

'I'm more excited by the minute,' Holly told her. 'Let's get the dining room set up for the post-hunt supper on Sunday night.'

Holly began to relax as they piled plates and cutlery on the sideboard and fished out a packet of napkins. 'The hostess trolley must be thirty years old if it's a day, Sadie,' she said, as she pulled it into place.

'It certainly doesn't owe us anything, does it? Still, we'd be lost without it. It'll keep the rice warm and any leftover stew for the inevitable latecomer.'

'I'm planning on making a big bowl of coleslaw and we'll leave it at that,' Holly mused.

'That'll be gorgeous – simple and tasty.'

'We were down at McBrides' the other night. Remember I told you they were having a buffet for Mary?'

'How was it?' Sadie asked. 'That woman always did think she was above the Lord, I've no idea why. She doesn't even bother to bake for any of the parish cake sales so where she gets her notions from I'll never know.'

Holly stifled a grin and filled Sadie in on the evening.

'That sounds very fancy altogether. And why did she think she needed to do all those courses?' Sadie asked. 'I never understood the sorbet thing, especially in the depths of winter when you're feeding farmers and young fellas who want a good, hearty dinner.'

'It's not even that. I'm all about making people feel welcome. I hate nothing more than going to a person's house and being made to feel the hostess has spent all day and night slaving over a hot stove. Mary was a like a woman possessed and she never sat at the table the entire night.'

'Ah, sure that's the way she is. Different strokes for different folks, eh?'

'I'm going to grab a box of decorations, Sadie. Would you have a minute to help me with a few bits in here?'

'Of course.'

As Holly left the room, she felt a stab of longing for her mother. She'd always been here to back her up and give her a dig-out. Sadie was fantastic, but it wasn't the same as having her mum by her side. She felt guilty for being rude about her to Sadie just now, but she was deeply hurt that her mother had chosen to move so far away. Now, opening a cupboard in the office, she pulled out the large cardboard box of decorations and made her way back to Sadie.

'I'm sorry for biting your head off earlier on,' she said, as they began to sift through the contents of the box. 'I'm too old to behave like a spoilt child.'

'Ah, don't you worry, love. I know you don't mean any harm. Christmas always makes us feel nostalgic, doesn't it?' Sadie patted her hand. 'I'd another email from Maggie,' she said, without looking up. She waited for the usual reaction. She wasn't disappointed.

'As long as Mum is healthy and happy I don't want to know any details.'

Deep down Holly knew that she'd be on the first plane to Australia should anything untoward happen to Maggie, but now, eleven months on, she was still struggling with her mother's departure. She still woke some mornings expecting her to be there until it dawned on her yet again that Maggie was gone.

'Indeed she's healthy and happy,' Sadie said firmly.

'Great.' Holly recalled the conversation she'd had with her mother just prior to her sudden departure.

'You don't need me here in the background all the time. You're well able to carry on without me,' Maggie had argued.

'But it won't be the same.'

'Different doesn't have to mean awful,' Maggie had said dismissively.

Holly's fears had swiftly turned to anger. Her mother had told them all in no uncertain terms that she had given enough of her life to Huntersbrook House and all who resided there.

'I didn't realise we were such a penance,' Holly had said icily.

'Now, stop behaving like a spoilt toddler.' Maggie had laughed. Holly had wanted to thump her. As her mother had gleefully boarded a plane with a man she barely knew to travel as far away as she could without leaving the planet, she'd managed to make them all feel she was ridding herself of an irritating thorn.

That thorn had lodged itself in Holly. As the weeks had turned to months it had caused untold pain. Holly had known change was afoot – it was inevitable – but she couldn't help resenting her mother for abandoning her when things were so precarious.

3

The Fairytale of New York

Pippa felt like Carrie from *Sex and the City*. 'Cheers, girlies,' she said, as they clinked glasses. 'Can you believe we're actually here, drinking cosmopolitans and being New Yorkers?'

'I thought this trip would never actually happen,' Skye said. 'The fact that we were flying on a Thursday made the week go a bit quicker at least. But now that we're here it's kind of surreal! I've been saving for this for nearly a year!'

'Me too,' Lucy said. 'It was worth all those nights in so we could make it here. I can see why people fall in love with New York. It's just so special, isn't it?'

'Totally,' Pippa agreed. 'I was worried it might be a bit of a let-down when we got here, but it's even better than I'd imagined.'

'The scale of everything is just mega,' Skye said. 'I had a total out-of-body experience this afternoon while we were sitting in the horse and carriage going around Central Park. I looked down at the Macy's bags and thought I was going to pass out from the joy of it all!'

'And here we are, drinking Cosmos like the local gals,' Pippa carolled. 'Uh, hello! Divine hunk of gorgeousness at six o'clock.'

'Now, now. What about Jay? Skye asked. 'I thought you said last night that he was the first guy you've met who makes you want to settle down, that you're amazed to have finally managed a full year with the same boyfriend.'

'That was then, this is now, and that guy is so happening and so right beside me, it'd be sacrilege to ignore him,' Pippa said, winking at him. 'Oh, Jesus, he's coming over,' she said, elbowing Skye.

'Hi there, ladies,' he said, with an unmistakable New York twang. 'Where are you from?'

'Ireland,' Pippa said.

'Oh, really?' He nodded appreciatively. 'My great-grandmother was from Galway. Wanna join us over here?' He gestured towards the neighbouring table where some other guys were waving. 'We'd all love to take you girls to a club, if you're interested.'

'Well, we'd love to come with you. And you're the type of tour guide I had in mind,' Pippa said.

'We'll follow you over in a moment,' Skye said, flashing a smile.

'Sure,' said Mr Gorgeous. Pippa gave him a little wave and held his gaze for a moment too long.

'Pippa!' Skye hissed.

'What's up?' Pippa said, dipping under the table to grab her lip gloss from her handbag. 'That guy is hot and look at his friends,' she said, as she rolled her lips together. 'Do I have lip gloss on my teeth?'

'What? No. Listen, we don't want to end up in some crazy situation,' Skye said. 'New York is a dangerous place and, besides, I don't want to spend all my money on drink. I want to have as much as possible for the discount outlets tomorrow. The stuff you can get is meant to be a third of the prices back home. It's going to be so amazing!'

Lucy agreed. 'I'd love to go for a quick bop but let's just keep our heads, yeah?'

'Ladies, ladies, you need to chill. We're in the Big Apple. We're having cocktails and some guys want to take us clubbing. Correct me if I'm wrong, but isn't this meant to be a fun trip? Aren't we here to live it up a little? You both worry too much.' Pippa pulled her credit card from her bag. 'The drinks are on me!'

The girls squealed and picked up their cocktail glasses.

'Come on, then. Let's show those New Yorkers that we Irish really know how to rock a party.' Pippa picked up her cocktail glass and stood up, smoothing down her short, flirty dress. Her shoes were skyscraper high, but her need to command a bit of male attention meant she'd suck up the crushing pain in her toes.

'Bloody hell, these shoes are killers. I need more drink and a good-looking man to take the pain away. Right, girls, let's walk the walk and talk the talk,' she said, swishing her glossy hair back as she pulled her tummy in, thrust her boobs out and did the best impression of Jessica Rabbit her friends had ever seen.

'Those fellas are practically drooling,' Skye muttered to Lucy. 'I know I was raised by hippies so I'm probably the opposite end of the scale when it comes to being streetwise, but Pippa's a force to be reckoned with.'

'God only knows what she's going to tell them now.' Lucy

laughed. Pippa, her friends knew, would simply *have* to stretch the truth with these poor unsuspecting fellas.

'Ready to nod and smile a lot?' Skye asked Lucy, as they followed Pippa's lead. They knew they didn't have the 'model walk' sorted, as Pippa had.

'It's so great to be here,' Pippa said, as she bent to deposit her bag on the floor. Keeping her legs straight, she made sure the men got a good view of her toned thighs.

'Charlie here tells us you gals are from Ireland.'

'Sure are,' Pippa said, holding out her hand so he could take it and kiss it. 'I'm Pippa, and my friends are Lucy and Skye. We've come all the way from Dublin in search of some New York magic. We'd seriously appreciate some chaperones. Obviously we don't know where we should be hitting tonight.' Putting her finger to her lips, Pippa opened her eyes wide and did her helpless-little-girl act.

'We all work and live right here in the city so it'd be our pleasure to show you gals around. I'm Bill, you've already spoken with Charlie and this is Zack.'

'We're here for a bit of relaxation and retail therapy,' Pippa said. 'We run our own company back home. I'm a lawyer, Lucy is a detective and Skye is an IT specialist. As you can imagine, we like to work hard and play hard. We're Dublin's answer to Charlie's Angels.'

'Wow, that's pretty impressive.' Bill was nodding enthusiastically.

Skye gave Pippa a dig in the ribs. Pippa carried on: 'We go on mini breaks every couple of months. It's good for us to get away from the pressures of our day-to-day lives and let our hair down.' She ran her fingers through her mane slowly, smiling sexily at Zack.

'I'd say you get lots of clients,' Charlie said appreciatively.

'We're very talented,' Pippa said, draining her glass.

'Would you ladies like another drink?' Zack asked.

'We'll get our own—' Skye began.

'That sounds lovely,' Pippa interrupted, flashing a wide smile. 'Let me come and help you carry them.' As she tottered towards the bar, linking Zack's arm, Lucy and Skye tried not to giggle.

Their conversation with Charlie and Bill was rather stilted.

'Your friend's quite a live wire, isn't she?' Bill said, unabashedly checking Pippa out as she stood and chatted at the bar.

'She's always the life and soul of the party,' Skye agreed.

Moments later they were back. 'Look what Zack's bought us, girls!' Pippa chirped. 'He's so generous! Cheers, boys, we're thrilled to have met you.'

'So much for Jay being the love of your life,' Lucy whispered to Pippa, who grinned back.

'That was last night, Lucy – keep up!' Pippa swatted her friend's arm. 'There's no ring on my finger. We're in New York, baby, and the boys are smokin',' she said, with a little shimmy.

'How long have you girls been in business?' Bill asked.

'How long is it now?' Skye said, staring at Pippa. She added, in a whisper, 'I can't believe you told them that lie. What's wrong with saying I design websites and Lucy works for the bank? You're still in the PR company, aren't you?'

'Not really. I sort of got fired. Long story, so I'll tell you another time,' Pippa said. 'We'll never see these guys again and it's all a bit of fun. So what if I told a little fib? They're wildly impressed with us and it'll do them no harm to believe they're privileged to be standing here with us. Don't you love being a Charlie's Angel even for one night?'

Skye wouldn't have chosen to lie to the boys but she had to admit they were hanging on their every word. Pippa was incorrigible but she certainly knew how to have a good time.

'When we graduated jobs weren't easy to come by in Ireland, due to the economic downturn, so we figured there was no point waiting for work to come to us. We set up our company and our feet have barely touched the ground,' Pippa said.

'That's impressive,' Charlie said. 'How many clients have you?'

'Much as we all adore talking shop,' Pippa said, 'we have a little rule that when we're away we leave the business in the office. So if it's all the same to you, the only agenda we have here is fun, fun and more fun!'

'That sounds good to me!' Zack said.

As the guys ordered yet another round of cocktails, Pippa announced that she, Skye and Lucy were going to the ladies' room.

'They're so charming, aren't they?' she said, as they fixed their hair and makeup.

'They're not like some of the Irish guys who get blotto and start trying it on before you've even told them your name,' Lucy agreed.

'They're not really my type. I hate to rain on the parade but I find them a bit staged,' Skye put in.

'Don't you want to go home knowing you broke a New York guy's heart?' Pippa asked.

'Not really,' Skye admitted.

'What about you, Lucy? Keep talking – I'm running into a cubicle but I can still hear you.' Pippa was hoping for a little more enthusiasm from Lucy. Skye was a lovely girl, but she'd always found her a bit sensible. Skye had been raised in a vegan commune, which was a million miles away from anything Pippa could understand. Sure she'd grown up at Huntersbrook, in Wicklow, but it was close to Dublin City and always full of fun visitors. Pippa liked Skye but found her a bit too level-headed.

'Zack's so cute,' Lucy said. 'I know where you're coming from, too, Skye, but as Pippa said, we're only here for two nights and it's a bit different from the usual banter, isn't it?'

'Attagirl!' Pippa said, as she emerged from the loo. Once she'd washed her hands she leaned forward and stared into the mirror. 'I need to fix my face again,' she said, examining herself critically. As she brushed on some more eye shadow and fished in her bag for her lip liner, she thanked God for the millionth time that makeup had been invented. 'Well,' she pouted, happier now with her reflection, 'I happen to find the clean-cut American businessman thing wildly attractive. I'm not planning a wedding or anything but I'm loving the cocktails – and I don't care what anyone says, I think their accents are *hot*!'

The two girls had finished their own patch jobs and seemed ready to head back to the table.

'Right then, let's show them what Irish girls are made of!' Pippa said. She twirled to check that her dress wasn't tucked into her knickers, gave her hair a final flick, then flung the door open and did her best runway-model walk back to the boys.

'Would you gals like to come to a club now?' Bill asked. 'There's a really cool place on the next block. We're members of the VIP lounge so we could check it out if you're interested.'

'Ooh, that sounds like a plan,' Pippa said. 'Ladies?' She raised an eyebrow.

'Sounds great,' Lucy said, smiling.

'Yeah, sure.' Skye looked far from keen. Pippa chose to ignore the hesitation in her friend's voice. They were in New York and it wasn't the time for an early night with slippers and a mug of cocoa.

As they pulled on their jackets and stepped out into the freezing air, the icy wind was instantly sobering. If she hadn't been so intent on flirting, Pippa would've cursed like a tinker and insisted on going back into the warmth of the bar. 'It's pretty cold out here,' she said, snuggling up to Bill. She'd decided he was the most fun.

'You're freezing,' Bill said, removing his coat and draping it around her shoulders.

'Thanks, Bill,' she said. 'You're a gentleman.'

'My pleasure,' he answered.

I could get used to this kind of chivalry, Pippa decided.

Thankfully, the club was literally just around the block. The large queue made Pippa want to cry as she pictured them having to stand and wait, followed by the usual arguing with bouncers.

'Evening, sir,' the tuxedo-clad doorman said to Bill, as he stood to the side and beckoned them in.

'Evening. We've three guests,' Bill said.

'Of course. Enjoy your evening, ladies.' The man smiled.

The steep stairs led to a contemporary balcony area with clusters of chrome tables and high stools. Several waitresses, dressed head to toe in white, were dashing around the room with trays held high.

'We'd like a table overlooking the dance floor, if possible,' Bill said to the hostess.

'Sure, sir. Follow me.'

'This is fabulous,' Lucy said excitedly.

'It's one of the best clubs in the city,' Bill told her. 'I bring clients here on a regular basis – or charming ladies such as yourselves.'

'Let's have some champagne.' Pippa had been swept along with the brilliance of it all. 'My treat!'

'That's very generous of you. Thank you, Pippa,' Bill said.

'Would you prefer Moët, Taittinger, Bollinger or Krug, ma'am?' A waitress had materialised beside them.

'Oh, which do you recommend?' Pippa asked, who had no idea of the difference between them.

'Well, not the Krug, unless you're making so much dough you don't know what to do with it!' Bill laughed.

'Yeah.' Pippa wrinkled her nose. 'We'll go for the Bollinger,' she said.

'Nice choice, little lady,' Bill said. 'I think they charge five hundred dollars for a bottle of Krug in this joint. But the Bollinger shouldn't be quite as bad,' he said. 'It's kind of you to make the gesture, though. Shows a real lady.'

Pippa did her best to hide her shock. How much was this going to cost her?

'I agree,' Zack said. 'Some girls we meet are totally at ease with taking drinks and being brought to funky places but never reciprocate. You Irish are different. I like that.'

'Oh, we'd never want anyone to think we're after their money,' Pippa said. She had to resist the urge to yelp when the waitress brought the bill. 'Do you accept Visa?' she asked, trying not to sound strangled.

'Sure. Would you mind coming to the counter?' the waitress asked. 'The mobile card machine has just malfunctioned so my apologies for dragging you away from your table.'

'No worries,' Pippa said, grabbing her bag.

'There seems to be an issue with this card, ma'am,' the waitress said, moments later. 'I'm afraid it's been declined.'

'Oh, shoot!' Pippa said, smiling. 'Try this one,' she said, handing over her American Express. She was beyond relieved when the transaction went through. Stuffing the receipt into her bag, she went back to the table where the Champagne was being poured into flutes.

'Pippa, I just looked at the prices. One hundred and sixty dollars for a bottle of champagne! I won't be getting pissed in here.' Skye was clearly horrified as she put the white-leather drinks menu back on the table.

'Isn't this place just ice-box, though?' Pippa replied. 'Look at the bright blue dance floor!' Skye was beginning to irritate her. The prices were extortionate but the transaction had gone through so they might as well enjoy it. What was the point in harping on about it and making them look like paupers?

'They do a foam party in here sometimes,' Zack said. 'There's, like, an under-the-sea type vibe.'

'This is worth celebrating,' Pippa said, brushing off the twinge of fear that had just assailed her over her maxed-out Visa.

'To Irish lassies!' Bill grinned.

'To New York and the wonderful views she boasts,' Pippa said, giggling as she winked back at Bill.

Rihanna's 'Only Girl (In The World)' poured out of the speakers, bringing Pippa to her feet. 'I *love* this song!' she said. With one hand on her hip, she beckoned Bill slowly with the index finger of her other hand. 'Dance with me,' she whispered, as he put an arm around her waist. As they made their way down to the dance floor below via a Perspex staircase, Pippa drank in the heaving atmosphere and cool dancers. The girls were dressed to kill and so were the men. This was what it was all about. She gazed back up towards the VIP area to see the remaining four waving down at them. A couple of people dancing beside them clocked her friends and gazed at her and Bill with obvious envy.

As far as Pippa was concerned, that bottle of bubbly had been a sound business investment. Once she'd had enough of dancing, Bill led her back up the stairs to rejoin the others. For the remainder of the evening, the men wouldn't allow them pay for a single thing.

Skye was chatting to Charlie but from her uptight body language it was clear that she wasn't interested in staying for much longer. Lucy, though, was wrapped around Zack and seemed to be making the most of the night.

Pippa had thought her heart would burst out of her chest when Bill kissed her as they went up the stairs to join the others after yet another fling on the dance floor, but no. Any potential fireworks were well and truly quenched by the slobber. It was like snogging a fish.

'Want to go back to my place?' Bill asked, with a slight slur. Had he known how to kiss, Pippa might've gone, but suddenly the shared hotel room with her friends and the potential for a bit of girly gossip seemed the better option. Maybe she'd been right last night when she'd said she was smitten by Jay, she mused drunkenly.

'I'd better stay with the girls. We're only here for a couple of nights and it might be rude of me to abandon ship.' She injected as much regret into her face as she could muster.

'Sure thing,' Bill said, holding his hands up. 'I didn't think you would but it was worth asking!'

As they rejoined the others, Pippa caught Skye yawning. 'Skye, you poor love, you're exhausted,' she said, full of concern. 'I think we should get you back to the hotel right now.'

'I'm fine for another while if you girls want to stay on,' Skye offered.

'Oh, no,' Pippa said, patting her hand.

'Well, if you're sure ...'

'Sorry to break up the party, guys,' Pippa said, after the style of a boxing referee. 'Lucy, it's really late and poor Skye's had it.'

'Aw, seriously?' Lucy said, disappointment etched across her face.

'You can always stay with me?' Zack said hopefully.

'Ah, no. This hen party is sticking together,' Skye interjected.

Pippa pulled her coat on and hugged Zack and Charlie, leaving Bill until last. Knowing she wanted to keep their goodbyes brief, she gave him a quick kiss on the lips, then made a big song and dance of how sad it was they had to leave, arms flailing to discourage too much intimacy. 'Double boo-hoo that we can't meet up tomorrow night – we're hooking up with some distant cousins,' she fibbed.

'That's a shame.' Bill looked a little crushed.

'Take care, boys, and thanks so much for the club,' Pippa said.

The girls linked arms and strode up the road towards their hotel.

'You're such a liar, Pippa Craig!' Skye chided her, as they went out of earshot of the boys.

'Yes, and I quite liked Zack, thank you very much!' Lucy said, swiping her.

'Sorry, Lucy, I wasn't thinking,' Pippa said. 'Bill was nice but he kissed me and it was so vile I knew I had to ditch him. He was like a Dyson crossed with a slug. Bleuch!'

'Ah, I'm only messing with you,' Lucy said. 'I could've stayed with him if I'd thought he was going to be The One.'

'It's hardly wise to go hotfooting off with a strange man in a massive city like this,' Skye said.

'True,' Pippa said, elbowing Lucy. 'Listen to Mummy Skye.'

'You can tease me all you like but it's not a good plan to go off with strange men.' Skye bristled.

By the time they'd bundled into the hotel room and got ready for bed the mess was astonishing. Shoes, clothes and makeup littered the floor and all of the surfaces.

'I'm wrecked,' Pippa croaked. 'I need to crash. Night.'

The next morning Skye groaned as she staggered bleary-eyed across the room to answer the phone. 'Hello?'

'Good morning,' the receptionist chirruped. 'This is your wake-up call.'

'Thank you,' Skye replied before putting the phone down. 'It's lucky I ordered a call or I reckon I would've slept all day. You two conked almost immediately last night. I was wide awake for ages.'

'Poor you,' Pippa said, peeling herself up from her pillow. 'We'd better get up, girls, if we want to get to the outlets. The flight back is so early tomorrow morning we won't have time to do anything. Next time we need to come for a week.' She yawned.

'Only if we have about two years to save!' Lucy said. 'I was stretched to my limit just to manage this. With Christmas around the corner, I couldn't have stayed any longer. Is it just me or does anyone else feel rough?'

'Yup,' Pippa answered, and pulled her sheet over her face. 'I've no idea how many drinks I had last night. It was a great idea at the time but I'm feeling pretty horrendous now.'

'I'm going to have a quick shower. At least if one of us is ready we might have a chance of getting something done today,' Skye said, marching into the en-suite. 'Come on, girls,' she said, exasperated. 'Friday is our only full day here so let's not waste it moaning.'

'Uh, are we in trouble?' Pippa rolled over and faced Lucy in the adjoining bed.

'I don't think Skye went past her usual two-drinks limit and she didn't score with what's-his-face,' Lucy said.

'We weren't that bad, though, were we?' Pippa asked, as she tried sitting up. She lay down again: the room was spinning.

'Ah, no. Skye will be fine. She's just excited to be here, that's all,' Lucy explained. 'I've known her for years. She's a sweetheart.'

'Come on, girls, up you get!' Skye appeared from the bathroom wrapped in a towel. 'The shower is more dribble than power so don't expect any water jets to massage your aching heads.'

'Right, I'm awake. I'll have a quick shower,' Pippa said, and staggered towards the bathroom. 'I need to find a cashpoint too,' she said, as she kicked the door shut. She couldn't remember getting into bed but, judging from the pile of clothing in the corner of the bathroom, she'd made it to the toilet, stripped and found the nightdress she was wearing. Her stale makeup was well and truly welded to her face. Black beads of dried-in mascara weren't helping the slightly green pallor with which the drink had left her.

The bathroom was pretty drab, with cracked tiles and an avocado suite. Still, the hotel was cheap and the management had agreed to slot in a third bed so they could all be together.

Skye hadn't been lying when she'd said the shower was

dribbly. Pippa was cold when she emerged and found a towel. She grabbed a facecloth and scrubbed the remainder of last night from her eyes and cheeks. 'I need some food,' she moaned, as she shuffled back into the room.

'Me too,' Skye said, applying lip balm.

The room was like a war zone by the time they were ready to head down to the hotel restaurant for breakfast. 'We'll clean up later,' Pippa said.

'I'd hate to be the maid walking in here,' Skye said guiltily.

'I'll put the do-not-disturb sign up,' Pippa suggested. 'That way we don't have to inflict our pig sty on anyone.'

After several cups of coffee and a plate of pancakes dripping in syrup, they all felt a lot more enthusiastic about heading to the outlets.

'I'm glad the food's good, seeing as tonight's dinner is included in the package,' Skye said, as she finished her last mouthful of breakfast. 'I'm actually a bit stressed about money at the moment,' she added. 'I've been renting a place but I couldn't stay there on my own any longer. The website designing's going better than I ever dreamed, but the landlord jacked my rent up.'

'Just find somewhere else, why don't you?' Pippa wondered, as they made their way out of the hotel in search of a cab.

'I'll have to, but it's probably not the ideal time of year to move,' Skye said. 'I moved out a couple of days ago – my cousin let me bring my stuff to his place but the thought of sleeping on the sofa in a flat with three grungy guys doesn't exactly fill me with joy.'

'I'll let you know if I hear of anywhere,' Lucy said.

'Me too,' Pippa said, as they bundled into the warmth of a taxi.

A short while later their hangovers were forgotten as they pulled up at the outlets.

'This is fabulous!' Pippa squealed, as she spotted row after row of her favourite stores. 'They have Juicy and Max Mara – and there's Hollister! Hold me back! I feel a splurge coming on.'

The mall was a shopper's dream, spotlessly clean and divided into identical-sized units. Inside, the rails were clearly marked, according to the discount offered.

'Look at this! Chanel with eighty-five per cent off the original price tags,' Pippa exclaimed to Skye.

'Yeah, but it's still crazy money,' she said, stroking a jacket longingly.

'Wouldn't you just kill for a Chanel jacket all the same?' Pippa took one off its hanger.

'Totally,' Lucy agreed immediately. 'I know it's a cliché but it really is an investment piece. One of my college friends has one that belonged to her grandmother. It's still as amazing today as it was when she bought it. It's timeless style at its best.'

Reluctantly Pippa put back the jacket and they moved from Chanel to the other stores. After two hours of manic trawling through stores and rails, they collapsed at the coffee shop with coffee and cake.

'I've bought four pairs of jeans for the price of one crappy pair at home,' Pippa said, as she sipped her cappuccino. 'It's so cheap here it's a joke. We're so ripped off, aren't we?'

'Totally,' Skye agreed. 'You'd better be a bit careful with how much you buy all the same, though, Pippa. They'll charge you a fortune if you're over the allotted weight when we check in.'

By the time they got back to the hotel it was snowing and minus three degrees centigrade.

'Let's dump our treasures and head down to the hotel bar. The windows will give us a bird's eye view of the passers-by and the snow falling!' Pippa said excitedly.

'Oh, my God, the mess in here!' Skye gasped, as they shoved the door of their room open. 'How about we do a quick pack and then we'll be sorted? At least we won't have to do it all later or, worse, at four in the morning before we go to the airport.'

'Do we have to?' Pippa moaned.

'I'm going to,' Lucy said, staring at the debris on the floor. 'I certainly won't feel like it later.'

Reluctantly Pippa joined forces with the others and found her bits and pieces. She stuffed them into her bag, which didn't want to close. She didn't want to admit it to Skye but she was having serious trouble closing her bag. It weighed as much as a small mammal too. Figuring she could go for the layered look, she took out two sweatshirts, a coat and one of her new pairs of jeans. She'd need to be well wrapped up against the biting cold. She flung her shampoo and conditioner, with a pile of other toiletries, into the bath, and allowed herself to feel a little smug.

'I've just saved myself loads of space and suitcase weight,' she said, looking a bit florid in the face.

'But they're full bottles – expensive ones too,' Lucy said. 'You're something else, Pippa! I'm too broke to buy that brand of shampoo, let alone throw it away.'

'I get them when I'm having my hair done so it never seems that expensive,' she said. 'Feel free to take it if you have space.'

When they left the room to go down to the bar for a well-earned drink, it looked much more organised. As they toasted a wonderful day of shopping, the snow was beginning to stick outside.

'This is like being *inside* a snow globe, isn't it?' Pippa said. 'I think I'd like to live here for a while.'

'I wouldn't,' Skye admitted. 'Don't get me wrong, I've had a total blast, but I find the speed of it all and the vast amounts of space and crowds of people sort of scary.'

'I know what you mean,' Lucy agreed. 'But I'd happily come and visit Pippa a few times a year if she's planning on being here!'

The evening went far too quickly as Pippa managed to attract another group of men. 'I just can't get enough of the New York accent,' she said.

'Well, your Irish accent is just the cutest thing,' one said, taking the bait instantly.

'Really?' Pippa said. 'I didn't even think I had an accent!'

'Oh, you certainly do,' another man joined in.

'Do any of you have Irish roots?' Pippa asked.

As they all tried to answer at once, Skye grinned at Lucy. 'What will we do with her?' she murmured. 'She's irrepressible, isn't she? You could dump Pippa on the edge of the earth with nothing but a smile and she'd get herself invited to a party within half an hour.'

'I think the big blue eyes, ski-slope nose and perfect figure help,' Lucy said. 'I'm bursting out of my skinny jeans after all the carbs and booze we've had since we got here.'

'I've a massive zit coming up on the side of my nose. I always end up with manky skin when I travel,' Skye said.

'I know the feeling. But Miss Ireland here seems to flourish,' Lucy said. 'She certainly knows how to pull, doesn't she?'

'Hell, yeah!' Skye said, in a mock-American accent. 'As I said before, she'd draw a crowd even if she were in solitary confinement!'

They decided to call it a night at just after one o'clock. As Skye and Lucy drifted off to sleep, Pippa's jetlag kicked in and she was suddenly wide awake. Without disturbing Lucy and Skye, she tiptoed to perch on the window seat and gaze out at the lights and hubbub of New York below. It was still snowing but she had a good view, and could see dozens of people still wandering around.

She tried to picture what it might be like to live here, and suddenly felt unsure. Maybe it wouldn't be that great. The snow and bright lights were exciting, but New York didn't hold a torch to Huntersbrook House. She couldn't imagine being anywhere else on Christmas morning. Tomorrow night she'd be missing Lainey's birthday dinner. Now that she was awake, alone and with nobody to chat to, she felt stupidly homesick.

In the taxi on the way to the airport they were quiet as they huddled together for warmth. The roads were snowed over but they made it on time for check-in. Pippa rooted in her purse for her third of the taxi fare. 'Girls, I'm so embarrassed but I haven't a bean left. Can I pay you back when we get home?'

'I'll put in your share. I have cash,' Skye said.

'Thanks,' Pippa said, cringing. She hated not having money of her own.

They went into the airport and found the right desk. Pippa heaved her bag on to the scales. 'This one is over the allocated weight. There's a charge of eighty dollars,' the check-in woman announced, in a voice that didn't invite argument.

'Holy cow, Pippa.' Skye giggled. 'You'd have been better off buying the stuff in Dublin! Any savings you might have made are going straight back on.'

Pippa produced her trusty American Express card and paid the charge.

Once they were rid of the luggage, they went through Security and wandered towards the duty-free area. 'I'm going to pick up some makeup. Clinique's really cheap here,' Pippa said knowledgeably. 'Come on – I'll treat you both to a lipstick and nail polish, seeing as you had to use your cash to pay the taxi driver.'

'Thanks, Pippa. That sounds like a fair trade,' Skye said. 'I'd love a nice new lippy for the Christmas-party season.'

'Me too,' Lucy chimed in.

They chose their lipsticks and nail polish, then glanced at the time, squealed and ran. They should have been at the gate, ready to board the aircraft.

'Oh, my God, imagine if we missed the plane because we were so busy trying on lipstick!' Pippa panted.

'Don't joke, we're not on it yet,' Skye said. 'I feel like I'm going to puke from running.'

'You were cutting it fine, ladies,' the air stewardess said, with a grin. 'We literally just did our final call before shutting the aircraft doors.'

'We were in the Land of Lippy,' Pippa gasped.

'Oh you won't be the last ones to be sucked in by the mystique of Clinique!' the lady said, as she tore off their boarding-card stubs and ushered them towards their plane.

'It's so handy that you had your car at the airport, Pippa,' Lucy said. 'Thanks for offering to drive us both home. I couldn't bear the thought of getting on the bus right now.'

'Ugh! Neither could I,' Skye agreed.

By the time she'd dropped them off and driven to her own apartment, all Pippa was fit for was her bed. Somewhere in the back of her exhausted mind she had an inkling that she might soon have to sit down and sort out her finances. But she was far too wrecked to go there. That little matter could wait until another day.

4

Little Drummer Boy

Joey was delighted that Sophia had agreed to spend the weekend at Huntersbrook House. Dublin was fun and buzzy on a Friday or Saturday night but every now and again he craved the calmer pace of home. 'There's nothing like the view of a frosty Wicklow field in winter,' he said, as he put his foot to the floor and raced up the straight stretch of the N11 that Saturday morning.

'We have frost in Dublin too,' Sophia said, sounding irritated.

'I know, but it's not the same when it's on rooftops rather than paddocks,' Joey said, with a faraway expression on his face. 'Mum will be like a child. She gets so into the build-up to Christmas,' he said, laughing. 'If she could cover the entire place with decorations, she would! Dad pretends to get narky with her about it, but deep down I reckon he's as bad as she is.'

'Maybe he genuinely hates the tackiness,' Sophia pointed out. 'Just because your mother likes defacing the place with tat doesn't mean he has to love it too.'

'Perhaps not, but he enjoys watching Mum. She's infectious when she gets going.'

'Hm.' Sophia pulled on her shades and relaxed into her seat.

'I know it probably sounds silly to you, but I still get butterflies in my stomach when I think about Christmas,' Joey continued. 'It's such a magical time, isn't it?'

The silence made him look to the passenger seat. Sophia was having a power nap. He knew she was using the journey time to recharge her batteries but he couldn't help feeling a little stung that she didn't want to share his buzz.

Fifteen minutes later, the sound of Joey's tyres on the gravel outside the house brought Holly to the front door.

'There's Mum to greet us,' Joey said, patting Sophia's leg to rouse her before he leaped out of the car.

'Joey!' Holly said, rushing to hug him. 'How are you, son?'

'Good, thanks, Mum. Yourself?' Joey had inherited his parents' best features: he had Paddy's strong frame and height, with Holly's dark hair and sallow features. His cheeky grin and happy-go-lucky nature made him a real hit with the ladies, not least his mother.

'The Christmas transformation is under way, I see.' He gestured towards the front door, on which the wreath was displayed.

'You like?' Holly said.

'Looking good, Mum.' He hugged her again, then stepped back to open the car door for Sophia. 'You awake, sleepy-head?'

'Yup,' Sophia said. She clambered out and stretched her arms high above her head.

'Sophia dear, how are you?' Holly was keeping her smile in place as Sophia came towards her.

'Hi,' Sophia said, with a limp wave.

'How was the journey?'

'All right. It's very cold here, isn't it?'

'Yes, but I guess that goes with the time of year. It is December after all,' Holly said.

Joey was desperate for the weekend to be fun. He knew Sophia wasn't ecstatic to be here – she'd told him often enough that she didn't want to come: 'I'm a town mouse, not a country mouse. You go on down to Huntersbrook and I'll see you when you get back.' Her favourite excuse was, 'My lungs aren't used to all that clear air. I always end up with a cough or cold.'

They'd been dating for almost a year and living together for the past five months. It had all happened so quickly. Joey had joined the work triathlon team. In the beginning it had been a calculated move to keep in with his boss, who was triathlon crazy, but he'd quickly discovered he enjoyed it. The fitness level required to race was high, though, so he'd sought the help of a personal trainer through his local gym.

He'd automatically expected an ex-army type or an oiled muscle man and had been over the moon when Sophia had greeted him. With her pert bottom and breasts, she was everything he'd wanted in a woman.

'Take your running up a few paces,' she'd called over her shoulder as they'd ventured onto the running track the first time. 'You need to push yourself. Get that heart pumping.'

If he hadn't been so desperate to impress her, Joey might've caved and told her it was too energetic, but she was the best reason he had to get fit, never mind the triathlon.

They'd clicked immediately. She'd giggled at his jokes and he'd noticed she was quite touchy-feely with him. After three weeks, and at the end of a particularly rough track session, he'd poured what remained in his water bottle over his head to cool himself down, and said breathlessly, 'Fancy going for a bite to eat with me some time?' He'd been pacing up and down, trying to look as if he wasn't bricking himself.

'I thought you'd never ask,' she replied, smiling.

'Tomorrow night? I'll meet you in Pasta Italiano at eight?'

'See you then. It'll be nice to discover what you look like when you're not chasing me and dressed in Lycra.'

The date couldn't have gone better. The food and wine, then the dancing blew him away. As did what had happened later at his place.

'You don't hold back once you get going, do you?' Joey observed, as he lay propped on his elbow beside her in bed.

'I like speed and excitement. Why do you think I eat, sleep and breathe triathlon?'

His colleagues and friends were wildly impressed the first time he'd brought her to the pub.

'You're some snake, Joey,' his boss, Clive, had said, bashing him on the back. 'She's a total babe and I've seen her shoot past me on the bike during a number of races. She can move when she needs to.'

'That's my honey,' Joey said proudly. The only time Sophia wasn't herself was with his family. But he was hoping that Christmas at Huntersbrook would help to change her mind about country living. They always had plenty of people buzzing around and Mum would have the place done up like a Victorian Christmas card. Sophia hadn't had a chance to get to know Lainey and Pippa properly either. He was certain they'd love each other once they bonded. Whatever about Lainey, with her shy and slightly conservative approach to life, Joey was sure Sophia would love Pippa once she'd spent some time with her.

As Sophia stood on the steps up to the front door, shivering with her arms wrapped around herself, he urged her to go in and get warm. 'But the bags and the rest of the stuff ...' She trailed off.

'I've got them. Go on into the kitchen. Is Sadie there?' Joey asked Holly.

'Certainly is, and I'd say she's pulling a loaf of soda bread out of the Aga as we speak. She has gorgeous soup ready, so we'll have you warm and relaxed in no time,' Holly promised.

As the women went ahead, Joey took deep gulps of fresh air and rubbed his hands. He'd a good feeling about this weekend.

By the time he'd deposited their things in his old bedroom and ventured into the kitchen, Sophia was sitting at the table having a bowl of soup with his dad.

'Ah, Joey, there you are, son,' Paddy greeted him. 'Come and join us.'

'I certainly will,' Joey said. 'Sadie! How's it going?' he asked.

'Ah, sure I'm great, love. All the better for seeing you. Soup?'

'Love some, thanks,' Joey said. 'There's nothing like your soda bread straight from the oven either,' he said through a mouthful. 'It's rather chilly upstairs.'

'I must've forgotten to turn on the heating up there,' Paddy said apologetically. 'I've had the radiators off in a lot of the upstairs rooms. No point in heating them if they're empty.'

'True,' Joey said, as he joined them at the table with his soup. 'It'll end up damp if you're not careful, though.'

'Here you all are,' Holly said as she arrived. 'I'll have a cup of tea with you before I go and finish off in the dining room. It's Lainey's birthday so we've a few people popping in for supper this evening,' she explained to Sophia.

'Aw, shoot, I totally forgot to get her anything,' Joey said.

'I'm sure I've a trinket in the pantry you could give her,' Holly said. 'She'll be delighted you and Sophia are here. I wouldn't worry.'

'You never told me it was your sister's birthday,' Sophia snapped.

'Sorry, babe, it went out of my head,' he said. 'It's no hassle. Lainey's very chilled. She won't be looking for a pile of expensive gifts.'

'That's right,' Paddy said. 'As Joey pointed out, the main thing is that you're both here to celebrate and have a slice of cake.'

'I've only brought jeans and a top, Joey,' Sophia said, glowering at him.

'That's cool. It won't be fancy,' Joey said, grabbing the newspaper.

Sophia sighed and clenched her fists.

'What?' Joey asked, with a grin. 'Am I in trouble?'

'I'm going to head out for a run, if that's okay with all of you,' Sophia said tightly.

'It's a lovely day for it. You do that,' Sadie said, as she picked up Sophia's barely touched bowl of soup. 'Are you finished with this, then?' she asked.

'Eh, yeah, thanks. I'm not that hungry. I'll go and get changed.'

'Right so,' Joey said, returning to the paper.

There was brief silence after Sophia left the room.

'I think you'd better go and see if she's okay,' Holly suggested.

'Ah, she's fine. I'll finish this and check on her.'

'I'll see you later then. I'm off to do my jobs outside,' Paddy announced. 'Thanks for lunch, Sadie.'

'You're welcome, dear. At least you seemed to enjoy it,' she remarked, as she cleared away his empty bowl.

'I'll be in the dining room if you're looking for me,' Holly said, over her shoulder.

Joey wandered upstairs to his room. Sophia had emptied her bags over the bed and was pulling on her trainers. 'Okay?' he said. He was about to throw himself onto the bed for a quick snooze when she lit into him.

'Not really,' she snarled. 'Why didn't you tell me it was Lainey's birthday? I've a two-hour run to do now and I need to be back to Dublin at a reasonable hour to get a decent cycle in tomorrow.'

'Whoa! What's this about?' Joey said, confused. 'I'll bring you back whatever time you like tomorrow. Although I'd thought we'd stay and have Sunday lunch with my folks. If you're hassled we don't have to.'

'I'm training for the Ironman race in September. It means a lot to me, Joey. I know you've only been racing a few short months but I'm serious about my sport,' she explained. 'It's my livelihood and my passion and I need to stay focused and disciplined.'

'I know all that and it's cool with me. I didn't tell you about Lainey's birthday because I forgot. Sorry, but I'm crap like that. I'm a bloke.' He grinned. 'You won't need to get dressed up either – you'll be gorgeous in your jeans. And, besides, I thought you were passionate about me,' he said, sliding off the bed and pulling her into his arms.

'Not now, Joey.' She pushed him away. 'I just don't really need to have to stay up till all hours at a party tonight, that's all.' He must have looked as crushed as he felt because she softened and gave him a slow kiss on the lips. 'I'll see you when I get back.'

'I'll be waiting,' he said. 'Tonight won't be a late one. You can go to bed whenever suits you, okay?'

'Fine,' she conceded.

As she walked out of the room, shoving her headphones on, he relaxed. Sophia was just feisty. But that was one of the things he liked about her. He'd had quite a few girlfriends in the past and none of them had held his attention as she did.

He knew he should go for a run himself. He rarely went with Sophia because she was at a different level: he'd end up telling her to go on ahead and he hated feeling like a dweeb beside her. Unless she was coaching him, which was rare now that they were a couple, they kept their training separate.

He figured he'd spend a bit of time with his folks and then go for a jog.

'Joey?' Holly called, from the landing outside his door.

'I'm coming!'

'Would you be able to grab some of the big boxes of Christmas decorations from the attic for me? Sadie and I got out the ones that live in the office earlier in the week but the bulk of them are up there.'

'Of course,' he said. 'Are you about to turn into Mrs Claus again?' he teased. He'd never met a woman like his mother when it came to decorating.

'I just love the weeks before Christmas,' she said, as he pulled the attic staircase down, climbed it and began to pass things down to her. 'I've the thrill of rooting through all the treasures that've been packed away all year.'

'You're mad.' Joey chuckled. 'Is that enough for now or do you want me to take them all down while I'm at it?' he asked.

'Sure you might as well give me the whole lot. It'll save Dad and me doing it. We're not as young as we used to be.'

Joey walked around the attic space. It was probably twice the size of his apartment. In one corner he spotted some of his old toys. A dusty Action Man waited in his jeep to be brought to an imaginary battle. His teddy, loved to within an inch of his faded plush fur, sat winking, with one eye missing. As he stooped to touch him, memories of his childhood flashed through Joey's mind.

He and his sisters had enjoyed the most idyllic times here at Huntersbrook, but he had embraced his new life in Dublin. His job was fulfilling and he knew he'd been lucky to get such a good position when he graduated. Loads of guys he'd gone to college with were just as good as he was at accountancy yet they were sitting at home with no work to go to. He liked to think his get-up-and-go attitude had contributed to his success. That was down to his family and this place, he mused.

He straightened and went to rejoin his mother. He was fortunate to have been raised in a home where social skills were deemed just as important as academic ones. He hoped that if he and Sophia had children, they would be able to spend lots of time here with their grandparents.

He folded the ladder back into the attic and clicked the door shut using the special pole. Then he turned and laughed. 'Mum, you're like a mad bag-lady sifting through a bin.'

'I'm itching to get the Christmas tree up now,' she said. 'Would you both do the lights at the front door for me?'

'What – now this minute?'

'Please?'

'Sure.' His jog could wait. If they had to go back to Dublin early in the morning, he could put in a couple of hours at the gym or even in the park. He'd have loved to get out into the fresh, clear Wicklow air, but he knew how important Christmas was to his mum. She hadn't said so, but she must be missing Grandma. The least he could do was give her a hand.

'I'll go and find Dad. I can't do those big pillars on my own,' he said.

'Okay,' Holly said, with her arse in the air and her head stuck in another box of decorations.

Just as Joey and Paddy had untangled the lights, straightened them out and got them going, Lainey roared up on her bike. 'Hey, you two,' she said. 'Mum cracking the Christmas whip already?'

'Lainey! Happy birthday.' Joey kissed her on both cheeks.

'Hi, love,' Paddy said, pulling her into a bear-hug. 'Happy birthday.'

'Thanks.' She grabbed her saddlebag from the back of the bike. 'Where's everyone?'

'Mum's inside with Sadie and Sophia's out running,' Joey said. 'Ah, crap! The lights have gone off again. Right. Back to the beginning. We'll have to wiggle them until we find the dodgy one.'

'I'll leave you to it,' Lainey said. 'Enjoy!'

It was growing dark by the time they eventually got the lights working and attached to both pillars. 'That looks fantastic even if I say so myself.' Joey stood back to gaze at their handiwork.

Sophia felt calmer once she was out of sight of the house. She couldn't stand being here. It was just so jolly and down-by-the-farm. She liked order and routine. Joey's family were all about letting the day unfold as it would. There was never any agenda or schedule.

Take this birthday party for lame Lainey tonight. Joey hadn't even told her it was on. She didn't know who was coming. There was no dress code and there had been no proper planning. She wanted to scream.

Whatever about Pippa, who was a spoiled little cow, Sophia just didn't *get* Lainey. She was so limp and bland. Her short, dark hair was styled in a way that reminded Sophia of the old nuns who'd taught her in school. She needed several layers of fake tan to liven up her pasty skin – and as for the scrubbed-with-no-makeup look! Ugh, she was way too old to rock it.

She hadn't a bad figure, Sophia admitted grudgingly. She was probably quite toned from the horse-riding, not that that mattered when she paraded around in awful butch biking gear or outdated jeans and baggy sweaters. In a word, Lainey was beige.

But Joey didn't see it. He thought they were all fabulous and acted like he was descended from the royal family or something. He was different when they were in Dublin. He was seriously focused at work, and getting into his training, too, which pleased her. But every now and again he'd want to come down here for the weekend. As soon as they drove through the gates – which might have been fantastic a hundred years ago but now looked dilapidated as well as ancient – he turned into this sappy version of himself. It was like he'd left cool Joey in Dublin.

He was in awe of his family. Enraptured by his parents and entertained by his sisters. They'd sit and talk about pointless stuff, like Christmas trees, for hours. It got on her wick to the extent that she had to bite her tongue to stop herself yelling at them to get with the real world and stop faffing about.

The biggest advantage of her irritation was the difference it made to her run times. She'd just done a really good couple of hours without dropping her pace. As the house came into view, she grimaced. Joey was still pissing about at the front door with his father. She hoped for his sake he'd gone for at least a short run. Still, who was she to nag? He'd know all about it when race season started and he was being passed on the road by the people who'd put in the effort.

'Hey,' Sophia said, jogging to a halt at the front door. Red in the face and bathed in sweat, despite the plummeting temperature, she immediately checked her heart monitor.

'Nice run?' Joey asked.

'Great. I need to do some stretches so I'll go on up to your room,' she said. 'I'll get cold pretty quickly standing around here.' She made for the door.

'Didn't you notice the fantastic job we've done with the lights?' Joey asked, a little hurt.

'Did you not bother training?' she shot back at him, exasperated.

'He did,' Paddy said. 'He ran in and out the front door at least twenty times and up and down the stepladder too!'

'Right,' she said, raising her eyes to heaven.

'What?' Joey said, clearly uncomfortable. 'Dad was only joking. We got carried away here. I thought it'd take a few minutes but every time we tipped off them they went out.

Christmas lights were designed by some sadist who likes testing people's patience! But we're feeling more than a little proud of ourselves now, aren't we, Dad?' Joey banged his dad on the back.

'So I see.' Sophia held her hands up. 'We're not that into the Christmas thing in our house. My mum thinks decorations are tacky.'

'Oh dear.' Joey grinned. 'Well, you're most definitely in the wrong house, is all I can say. Believe me, when you see this place on Christmas Day, you'll be cured or cursed for ever.'

'Eh, right,' Sophia muttered.

'Go on, you'll freeze,' Joey said. 'I'll catch you in a minute, yeah?'

'Cool,' she said, striding inside and up the stairs.

'She loves her training, doesn't she?' Paddy said, trying to defuse the awkwardness.

'Sure does,' Joey answered. 'I'll go and have a shower and get changed. What time are the guests arriving for supper?'

'I think your mother said around six thirty or seven. There's a hunt in the morning so it won't be a late one.'

'Great. See you shortly,' Joey said.

When he found Sophia she was on the floor in his bedroom, stretching. 'All okay?' he asked.

'Yeah. I'll jump into the shower, and then I'd love to grab some pasta or something, if that's okay?'

'Well, dinner won't be long. Can you make do with a piece of toast or something to keep you going?' he asked.

'What are we having?'

'I don't know. Why?'

'I'm not really into those stews with random bits of God knows what in them that Sadie likes making,' she said, chewing her lip.

'Sadie's a brilliant cook,' Joey said. 'She uses mostly home-grown veggies, and the meat is locally produced and a hell of a lot healthier than most shop-bought stuff.'

'No need to get so uppity,' she said, chucking him under the chin. 'I'll have my shower. Then we can go and investigate.' Planting a kiss on his lips, she disappeared.

Joey was torn. He adored Sophia. She was great in bed and most of the time she was easy enough to get on with. But every time they came to Huntersbrook there was tension between them. He'd have to chat to her and see if they could get to the bottom of it.

When she tiptoed back in to his room, wrapped in a towel and looking extremely sexy, his woes disappeared and he remembered all the reasons he'd fallen in love with her. 'You're amazing, you know that, don't you?' he said, stroking her face as he held her close under the duvet.

'I do my best,' she said, smiling brightly. 'Now, I don't mean to be rude, Joey, but I was starving before and right now I feel like I'm going to die if I don't eat.'

'Yes, ma'am!' Joey said, reluctantly peeling himself out of his bed. 'Let me jump in the shower for two minutes and I'll be with you. Sure you go on down to the kitchen and help yourself.'

'Ah, no. I'll wait for you here,' she said, burying her head in her overnight bag. 'By the time I've done my makeup and got dressed you'll be ready.'

Joey trotted into the bathroom and stood under the shower. As he blew the water off his face and lathered himself, he wondered how to approach Sophia's reluctance to chill out with his family. He wanted her to feel at home here. Christmas was only weeks away. It was their first together and he hoped she'd get into the spirit and enjoy the break with him here.

A tap on the door made him jump. 'Yeah?' he called.

'Are you nearly finished?' Sophia shouted.

'There now, babe,' he said. Christ, she was keen to get to the kitchen. He turned off the shower, tied the towel around his waist like a sarong and padded back in to his room. 'Go on ahead and I'll follow you,' he suggested again.

'I'm fine,' she said tightly, perching on the edge of the bed.

'Nobody will mind if you help yourself to some food. Go on, make yourself at home,' he continued. 'In fact, Mum and Dad would be delighted if you acted like you were at ease here.'

'I said I'd wait.'

'When we're here over Christmas I want you to feel you belong,' he said. 'It's always a real family and friends get-together. But it's not going to be fun if you're not a bit more chilled.'

'Eh, right,' she said, her eyes on the floor. 'I meant to chat to you about that. I've a surprise for you.' She put her arms around him.

'Oh?'

'I've booked us onto a training camp over Christmas. I was going to tell you about it closer to the time, but now that it's come up ...'

'A training camp? Won't it be a bit Baltic? Especially if this cold snap keeps up,' Joey said.

'That won't be a problem where we're going.'

'Where have you booked?' he asked.

'Lanzarote!' she announced. 'We leave on the twenty-third and get back on the second!' She squealed and jumped up and down, making tiny claps with her hands. Instead of thinking how cutesy and gorgeous she looked, as he usually did at such times, Joey found her mildly annoying. He was reminded of an over-enthusiastic performing seal.

'I'll have to think about that,' he said flatly, as he pulled his jeans and sweatshirt on. 'I'm not sure my folks would ever forgive me if I bailed on them for Christmas. And this year it'll be hard enough for them with Grandma gone.'

'Joey! Are you serious?' she scoffed. 'You're twenty-five, for crying out loud! Are you afraid Santa Claus won't find you in Lanzarote?'

'Family is important to me and so is Christmas. That's all,' he said evenly.

'Uh, whatever,' Sophia said. 'Come on, we can sort this out another time. I need some food.'

Sophia was seething. She'd thought she had it all sussed when she'd booked the camp in Lanzarote. It was the perfect way to get out of being bored senseless down here over Christmas without causing an out-and-out row with Joey. All their Dublin friends were so impressed that Joey was from this big manor house, but the reality was mind-numbingly boring and Joey's family so parochial. They wouldn't know what hit them if they were to try and fit in at The Shelbourne or any of the cool places in Dublin.

As she and Joey made their way to the kitchen, a load of guests were chatting in the hallway beside the fire. She almost had to stifle a snigger: they hadn't a shred of style between them. She bet they'd never even heard of a GHD and as for their clothes – uh, call the fashion police! Paddy and Holly were fine, but she found the entire set-up too much like The Partridge Family. There was no way she was getting stuck here for Christmas. Joey had surprised her, though. She hadn't anticipated that he'd rather be here than going away. Still, she'd get around him. He was a big teddy bear when all was said and done. He might think he was better off being Prince of the Manor, but that was because he'd never been encouraged to do anything else. She'd bide her time and let him come around to her way of thinking. It'd be a cinch.

'Here you go, son.' Paddy handed Joey a beer.

'Thanks, Dad,' he said gratefully. 'I need this.' He drained half the bottle in one go.

'Will you have a glass of wine or a beer, Sophia?' Paddy asked.

'No, thanks. I'll grab some water in a while. I'm fine for the moment.'

'Ah, John . . .' Paddy was already greeting another guest.

As he waved at an old friend, Joey felt Sophia tugging at his sleeve. 'Will you come into the kitchen with me? I'm starving, remember?'

'Don't you look divine?' Holly had come over to them before they could make it out of the hallway. 'Wow, I'd be arrested if I went out in those skinny jeans! They'd show up all my wobbly bits. All that training certainly pays off when you end up with a figure like yours.'

'You look gorgeous, too,' Joey said, kissing her. 'We're starving, Mum, so we're going to grab something to eat, if you don't mind?'

'Sure, love. I'd say we'll all sit down to eat fairly soon but go on ahead. Sadie's lamb casserole is in the bottom oven of the Aga and there's rice just strained on the hob.'

'Thanks, Mum,' he said, and they marched into the kitchen, avoiding any further conversations.

'Joey, no offence, but I hate lamb. It's too fatty and I'm really not into that type of thing. Whatever about eating lean meat, I don't do the babies of any species. That's just gross,' Sophia whined.

Joey closed his eyes and tried not to lose his temper. 'I can easily make you pasta but Sadie's lamb is really tasty. Why don't you just try it?'

'Pasta would be great.' She smiled sweetly.

He could feel a row brewing so he grabbed a saucepan and filled it with water. 'Is pesto okay for you?'

'I'll take it dry, thanks.'

'Don't you ever get fed up eating dry pasta? I honestly think you should try to vary your diet a bit,' he said. 'It's one thing eating like this when you're in the middle of racing but I'd worry about your bones and general health. You rarely eat meat or fish and you're not even great with vegetables.'

'Joey,' she smirked, 'with all due respect, I'm the one who works as a personal trainer. I'm the one who got you into triathlon in the first place. I think I know how to work with my own body so I don't need a lecture.'

'Fine.'

Holly swept in. 'I'm going to serve the food now. Would you bring in the big casserole dish for me, love?' she asked Joey.

'Sure, Mum,' he said, glad to end the conversation with Sophia. 'You might like to put your pasta on – there's some that cooks in about two minutes in there,' he said, gesturing to a cupboard as he left the kitchen. He was waylaid several times by old friends en route to the dining room, but when he got back to collect the rice, Sophia was perched on the sideboard eating her pasta.

'Need a hand?' she asked, without moving.

'I'm doing just fine, thank you,' he said curtly. As far as he was concerned, she could stay in the kitchen by herself if that was what made her happy.

In the dining room, the difference in atmosphere was marked, with laughter and easy banter. Joey put the rice on the hostess trolley and wondered where to sit.

'I'd like to propose a birthday toast to our eldest child,' Paddy said above the hum of conversation, and the room hushed. 'Thank you, Sadie and Holly, for the delicious meal and we hope you all enjoy it. Cheers!' he said.

'Cheers!' the crowd joined him.

Lainey had sat down at the head of the large table so Joey went over and perched beside her. 'Sorry I didn't get you a pressie,' he said.

'Joey, I'd think there was something wrong if you did! In all my thirty-one years on this planet you've never managed it so why start now?'

He grinned, shame-faced.

'Where's Sophia?' she added.

'In the kitchen.' He tried not to sound pissed off. 'She hates lamb so she's made her own food.'

'Right.' Lainey changed the subject. 'Did you see what Grandma sent me?' She held up her wrist for him to admire the silver charm bracelet.

'So she hasn't forgotten us altogether,' Joey commented.

'I suppose. And I do love it but I'd rather see her. It'll be weird not having her here for Christmas, won't it?'

As Joey looked around the room at his family and friends, he knew he didn't want to miss out either. He got up, grabbed another beer and went to join his dad. He was getting tired of Sophia's moodiness. He wondered if he was having an off day or whether the cracks that were beginning to show in their relationship were more serious than he'd first thought.

A little later he went into the kitchen to see if she was all right.

'Are you looking for Sophia?' Holly asked, as she crashed in behind him with a pile of dirty plates.

'Have you seen her?' he asked.

'She said she was going to bed a while ago. Didn't she tell you?'

'No, she didn't,' Joey said. He could go up and find her but he figured he'd rather have another beer.

5

Last Christmas

❄❄❄

Sunday morning dawned with a heavy frost and Lainey pulled the duvet up to her chin. Her eyes fell on her nightstand where the photo of her and Seth used to be. She wished she could reach the point where she didn't think about him any more.

They'd broken up a year ago yet she still found it hard to move on. He'd been her first serious boyfriend and, although she'd known deep down that he was wrong for her, she hadn't seen the break-up coming. In fact, she'd been half expecting, half hoping he'd propose. Instead he'd been seeing someone else.

When he'd finally come clean Lainey had tried to hold on to him, saying she'd forgive him. In fact, she'd have done anything to keep him. But he hadn't given her the choice. He'd told her it was over – dumped her without so much as a backward glance. Her emotions had been all over the place: she'd gone from heartbroken mess to vague relief in the understanding that she'd had a lucky escape.

Old habits die hard, though, and now she flicked to the Facebook app on her phone. She felt like she'd been slapped. Seth had just updated his status to engaged. She knew she should unfriend him and stop torturing herself, but Lainey couldn't resist checking on him. After all, he'd been the centre of her universe for the three years they'd been dating.

Lainey tried to force back tears as she lay on her bed and stared at the ceiling. Seth had dumped her. Grandma had run to the other side of the world. The two people who'd filled her life were both gone.

She needed to talk to someone about this latest revelation. Without thinking, she dialled Jules's number.

'Hiya!' Jules answered on the first ring. 'What are you up to so early on a Sunday morning?'

'I could ask you the same thing,' Lainey said, feeling instantly cheered.

'Oh, I'm out for a walk. I couldn't sleep so I got up and out,' she explained. 'How was your birthday dinner last night? Sorry again that I couldn't make it.'

'It was a lovely evening, very chilled, and I didn't drink too much. I'm hunting today so I didn't go too crazy. The thing is … I was looking at Facebook and it turns out Seth is engaged.'

'Seriously? Are you okay?'

'Yeah, but it feels weird.'

'Poor you. It's always hard when an ex moves on, isn't it?'

'I hope you don't mind me ringing you,' Lainey said. 'You didn't even know the guy – but it's so long since I was in touch with most of my old friends.'

'Didn't he get on with them?'

'He complained when I arranged for any of my pals to hook up with us, so I stopped asking them,' she admitted. 'In the end, most things we did were on his terms, and where did it get me?'

'We all have dodgy exes,' Jules told her. 'That's why they're exes. Don't beat yourself up, Lainz. And as for the Facebook habit, I'd say a million other broken-hearted people do the exact same thing.'

'I really should have the sense to swat myself at this stage, shouldn't I?'

'I'm no expert on relationships so don't look to me for the answers.' Jules laughed.

'You're so kind just listening to me.'

'We're friends, silly!' Jules reminded her. 'Next time I'm having a crisis I'll call you! How's that?'

'Deal! And now I'd better get up and saddle my horse if I'm going hunting.' Lainey was feeling much better.

In the kitchen, Holly and Paddy were finishing breakfast, on the verge of going outside to welcome the hunt.

'Hi, love,' Paddy said, when Lainey appeared. 'You'd want to get your skates on if you're joining the hunt. Will I grab Kizzy from the stable and make a start on her?'

'Thanks, Dad. I won't be long,' she said.

'There's tea in the pot,' Holly said. 'I'll be out the front directing the boxes. A few eager beavers have arrived already. It looks like we're going to have a good turn-out this morning. It might be an idea for you to think about hurrying yourself there. It's hardly your father's responsibility to saddle up your horse. You're not a child any longer, in case you haven't noticed.'

'Okay, Mum. I won't be long,' Lainey said, bristling. 'Dad offered to get started on Kizzy. I didn't assume he would.'

'No, of course you didn't,' Holly said tightly. 'So I'll see you shortly?'

'Great,' Lainey said, trying to keep her frustration from her voice. She poured some tea and hacked a chunk of bread off a loaf, then meandered back to her room to get dressed.

By the time she made it outside, Paddy had a rather excited Kizzy ready to go. 'Thanks, Dad. I didn't mean you to do the whole job for me.' He gave her a leg up, and she gathered her reins.

'Ah, sure it's like old times when you were little,' he said. 'I like to do it for you. Especially seeing as your brother and sister don't ride out now. Enjoy yourself and try to stay on.'

Excited hounds poured out of a horsebox and Kizzy danced on the spot. 'Good girl,' Lainey said, patting her neck to calm her. Her mother appeared beside her.

'The dragsman's gone on ahead to lay the scent,' Holly told her, 'so you'll be pushing off in five minutes.'

The whinnying of the horses mixed with the hounds' yelping gave Lainey butterflies.

'Tally-ho!' the Master shouted, and blew on his horn.

'See you later, Lainey!' her father called after her, as she trotted away.

Once they headed out across the field Lainey felt her shoulders relax. When she and Kizzy were out together, she always felt carefree and happy. She'd missed Grandma this weekend. They usually shared a slice of birthday cake and several cups of coffee together. Maggie could be rather abrasive, as many who had experienced her sharp tongue knew, but Lainey had always seen a different side of her.

The hunt was fast and furious but there were no casualties. By the time they returned, and Lainey had brushed her mare down, it was lunchtime. She gave Kizzy a bucket of nuts and went into the house.

Sadie had appeared, as she did most Sundays. Officially she was there to help, but she always had lunch too. 'I've run you a nice deep bubble bath,' she said, as Lainey came in. 'How was it?'

'Great, and thanks for the bath. How far away is lunch?' she asked Holly, who was at the table reading the papers with Paddy.

'Just as soon as you're ready. The meat is out resting,' Holly said.

'Are Joey and Sophia still here?' Lainey asked.

'They had to head back to Dublin in a hurry,' Paddy answered. 'Seems young Sophia had a lot of training on.'

'I see,' Lainey said. 'Well, I'll eat enough to make up for them.'

'Can you eat enough to make up for Grandma too?' Holly asked acidly. 'I still don't understand why she's chosen to abandon us and live so far away.'

'She didn't abandon us, Mum, and I'd love her to be here, too, but she's entitled to have fun just like the rest of us.'

'It was you who softened her, Lainey,' Holly mused reflectively. 'She was a tough old bird. I suppose she got that way when Daddy died. You were the one who broke the ice that had formed around her heart.'

'Indeed you were,' Sadie confirmed. 'Maggie did everything with one hand when you were born. She brought you here, there and everywhere. She talked to you as if you and she were the same age. She told you her innermost thoughts. You were her life blood.'

As her daughter and Sadie chatted, Holly allowed herself to dwell on the past.

The whole village and town had known how fabulous

Maggie was with the baby, but Holly often wondered if that *help* had cost her in the long run. She didn't feel as close to Lainey as she did to Joey and Pippa. Here she was, thirty-one years later, and there was still an invisible barrier between them. She blamed her mother for it and had unleashed her anger eleven months previously. This was something she'd never been able to admit. Not even to Paddy.

'What do you mean you're going to live with Sid?' Holly had asked, aghast.

'It's probably the most frivolous thing I've ever done but I'm getting on, Holly,' Maggie had said. 'If I don't do this now I'll regret it.'

'God forbid that you should have any regrets in life, Mum,' Holly had scoffed.

'I don't have time to wait around for you to decide whether or not you can forgive me, Holly. I've made my decision. Try to be happy for me,' Maggie had said.

Her mother's unusually gentle tone had disarmed Holly, until she discovered how soon Maggie would leave.

'It's not up to us what your mother does, love,' Paddy had said, on the night before Maggie caught her plane.

'Oh, don't I know it?' Holly had raved. 'But what about us, Paddy? Mum is making out she's being all noble and wonderful handing us the deeds to Huntersbrook House. As usual she'll emerge looking like a superhero.'

'How do you mean?' Paddy looked perplexed.

'Oh, what's the use? Forget it. I'm just being awkward as usual. I suppose it's just that Mum's always been here,' she'd fibbed. 'I'm a typical only child.'

Now as she watched Lainey's face light up, reading her grandma's card, a raw nerve twanged inside Holly for the umpteenth time.

It's the Most Wonderful Time of the Year!

Pippa wanted to put her hands over her ears and rock, making mildly insane crooning noises. It was only Monday morning and the week had got off to a disastrous start. She'd just pressed play on her answer machine and every caller was irate.

As she sat on her recently acquired sofa, positioned alongside a nest of tables to face the stupidly large flatscreen TV, she wasn't experiencing the same glow as she had when the friendly chaps had delivered all of it a couple of months previously.

She'd seen the advert that showed where you could go and pick out the contents of a living room and get a giant TV thrown in. They'd promised she wouldn't have to pay until the next decade, or some time way off in the future at any rate. It would've been rude not to take them up on the offer.

She hadn't bothered about the price at the time, but she knew it was buttons.

In Pippa's view, they'd been extremely sneaky and underhand about the whole thing. Now it appeared, from the snotty voice message, that they wanted some of the money immediately – as in today.

Joey, Pippa thought. He'd sort it. He could tell them to bog off with their request for payments. Did they not know there were only a handful of shopping days left until Christmas? Where was the season-of-goodwill thing?

'Did you read the terms and conditions?' Joey asked moments later, when she'd explained the situation to him.

'Of course I didn't!' she scoffed. 'I watched the TV advert, went to the store, signed the bit of paper and all the lovely new stuff arrived. Why should I have to hire an accountant and lawyer to buy a sofa? Nobody takes any notice of terms and conditions,' she reasoned. 'Why else do you think they're written so small at the bottom of the page?'

'You're precisely the type of numbskull these companies are hoping to trap. In the real world, you're meant to check these things. The fact of the matter is that you have to pay. Furniture and electrical equipment aren't free. Even to you.'

'I see. Well, you're not much bloody help, are you?' Pippa spat. 'Thanks for nothing, Joey.'

'Hey! It's not my fault.' Joey sounded angry. 'I didn't tell you to do it, and if you'd asked me before now I could've explained what you were letting yourself in for. I give up, do you know that? I don't understand women. Never have and never will.'

'Okay. Jeez!' Pippa said. 'Congratulations! You've bitten my head off. Don't choke on it.' She slammed the phone down. She'd no idea what was eating Joey but he'd want to get himself sorted. He wasn't usually that cranky in fairness to him. But she'd wait for an apology from him all the same.

The second message was from Jay, all whiny and needy. She wasn't able for him any more. He had been good craic in the beginning but the relationship had run its course. Fair enough, they'd been together over a year, which was a personal record for her, but Pippa figured all good things must come to an end. Jay and she were another example of that theory. She was also of the opinion that once something was over it was dead in the water, so what was the point in prolonging the pain? Jay was a good guy but she'd moved on. It happened. She texted him: *Hi J – we need 2 talk. Can u come 2 my place this avo @ 3?*

He answered immediately. He always answered on the first ring or would text back instantly. When she'd first met him she'd thought that was really cute. Now it seemed a bit too eager. As she pictured Jay, with his neat brown hair, Italian suits and smart, brightly coloured shirts, she knew he was too clean-cut and predictable for her. She'd enjoyed her time with him but he was too bloody nice! She didn't want to date Jack the Ripper, but she felt she could do better.

I'm working – it's Monday, remember? Jetlag obviously getting 2 u! C u @ 6 ok? Xxxx

Great, she thought. I'll have it sorted by seven. *Cool c u then J* She did a smiley rather than a kiss to start the 'dumping' process, and ticked that box on the 'to do' list in her head.

The next message was from her landlord. Now he was a first-class git. Any correlation between him and humans was purely coincidental. He wore head-to-foot grey nylon and spoke in a zero-punctuation monotone. Pippa wondered if he breathed through a secret hole in the back of his head.

'This is a voice message for Pippa Craig,' he began. Duh, Pippa thought, making a face. Nobody else lived here – who else could it be aimed at? Miss Piggy?

'Your rent is currently overdue by two weeks as per the agreement you have until the end of this week to submit the full amount or I will be forced to ask you to remove yourself from the flat [which he pronounced *fla-sh*] please call me by end of business today to confirm that you are in a position to uphold your end of the agreement obviously it would be ideal for both parties if we can get this sorted and have the payment processed as it's getting very close to Christmas.'

Pippa had to marvel at his ability to say all that in one breath. Perhaps he'd been practising, by sinking under the bathwater and holding his breath for as long as he could, since the age of four.

The final two messages were probably the worst. 'Good morning, Miss Craig, Ryan here from Credit Control Services. For your information, your cards have been frozen.'

He asked her to call immediately, as did the man who had left the last, and worst, message.

'Miss Craig, this is Sean from Bank of Ireland. There are a number of transactions pending and your account is overdrawn so I would strongly advise you to be in touch forthwith. If these pending sums are to be met, we'd need to have some immediate funds lodged.'

She'd make some coffee and phone the bank bloke and the credit card shark. God, these people were so dramatic! If the stupid promotions company hadn't fired her, everything would have been fine. This was their fault. They'd been so up themselves from the start that it was inevitable the whole thing would end in tears.

'How was I to know people would want actual names of who won the bloody iPod?' Pippa had yelled.

'If you're standing in a shopping centre dressed in a carrot costume and asking people to sign up for a loyalty card, stating there are a number of prizes on offer, the company has to stand by its word,' Mr Nugent had yelled back. 'We have a legal obligation to do as we promised. You cannot help yourself to one of the prizes and tell one of the punters how brilliant you're finding it.'

Pippa knew she probably shouldn't have asked for time off to go to New York at that exact moment. She should've stuck to her original idea of not telling Mr Nugent and getting Lainey to phone and say she had a tummy bug. But hindsight was a great thing.

She was in a right mess. She had to sort her life out. She'd clean up her current financial disorder and start the new year with a whole new attitude.

Pippa Craig was going to become organised and businesslike.

She put on the kettle. Everything would run more smoothly with a cup of coffee.

She returned to the sofa with her mug and dialled Sean at the bank. 'Ah, hello, Pippa Craig here,' she said, in her most professional voice.

Sean wasn't at all like his voicemail. He turned out to be rather an aggressive little man. Well, Pippa had no idea how tall he was but she had strong suspicions, from his angry terrier-like attitude, that he had a very small penis, regardless of his height.

She had to hold the phone away from her ear as he insisted on going through her account – very loudly.

'Right so,' Pippa said, at the end of it. 'I'll get it back on track.' She wished she hadn't bothered to phone him.

The woman she had to chat to at Credit Control Services was even worse. 'Can you give me your Visa card number and I'll deal with your query?' she asked, sounding clipped.

'Well, I'd prefer to talk to Ryan, seeing as he left the message.'

'Ryan is dealing with another client right now so I'll help you. This is Frieda,' she said.

'Right,' Pippa began. 'It seems I've fallen behind with my repayments—'

'Just quote your credit card number, Miss Craig, and we'll deal with this,' Frieda interrupted. Pippa did so, then listened as Frieda made lots of typing noises. 'Your last payment was eleven weeks ago,' she deadpanned.

'Is it that long?' Pippa said, trying to sound jokey about it. 'Ah, you know yourself, time flies when you're having fun, eh?'

'I need a percentage of the money paid off by Friday or we'll be forced to pass your debt to our legal department.'

'What?'

'You heard.'

'That's a bit harsh,' Pippa said, dropping the routine.

'Unfortunately that's the stage this account has reached,' Frieda said, bereft of emotion.

Pippa put the phone down. She hadn't had a notion that she'd racked up so much debt.

She'd known her funds must be running quite low but not to this extent. Two years previously she'd had a really good job in PR. She'd been well paid and in the boom times she'd secured a long-term lease on the upscale two-bedroom apartment overlooking Herbert Park. Now, confronted by the white walls with the designer prints, she began to panic. When the PR company had folded, they'd given her a really decent redundancy package. She'd added to that little nest egg by doing the odd promotional job. She'd honestly figured she was still financially sound.

She thought back to her recent trip to New York, and bit her lip guiltily. She hadn't gone too mad there. She'd really only bought jeans. And the bottle of champagne. And the makeup, and a few bits and bobs in Macy's.

Fleetingly she considered phoning her parents and asking them for a short-term loan. But she was twenty-three. She needed to sort herself out. Flicking through the freebie paper that had been pushed through her door, she circled a couple of job adverts. This recession lark was all in people's heads: there were loads of jobs on offer. People just didn't want to do them.

Lucy was always great for calming advice so Pippa phoned her.

'I can't talk right now, Pippa,' she said. 'My boss has just called me in for a meeting and I've a pile of emails to answer.'

'Fair enough.'

'Sorry, Pippa, but I'm genuinely busy.' Lucy sighed.

'It's all right for some,' Pippa said grumpily.

'Why don't you come into town and we'll go for a coffee?' Lucy offered. 'I'll see you in Starbucks at half past one. How's that?'

'You're brilliant,' Pippa said, instantly cheered. Now she could go and have a shower and feel as if she'd accomplished something.

Her feeling of euphoria didn't last long. By the time Lucy flew into the café that lunchtime things had taken a nosedive.

'You look like you've just come from Santa's grave.' Lucy chuckled. 'Sorr-ee! I thought that was quite witty of me. Not to mention seasonal.'

'Some of us aren't in the mood for jokes, or Christmas for that matter,' Pippa snapped.

'Whoop-di-do,' Lucy said tartly. 'I think I need a coffee. Want one?'

'You bet.' Pippa plonked her elbows on to the empty table dramatically.

'Would you like something to eat?' Lucy called from the spiralling queue.

'Yeah, get me whatever you're having. I'm too depressed to think,' Pippa shouted back. She gazed around the café. Lots of people in work suits had shopping bags shoehorned under their chairs and between their knees as they glanced anxiously at their watches. Some people had all the luck. They clearly had well-paid jobs and were off spending money like water, buying gorgeous Christmas gifts for their loved ones. All she had to look forward to this year was living in a homeless shelter. Life just wasn't fair.

'Here we go.' Lucy had arrived back at the table.

'You're a star, Luce,' Pippa said, as the other girl balanced the tray in one hand and attempted to transfer their bucket-sized cups of coffee and sandwiches to the table. 'I'm so depressed. All I've had is stress since I got back from New York. It's as if I'm being punished for having a crappy couple of days away.'

'Well, it was hardly crappy,' Lucy said. 'I thought we had a pretty amazing time. You're probably just experiencing post-holiday blues. It happens.'

'I'm in dire straits, Lucy,' Pippa blurted. 'I've bills coming out my ears. I feel like a criminal. Every time the phone rings it's another person out to get me. I tried to get a job this morning and every advert I answered was a dead end.'

'Things are rough out there right now,' Lucy said. 'Loads of our friends are in the same boat.'

Pippa sipped her coffee. 'Ugh!' she said. 'You didn't put any sugar in this.'

'No,' Lucy said. 'I'm starving, dying for a coffee, and all I was thinking about was sitting down and eating.'

'I'll go and get some sugar.' Pippa wasn't going to be snappy, but Lucy could be quite difficult at times. Not to mention unfeeling. Here Pippa was, upset about her financial crisis, and all Lucy could do was witter on about food.

'I've been thinking,' Lucy said, scrunching up the paper from her sandwich. 'Why don't you give Skye a call?'

'Skye?' Pippa was pouring the contents of three long, thin sugar sachets into her coffee and creating a tiny whirlpool with a wooden stick.

'Didn't she say that she'd had to move from her place? Isn't she camping with her cousin at the moment?'

'Oh, my God, you're a genius!' Pippa said. She was glad she hadn't started a row with Lucy now.

'I have to run, Pippa.' Lucy downed the rest of her coffee.

'Already? I've barely started this,' she said, pointing to her cup.

'Believe me, I'd love to sit and chat for the afternoon, but I've a meeting in forty minutes and I need to go through my notes first.' She swooped down and kissed Pippa's cheek. 'Good luck with sorting yourself out. I'll ask around about jobs, needless to say.'

'Okay. See you soon, I suppose.' Pippa felt neglected once more.

'You're welcome,' Lucy said, looking at her from beneath her eyelashes.

'Why are you giving me the headmistress stare?' Pippa asked.

'Well, I bought you lunch and you seem to have forgotten to say thank you or even acknowledge the fact.'

'I did!'

'I don't think so,' Lucy shot back. 'Ciao.'

Jeez, Pippa mused. Lucy must have PMT or some sort of jet-lag-associated mood-swing thing. She settled back to enjoy her coffee and dialled Skye's number. 'Hello, Skye. How's it going?'

'Not great. I'm not cut out for camping on sofas.'

'That's the right answer!' Pippa exclaimed.

'Sorry?'

'How would you like to move in with me?'

'Seriously? Just for a dig-out or long-term?' Skye asked. 'Not that I'm choosy right now.'

'Long-term. As in split the rent and the bills, take the spare room, half the cupboards in the kitchen, two shelves of the fridge and a wheelie trolley rack in the bathroom!'

'Can I come and have a look later this evening?' Skye asked.

'Yes, if you make it after seven. I've a small break-up to execute with Jay so you might prefer to wait until the coast is clear.'

'Are you sure about that? I think he's a really lovely guy, Pippa.'

'Why don't you go out with him, then?' Pippa asked.

'I didn't mean it like that.' Skye giggled. 'I just think you'll regret letting him go. He's crazy about you, and before we went away you were singing his praises. I think you two are made for each other. Are you certain you're not being a bit hasty?'

'Thanks for the advice but I know my own mind.' Pippa tried to keep the edge from her voice.

'Fair enough. I'll text you around seven to make sure he's gone before I pop over.'

Pippa hung up, feeling much more positive. She knew she hadn't actually paid her rent or cleared her credit cards – or her overdraft, for that matter – but she was on the right road. That was enough for one day.

She was seriously fed up with being cross-examined by her friends, though. Skye had been looking for a man for ages. She'd spent the weekend telling Pippa she was too shy to talk to guys. That guy in New York would've been fine but she'd turned up her nose at him. *And*, to top it all off, she was practically homeless.

Lucy seemed to think she was a financial wizard. Maybe she was, but she was so damn careful all the time. Every move she made had to be planned and thought through. Pippa didn't appreciate being made to feel as if she was the disaster of the gang.

She was having a small blip currently. No biggie. She'd dig herself out of it once she'd set her mind to it. Lucy would never be impulsive, God bless her, and Skye would be afraid of her own shadow for eternity.

Feeling sensible and grown-up, Pippa bypassed Top Shop, and didn't even try on the pale pink Ugg boots in the shoe shop, even though they were half price and she'd wanted them for ages. All she bought was the newspaper and a sparkly pink pen with strawberry-scented ink. She figured it would encourage her to circle more job ads.

As she parked outside her apartment she looked around the modern complex proudly. Not everyone lived in such a salubrious place. Let the girls look down their noses if they liked, but she, Pippa Craig, was doing all right, thank you very much.

By the time she'd let herself in and cleared up the spare room, jetlag had set in. Seeing as the sofa was now going to cost so much, she put it to good use by lying on it and watching *Oprah* on the equally expensive television.

The buzzing of her intercom woke her. It seemed like she'd only just drifted off, yet it was dark outside. When she checked her watch she discovered it was already after six. She'd never get rid of the jetlag if she kept conking out.

'Hello?' she croaked into the intercom.

'It's only me!' Jay said cheerfully. 'I didn't bring the car to work with me today so I don't have my key, sorry honey.'

'Come up,' she said, pressing the button. She pulled her matted hair into a ponytail, stretched and unlocked the door, leaving it on the latch.

'Hi!' he said, rushing in and wrapping himself around her.

'Hi,' she said, smothered by his enthusiastic embrace.

Before she could speak he'd engaged her in a full-on snog. She pulled away, stepped back and sat on the sofa, indicating that he should sit beside her. 'I need to say something,' she said.

'Me too,' he said, looking sheepish.

'You go first,' she said, hoping against hope he'd break up with her. That way she could look all sad until he left and the guilt would be his.

Dropping onto the sofa beside her, Jay took an envelope out of his pocket and held it out. 'Open it.' He grinned.

'What is it?' she asked, suddenly worried.

'I've booked us a two-week break in the Seychelles,' he said.

'What?' She almost choked. 'When?'

'It's not until February but I couldn't wait to tell you. I've always wanted to go but never had the right person to share it with. I know you were only gone for a couple of days, but while you were in New York I realised that I'm totally in love with you, Pippa.'

'Oh,' was all she could muster.

'I can see you're in shock. I know it might be a bit sudden but we've been together over a year, which, as you keep telling me, is a record for you! Why shouldn't I treat us?'

'Oh, God.' She swallowed. 'I feel really bad about this.' She honestly did. 'I was going to tell you I think we should break up.' She waited for the hurt and anger to pour forth.

'Wow,' he said, running his fingers through his hair. 'I can't say I was expecting that.' He leaned forward and stared at the floor.

'I'm sorry,' she said feebly.

'Not as sorry as I am.' He stood up and walked slowly towards the door. 'I really misread this one. I honestly thought we had something special ... I'd never have done this if I'd known.'

'Jay, I feel so bad . . .'

'So you've said.'

'I'd no idea you were so serious about us. I thought we were just having fun.'

'We were. That was the whole point, Pippa,' he said. 'You were the first girl I could really be myself with. I've never met anyone like you. I stupidly thought you were happy with me too. I'm not usually that spontaneous but you brought out a different side to me.'

Jay strode out of the apartment and shut the door quietly.

Pippa was alone, engulfed in uneasy silence. Wrapping her arms around herself, she felt suddenly cold and guiltier than she ever had before. Her gaze rested on the unopened envelope Jay had left on the sofa. Grabbing it, she ran out the door to catch him, but he had gone.

Her phone pinged. *Coast clear? Can I drop round? S x*

Pippa told Skye to come straight over and gave her the code for the door downstairs. Then she opened a bottle of wine from the fridge. She tore off the flap of the A4 envelope and felt sick. Jay had booked an all-inclusive luxury resort hotel. This was the trip of a lifetime.

Still, she had to be true to herself. She wasn't into Jay and that was it. He was too into her, too kind, too needy and not her type.

As she slumped on the sofa waiting for Skye to arrive, she quashed the thought that maybe she'd been a bit rash.

7

Rudolf, the Red-nosed Reindeer

Lainey hated going to the Limerick office at this time of year. Even though she knew their clerk, Evelyn, of old, the office wasn't as friendly as her own and she always felt that everyone was staring at her.

This year Drake had told her to bring Jules along. 'She needs the experience and it might give her a bit of insight into the reason why reports have to be delivered on time,' he'd barked. 'She doesn't seem to get the fact that we need to keep up with the other parts of the country. That when she's too busy filing her nails to bother getting stuff done for me, it affects people in Limerick or Cork or Waterford or whoever is waiting for the information.'

Lainey wanted to point out that Jules never did her nails in the office and that her work was flawlessly accurate, albeit a little slower than some. 'She rarely makes mistakes, Mr Drake. She's meticulous in her work. I don't think that's a fair comment.'

'Whatever. If she's so great you'll enjoy having her with you.'

Lainey hadn't a violent bone in her body but Drake brought out such anger in her that she often found it hard to control herself when she was with him. Just because Jules was pretty and glamorous, their boss assumed she was an airhead.

The Limerick office was close to the station so the girls decided to take the train. As it turned out, the job that day was more straightforward than they'd expected so they were done and dusted by four o'clock. 'Our return train isn't until seven. I've stupidly booked the seats so we'll have to kill time,' Lainey apologised. 'I'm ravenous – will we go for a meal?'

'Ooh, that sounds gorgeous!'

'And we'll charge it to the office, which is even better,' Lainey said, winking. She'd only ever used her work credit card for the odd overnight stay in a cheap hotel. Her shyness had meant she'd never eat out alone while on business, preferring to have a room-service snack or zoom home on the bike even if it was late. 'There are a few places on the way to the station, so let's park ourselves in one of those and that way we won't be hassled about missing the train,' she suggested.

A few moments later they walked up to a buzzy traditional Italian restaurant. 'This looks nice,' Jules remarked.

It was beginning to rain as the girls shuffled inside. The smell of garlic mixed with warm air was welcoming.

'Ladies, please, find a table and sit!' the waiter called across the room.

The small square tables were so close together that Lainey had to pull theirs out from the window so Jules could squeeze in to sit down. 'Are you all right in there?' she asked. 'They certainly know how to pack us all in, don't they?'

'Sure do, but it's busy so I reckon that's a good indication,' Jules said, and began to scan the menu, which was slotted between the salt and pepper mills.

'I've no idea if the food is going to be tasty but the staff certainly are!' Lainey joked. 'Isn't the waiter just divine? I love that dark curly hair and his cross expression. He's acting as if we're interrupting his day by being here. If he was Irish and pale with spots, I'd think he was a rude upstart, but it's almost sexy when someone's awful to you in Italian!'

'He doesn't do it for me, I'm afraid,' Jules confessed.

The waiter approached and asked if they'd like bread.

'Yes, please,' Lainey answered, and he fired a basket onto the table.

'So, what is your type, then?' Lainey asked, as they dipped crusty bread into olive oil.

'Oh, I go for a prettier look.'

'My sister Pippa's like you. She loves the fresh-faced boyish kind. Beautiful rather than rugged.'

'Right.' Jules was looking uncomfortable. 'Tell me about the Christmas party in work. Is it fun?' she asked, changing the subject.

'Oh, it's the usual large function-room event. I can't bear it, as I told you before, but my life wouldn't be worth living if I didn't turn up.' Lainey rolled her eyes. 'That reminds me – do you need any more info on the Kris Kindle thing?'

'You said the gift has to be around twenty euro?' said Jules.

'Yeah. You'll match people up once you have the names of the attendees.'

'I'm getting Mr Poo-face Drake,' Jules said, with a twinkle in her eye.

'Why don't you fix it that someone else gets him? He's such a git to you. Pick someone nicer.'

'I'm making sure I get him and I'm going to buy him stuff that'll mortify him.' She giggled. 'He's a real lad when he's in the office, throwing his weight around, but I'm going to buy him things like plastic boobs and a knitted willy-warmer to make a show of him.'

'You're really not as sweet as you look, are you?' Lainey was laughing.

'I have my ways of getting revenge on nasty people.'

'Yes, ladies, what will you eat?' the waiter asked, almost skidding to a halt at their table.

'I'll have tagliatelle and a side salad,' Lainey said, smiling at him.

'And you?' He pointed at Jules.

'The lasagne,' she said, clearly not enjoying his antics.

'Red or white wine?' Lainey asked Jules.

'White, if that's okay with you,' she said.

'And a bottle of house white, please.' Lainey flashed the waiter a smile, but too late – he'd already darted across the restaurant shouting their order to the gaggle of staff behind the counter.

'Is this your first Christmas being single for a while?' Lainey asked, dipping another piece of ciabatta into the oil.

'Yes,' Jules answered. 'I had a boyfriend last year.'

A different waiter pitched up with their wine, flashing the label at Lainey, flicking the screw-top open and pouring from such a height it was like a waterfall. '*Salute!* Cheers!' he shouted.

'I've only ever had Seth at Christmas. But he was very into

lists. We'd both have to write one and give it to the other by the first of December,' Lainey recalled. 'Five expensive things and five cheap things. We'd pick one from each category.'

'Wow. That's bunny-boiler stuff, Lainz. Didn't it kind of take away any sense of magic?'

'I suppose now you put it that way it was kind of contrived. But that was Seth all over,' she said, shrugging. 'He liked to have things done a certain way. Anyway, cheers!' They clinked glasses.

The first waiter returned and almost frisbeed their plates onto the table.

Jules jumped. 'Jeez, he nearly smashed yours.'

'He's pretty narky all right.' Lainey smiled. 'Christmas is going to be different in more ways than one this year, though. My grandma has gone away so it'll be my first Christmas without her too.'

'You seem really sad about that. Are you guys close?'

'Yeah. She's a tough old bird by anyone's standards but she and I always understood one another. I really miss her,' Lainey said, looking down.

'As I don't even get on with my mother, I find it hard to imagine how you feel. What's the story with Huntersbrook? Is it your grandma's house?'

'It was until she met an Australian called Sid and made this random decision to up sticks and go to live with him on his vineyard just after Christmas last year.' Lainey's eyes moistened. 'She's eighty, Jules, so I can't say any of us expected her to do what she did.'

'I can see you're upset about it, but I think she sounds pretty amazing. I hope I can do stuff like that when I'm old,' Jules said. 'You have to admit she's pretty out there!'

'I understand why she did it and I wish her well, but she

shocked the hell out of us in the process. You've got to see it from my point of view too. She was the one who held our family together. She was head of the house, and imposing with it. She always made her presence felt so it was like someone else appeared from her room one morning and said she was going off to be a flibbertigibbet.' Lainey scowled.

'A what?' Jules asked.

'A fly-by-night who turned her back on us all,' Lainey said forcefully.

'Have you spoken to her much since she went?'

'Not at all. She sent me this for my birthday,' she said, showing Jules her bracelet.

'That's gorgeous. Listen, it's none of my business and I don't even know her but you should try and see things from her perspective. She probably got tired of doing the right thing. It happens to the best of us,' Jules said. 'Maybe she met this guy, realised her life wasn't over quite yet and decided to grab the bull by the horns.'

'I know all that and I wish her well, of course I do. I just miss her. We used to sit and talk for hours. Then she was gone. It was literally as quick as that.'

'I'm no expert on families. But I do understand what it's like to feel resentment when you make a choice,' Jules said.

'What do you mean?'

'I'll tell you some other time, if that's okay?' Jules held her gaze. 'I know it must hurt like hell that your grandma moved so far away, but we all need to live. We all deserve to be happy too. Some people never find happiness. It took your grandma a long time but perhaps she's finally doing what she enjoys.'

'I guess,' Lainey said hesitantly. 'I sound like a horrible spoilt child when you put it like that, but it was so sudden.

It's been months now and I've let this silence come between us.'

'Maybe you can sort it out now. New year and all that? Contact her and start afresh,' Jules suggested. 'Anyway, I'm a right one to talk! I won't be in touch with my mother so that's that! On a more cheerful note, I'm really looking forward to Christmas at Huntersbrook.'

Lainey was delighted Jules was joining them, if baffled as to why her mother wasn't speaking to her. She was such a lovely girl, and so diplomatic. She could easily have entered into a let's-slag-Grandma conversation just now, but she hadn't. In Lainey's opinion Jules's mother was missing out by not talking to her daughter.

The girls finished their meal and made their way to the station. As they settled into their seats on the train, Lainey couldn't recall a business trip she'd enjoyed as much.

It was dark and lashing rain by the time they pulled into Heuston station in Dublin. 'I'm going to jump in a taxi,' Lainey said. 'It's so disgusting – I can't bear the thought of messing around on buses.'

'I'm near the city centre so I'll hop in a taxi too,' Jules said. 'Thanks for today. My first business trip with the county council!'

'Great to have your company,' Lainey said, kissing Jules on both cheeks.

Moments later, as she settled into the warmth of the taxi, she felt happier than she had for ages. In general she liked her job, but until Jules had joined she'd often felt a bit lonely at the office. Days like today made her feel hopeful that she'd get over Seth and move on with her life.

When the driver stopped outside her apartment complex, she realised she was exhausted. She paid him, stashed the receipt so she could claim the money back, then let herself into the dark flat. The one-bedroom first-floor unit was far from luxurious. The developers had described it as compact, which translated as poky yet functional. Lainey had bought it at the right time, just before the whole country had gone mad, paying extortionate prices. It was in one of those purpose-built complexes halfway between Dublin and Wicklow so there was little in the way of community spirit. Lainey knew none of her neighbours and she'd often thought that she could be lying there dead for a week and nobody would notice or care.

'It's a glorified cubbyhole,' Grandma had said, the first time she saw the place. 'I'd go stark raving mad in here.'

'Well, you're Manor House Maggie!' Lainey had teased. All the same, she'd been bowled over when her grandma had arrived the following day with a large picture in a frame.

'It's your moving-in gift. I'd call it a house-warmer but this isn't a house.' Grandma had sniffed.

Lainey had peeled off the newspaper wrapping (Grandma didn't believe in waste and had recycled unwittingly all her life) and gasped at the blown-up photo.

'Do you recognise it?' Grandma asked, smiling.

'It's the view from my bedroom window at Huntersbrook,' Lainey said, with tears in her eyes.

'At least you can still see a bit of greenery to keep you going until the weekends.'

Grandma always did things like that. She made thoughtful gestures that nobody else would ever consider. Well, she used to, until she'd gone with Sid to the other side of the planet without so much as a backward glance. Maybe it was the chilly air in the unheated apartment or maybe her hangover had set in, but Lainey was suddenly wide awake.

She scolded herself for falling back into a grouch about Grandma's defection, and tried to put herself into the positive zone Jules had talked about earlier. She needed to become a little more glass-half-full about everything.

She turned on the washing machine and vacuumed the apartment. Then she put on her pyjamas and decided to have a quick practice in her new shoes. The high heels still made her feel a bit scared as she slid them on. She had to learn to walk in them before she ventured out in public or she'd be face down with her dress over her head in spitting time.

Jules probably hadn't meant for her to clean the oven with them on, but Lainey wasn't going to cease being practical overnight. She was cleaning when her mobile rang so she forgot she was wearing the new shoes and nearly poleaxed herself as she staggered towards the coffee table. 'Hello,' she gasped.

'Lainz, it's only me. Is everything okay?' Jules asked.

'You don't want to know! I think you'd have me locked up if you saw me now. I'm in my pyjamas with a pair of rubber gloves on and my new high heels. I nearly killed myself answering the phone. I'm not holding out much hope for making it through the Christmas party in these, Jules.'

'Listen, tell me if you hate him,' Jules said, 'but I just got a call from a girly mate who has two Michael Bublé tickets from her ex-boyfriend, as of this afternoon, and they're going begging for zero euros.'

'Free?' Lainey was aghast.

'The only condition is that she might get back with him and need them again. But seeing as he's been shagging her flatmate, I reckon we're fairly safe.'

'Are you sure you don't have anyone else to bring?' Lainey said doubtfully.

'Oh! You're allergic to him, aren't you?' she said. 'I know he's a bit of a Marmite type – some people love him and others hate him.'

'No! It's not that.' Lainey was giggling. 'I'd love to see him. Thank you.' She needed to get out more and Jules was fun. It was time to push through the barrier of uncertainty Seth had left her with. I'm going to be a glass-half-full girl, she reminded herself.

'If you want to stay over at my place you're most welcome. It'll be a blow-up bed on the living-room floor but it'd save you a taxi fare to your own place,' Jules offered.

'Thanks, Jules.' She shook off her shoes and flopped onto the sofa.

'Brilliant!' Jules said happily. 'See you tomorrow at the office and thanks again for a great day today.'

Lainey said goodbye, then decided to log on to Facebook and post something cheerful.

Happy Monday one and all. Just home from a successful business trip where I was joined by a great friend along with the Chardonnay fairy! Oops – shouldn't drink on a work night but what the heck? It's nearly Christmas! Off to Mr Bublé on Sat night! Can't wait!

As she hit the share button her gaze rested on Seth's latest post.

My fiancée made a serious faux pas today & brought a wedding dress home to hide in the wardrobe. Luckily I came across it – suffice it to say she'll be taking it back tomorrow. I mean, who wants to marry a girl dressed in an old-fashioned toilet-roll holder? Ugh! It's vile! I told her she's lucky I'm willing to wipe the image of her wearing it from my mind!

Some of Seth's mates had added comments about him being like Hitler, and one even suggested he should consider locking the girl in the attic. The whole exchange made Lainey's blood run cold. She knew Seth wasn't joking about any of it. She could clearly imagine his flaring nostrils as he'd found that poor girl's dress. She was probably sobbing silently in their room at this very moment broken-hearted that he had slated the dress she'd thought was *the one*.

Closing her laptop, Lainey glanced at her watch and decided to give her parents a quick call before she went to bed.

'Hi, love,' her dad answered. 'Are you not watching *NCIS*?'

'I forgot it was on.'

'Are you ill? It's not like you to miss it,' Paddy said.

'I was at the Limerick office all day. I'm not long back,' she said, yawning. 'I was just calling to tell you and Mum I've been invited to the Michael Bublé concert with a friend on Saturday.'

'God love you,' Paddy said. 'I think I'd rather stab myself with the pitchfork, but I suppose he's more for the ladies than rough old farmers like myself.'

'That's enough.' Holly was on the line. 'I'm envious, Lainey,' Holly continued. 'I'd love to see Mr Bublé. Ignore your father, he's in one of his silly moods. Hold on till I give him a quick thump. Who are you going with? Anyone nice?'

'Jules, my new friend in the office.'

'Oh. I thought for a moment there you might have a hot date.'

'Sorry to disappoint you,' Lainey said, smarting. 'Jules is really lovely and you'll like her. While I remember, I invited her for Christmas dinner. That's okay, isn't it?'

'Eh, yes, of course.' Holly sounded hesitant.

'You don't sound sure,' Lainey said. 'Is everything okay, Mum?'

'Everything's fine. I'm just tired. I was running around like a mad woman today, that's all.'

'Sure I'll chat to you later in the week. Get a good night's sleep – you sound exhausted,' Lainey said.

'I said I was fine!'

'Sorry.' Her mother was in one of her usual defensive moods. Lainey couldn't help but think that if Holly had been talking to Pippa or Joey she wouldn't have snapped. If she herself so much as attempted to voice an opinion her mother practically jumped down her throat.

She said goodbye, scooped up her new shoes and went into her bedroom to look in her wardrobe for something to wear to the concert. Nothing jumped out as being a 'gig' outfit. She vowed to call Pippa the following day for some fashion advice.

Grown-up Christmas Wish

✳✳✳

Joey was having one of those days when he was pretty short of patience. He needed to get to work and Sophia had been in the bathroom for at least half an hour. 'I'm late! What are you doing in there?' he asked, knocking on the door once more.

'I was putting on fake tan,' she said, coming out and brushing past him.

He went in and opened the window. He couldn't stand the smell of that stuff. The whole concept was beyond him at the best of times but it was December and they lived in Ireland: why did girls think they should have a tan?

'This place stinks,' he shouted, as he kicked the door shut. He turned on the shower, stood under the jets and lathered himself. At least he could breathe in the citrus scent rather than that awful burned-rashers pong. Folding his arms, he sighed deeply. He was still pissed off with Sophia. She'd made zero effort with his family last weekend. He'd given her the benefit of the doubt on the rare occasions they'd visited Huntersbrook over the past few months, but this time her selfish carry-on had bugged him.

He rubbed his hair dry, wrapped a towel around his waist and brushed his teeth. Sod it, he thought. Enough was enough. 'We need to talk,' he said, walking into the bedroom and beginning to get dressed.

'Not now,' she said, as she pulled on a puffa coat over her yoga gear. 'I'm going to the gym to meet a new client. I'll see you later. I've a bike session to do so I'll set up the turbo-trainer in the living room. You can talk to me then.'

'Sophia, can't you give me five minutes? I'm late for work too.'

'Then now isn't the time. Catch you later,' she said, pecking him on the lips and jogging out the door.

Joey thumped the bedroom wall, then finished dressing as quickly as he could. There was no way he could talk while he was in work and, besides, she never answered her phone during the day.

The Lanzarote thing was stressing him out too. He didn't want to go. He was enjoying his training and he certainly hoped he'd do a few races come the summer, but he wasn't as dedicated to it as Sophia was. He knew she needed to put in serious hours if she was to manage the Ironman race in September, but he had to explain to her that he wasn't happy about missing Christmas with his family. Maybe they could come to a compromise and go to the Canaries on 26 or 27 December instead.

Luckily the bus arrived quickly and he made it into the office on time.

'Ready to meet Mr Dunphy from Megavalue Supermarket?' Clive, his boss, greeted him. 'They should be here in a few minutes. I'll be along once you've gone over the initial figures with them.'

'See you shortly,' Joey said.

'I hope to have a bit of news for you later on too,' Clive added, banging Joey on the back.

'Thanks,' Joey said, brightening. Could this be what he'd been waiting for? A promotion, perhaps? He'd been working his arse off to make it in the accountancy firm. Times were really hard economically but they were weathering the storm so far. The client he was meeting this morning was a tricky fecker, but he and Joey had connected on the triathlon circuit last summer.

'Joey! Good morning. How are things?' Mr Dunphy emerged from the lift behind him.

'Good morning! Good to see you. Come on in and we'll get started,' he said. 'Coffee or tea?'

'I'm off caffeine. I've a new trainer and he's all about natural foods and avoiding artificial stimulants. Not sure how it'll all translate on the triathlon courses but I'm giving it a shot. Have you herbal tea in this place?' he asked, striding into the meeting room and bashing his briefcase onto the desk. He was pushing sixty but his training meant he was fit. He worked and trained hard, but although he was undoubtedly a sound businessman, he wasn't exactly popular with most of the accountants. He was loud and brash and had a habit of offending people.

'Certainly,' Joey said, buzzing his secretary's extension. 'Morning, Jemima. Can you bring me two herbal teas, please? Hold all my calls. I'm in room three with Mr Dunphy.'

He hung up, clipped open his briefcase and pulled out his laptop with the Megavalue books he'd finished working on.

'How's the training going yourself?' Dunphy asked.

'Not bad,' Joey said. 'Ticking away. I can't say I'll be as successful as you are come race season, but I'll do my best.'

'It's easier to win when you hit my age group. Most of the competition are heading towards Zimmer-frame territory so I'm at a bit of an advantage, I suppose,' he said gruffly.

'Ah, don't put yourself down. You're a fine athlete in your own right. I've seen you in the water and you're a machine!' Joey said, grateful to be able to tap into the other man's passion outside running one of the biggest local supermarkets in the country.

Dunphy cackled at the compliment. Then: 'Enough of that. Show me the money,' he said, all smiles gone.

Sophia was feeling even more irritated by the end of the morning. Her first client that day had been a total sap, a man sent to her by his wife to lose some of his beer belly.

'My good lady has gently told me I need to tone up, so I figured a few sessions before Christmas would keep her happy,' he boomed.

'Well, it's going to take a lot more than one or two jogs,' she said. 'I'm not going to kid you here. You're very out of shape. I can help you, certainly, but it won't be easy.'

He'd looked shocked and annoyed! Ha! As if it was her fault he'd stuffed his face for fifty years and spent his evenings drinking wine and pontificating.

She'd got him to pay up-front for the training so, as far as she was concerned, the rest was up to him. He was definitely one of the lazy sort who'd come once more, twice at a push, and she'd never see him again. She wasn't bothered what he did. She was a good trainer, everyone in south Dublin knew that, but she wasn't a 'coach'. If they wanted to discuss their feelings, her clients could go elsewhere. Her way of doing things involved pushing it, then finding the extra ten per cent and pushing it some more. Nothing else worked.

'You're a hard taskmaster,' Mr Blobby had said this morning.

'And I make no apologies for it,' she'd answered.

The next session was a group she'd been training for a while. They were a corporate set, like the crew from Joey's work, but this lot were women, who did their block session of planned training and disappeared. Perfect.

She saw she'd missed calls from Joey but she hadn't the headspace to talk to him today. He was only going to bleat on at her about Christmas again. He was really pissing her off. She'd counted on his usual easygoing nature to bring him round to her way of thinking, but he was digging in his heels and she didn't like it one bit. He kept saying, 'Mum'll be hurt,' or 'Dad'll be devastated,' and even 'Pippa would never get over it if I wasn't there.'

It was such arse in Sophia's opinion. It was Christmas – one day. Who gave a toss? He could go and sit by the fire and smell smouldering logs any other time he wished. Why did she have to do it too? Christmas to her meant time off from her clients. Time she needed to spend training. This camp only operated for a few weeks each year. It was vital she tapped into the expertise of the people who ran it. Ironman was a big deal and Joey needed to start seeing her point of view. If he didn't, she'd have to reconsider her position with regard to their relationship.

Stuffing her mobile phone to the bottom of her kitbag, she banished the scowl from her face and turned on a smile. Her ladies would be ready for action and they didn't need to be faced with a sourpuss. Damn Joey and his constant whining.

The day flew past, as Joey moved from one taxing meeting to another. By the time five o'clock came around he was starving. He grabbed a banana and a large packet of peanuts from his desk drawer and shovelled in as much as he could before he went to the lift.

'Ah, there you are,' Clive said, as he joined him. 'Are you coming to the track for a run?'

'Yup,' Joey said wearily. 'I can't say I'm in the mood but I'm sure it'll do me good once I get going. I'm starving – I didn't make it to the canteen for a proper lunch but I reckon the exercise will clear my throbbing head. It sounds pretty wild and windy out there. It'll blow the cobwebs off us if nothing else.'

'Certainly will,' Clive agreed. 'Did you bring your car today or do you want a lift?'

'I'd love a lift, as it happens,' Joey said. 'I knew I was in the office all day so I didn't bother with the car. Cheers,' he said. They descended in the lift to the underground level and he held the door to the car park open for his boss. Sitting inside Clive's Audi, Joey inhaled the earthy smell of the leather.

'God, this is some machine, Clive,' he said, with clear envy.

'Isn't she? I never tire of driving her. Which brings me on to you. Seeing as I have you on your own, I can let you in on a secret. You could be driving something similar yourself before too long.'

'Go on.'

'I've spoken with some of the senior partners,' Clive

said, navigating out of the car park and towards the nearby running track. 'The announcement won't come officially until January but I can tell you, totally on the QT, that you're going to be offered a promotion.'

'That's amazing news,' Joey exclaimed. 'Christ, I'm made up.'

'It's well deserved, son,' he said, as they pulled up at the track. 'Not a word for the moment, mind.'

'My lips are sealed,' Joey promised. 'Thanks for giving me the heads-up.'

Clive grinned as he got out and grabbed his kitbag. 'Watch this.' He pushed the car door gently. As it neared closing, it slowed and the car automatically sucked it shut, with a soft click.

'Deadly.' Joey followed suit with his own door. 'Sweet.'

'Let's get changed and I'll whoop your arse,' Clive said.

'We'll see about that,' Joey said, rising to the challenge.

Once they'd greeted the other runners and were on the track, it was starting to rain. All notions of not wanting to be there were firmly out. Joey was on a high. He was dying to tell Sophia about his imminent promotion. He could almost hear her squealing down the phone.

'Right, lads, let's get warmed up. It's bloody cold this evening so we'll get a good pace going,' the trainer called, as the floodlights came on. 'Don't stand around or your temperature will plummet. Let's get some stretches started.' He clapped his hands.

When they were ready to run around the track for the first time, Joey nudged Clive. 'Smell you later, old man,' he gibed.

'Hey, I'm your boss.' Clive swiped at him and missed as Joey bolted away.

'Not on the track you're not,' Joey said, laughing.

'You should be bowing to me, you young pup,' Clive said, catching him up. 'If it wasn't for my hiring Sophia to do that team-building day last year you'd still be single and sad, not to mention slow. You should have more respect!'

'Ah, sure you're my guardian angel, Clive,' Joey said, and tore off ahead of him.

Joey managed to stay at the front of the pack for the entire session, enjoying every stride.

'You'll be hard to catch in race season,' Clive said in the locker room afterwards.

'I'm feeling pretty buzzed. I'll have a quick shower and go find my girlfriend.'

'How is she? I haven't seen her for quite a while.'

'She's good, thanks. Training pretty hard herself. She's planning on doing an Ironman this year so it's fairly full on.'

'Good for her. She's a cracker. You're a lucky guy.'

'Ah, don't I know it.'

As soon as he'd showered and dressed, Joey called Sophia to see if there was any food in the fridge. He was famished and couldn't bear the prospect of a bowl of dry pasta, which was her idea of dinner.

'Hello,' she said, sounding out of breath.

'Hi, love. How's it going?'

'Good. Listen, I'm on the turbo-trainer in the living room.' When she'd moved in he'd found it endearing that she placed her bike on the special stand, which meant she could cycle on the spot for hours on end. Now it alienated him and pushed him into the bedroom – alone.

'Did you want something specific or can I talk to you in a while?' she asked.

'Eh, no. I was just calling to say I'm finished my run session.'

'Great. See you in a while,' she huffed.

'Do you want dinner? I could stop and—'

'Joey, I don't mean to be rude but I'm pushing really hard here and I can't talk on the phone at the same time. Get whatever you want and I'll sort myself.'

He knew it was totally off limits in the world according to Sophia but he had a mad urge for junk food. A call from Pippa sealed the deal.

'Hey, bro,' she said chirpily.

'Hi, Pippa! How are things?'

'Good! Where are you?'

'Just finished training. I'm starving and I'm headed for a greasy dose of the chipper. Will I call in with some for you too?' he asked. Pippa's apartment was less than a five-minute walk from his place and on his way home.

'I'd love that. Will you get me a double cheeseburger and garlic fries?' she asked. 'I've no money, though, so I'll have to owe you.'

'What's new?' Joey said. 'I'll be there in about fifteen minutes.'

'I'll have the telly on and the kitchen paper ready,' she said.

For all her faults, at least Pippa would be genuinely happy to see him. Sophia would probably be on her turbo-trainer in the middle of the living room for the next hour.

A text came through from Pippa when he was at the counter ordering his food: *Can you get chips for Skye as well? Cheers.*

Joey tried to remember if he'd met Skye. Knowing Pippa, she could be anyone from a new best friend to an orphaned hedgehog she'd found in the car park that evening. Either way, he ordered another bag of chips. She might be a bit of a messer but at least Pippa wouldn't lecture him about how many grams of fat he was consuming or how junk food would negatively affect his training the following day.

In the lift on the way up to Pippa's apartment he felt as if he was going to pass out with hunger. The door was on the latch so he let himself in. 'Knock, knock!' he called.

'Hello,' said a girl, long hair pulled back off her face in two plaits.

'Hi there,' he said. 'You must be Skye. I'm Joey, Pippa's brother.'

'I'm Pippa's new flatmate.'

'Cool. I didn't even know she was getting someone to join her here, but that means nothing where our Pip's concerned.' He dumped the brown-paper bag on the kitchen counter.

'Pippa's in the shower but she'll be out in a minute,' Skye said shyly.

'How do you know her?' Joey asked, as he rooted in the kitchen for plates.

'I met her through Lucy and we were in New York together last week,' Skye explained.

'Did you enjoy the trip? Knowing Pippa, you were up at the crack of dawn waiting for the shops to open. She's a force of nature when it comes to spending.'

'We didn't go too crazy, but it was fun,' Skye said. 'It's so much cheaper there that it's hard not to buy stuff just for the sake of it.'

'I can't say I'm mad about shopping, but I'm a bloke so there you have it,' Joey said.

'Hiya!' Pippa was in her pyjamas. 'That smells amazing, thanks, Joey.' She kissed his cheek. 'I presume you've met Skye and vice versa.' She popped a chip into her mouth.

'Sure did,' Joey said, tearing into his burger. 'God, this is angel food!'

'I could be a real cow and take a photo of you right now and mail it to Sophia,' Pippa said, winking.

Joey rolled his eyes.

'Who's Sophia?' Skye accepted a bag of chips.

'My girlfriend,' Joey said, with his mouth full. 'She's a personal trainer and very intense when it comes to this kind of thing.'

'Joey would be sleeping in the shed if she knew he was eating this,' Pippa said. 'She only eats organic healthy stuff and pasta, pasta and more pasta. *Total* pain in the arse.' She made a face.

'She's also my girlfriend, Pippa!' Joey was shocked. 'Don't be so rude about her.'

'She's bloody uptight and you know it,' Pippa said. 'I'm polite to her face, that'll do. Besides, she doesn't make any bones about the fact that she can't stick me, so feck her.'

Skye giggled as Joey looked at Pippa with narrowed eyes. 'She likes you just fine,' he said. 'You're just being nit-picky.'

'Yeah, sure!' Pippa said sarcastically. 'He has to come here to stuff his face because she'd beat him with that burger if he brought it home.'

'She probably would, you know,' Joey conceded. 'It's actually worth having to pay for this one's dinner rather than go home with it.' He shrugged his shoulders. 'When did you move in, Skye?'

'Just today,' she said.

'It was all a bit spur-of-the-moment,' Pippa interjected. 'I needed a lodger. Skye needed a place. Jigsaw fitted, so here we are.'

'Right.' Joey nodded. 'Tell me about your trip – was it amazing?'

'It was fine,' Pippa said, making it clear she didn't want to get into a chat about it.

'Are you all right?' he asked, looking at her intently. He knew Pippa was either up to or hiding something.

'Of course. Why?' Pippa said, busying herself with the chip wrappers. She flicked a glance at Skye. That meant she wasn't going to discuss anything in front of her new lodger.

Joey raised his eyebrows in a silent question. Pippa shook her head and put her hand to her face in a phone shape, indicating she'd call him another time.

Joey finished his food and pulled a toothbrush from his inside pocket.

'He has to brush his teeth and wash his hands and face now so Sophia won't go on at him,' Pippa explained.

'I think it's kind of nice that you care about her that much,' Skye said. 'You obviously want to keep her happy so you go to a lot of trouble to be the boyfriend she expects.'

'Precisely.' Joey grinned. 'I'm the best boyfriend on the planet!'

'More like the biggest sap going,' Pippa teased. 'I can't say I'd be bothered being with someone who was so bloody bossy.'

'Sophia's not that bad, Pippa,' Joey said, and made for the bathroom.

'Yes, she is,' Pippa shouted, as he brushed his teeth. Joey chose to ignore her.

'Okay, ladies, I'm off,' he said a few minutes later when he ducked back into the kitchen. 'Nice to meet you, Skye.'

'You too.'

'See ya.' Pippa followed him to the door. 'Hope Sophia doesn't smell the vinegar and make you run around the park for the rest of the night.'

'Shut up!' Joey was unable to hide his grin.

By the time he'd walked the short distance to his own apartment he was feeling kind of nervous but in an excited way. He was dying to tell Sophia about his promotion.

'Hello?' he called, as he went in. All the lights were off and the place was freezing and for a moment he thought Sophia had gone out. He switched on the hall light, then the one in their bedroom, and jumped as she sat bolt upright in the bed, screaming.

'What are you doing?' she spat. 'Couldn't you see I was asleep? I've had a full day and I'm up early. Have a bit of consideration, will you?'

Joey was stung. 'I came back to what looked like an empty flat. Sorry for existing,' he said, turned the light off and backed out the door.

As he flopped onto the sofa, chucking his training bag on the floor, he shoved his hands despondently into his jacket pockets. He fancied Sophia, and she certainly knew how to keep him on his toes. Any other girls he'd gone out with had bored him after a while so he'd ended up dumping them. But Sophia's selfishness was becoming too much.

He'd been in flying form earlier. His job couldn't be going better, he was loving the training, and he'd really enjoyed popping in to see Pippa and what's-her-name. Joey had to face facts: it wasn't right that every part of his day was great until he got home. Something had to give. He didn't want to be forced into a position where he had to choose between his family and his girlfriend. But it looked horribly as if that was on the cards. He knew which he'd choose if a gun was held to his head. He just didn't feel ready to go there yet.

9

Ding Dong
Merrily on High

❄❄❄

Pippa was all set to fall into bed. The burger and chips had been delicious, but now she felt like she'd a bag of quick-drying cement inside her.

Skye was boiling the kettle in the kitchen so Pippa padded in to join her. 'I'll have a peppermint tea,' she said, groaning. 'You only had chips so you're probably not as bunged up as I am.'

Skye was sitting at the table, looking guilty.

'What?' Pippa stopped dead.

'I'm really sorry, Pippa. I wasn't prying, honestly,' she said.

'What are you talking about?'

'I was looking for a teaspoon and when I opened the drawer over there I couldn't help but notice the pile of bills with bright red "overdue" stamps all over them.' Skye patted the spare chair beside her. 'Want to sit and tell me what's happening?'

'Oh … Right … I suppose so. I didn't want you to know all this stuff. I'll get it sorted. I've just got a bit behind with things, that's all. It's nothing to stress about.'

'Pippa, I know I've only just moved in, and I hope we'll be able to live together in perfect harmony and all that,' Skye smiled, 'but I don't agree that overdue bills aren't worth stressing over. They're not going to go away. Also, if I'm going to be living here, I need the fundamentals like electricity and heating. Call me narrow-minded, but I'm afraid that's the way I am.'

'I know this all looks really bad,' Pippa confided, 'but I'm in a bit of a pickle, as you've seen. I'm good at getting myself out of awkward situations, though. Ask Joey! He's always saying I'm a jammy cow.'

'That may be the case,' Skye said gently. 'But I don't conduct my life that way. I work for myself so I need to make certain I'm not left short.'

If she'd had her wits about her, Pippa thought, she'd have dumped those bills in the wheelie bin outside.

'I used to do my website designing part time and work in a coffee shop to boost my money, but last month I quit waitressing and went into designing full time.'

'Cool! And it's obviously going really well if you managed to go to New York and still have money to pay the deposit and first month's rent here. You do have that cash, right?'

'I told you I'd give it to you and I will,' Skye said firmly. 'Once we establish that I'll have a place to live.'

'Yeah, yeah, I get it. With lights and heat and all that.' Ugh, Pippa thought. She was doing it again. Skye was lovely but she was a bit of a mammy. Still, beggars couldn't be choosers and she needed to put up or shut up right now.

'How far behind are you with the rent?' Skye arched an eyebrow.

'Who told you I was?' Pippa pouted like a toddler.

'I guessed. Wouldn't take Einstein, in all fairness,' Skye added.

'Listen, if you can give me the deposit and your half of this month's rent I'll be bang up to date. The landlord is a real stickler for payment so I've never let it slip until this month.'

'Honestly?'

'Cross my heart and hope to die,' Pippa said, licking her finger and making a cross sign on her chest.

Skye grinned. 'I haven't seen anyone do that for about ten years!'

'I'll drop the rent off tomorrow and go down to the job centre straight afterwards. I promise I'll get myself together.'

'Pippa, I'm not your teacher or your mother,' Skye said. 'I just need to make sure I'm not going to use all my savings and end up homeless. I'd rather not spend Christmas in an alleyway alone.'

'Won't you be going home to your family for Christmas?' Pippa asked, flushing with mild embarrassment that Skye had picked up on what she'd been thinking.

'Nah. We don't see eye to eye so I'll be sticking around here. Sorry, I should've mentioned that.' She was cringing. 'Is that cool?'

'You're not planning on sitting here by yourself, are you?'

'Well, yeah, I was. Is that a problem?'

'Don't do that, Skye. Come down to Huntersbrook with me,' Pippa said automatically.

'Huntersbrook?'

'My family home in Wicklow. There'll be a gang and a ton of food. My folks would be furious if I didn't insist on you coming. Joey will be there too so you'll know him and me.'

'You're really sweet to offer …'

'So you'll come?'

'Leave it with me,' Skye said.

'Listen, you're helping me out here so at least let me repay the compliment. You can't sit here like a sad loner on Christmas Day!'

'I hadn't viewed myself like that.' Skye burst out laughing.

'What are you going to do? Ram half of a cracker in the door and pull the other end? Seriously! Come! Please!' She wasn't the most wild and wacky person Pippa had ever met, but she couldn't bear the thought of leaving the poor girl here by herself at Christmas. She found the image horrendous.

'On one condition,' Skye said.

'What's that?' Pippa asked.

'That you'll try out a job I'm about to get you,' she said, looking mischievous.

'Sure! What is it?'

'My aunt Sue called me today to see if I could give her a dig-out over Christmas in her clothes shop. I saw the way you operate in shops when we were in New York and I reckon you're the perfect candidate.'

'Sounds great!' Pippa said instantly.

'I had to say no because I've quite a bit of work on but Sue is really good to me and has kind of looked out for me over the years,' Skye explained. 'My parents were into home-schooling and living an alternative life but I wanted to live in Dublin so Sue took me in for a while. She was the voice of reason on my behalf with my parents.'

'She sounds great,' Pippa said. 'Where's her shop?'

'It's Boutique Belle on Grafton Street,' Skye said. 'Have you heard of it?'

'Have I heard of it?' Pippa shrieked. 'That place is the Mecca of fashion in Ireland! I've drooled outside the window so many times! And the owner's your aunt?' Pippa couldn't hide her surprise. And she was wildly impressed. Here was Skye, the most unassuming and laidback girl, and all the while she was related to the owner of Boutique Belle. It was almost too good to be true. 'Doesn't she have a host of fashionistas and wannabes queuing up to work there?'

'Probably,' Skye agreed. 'But the problem is finding someone who only wants a few weeks' work who she can trust. She finds it hard to get girls who know about the labels without being utterly useless spoiled divas.'

'Well, tell her I'm desperate, broke and a total expert on labels!'

Skye giggled as she grabbed her phone. 'I'll text her. It's after eleven so she might be asleep. Hopefully, she's still looking for someone.'

Pippa jumped up and hugged her. 'You're my guardian angel, do you know that?'

'Nothing's certain yet.'

As they finished going through the bills, Skye's phone bleeped.

'She's thrilled. Go in and have a chat with her at nine tomorrow morning,' Skye reported.

'Thank you, thank you, thank you!' Pippa said, bouncing around the room, like Winnie-the-Pooh's friend Tigger.

'What day is the bin collection?' Skye asked, pen and notebook poised.

'Eh, Wednesday. No, Friday, I think.' Pippa was tired of the housekeeping conversation. 'It doesn't really matter.

I usually just put the odd black bag I fill in someone else's wheelie bin in the basement. It's never a big issue.'

'Oh, we can't do that,' Skye said, clearly shocked. 'Leave it with me and I'll find out about it.'

'You're amazing!' Pippa said, and bounced into her bedroom to find something to wear the next day.

Pippa was meant to meet Sue at nine, but found herself pressing her nose up against the window at half past eight.

A tall, elegant blonde woman was inside the locked shop, thumbing through a large book on the counter. Catching Pippa's eye, she walked towards the door and opened it. 'Pippa?' she asked.

'Yes, you must be Sue.' She stood up straight. 'I'm sorry I'm a bit early. I was so excited I couldn't wait to see you,' she gushed.

'Well, that's a good start. I love your outfit,' Sue said, taking in Pippa's city shorts with the sheer dark tights and high-heeled ankle boots, the metallic top and leather blazer.

'Thanks.' Pippa smiled. 'And I love your Moschino dress. I saw it in *Harper's Bazaar* last month. It's amazing on you.'

'Come in,' Sue said, grinning. 'I've a feeling you're going to fit right in here. Do you have any retail experience?'

'Only on the spending side of the fence,' Pippa admitted. 'But I did a portfolio course in art and design last year, along with working for a promotions company at weekends and in the evenings, so I'd love to do window displays for you – and I know I'd have no trouble selling anything in this store.' She couldn't take her eyes off the rails. '"Be still, my beating heart"! Is that the new capsule collection from

Donna Karan? I thought Harrods was the nearest retailer for that.'

'They were until last week.' Sue smiled. 'Pippa? You're hired! When can you start?'

'Now?' Pippa offered. 'Or is that too late?'

Both women laughed.

Pippa took Sue up on her suggestion to have a good look at the stock. 'Ask any questions you like, but I reckon after a day, two tops, of being in here you'll know the lie of the land.'

Pippa didn't want to create a bad impression by using her phone so she texted Skye discreetly to let her know she'd secured the job: *Deadly! Well done! Isn't Sue the best?!*

Pippa responded quickly and put her phone firmly in her coat pocket in the stockroom.

Unlike any other job she'd ever had, Pippa took to this one instantly. Sue had to tell her to go and have lunch. 'You'll be no good to me if you collapse in a heap.'

'I know, but I've so many ideas for the window display,' she answered.

'Well, hold on to them and you can get going when you've eaten. Well done on handling Mrs Camden just now. She can be very tricky, and you did well to steer her towards the shift dress. She'll wear that and it was so much better on her than the velvet.'

'I didn't want to say it to her but the velvet was far too young-looking. She'd have been a laughing stock at the lunch she wanted it for.'

'I agree,' Sue said. 'You've a wonderful eye for fashion and know instinctively what suits people. I'm delighted Skye sent you my way. Now, go and take your lunch break.'

'Yes, ma'am!' Pippa saluted. As she meandered through

the crowded street, Pippa took a deep breath. This was brilliant! Although Sue hadn't offered her enough money to cover all her bills, she'd also said she could have a small commission. Along with Skye's rent and the fact the bills would be halved now, Pippa felt she'd made great strides to stop herself sinking even further into debt.

'Can you leave that with me for now? I need to work it out properly,' she had said.

'Sure,' Pippa had agreed, wanting to pinch herself in case she was dreaming. If the truth be known, she'd have worked there for free, but she nodded in a way she hoped hid her inner excitement.

Pippa had well and truly landed on her feet. If she played her cards right, maybe Sue would consider keeping her on after Christmas.

10

Hark, the Herald Angels Sing

✳✳✳

It was the Thursday before the Michael Bublé gig. Lainey was finding it really difficult to apply herself at work. She had loads of stuff to do but kept finding herself drifting to her wardrobe crisis. Eventually she dialled Pippa's number. The phone rang out so she tried her mobile instead.

'Hello?' Pippa whispered.

'Hi, it's me,' Lainey stated. 'Where are you?'

'Boutique Belle in Grafton Street.'

'Where do you get the money? I thought you were just back from shopping in New York.' Lainey was astonished.

'I am. But I'm not buying, I work here,' Pippa explained.

'Since when?' She really couldn't keep up with Pippa.

'Yesterday. It's great. I'll explain later,' she said. 'I'm literally just in the door so I have to go. I don't want my new

127

boss thinking I'm going to stand in the stockroom gossiping on my phone all day.'

'Okay,' Lainey said. 'I'm going to a gig on Saturday night with a friend from work and I've nothing to wear. Do you have any suggestions?'

'Do you want to borrow something?'

'Thanks, Pippa, but the last time I wore any clothing with the number eight on the label it had the word "age" beside it. Your stuff wouldn't go up one leg on me.' Lainey had come a long way in agreeing to wear the red 'siren' dress to the Christmas party, but she was acutely aware that she and Pippa would never be able to share their clothes. Shortly before she'd gone away, Grandma had put it delicately: Lainey had the build of a fine horsewoman, just like herself, while Pippa could dress as a fairy and might even grow wings.

'I hope you're not suggesting my nose would suit a bridle, Grandma?' Lainey had joked.

'Don't be touchy, darling. You've fine strong features. You and I are what your grandfather, Lord rest him, would've called handsome women. You and I,' Grandma had pulled her into a hug, 'are sturdy while Miss Pippa here,' Grandma tweaked her ski-slope nose, 'is dainty, like a ballerina.'

'Until she opens her mouth and all those illusions of petite charm are swiftly banished.' Lainey had giggled.

'I never thought of it like that,' Grandma said. 'I suppose your personalities do complement your physique. Pippa strives to fight her corner, making her a feisty little bundle, while you, my dear, are steady and more cautious.'

Grandma had had a way of making Lainey feel she fitted in. As if she was just right the way she was. Now she wished Maggie was around so she could turn to her for some much-needed bolstering and advice.

'Do you want me to see if there's anything in here you might like?' Pippa offered. 'That'd be great kudos for me if I could sell stuff over the phone on my second day.'

'Eh, not likely,' Lainey said. 'Isn't it like a hundred euro for a pair of tights in there?'

'Yeah, pretty much,' Pippa agreed. 'Why don't you meet me in Grafton Street during your lunch break? I'll help you find some stuff.'

'I can't leave the office today. I've so much on and I've already ordered a sandwich at my desk,' Lainey said, chewing her pen.

'Will I call up during my lunch break, then?'

'What good would that do?' Lainey was confused.

'We can go through some websites and if there's anything you like I'll pick it up for you.'

'Are you sure, Pippa? That'd be brilliant.'

'See you then.' Pippa hung up.

Lainey knew she could ask Jules to go shopping with her again, but she wanted her to be her friend, not her personal dresser. She also felt embarrassed by how untrendy she was. She wanted to be a shiny, happier version of herself.

As she got on with her work, Lainey was pleased that she and her sister had had that chat. She'd never have thought of turning to Pippa before. In fact, she'd have been the last person on her list of advisers. Grandma would have been delighted to see the two sisters beginning to find common ground.

The morning dragged on. By the time Pippa pitched up, Lainey was delighted to have an excuse to abandon her work for a while.

'God, it's so stuffy,' Pippa said, as she sat into the second seat in Lainey's section. 'I don't know how you work in here day in, day out. I'd go stir crazy.'

'It's fine most of the time,' Lainey said. 'So what's the story with this new job you have? The last I heard you were dressing up as a red pepper to sell soup in Bray.'

'You know Lucy who I was in school with? Well, her friend Skye came to New York with me last week. She's moved into my place.'

'When?' Lainey was stunned.

'The other day. Keep up!' Pippa giggled. 'Anyway, it turns out Skye's aunt owns Boutique Belle and she was looking for someone to do some extra hours over Christmas. Skye gave me the nod, I got the job and the rest is history.'

'Great.' Lainey was impressed. 'What's it like having a flatmate? I'm not sure I'd be that great at living with someone. I've got so set in my ways. God, that makes me sound like an old lady, doesn't it?'

'Yes!' Pippa grinned. 'Now, let's get down to brass tacks. I don't have much time and it's only my second day so I'd better get my skates on.' She flicked to the Internet on Lainey's desktop.

Lainey sat in awe as her sister flew through website after website of clothes.

'Do you want glitzy dressy or more smart-casual?' Pippa asked.

'I suppose more cool concert clothes than ball gown,' Lainey said. She honestly wasn't sure what she wanted and hoped Pippa would happen upon the right thing.

Lainey soon realised there was more to it than glimpsing stuff and hoping for the best. Not that it seemed to pose a problem for Pippa.

'Can't we just agree to go for the jumpsuit?' Pippa pleaded a little later, after they'd disagreed on every suggestion that far.

'I'd look like something from *Ghostbusters* in that,' Lainey said. 'I quite like the dress on the right,' She pointed at a floral thing.

'Christ, Lainey, you'd get a pensioner's ticket on the bus if you wore that. Grandma wouldn't give it house room,' Pippa hooted. 'You have a great figure, especially your arms. You've no bingo wings going on – all the riding's seen to that – so use it to your advantage. Let's look at Trendy Girl.'

'Right.' Lainey was attempting to keep up with her sister. 'Flaming Nora, I thought you weren't into computers. You're like a bolt of lightning when it comes to shopping.'

'Too right.' Pippa was barely listening. 'That's it! I've found the perfect outfit for you. Look at the blue top with the roses across the slash neckline, the skinny jeans and the smart blazer. Love it.'

'I'm not sure, Pippa. It looks a bit summery,' Lainey said uncertainly.

'You're going to the O₂, not the North Pole,' Pippa said. 'Now stop being all sensible and give it a go. I'll fly up to Trendy Girl and get it for you today. Can you pop over to my flat and pick it up tonight?'

'I suppose so,' Lainey said.

'Cool. Who are you going with? Is it a fella? I won't tell anyone.'

'It's Jules, who usually sits over there.' Lainey stood up to see if she'd returned from lunch. 'You can meet her another time. She's great fun. You'll love her.'

'Have you decided to be a laser beam?' Pippa asked.

'No. Jules started in the office recently and we get on well. Just because I have a friend it doesn't mean I'm gay.'

'Fair enough! I'm off. I'll get you the stuff and bring it

home. I'm totally smashed after New York, though. Can you give me the money?'

'I don't have any cash on me,' Lainey said apologetically. 'I'll tell you what, I'll give you my credit card and the PIN. You get me the things and for goodness' sake don't lose it.'

As she pulled out her card and wrote the PIN on a yellow Post-it, she felt a rush of gratitude towards her younger sister. 'Thanks for doing this, Pip,' she said, hugging her.

'No worries. I'm delighted. This is my idea of heaven – shopping with other people's money! Fabulous!' she said, in a mock-American accent.

As she waved to Pippa, Lainey clicked on to Facebook to post a comment. She was horrified by a conversation between Seth and one of his friends, Chris. There was a photo of some saucy underwear and a caption from Seth saying: 'Why wait until after we're married? Look what I've bought my fiancée for tonight.'

Understandably all the lads had posted lurid comments egging him on. They were pretty harmless until the one from Chris.

Your girlfriend must be a right saucy minx behind closed doors. It's obviously true what they say about the quiet ones being the ones to watch.

But Seth's response made her want to cry.

Dead right mate! The quiet ones put up with plenty of playing away from home too. As you know only too well I tend to have it sussed with the ladies. The last one wouldn't say boo to a goose and never had a clue what I was up to or WHO more to the point!!!

Lainey looked around feeling as if the whole office could see his comment. An awful feeling of shame and panic engulfed her. She'd had several rows with Seth before they'd finally split up. She'd suspected him of cheating on her but he'd ridiculed her and said she was crazy. Swallowing hard and fighting tears, she clicked out of Facebook.

'Hi, Lainz,' Jules said, popping her head over the workstation divider. 'How's it going?'

'Hi, Jules,' she managed. Perhaps it was because Jules was so friendly, but Lainey suddenly felt as if a dam had burst inside her. Tears poured down her cheeks.

'Hey, what's wrong?' Jules said, shooting around to give her a hug.

'Lainey, is that report done yet?' Drake barked. He was striding towards her.

'No ... I ...' Lainey wiped her eyes with the sleeve of her blouse. 'I'll have it done shortly.'

'What's going on here? Did someone die?' Drake said nastily.

'No, but you're just about to if you don't bugger off and stop being such a pig,' Jules shouted.

'Don't talk to me like that, Barbie,' he said, affronted.

'If I were you I'd go back into your office and wait until Lainey has gathered herself,' Jules said very slowly and menacingly. 'See these shoes?' She swivelled around to show him her stiletto heels.

Drake nodded appreciatively.

'I'll be forced to see if they fit in your rear orifice if you don't go away.'

As Jules led her to the bathroom Lainey couldn't help dissolving into snot-infested giggles.

'Jules, stop!' she managed desperately. 'He's such a snake he'll get you fired if you annoy him.'

'Ah, fuck him,' Jules said, oblivious to the gaping onlookers in the office.

'Oh dear.' Lainey splashed cold water on her face in the privacy of the Ladies. Her mirth had dissolved when she'd told Jules what she'd just seen on Facebook.

'He sounds like such a slime ball. I'm glad you broke up with him. At least you got away,' Jules said. 'I feel sorry for the poor girl he's marrying.'

Lainey managed to pull herself together, fix her face and make her way back into the office. The thing that upset her more than anything else was that she'd known Seth was cheating on her yet she hadn't trusted her instincts. She'd let him convince her she was the one with the problems.

In the interest of saving face she hadn't even been able to admit to Jules just now that the reason they'd split in the end was because Seth had dumped her.

As she settled back at her workstation to finish Drake's report she remembered Pippa was off getting her new clothes. Onwards and upwards. This weekend would be fun at the concert. She needed to grow a thicker skin and concentrate on that glass-half-full attitude.

11

Joy to the World

Pippa dashed down Grafton Street clutching Lainey's credit card. Running into Trendy Girl, she was thrilled to find all the things they'd chosen online.

'That'll be one hundred and twenty euro, please,' the assistant said, as she shoved Lainey's card into the machine.

Her mobile phone rang in her pocket. Jay's name flashed up. Get lost, Pippa thought, pressing the red button. She'd deal with him later on. She wasn't into him any more and the sooner he got the message the better.

'Thanks for shopping at Trendy Girl,' the assistant said cheerfully. 'Have a great day!'

'Thank you,' Pippa said, flashing a smile.

Trendy Girl seemed so cheap after the exorbitant prices in Boutique Belle. The upmarket Grafton Street shop was well known all over Ireland as being *the* place for serious fashionistas to shop and be seen. Grabbing Lainey's outfit, she ran as fast as her high wedges would carry her back to her new job.

'Hi, Sue,' she called to her boss.

'Ah, there you are,' Sue said, poking her head out of the stockroom. 'Come and see the new delivery I've just signed for.' Her smile faded. 'For goodness' sake, Pippa, don't come in here brandishing that Trendy Girl bag! That's hardly the image we want to project to my discerning customers.'

'Sorry. It's for my sister. I'll stash it in the back under my coat. Do show me the new delivery,' she said excitedly. The huge box with the famous black lettering on the side made Pippa want to dance with excitement.

'I love this entire D&G collection,' Sue oozed.

'Me too,' Pippa said. 'The colour popping is just magnificent. You should have these pieces in the window. I know I only put the other stuff in yesterday but the strong colours in this collection are crying out to be on show.'

'Go for it,' Sue said, grinning from ear to ear. 'I think I hit the jackpot when Skye recommended you. How you two are friends is beyond me, but I guess opposites attract. Her father and I are brother and sister. We couldn't be more different and we don't get on at all. That home-schooling nonsense just isn't me.'

'No,' Pippa said. She found the whole notion slightly disturbing too. Blood was thicker than water and she didn't want Sue or even Skye to think she was judging their family.

Her mobile rang. Fishing it out, she saw Jay's name once again. Hitting the silent button, she knew she was being cowardly, avoiding a conversation with him. She owed him a phone call at the very least because the tickets were still sitting beside the lamp in the living room and she needed to return them. But she couldn't have that kind of chat in front of Sue. She was too busy trying to become an irreplaceable asset to Boutique Belle. And the notion that she was also a heartless bitch didn't quite fit in with her shiny new image. Shoving her phone into her handbag, she widened her smile and quashed the guilty feelings inside her.

Pippa turned her attention to the new collection. She felt like a child in a sweet shop as she expertly picked out five gorgeous pieces to display.

'Did you have a window theme in mind?' Pippa asked Sue.

'Just keep it fresh and funky. I'll get you to do a Christmassy one in a couple of days,' she said. 'I'll let you into a little secret.' She dropped her voice so the two browsing customers wouldn't hear. 'I've some Chanel arriving any minute now so I'll want to promote that big-time. It's my first collection from them so I need to try and sell it.'

'Well,' Pippa said, sidling up close, 'when Skye and I were in New York I saw the most amazing Chanel stuff. I'm still raging I didn't take a jacket I saw there. You've met the right girl to inject all the love and passion those pieces deserve.'

'Pippa, where have you been all my life?' Sue said, throwing her head back and laughing. She went off to serve the customers as Pippa disappeared into the stockroom to find some props to use for the window.

She was having so much fun. Sue was amazing too. So sophisticated and cool. Pippa could barely believe how this week had turned out. On Monday she'd been plagued by awful Sean from the bank and the landlord. Now she was elbow-deep in designer clothes at Boutique Belle and in full view of the admiring glances of passers-by! Skye had promised to have her first month's rent, along with a deposit, by this evening so Pippa would be able to pay off the rent on time.

Joey was always telling her she was a jammy cow and now she had to agree with him.

The rest of the afternoon flew by as Pippa worked like a demon. 'Wow,' Sue said, as they went outside to admire her new display in the window. 'I love those moons and stars you've made from that bright yellow card,' Sue marvelled. 'I'd never have thought of doing the midnight-sky effect with the dark fabric either.'

'I'm so glad you like it,' Pippa said.

'Someone was watching over me when you were sent my way yesterday. Now, I told you I'd come up with what I hope is a fair way of paying you,' Sue continued. 'I'd love to be in a position to give you shedloads but obviously there's a recession on.'

'Right.' Pippa waited for the dampener.

'Would you work for the minimum wage with three per cent commission? *Aaaand* ...' she led Pippa back into the shop and towards the counter '. . . seeing you're a perfect size eight I'd like to give you these two outfits as well.'

'Oh, my God!' Pippa squealed, as she looked at the black D&G dress with the bright orange shrug, and the chocolate Max Mara cigarette trousers with a co-ordinating frothy chiffon blouse with tiny polka dots and pussy bow.

'They were samples,' Sue was quick to admit, 'but I still had to pay for them.'

'Sue, I've never owned anything like these before. Thank you,' she said, exhilarated.

'Welcome. Besides,' she arched an eyebrow, 'I can't have my staff looking out of place! Be sure to wear the stuff now. My clients really notice attention to detail so I'd prefer you to look the part.'

'No problem. I'll have no issue with looking like I fit in here,' Pippa said.

On her way back to the apartment, which involved plenty

of skipping and squealing, Pippa pulled her phone out of her bag. The missed calls from Jay taunted her. She'd talk to him once she'd had a few minutes to kick her shoes off at home and relax. She jumped as her phone rang.

'Hi, Mum,' she said, seeing Huntersbrook's number flash up. 'Guess what I've been up to!' She was in danger of exploding with delight. Pippa furnished Holly with the edited-for-Mother version of the past few days' events. Obviously she skipped the narky phone calls, debts and teetering on the edge of being thrown out of her apartment part.

'And how did you sort it out with your old boss?' Holly wanted to know. 'I hope you went in and spoke to them and explained that you were doing Skye's auntie this favour because her assistant had been knocked down by a car.'

'Of course I did,' Pippa lied. 'They were sorry to see me go but said they could find someone else to dress as a bumble-bee and sell Christmas hampers of honey at the food hall.'

'That's good,' Holly said. 'Any other news?' She was unable to hide a sigh.

'No. Are you okay, Mum?' Pippa asked. 'You sound tired and fed up.'

'I'm a bit of both, actually,' Holly admitted. 'Nothing a glass of wine and a soak in the bath won't fix. You go on and get yourself home. It's freezing out, isn't it?'

'Baltic,' Pippa agreed. 'Chat to you soon and give Dad a hug for me.' By the time she made it inside the apartment building half an hour later she was shivering. 'Hello?' she called, as she let herself in. Skye was thudding about in her room. 'How are you getting on?' she asked as the other girl came into the living room.

'Great, thanks. I moved the rest of my stuff in earlier on and got the bills sorted out. Bin day, in case you were wondering, is Monday and we've got the special black bags required. They're in the drawer in the kitchen.

'*Vino*?' Pippa offered.

'I'd love a glass. I noticed you always seem to have the essentials in stock – like wine and crisps!' she added, as Pippa pulled a large packet of sweet chilli Kettle chips from the cupboard.

'Well, you have to get your priorities right, don't you know?' Pippa said gleefully. 'This is great fun! I'm so glad to have you here. It's really nice to have someone to chat to when I get home.'

'Thanks for saving my arse. I couldn't have spent much longer living with Echo. He's disgustingly messy and his friends are worse,' she said, gulping her wine.

Pippa nearly choked. 'Your cousin isn't really called Echo, is he?'

'Don't go there,' Skye said, holding her hand up. 'Most of my dad's family are of the hippie-dippy variety, Echo's father included. In fact, Sue is the only one who wasn't into the whole alternative lifestyle thing.'

'How come your dad and Sue are so different?' Pippa asked, plonking herself on the sofa.

'Mum and Dad have always been alternative. He and Echo's dad were the typical spoiled and doted on sons who never really grew up or wanted to find a job,' Skye explained. 'They both met their girlfriends around the same time, then Echo and I came along and they all decided to live in a commune together. They figured being Friends of the Earth and doing the whole self-sufficient vibe was a great way to avoid living in the real world. My grandparents were pretty disgusted and never forgave them. It made a real rift in the family, which is sad, I guess.'

'Wow,' Pippa said. 'And what about Sue? Did you see much of her while you were growing up?'

'Yeah. She did her own thing and didn't judge her brothers too harshly. I used to go and stay with her the odd time and when I wanted to go to mainstream school she stood up for me.'

'I must say I've thoroughly enjoyed the last two days in the shop with her,' Pippa said. 'She's pretty cool.'

'I've always thought so. By the way, Jay called,' Skye said. 'I told him to catch you on the mobile. He sounded really down.'

'I'm sorry if he disturbed you,' Pippa said. 'I need to chat to him and sort out all this mess with the tickets.' She sighed. 'He did call all right, but I couldn't answer because I was in the middle of doing a window display.'

'Fair enough,' Skye said. 'I know I'm only here spitting time and tell me to bog off if you like …'

'But …' Pippa grinned.

'But he's a really decent guy, Pippa.'

'Oh, I know,' she said. 'Don't you think I'm feeling guilty?' she said dramatically. 'Normally I dump boys and never hear from them again. It's no big deal. But I wasn't to know he was going to book that mega-holiday, was I?'

'Can you imagine how gutted you'd feel if you'd spent thousands on a holiday and he'd dumped you but hadn't bothered to return the tickets or even call?'

'We'd have had a crowd complete with pitchforks and flaming torches to hunt him out of town,' Pippa told her.

'Pretty much,' Skye said.

'I hear ya. I'll meet him and give back the tickets.'

'Don't do it in a bar or anywhere the poor fella can be humiliated any further,' Skye begged.

'Okay.' Pippa was getting a bit snappy. 'But there's a fine line that can't be crossed here. He's not the right guy for me. There are no fireworks going off. It's not lurve. I can't lead him on at the same time.'

Skye shrugged.

'What about you?' Pippa asked. 'Any men on the scene?'

'Not really,' Skye said. 'Anyone I fancy either has a girlfriend or turns out to be gay. I haven't had much luck with men in recent times. Sometimes I figure it's safer to be single.'

'Ah, Jesus!' Pippa said, shaking her head. 'That's so depressing! There must be someone you can aim for. The chase and flirting part is the most fun. I tend to lose interest once I know I have a guy,' she admitted. 'For now, though, let's just have another glass of wine!' she said, tottering to the fridge.

As they sipped their wine, Lainey texted to say she was heading straight home and would call in tomorrow for her clothes and credit card. *Can u bring them into work & I'll grab them at lunch time? Sorry am knackered & need to get home. Crap day. Lainey x*

R u ok? Pippa x

Not really.

Want to call me?

'Sorry to cut you off, Skye, but this is my sister. She needs a bit of advice. You won't be offended if I pop into my room, will you?'

'Sure, go ahead,' Skye said, gathering up her things at the table.

Putting on her iPod in the docking station to muffle the sound, Pippa answered Lainey's call.

'So what's up?' she asked, and heard a garbled story about Seth and Facebook and how Lainey had ended up crying at the office.

'Who cares?' she said easily. 'Everyone has meltdowns every now and again. I'm sure nobody noticed. Besides, you're Miss Together. People don't view you as a basket case. They'll have forgotten by tomorrow. If it makes you feel any better, I'm up Shit Creek without a paddle.'

She hadn't meant to tell Lainey about her debts but it had tumbled out before she knew it.

'How much do you owe the bank and credit card company in total?' Lainey asked.

'Nearly three grand.' Pippa winced.

'What? How could you be so irresponsible?'

'It'll be fine. I've got this new job now. Skye will pay half the rent. Chill,' she said, wishing to God she hadn't said anything.

'Pippa, you need to sort yourself out.'

'I know that, Lainey. Please don't nag. I prefer it when you ask for advice on clothes. You sound like Grandma now, wittering on. The responsibility and forward planning speech is probably next!'

'You need to get your head out of your arse. I was amazed at how you were managing to jet off for a shopping weekend and live the life you do when you barely work,' Lainey said despairingly. 'Now I know. You just owe it all.'

'I had a good job,' she said defensively.

'Yeah, more than a year ago,' Lainey said, not letting her away with it. 'What have you done since? Got Mum and Dad to pay for an art course while you dressed up as a vegetable at weekends? You couldn't even do that without getting fired.'

'Shut up!' Pippa shouted angrily. 'We're not all as perfect as you are.'

'I never said I was perfect and I don't want to argue with you.' Lainey sounded beat. 'Do you want me to loan you the money to pay off your credit cards and sort your bank account?'

'*Would* you?' Pippa was astonished.

'It'll pretty much clear out my savings fund, but it's yours if you promise to pay me back.'

'I will.' Pippa punched the air. 'Thank you so much, Lainey. You're the best sister in the whole world.'

'I'm the only one you've got.' Lainey laughed.

'Seth was a right creep. Don't look at Facebook any more. You're better than that,' Pippa assured her. 'You'll meet someone fabulous soon. I just know it.'

'Thanks. I'll see you tomorrow. I'll call into the shop to collect my clothes and card, and I'll give you a cheque to clear your credit cards.'

By the time Pippa had said good night to Skye, laid out her clothes for the following morning and fallen into bed, she was wrecked. As she closed her eyes, she tried to imagine where she could be this time next year. Maybe she'd be Sue's chief buyer. Or perhaps she'd have a shop of her own.

One thing was for certain: she was absolutely determined to turn her life around. She'd messed up big-style over the last while. Now she was going to concentrate really hard on being together and independent.

12
Mary's Boy Child
❄❄❄

He could hear her but Joey wasn't going to acknowledge Sophia as she performed her usual crack-of-dawn routine. Opening one eye, he took in the time on his digital alarm clock. It wasn't even five. She was getting worse.

The shower would probably have woken him anyway but Sophia had the radio blaring as well, which he was certain must wake their neighbours too.

'Morning!' she said, turning the main light on in the bedroom.

'You are aware it's just gone five, are you?' he asked, burying his face in the duvet to shield his eyes.

'I need to get to the track. I'm doing a three-day intensive boot camp with a group from the engineering company. It's good money,' she said, as she fished her running leggings from the tub of clean washing. 'This place is getting seriously untidy. I'm working too hard right now so you'll have to sort it. Besides,' she said easily, 'your job isn't as tiring as mine. You're only sitting at a desk.'

'Oh, speaking of my job,' he said, suddenly remembering the promotion, 'I was talking to Clive last night on the way to the track—'

'How long did you stay at the track last night? You were very late,' she interrupted. 'I waited up, but when you didn't appear I had to go to bed.'

'I was back here by nine, Sophia,' he said crossly. 'That's hardly late.'

'In *your* opinion,' she said, as she tied her trainer laces.

'Anyway I was talking to Clive—'

'Before I forget,' she said, standing up and zipping up her running jacket, 'I need the money to pay for Lanzarote. Can you get it for me by this evening? It's working out at three grand each, okay?'

'What?' Joey said, sitting bolt upright. 'Three grand? Have you booked a five-star hotel or something?'

'It's more of a hostel, actually, but the price includes breakfast and dinner. Not to mention the coaching each day, which is the real reason we're going there. The coach in this particular camp does one-to-one training sessions with élite athletes during the season. He charges a fortune per hour. So, believe me, if you work it out this is cheap,' she said. 'Catch you later.' She pecked him on the forehead and bounded out.

Joey thumped his pillow. Sophia was making it very clear she wasn't interested in anything he had to say. What went on in his life was of no consequence to her unless it involved training. If she thought he was paying three thousand euro to spend Christmas in a flea-bitten hostel instead of at Huntersbrook with his family, she'd another think coming. Even if this man was meant to be the most amazing coach the triathlon world had ever borne witness to.

More than any of that, what was with this kissing him

on the forehead and nose shit? His grandma did that, for Christ's sake. If he wanted to live with a drill sergeant who treated him like a minion he'd have joined the army.

Knowing he wasn't going to sleep now, Joey got up and went into the shower. He'd go to the office and get some work done. At least they appreciated him there.

A short time later, he was pushing open the door to go out of his apartment complex. He decided to take the car, and was surprised by how quickly he got to work. Still, he mused, if he got up at five each morning and made it in here for six, it'd probably be like this every day.

Once he'd made a cup of coffee and settled at his desk his concentration went straight to the job in hand. By the time the rest of the building began to fill and lights flickered on across his floor he'd flown through a decent amount of work.

'Did you sleep here?' Clive asked, as he came through the door with wet hair.

'Nah. I was awake at an ungodly hour so I decided to schlep straight in. Were you at the gym?' he said, indicating his boss's hair.

'Yeah. We had that swim session, remember?'

'Oh, damn!' Joey said, bashing his head with the heel of his hand. 'I totally forgot. How was it?'

'Tough. That new trainer really knows his stuff. He was helpful, though. I'd say if we get a few months in with him before racing starts we'll be in a much better position in the water.'

'Sounds good. I'll definitely be at the next one,' Joey said. Irritation bubbled inside him. It was Sophia's fault he'd missed this morning's coaching. If she hadn't been so bloody selfish he would've been up at his normal time and into his usual routine.

When her name flashed up on the screen of his mobile phone at just after ten that morning he was sorely tempted not to answer. 'Hello,' he said evenly. He wasn't going to sound snotty but he'd no intention of being all airy-fairy either.

'Hi,' she shouted, above the din of traffic in the background. 'I'm just calling to remind you to get the money for Lanzarote, okay? I've been to the credit union to get mine.'

'Right,' was all he said.

'See you later.'

Joey was tapping his phone against his teeth when Jemima brought him a cup of coffee. 'Would you like a toasted sambo or anything with it?' she asked.

'No, thanks,' he said.

'Everything okay? You look kind of odd.'

'I'm fine, thanks, just deep in thought. Numbers whizzing around my brain, the usual.' Even his secretary had noticed he was pissed off. Joey was aware that some men's secretaries knew more about them than their wives did, but he shared Jemima with someone else and they had little contact other than general pleasantries.

He and Sophia needed to sit down and figure out where their relationship was going. He'd a fair idea where he thought it *should* go, but he was interested to know what she was thinking.

O Christmas Tree

Dear Maggie

I will certainly send you another box of Tayto crisps. It's no trouble at all. It gave Mrs Brennan in the post office something to talk about the last time. She's terribly nosy but she means no harm. Still, I did point out that I was glad there was nothing personal in the box seeing as she'd gone ahead and opened it.

Lainey loved her birthday present and I know she appreciated it. I'm sorry to hear she hasn't been in touch. All I can say is that you still come up in conversation all the time. Just because they're not talking to you doesn't mean they don't miss or love you.

Joey is like a muscle with eyes. All he does is train and work. I know triathlon is the new golf these days, and he has to be seen to be in with the lads in his job, but he's taken it all to extremes, Maggie. He was here with Sophia for the night the other week. Well, the girl was barely inside the house. She went off running and cycling for hours on end.

She eats nothing but pasta. Of all the things in the world I could pick to eat non-stop pasta wouldn't be it. I think it's like rubber. But that's just me. She turned her nose up at my stew. She acted like she'd been offered heroin when I produced a brown soda loaf from the oven. The worst part is that she's diminishing poor Joey's spirit. I don't like to see the lad being treated like she treats him. The dogs get more attention than he does. They say love is blind. Well, if you ask me the poor boy should sign up for a Labrador and his own white stick. I wouldn't mind if I felt she was worth it, but from what I can make out Joey would have more fun with a dead duck.

There hasn't been a sniff of Pippa. She was in New York with the girls and she's been on the phone all right but we haven't seen her for weeks. Holly tells me she's got another new job. You know I told you she was doing promotions? Well, she's now in Boutique Belle of all places. Maybe she'll stay there a while. She always loved her fashion so perhaps this is the right job for her now. Please, God. No doubt she'll be down when she gets herself into hot water again. If I know Pippa, that won't be too far away.

Lainey is off to see Michael Bublé at the weekend. Not for a date now, just the concert. Bridey from Moneystown went with her daughter last June twelve months. Sure you'll remember her gaffing on about it. Said she felt like he was singing to her alone. Silly old bat, weren't there forty thousand at it? Lainey's going with her new friend from the job. She's a great girl by all accounts. I'll get a look at her soon enough. Seems Lainey's bringing her to Huntersbrook for Christmas.

Holly is getting the decorations out, and although she's still excited, the sparkle's missing this year, Maggie. I can't help feeling there's something she's not telling me. She's being very snappy with poor Paddy too. He was out the back barrowing the fresh straw down to the livery yard yesterday and she nearly tore the head off him for no reason.

I could see he was trying to work out what he'd done wrong. If

I'd known I'd have tipped him off afterwards but I'm as much in the dark as he is. Maybe it's the change.

There's a Christmas market starting up in Delia's field. Apparently there'll be loads of homemade goods on the stalls. If you were here you could've had a pudding stall. There's nothing like your Christmas puds.

I'll get going and post you the crisps. Let me know if there's anything else you need. If I figure out what's ailing Holly I'll be sure to let you know.

Bye for now,

Sadie

'Paddy!' Holly called from inside the house. She'd been wandering around the rooms, shouting like a mad woman, for what felt like the entire morning looking for him. Normally by the second week in December the whole house would be decorated and ready for Christmas. This year little was getting done. Holly's heart just wasn't in it. She'd get up in the morning, full of great plans and intentions, and before she knew it, the day would end and she'd have achieved nothing. Her lacklustre mood was sapping her energy and stifling her creativity, and she hadn't the faintest idea of what she could do about it.

'Out here!' he answered.

'There you are!' she barked. 'I've a list of jobs I need doing. Can you get Scott to come and do a few hours with us today?'

'I'll give him a shout.'

'Can you get the tree this morning? I feel like we've nothing ready,' she said, irritated.

'Yup, I'll get hold of Scott. Sure if I'd chopped one down before now it'd only be dead by Christmas Day. They tend to smell like cat pee when they die off.'

'Well, I'll hardly let that happen,' Holly said, moving back towards the house. 'I have that special spray I use to keep the wreath fresh. I'll put the tree in a bucket, which I'll top up with water every day. I've managed to keep all the greenery alive for the last number of years and I reckon I'll manage it again this year. Let me know when you're going to get it because I want to come. I saw a good one while I was walking with the dogs the other day.'

'Holly,' Paddy said hesitantly.

'What?'

'What's up?'

'I think you know very well,' she said. 'There's no point in harping on about it constantly. What will be will be, and there's nothing we can do now.'

'Why don't you contact Maggie and see if she can help?' he asked.

'No.' Holly's tone was icy. 'Mum made her position clear. Leave her out of this.'

Holly had thought she knew her mother well, that Maggie would've done anything for her. She'd adored and lived for her grandchildren. Until she'd left them all without a backward glance. Well, if that was the way she wanted to play it, Holly would just have to accept it and do her best.

While she waited for the men to help her get the Christmas tree, Holly decided to make a start on the main living room. This was where the presents would be opened on Christmas morning and where they'd play games, drink wine and relax before and after dinner. Holly adored the fireplace with the intricately carved marble and gold leaf, which mirrored the etching in the ceiling. Each year she decorated it so that it glistened and shone in the warm glow of the log fire.

All her Christmas decorations were carefully boxed away

at the end of each season and labelled so she could find them the following year. She knew Joey had taken everything out of the attic for her when he was last at home so it was just a matter of putting her hand on the right box.

The familiarity of the red crate in which she'd always laid the swathes to surround the fireplace gave her a warm feeling inside. She peeled off the clingfilm that covered it (Paddy's brainwave to keep the dust out), opened the lid and gazed at the contents.

'Can I help at all?' Sadie's voice made her jump.

'Good morning, Sadie. I didn't know you were here. I'd love a hand, thank you.'

'Oh, look! It's the birds Maggie bought in Liberty of London many moons ago,' Sadie said, getting choked up. 'They cost a small fortune at the time, but she just had to have them.' As they carefully unwrapped the tissue paper, Holly couldn't hide her tears.

'Oh, would you look at the two of us?' Sadie said, laughing. 'Getting all soft over a pile of fake birds and a box of pretend greenery. What are we like?'

'I miss Mum terribly. It's going to be so strange not having her here this Christmas. I still keep expecting her to walk in the door.' Holly sniffed.

'We all do. But once you have the usual decorations up, so much of her will still be with us. Let's get these birds sorted for starters,' Sadie said, practicality kicking in once more. 'Why don't you phone Maggie?' she suggested.

'We both know I'm not going to do that,' Holly said firmly. 'She made her choice when she abandoned us all.'

As the main colour in the living room was sea green, Holly had always decorated to complement it. Sadie helped her attach the thick fuzzy artificial swag to the top of the mantelpiece. Once upon a time, they'd only used real foliage, but the central heating and indeed the fire meant it dried up and died far too quickly. Holly had gone to Dublin one year and invested in some good-quality artificial.

'I'll do the lights if you want to start attaching the birds?' Holly suggested.

'Right you are, love,' Sadie said, and began to clip each little bird to a perch she deemed suitable.

'Well, I'll be damned!' Holly said. 'The lights are working! That's nearly against the rules, isn't it?'

'It does seem a bit smooth.' Sadie's eyes crinkled at the corners. 'Maybe they'll blow up later on and give us all heart failure.'

'Don't say that!' Holly laughed. Flinging the lights on top of the swag, she negotiated the wire until it reached the socket. 'If Paddy were doing this he'd leave them strewn on top like that,' she said. 'He has a knack of making them look like he threw them from the doorway!' she said. 'I like to wind them carefully in and out of the branches so they look like they're meant to be there.'

Sadie continued to position the little birds. 'Paddy's argument is that none of this makes sense anyway. He's forever saying he's never seen a tree in the woods with pale green sparkly birds and twinkling lights attached to it.' Sadie giggled.

'Yes, he does say that,' Holly said. 'Men are very black and white about things, aren't they? I can see his point but it's lovely to use a bit of imagination every now and again. Instil a bit of magic in our often mundane existence.' She felt more cheerful now. 'And Paddy knows full well that if he does a shoddy job on the lights I'll run him out of the place and let him off the hook.'

'Ah, sure you can't blame him for that,' Sadie said diplomatically. 'If he was elbowing you out of the way and wanting to do everything you'd be even crosser. He's a good man, your Paddy.'

'I know he is,' Holly said pensively.

'Any news from Joey and the girls?' Sadie enquired.

'Nothing,' Holly said. 'I'm glad Lainey's getting out and about a bit. At times she makes me feel young, she's so intense and strait-laced. Still, she seems to have found a good pal in this Jules girl. Did I tell you she's joining us for Christmas?'

'That's good. I'll be able to have a chat with her,' Sadie said. 'What about Joey and Sophia? Are they gracing us with their presence?'

'I assume so,' Holly said. 'I haven't heard anything to the contrary.'

'It's awfully cold in here, Holly. Did you not bother turning the heating on today?' Sadie wondered.

'I thought it was on the timer,' Holly said. 'I know Paddy turned the radiators off upstairs. We figured there was no point in heating empty bedrooms.'

'Understandable,' Sadie said, zipping up her fleece jacket. 'Let me go and have a look at the heating controls.'

As she went to the panel, which was in the kitchen, she met Paddy coming in the back door.

'Is Holly ready to go for the tree?' he asked. 'Scott's on the way now. What are you looking at there?'

'The heating didn't come on and it's freezing. I'm just looking to see if the timer switch was changed by mistake,' Sadie explained.

'I'll check for you,' Paddy said, and Sadie went to give Holly a shout.

'That's odd,' he said, as the women joined him in the

kitchen. 'The heating should be on. I'll go and dip the oil tank. Ready to get this tree?' he said to Holly.

'Certainly am,' she said. 'Sadie and I have nearly finished the fireplace. It's like a scene from Fairy Land!'

'Meet me out the back, will you?' Paddy said, going on ahead.

'Right you are.'

Holly found a hat and her jacket, then wound a scarf around her neck. 'Are you staying here, Sadie?' she asked.

'Indeed I am. Whatever about decorating the tree, I'm not hiking up those freezing fields, thank you very much.'

By the time Holly joined Paddy he'd climbed up the ladder on the side of the big old oil tank and dipped a stick inside. 'We're out of oil,' he concluded. 'I'll get on to the oil company immediately before we head out and see if they can come today.'

'No!' Holly yelped.

'What do you mean, no?' Paddy asked, concerned. He climbed down the ladder and put a hand on her arm. 'What's going on, Holly?'

'We can't afford to fill the tank,' she said simply. 'We're broke.'

'What?' Paddy whispered. 'I knew things were bad, especially seeing as Jacob next door has had to stop renting the fields and we've lost two livery horses in the last month, but I didn't think we were in quite such dire straits,' he said, pulling her towards him. 'Why didn't you tell me? We'll be all right, though, won't we?'

'Quite honestly, Paddy, I don't know.' She sighed heavily.

She'd always controlled the purse strings. Paddy did more than his fair share of chores. He brought plenty of business their way, too, by engaging with farmers and working the land. But he'd never entered into the finances of Huntersbrook House. That had been Maggie's affair. Now it was Holly's.

'Oh, Holly, I'd noticed a change in you over the last while. But I put it down to Maggie's departure or women's troubles.' They stood holding one another for what felt like the longest time. 'We need to have a serious talk,' Paddy said finally.

'I know we do,' Holly said, rubbing her temples. 'Not right now, though. I'll go inside and order a quarter-tank of oil. We should be able to cover that. Then let's just go ahead and get the tree.'

'Whatever you say, love.' Paddy kissed her tenderly.

Ever since the fateful day when Paddy had lain injured on the hunting field and Holly had brought him back to Huntersbrook, nearly thirty-two years ago, Paddy had been the man of the house. He could run the farming end of things with his eyes shut. He did the lion's share of the maintenance and was a loving husband and father, but he wasn't a number-cruncher.

They'd had their fair share of ups and downs over the years and managed to come out relatively unscathed. But this time, Holly thought, their financial situation was on a different level altogether. It was so bleak she couldn't see any way they could dig their way out.

She'd always adored Paddy. She'd never questioned their relationship. She'd accepted their roles within the marriage. Now, for the first time ever, she wished he had the capacity to click into businessman mode. She longed for him to take her in his arms and tell her to stop worrying about the future. That he had a cunning plan to save Huntersbrook from ruin. But that wasn't going to happen.

Kicking off her boots, she went into the kitchen feeling more defeated than she'd ever thought possible.

'Did you forget something?' Sadie asked.

'No, I just need to make a phone call,' Holly answered. She loved Sadie, but the last thing she wanted was for the older woman to know what was happening. She didn't want anyone to know. Not yet, at least. If they could have one more Christmas at Huntersbrook when everyone was happy and blissfully unaware of what might lie ahead, that was good enough for Holly.

Ducking into the small study at the front of the house, Holly called the oil company and asked for a leaner order than usual.

Both she and Paddy were glad of the commotion the dogs were making as she went back outside to the jeep. 'All right, Jess and Millie,' she said. 'Take it easy now. In you hop.' She opened the back door and let them jump in, with much hysterical tail wagging and licking.

'I'll drive,' she said to Paddy. She needed to feel in control of as many situations as possible, even if it was only a drive to find the right tree. As she steered the jeep over the churned-up frozen ground they were jolted from side to side. 'The mud is like rock, it's so cold out there,' she said to a nodding Paddy.

'The bright blue sky is fantastic, though. Once I see that, I feel I can keep going,' he said wistfully. 'We'll find a way to get through this, Holly,' he vowed, and patted her hand. 'Nothing is ever hopeless.'

Holly wished she could share his optimism but she'd never been able to see the world in as clear a light as her husband, much as she'd tried.

'Here's the tree I spotted. What do you think?' she asked, happy to change the subject.

'Well, it's a fine specimen but I'd have to chop the whole

thing down if we want it. Why aren't we topping one of the bigger ones like usual?'

'How on earth are you going to scale a large tree while manoeuvring the chainsaw by yourself?' Holly asked. 'And I want it in the stand today. I need to keep my mind off all my worries. Come what may, Christmas is on the way and we need to make this one count.'

'All right, love.' He pulled on his gloves and hat and hauled the chainsaw from the boot.

'It's still a good sixteen feet high so it'll be glorious in the hall,' Holly said, rubbing her hands together. 'It's so cold! That wind would cut you in half.'

'Stand back and keep the dogs to the side while I fell this creature.'

As it crashed to the ground, Scott pulled up alongside them. 'G'day,' he said, getting out and walking towards them. 'How's it going? I called into the house and Sadie said you were up here. Let me give you a hand there, Paddy,' he said, grabbing some of the lower branches of the tree. 'Hefty bugger. Beautiful, but . . .' He yanked the tree into the back of the jeep and helped Paddy secure it with rope. 'Can I follow you back to the house and give you a lift out with it?'

'That'd be brilliant, Scott. Then I can get going with decorating it.' Holly was looking happier by the second.

'I'll take those two back, unless you're planning on having them on your laps in the front?' Scott said to Paddy, as the dogs jumped around his feet.

'Thanks. I rather not do the journey inhaling dog breath!'

The mood in the jeep was decidedly less strained on the way back to the house. Holly pulled up at the front door and hopped out.

'I'll give you a shout once we have this tree in the stand,' Paddy promised. 'I'll do it out here, and then we can haul it inside.'

'I'll find the right boxes and see if Sadie and I can get the lights working.' Holly disappeared around the side of the house.

The sound of the oil truck crunching along the main driveway made Holly stop in her tracks. 'Hello,' she said, waving to the driver. 'That was quick,' she said, as he rolled down his window.

'I was in the area and the orders aren't exactly coming in thick and fast at the moment,' he said. 'I'd enough on board for you so here I am.'

'You know where the tank is at the side, don't you?'

'Yup.' He handed her a docket from his delivery book.

'I'll write you a cheque and meet you there,' she promised.

She hadn't had time to sit and work it all out cent for cent, but as she went into the house, Holly hoped she'd left enough funds to cover Christmas.

Sadie appeared, pink-faced.

'All right?' Holly was puzzled. 'You look like you've been on a treadmill since we were gone.'

'I had a sudden burst of energy so I took advantage and got a few jobs done. Did you get the tree at all?'

'Yes and a beauty it is too. The men are putting it in the stand out front. Remind me to get Paddy to pop a bucket under the trunk, won't you? If I can't water the poor thing it'll die. And thanks for sending Scott to help.' Holly was rooting in her handbag for her cheque book. 'The oil man has just arrived so I'll pay him and maybe you'd give me a hand with the decorating,' she called over her shoulder as she went back out to pay.

'Right you are, love.'

When the oil man had gone, Holly dragged the boxes of decorations into the hall where Sadie was directing Scott and Paddy through the front door. 'Over to the right a bit or you'll skin the paint off the skirting board,' she instructed. 'I'm like the sat-nav here.' She grinned at Holly. 'You weren't exaggerating when you said you'd picked a fine one this year. It's magnificent, Holly.'

'It never looked that big when it was against the backdrop of the sky!' Holly giggled. 'It's really huge, isn't it?' she said, with her hands on her hips. 'Oh, Sadie, look at the fire you've lit! All we're missing now is a bit of Christmassy music. I'll go and grab the CD player.'

As she went into the living room, Holly saw that a fire was roaring in the hearth there too. No wonder poor Sadie looked like she'd run a marathon. She'd gone around trying to heat the freezing house while they were out. Holly didn't know if she'd overheard her conversation with Paddy earlier, but either way she had taken it upon herself to make the place more comfortable.

Holly picked up the CD player, then rushed back to the hallway, closing the living-room door to keep the heat in. As the children weren't around, she'd keep the central heating off until they needed it. The kitchen was warmed by the Aga and if they kept the fires stoked in the hall and living room, they'd stretch the oil.

'Mighty job there, Paddy, good on ya,' Scott said, pumping his hand as Holly plugged in the music. 'That's what I call a real tree, eh, mate?'

'Thanks for your help,' Paddy answered. 'Come in and have a cuppa, why don't you?'

'Cheers, I will.'

'Did you remember to put the bucket under the trunk?' Holly asked.

'Yes, dear. It's all done,' Paddy said patiently.

'Well, then, I don't mean to be rude but I can't wait another second to start decorating the tree,' Holly said.

'You get going there, pet, and I'll give these men a cup of tea in the kitchen,' Sadie offered. 'Then I'll be back to help.'

As she shooed the men away, Holly felt a rush of love for Sadie. She was always there for her and the family.

By the time she'd taken the decorations she wanted out of the boxes and found the white lights she needed, Paddy, Scott and Sadie had returned.

'We'll get the lights up and the high decorations done, and leave you to spend hours fussing over the details,' Paddy said, as Scott set up the stepladder.

'I'll do the climbing,' Scott volunteered, and shinned up the stepladder. 'I'm steady now. Pass the lights up, Paddy,' he called down.

'Over a bit more … Don't just dump them all in one bunch on the left,' Holly interjected anxiously. 'It needs to look natural when it's lit, with well-distributed lights.'

'It's hardly going to look the way nature intended by the time you're finished dumping fairies and balls and God knows what on the poor beggar,' Scott shouted down with a grin.

He and Paddy were a good team. Within a short time they had the tree lit to Holly's satisfaction.

'Should we put one more set towards the bottom right-hand side?' she wondered.

'No!' the men chorused in unison. Paddy held the front door open and Scott ran through with the ladder under his arm before she could change her mind.

Most of the decorations were up and the tree was looking gorgeous when Holly exclaimed, 'Look, Sadie, it's the box of homemade ones from when the children were small.' Turning the first one over, she looked inside the cardboard toilet-roll insert. '*Lainey age 4*'. The cotton wool was more than a little matted, the cardboard sagging, and Santa was down to one bobbly eye, but he was still just about recognisable. Holly placed him on the tree, then fished out an equally dishevelled snowman with Joey's name written in bockety childish scrawl. His head had come off several times over the years and was being kept in place now by a threading of wire.

Pippa had always had a fixation with paper chains. Holly had kept her quiet for hours by cutting strips of anything from old wallpaper to Christmas wrapping. Her little fingers would deftly entwine the strips into chains. An entire box housed yards of them. They were faded in parts, but still much loved. Each year Holly insisted on starting at the top and winding them the whole way around the tree. She'd no doubt that Pippa would turn up over the next few days and grumble about how embarrassing it was to have them there and how crappy they were. But Holly didn't care.

'Look, here's the angel Mum made with Lainey,' Holly said. The year Joey was born a disgruntled five-year-old Lainey had been coaxed away from her exhausted mother by the 'angel project' with her grandma.

'Come, and we'll do a little more work on her,' Maggie used to say, holding her hand out for Lainey to take. They'd made the body out of clay, baking it in the oven to harden it. Several vitally important trips had followed: one to the haberdasher to find scraps of white tulle and lace to make her dress, another to the wool shop to buy the angel some hair just like Lainey's. The poor thing mightn't have looked quite so kooky if Lainey hadn't insisted on making her head out of a ping-pong ball.

'Don't laugh when you see it,' Maggie had warned Holly. 'I tried to encourage her to use something else but she was having none of it.'

The angel had ended up looking like a mutant boiled egg.

Holly might have considered making it mysteriously disappear but every time Lainey clapped eyes on it she glowed with pride.

The first year Paddy had climbed the ladder with little Lainey on his shoulders so she could 'stick the tree up the angel's frock', as Grandma had delicately put it.

'She's as unfortunate-looking as she was the day they made her,' Holly said now, and giggled with Sadie.

'She is sort of hideous, God bless her,' Sadie said, and laughed.

'Oh, God, I do miss Mum,' Holly sighed.

'Me too,' Sadie said gently. 'But we'll have a good Christmas as usual, won't we?' She raised an eyebrow.

'Of course,' Holly said, as she gathered the empty decoration boxes and stacked them.

'Did you think of inviting Scott at all? We'd do worse than have him to look at,' Sadie said with a wink.

'You're awful!' Holly laughed. 'He's young enough to be your grandson.'

'True, but that doesn't mean I can't enjoy the view!'

'You're a bad girl underneath that angelic exterior,' Holly teased. 'I'll invite him along with Jacob and Cynthia and their son. I'd say there won't be a massive amount of Christmas cheer next door. The more the merrier!' Holly snatched up the boxes to move them out of the way. 'Just inhale that pine scent. Isn't it gorgeous?'

'Yes, indeed. It's making my nose very happy,' Sadie replied.

By the time darkness fell that evening, Huntersbrook House had begun its transformation into a Christmas wonderland. Both sides of the impressive double doors between the hall and the living room were encased in greenery, and so were both fireplaces. Paddy had dutifully gone outside and come back with a huge pile of sticks, which they'd poked into the swags to make them more lifelike. The little birds were like tiny twinkling finches. Dozens of white lights poked out at intervals, illuminating the silver glitter that Holly had carefully shaken over the artificial foliage.

'I'll head off home now, if that's all right with you?' Sadie asked.

'Of course. Thank you for helping me today,' Holly said, hugging her. 'I don't know what I'd do without you.'

'I'd be a lost soul without you too, my dear,' Sadie said, patting her hand.

As Holly threw another log onto the fire in the hallway, Paddy came to join her. He put his arms around her and they stood mesmerised by the spectacle of the tree. Holly leaned her head against his chest and smiled. She had a lot to be thankful for, she knew that. But she wished she could get them through the financial crisis that was threatening to change their lives for ever.

Feeling Paddy's strong arm around her, she felt guilty for being so short with him earlier on. She wouldn't trade him for any other. He would never be Richard Branson, but he was the kindest and most supportive man she'd ever met.

If they lost Huntersbrook House, the fault would lie with herself, not Paddy. She was the one her mother had trusted to keep it in the family. She was the one who was hurtling swiftly towards failure. There was nobody to blame but herself.

Sorrow, guilt and regret washed over her, but she had to remember to count her blessings. If her worst fears were realised and she had to sell Huntersbrook, would Paddy and the children hate her? The children were all grown up now. They would make their own way in the world, God willing. And Holly hoped more than anything that Paddy would always love her the way he did today. No matter where they ended up living.

14

The Sounds of Christmas

Lainey was really looking forward to her Saturday night out. She'd never been to a concert at the O₂ and she was feeling good about her new outfit. She had to hand it to her younger sister, Pippa knew her fashion.

Examining herself in the mirror, Lainey felt both nervous and delighted. Jules had offered her a bed for the night but Lainey said she'd prefer to go home. 'I'll gladly take you up on the offer for the night of the work Christmas party, but I'm going to pop down to Wicklow tomorrow so I'll head back to my flat.'

'Sure, Lainz,' Jules had said. 'Whatever you prefer.'

She hadn't been to the hairdresser for ages, so Lainey's normally short hair had grown a little, softening her previously boyish look. With a bit of makeup, she had to admit she felt a damn sight better than before.

A text from Jules helped her relax during the taxi ride: *Text when you get here and I'll meet u outside the bar so u don't have to walk in on ur own. C u soon!*

She answered: *Thank u! Will do. Ur a star!*

It was so long since she'd been in this position – going out and meeting new people. Seth hadn't been a concert-goer. He'd had a boys' night every Friday but he'd discouraged her from going out when he wasn't there. She'd comforted herself with the thought that he loved her so much that he couldn't bear to share her. But in hindsight she couldn't help wondering if he was merely trying to control her.

As the driver approached the concert venue, Lainey texted Jules. 'There's a lot of ladies around tonight,' the taxi driver said with a grin. 'Mr Bublé certainly knows how to draw a crowd.' She agreed, paid him, then began to walk towards the bar where she and Jules were to meet. A moment later, she spotted her friend.

'Lainz!' Jules was trotting towards her on pencil-thin high heels. 'Hi! You look great, come on and meet some super-cool people.' She hugged Lainey and kissed her on both cheeks.

'Thanks,' Lainey said. 'You look great too.'

Jules was certainly attracting plenty of attention kitted out in her gold-sequined hot-pants with a matching bra and see-through black blouse, her signature killer heels and fishnet tights.

'I'm in Kylie-meets-Madonna mode, *circa* 1986,' she said. 'Let's grab a glass of wine and I'll bring you over to meet the troops.'

Lainey had to employ every shred of poker face she possessed as she concentrated on not staring at one of the people standing in the group Jules had led her to. 'Manus, Lori, Anna, Carrie, this is Lainz,' Jules announced.

'Hiya!' they cried in unison.

The girls all looked ordinary enough. Manus, though, stood out.

Built like a tank, he sported a ponytail, full beard, tattoos, thick biker boots and what appeared to be a vintage wedding gown. 'All right. How's it going?' he asked, holding out his fingerless-gloved hand for her to shake.

'Hello,' she said, trying not to sound like a disapproving headmistress.

'I'm Manus and this is my wife Lorraine,' he said, obviously comfortable to play the role of man and introduce people. Even if he did look deranged.

Lorraine was a little twinkly Tinkerbell in pale pink tulle. 'Lovely to meet you,' she chirped. 'Jules has told us all about you.'

'Good to meet you too,' Lainey said, gulping her white wine wishing it was brandy.

Anna towered above them all in a black catsuit, which left nothing to the imagination. She oozed sex appeal. She stepped forward, grasped Lainey's hand and shook it firmly.

Carrie was quiet and dowdy in a blouse the colour of a plaster with mammy-style jeans and battered suede ankle boots. As she sipped her drink, which was an alarming shade of blue with a stripy straw, she waved vaguely. Lainey waved back.

'So are you ready for Mr Smoothie, then?' Lorraine asked.

'Eh, yes,' Lainey managed, as she downed the rest of her wine.

'I'm not mad about him, but the tickets were free and I can fake it for the night,' Jules said.

'Well, Lorraine is totally obsessed with him, aren't you?' Manus said, smiling.

'I'm probably going to faint the minute he comes on stage,' she admitted.

'It's a lovely way to kick off the Christmas season, isn't it?' Lainey said. 'Can I get you all another drink?'

'We're fine, thanks,' they said, waving their hands over their glasses.

'Jules?' Lainey asked.

'Ah, go on, then. I'll have one more glass of wine too. We'll probably need to head inside then. It's a seated concert and I hate stumbling around in the dark, don't you?'

A passing bartender took their order so Lainey had to stay standing next to bridal Manus.

'Look at the state of him!' a passer-by said loudly, pointing and laughing.

Lainey caught Manus's eye. He didn't seem in the least bit bothered.

'We're used to that sort of reaction,' Lorraine explained. 'We're married the last ten years,' she said, looking up lovingly at Manus. 'He works as a forklift driver during the week. He only cross-dresses at weekends.'

'That's very ... modern of you,' Lainey said, stony-faced. When she saw that the others were grinning, she burst out laughing. 'Oh, I'm sorry, I know I'm meant to be unfazed by this, but I'm so bloody shocked I feel like I'm going to die.'

'At least you're honest,' Manus said. 'You can stay. Every now and again we meet new people who tell us they're cool with it. Then they excuse themselves to go to the bathroom and we see them running up the road.'

'Oh, no way!' Lainey said, relaxing. 'Let me have another stiff drink and I'll be fine, I promise.'

'Didn't I tell you she's cool?' Jules said proudly.

'Ah, you did indeed,' Lorraine answered. 'We've heard all about you, Lainey, and how kind you've been to Jules since she started the job. Your boss sounds like a right prick. She'd be a basket case by now if it wasn't for you.'

'Yeah, fair play to you for looking out for her,' Manus said, putting his arm around Jules protectively.

'It works both ways,' Lainey said. 'She's a good pal to have around too.'

Once she'd finished her second glass of wine, Lainey felt less freaked out. 'Are we all sitting together?' she asked.

'Yes,' Jules told her. 'It was Lorraine's sister who gave us the tickets.'

'She's at home heartbroken, the poor bitch,' Lorraine said. 'I told her to dump that dopey shite she was living with. He didn't give a toss about her. She needs a decent man like my Manus, isn't that right?' she said, looking up at her bearded bride. 'So we're all in beside each other. That cool with you, Lainey?'

'Sure,' Lainey said. This was certainly different from any night she'd had with Seth – or anyone else, for that matter. She was actually enjoying being part of the group. Even if they were a little alternative.

As they made their way into the auditorium for the show Jules linked her arm. 'Can I have a word?' she asked.

'Sure,' Lainey said, and they stood over to one side allowing the crowd to pass them by.

'We'll catch up with you in a sec,' Jules called to the others. Lorraine gave her the thumbs-up to let her know she'd heard.

'This is actually really hard for me,' Jules said, looking at the floor. 'I honestly hope that what I'm about to say doesn't ruin our friendship.'

'Okay.'

'The thing is, Lainz . . . well, I'm gay.'

'Really?' Lainey said. She'd thought meeting Manus was going to be the most outrageous thing that happened tonight but it seemed the surprises weren't over yet. 'Wow. I wasn't expecting that!'

'You're not annoyed with me?'

'Why would I be?' Lainey said, puzzled.

'You've been so good to me since I started my job and I was going to tell you before but it never seemed like the right time,' Jules continued. 'Then I figured you might guess when I told you my mum wasn't talking to me and I'd split with my boyfriend ...' She trailed off.

'Nope! I'd no idea. This is going to sound awful but I think I had a stereotypical image in my head of what a lesbian should look like and it's not you.'

'Because I don't have a shaved head and wear army-surplus gear?' she said, giggling.

'Precisely,' Lainey said. 'Listen, I meant what I said just now to Lorraine and Manus. You've been such a great friend to me. You're kind and thoughtful and I'd like to think we've clicked.' Suddenly she had a thought. 'You don't fancy me, do you?' she asked, before she could stop herself.

'No! Not at all! Eh ... I mean, that's not why I've been hanging around with you. Sorry, that sounds insulting. I didn't mean it to be. I know you're not gay, Lainz, so I don't think of you that way,' Jules said, looking mortified.

'Let's start this conversation again,' Lainey said calmly. 'You've told me you're gay. I have no issue with it. You don't fancy me. I hope we can continue being great friends. Does that just about sum it up?' she asked.

'Yes,' Jules said. 'That's exactly what I wanted to say!'

They both burst out laughing.

'Can you believe Pippa tells me all the time that I act like a pensioner and I'm too sensible,' Lainey said. 'And Mum's always saying how intense I am. Well, now I can tell both of them I was at a concert with a cross-dressed married man and a lesbian. Jules, you've done more for my street cred than you'll ever know.'

'Thank you,' Jules said, growing very serious suddenly. Tears shone in her eyes. 'Thank you,' she said again, taking Lainey's hand. 'Remember I told you my mum won't talk to me? She told me I'm a freak. She said she's ashamed of me and I make her sick. She thinks I'm doing this to get to her.'

'Well, I hope in time she'll come round,' Lainey said.

'Thanks, Lainz,' Jules said, hugging her. As the screams went up in the auditorium the girls jumped.

'Sounds like Michael's on his way. Let's get in there,' Jules said. She pulled Lainey's sleeve and tottered towards the entrance.

As they made their way to their seats Lainey tried to take it all in. She honestly didn't mind that Jules was gay. But she was totally stunned. She'd never have guessed in a million years. Although she was certainly surprised at her friend's news, Lainey was struck by how shoddily Jules's mum had behaved. No matter how bad things were at home, Lainey could never imagine her own family being so harsh. They weren't the Brady Bunch either, Lainey mused. They were far from perfect in actual fact. They didn't talk openly enough.

Yes, they had a wonderful open-door policy going, but so many things were brushed under the carpet. Look at the way they'd handled things since Grandma had left. They all said they missed her but that was where it ended. How come none of them had contacted her? It wasn't right. Months had gone by yet the rift between them still stood.

Lainey decided there and then that she would definitely drop down to Huntersbrook the following day. She wanted to talk to her mother. For a long time she'd been aware of a wedge between herself and Holly. Grandma had buffered that for years but since she'd left Lainey had felt the tension increase. She figured she was going to take her new friend's lead and try to be more open about her feelings.

The opportunity for further deep thought vanished as the auditorium lights dipped and the stage came alive.

The concert was fantastic. Lainey was surprised by how many of the songs she knew and found herself singing along happily with all the others.

'Let's go clubbing now,' Carrie suggested, as they filed out among the massive crowd.

Lainey felt nervous again. What if they wanted to go to some underground fetish place?

'We could go to the hotel over there,' Jules said, pointing to what looked like a very ordinary place. Lainey decided she should stay a while, out of politeness if nothing else.

The disco bar turned out to be totally kosher, with trendy tables and chairs and not a bondage whip in sight. Manus was the only man in a dress but the fact he could take down the entire front row of the Irish rugby team with one arm probably explained why people weren't jeering at him or picking fights.

The music was great, and Lainey even ventured on to the dance floor with Jules, Carrie and Anna.

'Seth hated dancing so I've never really been to clubs,' Lainey shouted to Jules, as they jumped around. 'This is so much fun! We'll have to organise some more nights out!'

'Well, my New Year's resolution is to let my hair down and be happy to be myself,' Jules vowed.

'That sounds like a great plan!' Lainey agreed.

By the time she got back to her flat it was after three in the morning. Lainey had enjoyed every minute of the night. She was still a bit floored by Jules's revelation, but she'd meant it when she'd said it wouldn't make any difference to their friendship.

Her heart went out to Jules when she thought of her mother shunning her. That woman was missing out on a relationship with a wonderful daughter.

As she drifted off to sleep, Grandma's face filled her mind. Sometimes other people's selfish actions highlighted our own, Lainey mused. She wasn't sure that Grandma would still want to chat to her but she needed to find out. She'd ask her mother for the number and pluck up the courage to phone her.

15

All I Want for Christmas Is ...

✳✳✳

That Sunday, as Pippa and Sue unpacked the stunning collection by Chanel at Boutique Belle, Pippa felt as if she was in the presence of royalty.

'Let's get this window all Chanelled up!' Pippa squeaked, unable to hide her excitement. 'This is the next best thing to owning the stuff.' Reverently she lifted a piece free of its tissue paper.

'Ha! You're as bad as I am!' Sue said, giving her a quick hug. 'And there was I thinking you'd be cursing me for getting you up at the crack of dawn on a Sunday to troop in here in the freezing cold.'

'Sue. Sweetie,' Pippa said, with one hand on her hip and the other waving in an exaggerated gesture. 'I'd walk to work backwards in my bare feet in the middle of the night if it meant I could touch the Chanel stuff.'

'I know you probably want to have some of your Sunday off all he same,' Sue said. 'You should be gone by two at the latest and I'll pay you double.'

'Great!' Pippa was delighted.

As it turned out, there were lots of early-morning shoppers milling around Grafton Street, so Sue wisely opened the doors ahead of the scheduled time. As she was caught up with serving customers, Pippa pretty much had free rein with the window dressing.

'Oh!' Sue exclaimed later, when Pippa dragged her out of the shop to view the finished window.

'You like?' she asked, as she scrutinised her own work.

'It's stunning! I love the monochrome effect. The oversized white glittery baubles on strings of tinsel are a far cry from a mannequin in a Santa hat and a family of penguins in a corner, which is what most shops do.'

'Most shops don't carry Chanel, dahling,' Pippa said. 'Nor do they have Pippa Craig at their service.'

Sue laughed and hugged her again. 'All jokes aside, you have an incredible eye for style, Pippa. You should put it to good use. I'm not here to lecture you, but you really have a talent.'

'Thanks.' Pippa grinned. She'd felt such a buzz as she'd dressed the window. She'd known instinctively that black-and-white would be the best backdrop against which to show off the gorgeous black bouclé Chanel suits, with the frothy white-and-black patterned silk blouses. Coco Chanel herself might have sent the life-sized porcelain Dalmatian she had found in the stockroom. Pippa had wanted to bring the glitz of Christmas to the window without being tacky, so the thin strings of silver tinsel had worked marvellously with the spotlighting to suspend the baubles and join the dog to the mannequin as a twinkling lead.

'I used my own lipstick on the mannequin and it's kind of sitting on top of her plastic face, so don't let it rub off on you if you're taking anything out of the window to sell,' Pippa warned.

'Good point, thank you. But you're so right to give her ruby red lips. It just lifts the whole look. Well done!'

As a customer approached, Sue and Pippa rushed back into the shop. Whether it was the striking window or just pre-Christmas indulgence, the shop was thronged for the next few hours.

By four o'clock it was getting dark and the wind had begun to whip down the street. 'You go on home, pet,' Sue said to Pippa. 'I'm sorry you had to stay so long, but I'm so glad you were here. I'd never have managed on my own.'

'My pleasure,' Pippa said. 'I love working with fashion. It's a brilliant way for me to stay out of debt! Shopping with other people's money is so much fun!' She giggled.

'Speaking of money, I'll give you cash for today,' Sue said. 'You could get yourself a little treat!' She handed Pippa a generous wedge.

'Thanks, Sue!' Pippa said. 'I think I will treat myself! I've been under a bit of financial stress lately but seeing as this is a bit of a bonus I might just blow it!'

'You only live once.' Sue grinned.

Pippa decided it would be rude not to make the most of this little windfall. Needless to say, Sue was totally unaware that Pippa had spent her entire life until that week treating herself. But that was immaterial.

It was freezing when she left the shop and made her way across town. She knew she should go home to avoid spending money, but she couldn't shake the idea that she was 'Chanel personnel' now.

She rang Skye, and was thrilled when she answered with the sound of glasses clinking and raised voices in the background.

'It's me!' Pippa shouted.

'Pippa! Where are you?' Skye shouted back.

'Just leaving work. Are you in town?'

'I'm in Diamonds bar with a few people. Do you want to come and join us?'

'Cool! See you in a few minutes.' That was exactly what Pippa felt like, an evening of chatting and laughing with a bit of flirting mixed in. Jay came fleetingly to mind. She still needed to speak to him. She brushed aside the image of his face when she'd rejected him, and strode quickly across the city centre to the bar.

The place was jammed. As the rain began to hammer down outside, the windows steamed up. Threading her way through the throng, Pippa nodded to the beat of the music. Spotting Skye waving at her, she smiled and waved back, then nudged her way to the far corner.

'Hi,' she said, kissing Skye. 'How did you manage to get seats?' she asked, impressed.

'I've been here since lunchtime!' Skye slurred. 'I met a client who bought me a bite to eat and we had wine and I should've gone home but I'm still here!' She put a hand to her mouth in mock shock. 'What'll you have?' She swayed as she slid off her stool to go to the bar.

'They're on me,' a guy Pippa had never seen before announced. He was about two stone overweight, with a slick of sweat across his brow and upper lip. She guessed he was in his early thirties, although he was already balding. 'I'm Vince,' he said, taking Pippa's hand in his doughy one.

'Hi, Vince, lovely to meet you,' she said, lurching backwards to avoid a slobbery kiss. 'I'm Pippa.'

'You're looking lovely, Pippa,' he said, with a slow grin. 'What can I get you to drink?'

'You're very kind. I'll have a gin and tonic, please.' He was pretty vile, but if he wanted to buy her drinks Pippa wasn't going to object.

As he'd vacated his stool to go to the bar, Pippa decided to sit on it for a minute. Sliding it beside Skye's, she settled down for a chat.

'Is he your client?' she asked.

'Nope,' Skye said, and her eyes crossed.

'You're totally pie-eyed!' Pippa laughed.

'Yeah. I think I need to move on to sparkling water. I'm not sure how much longer I'll last here. I'm so bad at drinking during the day. But it was one of those quick deals. The guy phoned me this morning looking to have a site done ASAP so I agreed to meet him today. He's very cool and he's given me the job.'

'Brilliant!' Pippa said.

'He's a serious mover and shaker too – I reckon it'll lead to lots more work so I'm stoked. He bought a glass of bubbly to celebrate and we had wine with lunch,' she explained. 'I was so nervous and delighted about the deal I couldn't really eat. And now I'm skuttered. I should get out of here before I fall in a heap on the floor.'

'Ah, it's Christmas! Live a little,' Pippa said. 'Here's what's-his-name with my drink. Do you know him?' she asked.

'No . . . He's just some randomer who pitched up a while ago with the two fellas just there,' Skye said, pointing behind. 'He seems okay, just a bit lechy.'

'Now, Princess,' Vince said, dumping the drink rather ungraciously in front of Pippa. 'Jesus, would you steal my grave as quick?' He gestured at his stool.

'Sorry.' Pippa began to get up.

A large sweaty paw clamped onto her shoulder. 'Not at all,' Vince said. 'I'm only slagging you. Stay where you are. What do you think I am? An ogre? You sit and enjoy your drink, darling.'

'Cheers!' Pippa said, flashing him one of her sexiest smiles.

Over the next hour the group surrounding them began to filter away one by one. Vince and his two mates had turned out to be great craic. 'We've had a liquid lunch,' Vince explained to Pippa. 'Ah, sure it's nearly Christmas!'

'I'm right there with you!' Pippa said, loving the attention, not to mention the free drinks.

By now Skye had gulped two pints of water, but still wanted to go home, and said as much to Pippa.

'No worries,' she said, unable to hide her disappointment. 'You stay here. I'll grab a taxi outside.'

'Are you sure?' Pippa asked. 'I know I should probably come with you, but it's a laugh in here and these guys are brilliant. I haven't put my hand in my pocket since I arrived. This is my kind of piss-up – flowing booze for free!'

'Will you be okay?' Skye asked uncertainly.

'You bet! I won't be too late. I've to work tomorrow so I don't want to be falling in the door looking like I've spent the night in a urinal.'

'I don't think Sue would appreciate that,' Skye confirmed.

'Especially now that we're a Chanel stockist,' Pippa said.

'Sue's tried to get me to come and work with her over the years and it's just not my scene. Sounds like your idea of heaven on earth, though.' Skye grinned.

'You said it!' Pippa shrilled, as she kissed Skye. 'Are you sure you don't want me to come with you now?'

'I'm not raining on your parade,' she said, as her eyes crossed again. 'Nighty-night.'

As Skye left, Vince slid in beside Pippa with a tray of shots. 'Tequila?' he offered.

'It's not really my scene but I'll give it a go.'

'Lick your hand and I'll pour salt on it for you. Here's the lemon,' he said, offering her a saucer of wedges.

Pippa clinked glasses with him. 'Down the hatch.' As she tossed back the putrid drink and shoved the lemon into her mouth, the burning in her throat and chest made her cough.

'One more?' Vince asked, laughing at her expression.

'I've had enough of that stuff, thanks. I'll just have my gin and tonic.' Her head began to spin and she thought she was going to vomit. She grabbed her glass and downed the remainder.

'Don't get all sensible on me now! Here, I'll do the last shot with you,' he promised. 'They'll only go to waste and I've paid for them.'

'Your friends didn't get one – would they not drink them?' Pippa asked.

'They're on pints.' He raised his eyes to heaven. 'They're boring, not like you.' He held up a lemon wedge in one hand and a full shot glass in the other. 'Go on, you know you want to!' he goaded.

'Okay, but this is the last one!' As soon as the tequila hit her stomach Pippa knew it was one drink too many. Retching, she was terrified she was going to barf all over Vince and the table. 'I don't feel too well,' she choked out.

'Oh, no! Come out into the fresh air for a minute and you'll be fine.' He used his bulk to manoeuvre her through the throng in the bar, like the parting of the Red Sea. 'Move it out, please! We've got a lady with a whitie!'

Pippa grabbed her bag and coat and darted towards the exit.

Outside, the freezing air shocked Pippa into near-sobriety. She leaned against the window beside the main door. 'Hey, move it! You're blocking the entrance, you stupid bint,' a man yelled. Pippa staggered sideways.

'Oh dear, you're pretty drunk, Princess,' Vince said with a grin.

'I'm actually locked,' Pippa agreed. 'I didn't realise how pissed I was until we came out here. It was all a great plan earlier on. Now I'd like to die.'

'Let's get out of the way in case anyone else shouts at you,' Vince said, taking her elbow and leading her to the roadside.

'I want to go home,' she said.

'Where do you live?'

'Just around from Lourdes Hospital,' she managed.

'Taxi!' Vince yelled, and a cab screeched to a halt beside them.

He helped her into the back seat, then slid in beside her.

'Uh, I'm not well,' she slurred.

'I was wondering how such a little thing could put away so much booze and not feel the effects,' Vince said. 'I'll ask this gentleman to pull in at the chipper on the way, run in and get you some food.' He leaned forward. 'Can you stop outside the kebab shop, mate?'

'Whatever. I'll leave the meter running, though. It's lashing rain, in case you hadn't noticed, and other punters are looking for cars tonight,' he said rudely.

'I'll pay, don't worry,' Vince scoffed. 'What'll I get you?' he asked Pippa.

'Anything … I don't care …' She slumped against the door.

As Vince dashed out into the wet night, the driver looked

at Pippa in the rear-view mirror. 'Your boyfriend is very good to you. I hope you appreciate him,' he said.

'He's not my boyfriend,' Pippa said, pulling a face. 'He's just a guy I met in a bar.'

'He seems to like you,' the man said.

'Maybe he does but he's barking up the wrong tree,' Pippa said. Vince was fine, but he was overweight, far too slobbery and certainly not her type. She wouldn't go for someone like him in a million years.

'That's a little harsh, isn't it?' the driver commented.

'What's it to you?' Pippa snapped. 'He's nice and all that. He bought me drinks and I appreciate it. End of ...' She trailed off as another wave of nausea hit her. Squashing her cheek against the cool glass of the window, she groaned. 'I shouldn't have drunk those tequilas he bought. It always makes me sick.'

'Yeah, he's a real selfish git all right, buying you all that booze and now getting you food while he drops you home,' the driver said nastily.

'Eh, it's none of your business, thank you,' Pippa said, as her head lurched forwards. 'Who asked you? Not me, that's for certain.'

The door was flung open and the wind and rain whooshed in. 'It's rough out there,' Vince said. 'I'm going to hop out at my own place. It's on the way to yours.' He handed Pippa a bag of food.

'Cool.' Pippa closed her eyes.

It seemed only a moment later that Vince was shaking her arm. 'Hey, Pippa?' he said. 'I'm going now. I've paid for the taxi.'

'Cheers,' she said, peeling her eyes open. The bag of chips was burning her lap as she waved haphazardly at him.

'I had a really fun time with you,' he said. 'Here's my phone number.' He posted a business card into her bag. 'Maybe give me a call and we could go for dinner or something.'

'Yeah … Great …' she said. 'I'll be sure to ring.'

''Bye, then,' he said, as a gust of wind and rain hit him.

'Geek,' Pippa muttered, as the taxi pulled back into the traffic.

'Why are you such a nasty little cow?' the taxi driver asked.

'Huh?'

'He was a decent bloke. There aren't many of them around, I can tell you,' the driver said. 'You should see the way some of them behave in the back of this car.'

'Right,' Pippa said, wishing he'd shut up. 'Good for them. Now can you just get me home? I need to sleep. I have work in the morning.'

When they pulled up outside her apartment block she was out cold.

'Here, Sleeping Beauty, time to get yourself out of my golden carriage,' said the driver, as he nudged her roughly.

'Ouch! Watch it,' Pippa swung her legs out of the car with her bag of chips and staggered into the foyer of her apartment block.

'Don't bother closing my car door!' the driver shouted after her.

'Why don't you just sod off?' Pippa called over her shoulder. Her head hurt. She just wanted to get into her room, kick her shoes off, eat a few chips and go to sleep.

The thought of being in the lift as it lurched up to the second floor made her want to puke so she made for the stairs. After the first flight, she stopped, took a few deep breaths and willed herself on. She really needed to stop getting this drunk. Still, it was Christmas time. Everyone was out having fun.

As she reached the door of her apartment she realised she'd left her bag in the taxi. 'Shit,' she said.

'Looking for this, were you?' the taxi driver said, appearing behind her.

'Uh, right. Yeah,' she said.

'Is that it?' the man sneered.

'What? Listen, I'm tired and I need to get in here. Can you just give me my stuff and leave me alone?'

'You really think you're something, don't you?' he said, balling his fists as he dumped her bag on the floor.

'Hey,' she said. 'Pick that up!'

'Only if you give me a little kiss first,' he said, as a grin spread across his face.

'You must be kidding! I might be drunk but I'm not desperate.'

The shock as he smacked her face nearly caused Pippa to black out. She heard her head bash against the closed apartment door.

As his mouth bore down on hers Pippa felt suffocated. She tried to shove him away. 'No!'

She began to panic. This guy was big and strong and, from the force he was using to hold her down, he had no intention of letting her go. She bit his bottom lip. He yelped and jumped back.

At that moment the apartment door was flung open and Pippa crumpled to the floor just inside the hallway.

'What the hell is going on?' Skye yelled, as the taxi driver fled.

Pippa crawled into the living room on her hands and knees. Skye picked up her things from the floor and went into the kitchen with the soggy bag of takeaway food. Then she said, 'Let me look at you. Oh, God – he must have hit you hard. I thought we were being broken into.'

Blood dripped from Pippa's nose. Skye found some kitchen paper and wiped her friend's face. 'I'm calling the police,' she said, and rushed for the phone.

'No!' Pippa sobbed. 'Leave it.'

'Pippa, that guy is a danger to society. If you don't report him, God knows what he could do to someone else.'

'It was my own fault,' Pippa cried.

'How can you say that?' Skye looked stunned. 'It's certainly not your fault that a big oaf of a man followed you up here and assaulted you.'

'I was being really obnoxious,' Pippa said. 'I left my bag in the car and he was returning it. I was really nasty about Vince and then that taxi driver came to give me my stuff and I was rude to him.' She put her hand to her face. 'I feel like I've been whacked with a hammer.'

'I hate to tell you but you look it too. You should go to hospital and have your nose X-rayed,' Skye told her.

Pippa burst into tears.

'It's not that late. Why don't I call Joey and ask him to come and get us? If we go to A&E I'm sure you'll get sorted pretty quickly.'

Pippa handed Skye her mobile and sat in a daze as her friend talked to Joey.

'He's on the way,' Skye said. 'You have to be checked and, more importantly, you need to report that man, Pippa.'

'Thank you for being so brilliant. You're my guardian angel.'

'Don't be silly, I'm glad I was here.'

The next couple of hours passed in a blur. Joey drove them

to the hospital where, mercifully, they seemed to hit a lull in the accident and emergency department.

'It's after the pubs have closed and before the nightclub lot are in,' the kindly nurse explained. 'Sometimes you can end up waiting half the night, so you're in luck.'

While Pippa had her X-ray done, Skye called the police, who arrived to take her and Pippa's statements. A male and female officer arrived, but the lady conducted the interview with Pippa.

'Can you remember the colour of the car? Did you notice the driver's ID card on the dashboard?' the policewoman asked a short while later.

'I didn't look at any of it,' Pippa admitted. 'I was leaning against the window behind the driver's seat most of the time.'

'Would the gentleman you were travelling with remember any details?' she probed.

'I dunno,' Pippa said miserably. 'I don't have his number. He's called Vince, but that's all I know.'

Joey was rooting through her bag for clues and came across a business card. 'Here you go,' he said, handing the policewoman the details.

'I don't even remember taking his card.' Pippa was shamefaced.

'I know you're not in the mood for a lecture right now,' Joey said, 'but ...'

'I know, Joey. You don't have to say it. I shouldn't get so pissed and I shouldn't go off with strangers.'

'We'll call Vince and hopefully he'll be able to remember some details. Sadly, the CCTV camera at your apartment block is out of service so we don't have that to fall back on,' the policewoman continued, 'but we'll be in touch if we have any leads.'

'Thanks.'

'Now, my dear,' the nurse said, 'that X-ray is through. Your nose isn't broken. You're just bruised. You'll have two black eyes by tomorrow, though.'

'My job!' Pippa shrilled. 'I can't go into Boutique Belle in this state. I know I've gone for the monochrome look with the window but I don't think Sue intended having a panda serving her customers.'

'No, you can't,' Joey said. 'It's bad now so I can't imagine how horrific you're going to look over the next few days.'

'Cheers, brother. Are you all right?' Pippa asked Skye. 'I bet you wish you'd never moved in with me now.' She tried to force a smile.

'Not at all. Quite the opposite. I was actually just thinking it was lucky I was there. Don't worry, I'm not going to move out and leave you,' she said. 'I'll call Sue and tell her what's happened.'

'Would you?' Pippa said quietly. 'I'm so mortified,' she said, beginning to cry once more. 'Please tell her I'll talk to her in the morning and I'm so sorry.'

Pippa cried when she rang her mother and heard her voice.

Holly was amazingly calm as Pippa explained where she was. 'We'll come up immediately. Who's there with you?' Holly asked.

'Skye, and she's been brilliant,' Pippa said. 'And Joey came and brought us to the hospital. There's no point in dragging yourselves all the way up here at this hour of the night, Mum.'

'We don't mind, love.'

'No, please – I feel like I've caused enough trouble for one night.' Her hangover was kicking in. Along with the smack on the head, she certainly wasn't feeling too hot. 'I really just need to crash out. I'll call you when I wake up in the morning,' she promised.

Joey dropped them back to the apartment. 'Thanks for being there tonight, Skye,' he said. 'This little minx thinks she has it all sorted but she was bloody lucky to have you to save her arse this time.'

'No worries,' Skye said, smiling. 'It was a horrible incident. We'll have to be more careful about going places on our own. Us single girls need to look after one another.'

'Well, knowing this one, she'll have some new beau on her arm shortly,' Joey said. 'I can't see you staying single for too long either.'

Skye blushed as she got out of the car. 'Thanks for the lift.'

'See you soon, Joey. I'll call you tomorrow. Hope Sophia isn't too annoyed with me for taking you away,' Pippa said.

'I didn't dare wake her,' Joey said. 'It's not a problem for her.'

As they made their way back into the apartment Pippa shuddered. She'd had a lucky escape tonight. She had to start taking responsibility for herself. Flitting along as if the world owed her a living wasn't right. She needed to get herself together before she made a total shambles of her life.

16

Hark! the Herald Angels Sing ...

✳✳✳

The following morning he was rudely awoken, as usual, by Sophia thundering around the apartment. The lashing sleet and darkness outside were not enticing.

'Nobody likes a lazy boy,' Sophia joked, before dashing into the kitchen to fill her water bottle. Joey watched her. Sophia never seemed to have trouble getting up. She was so driven and focused on what she was doing and never seemed to have a moment like the one he was currently experiencing where he'd have given his right ball to be able to turn over, pull the duvet up to his chin and sleep until noon.

'Pippa had a terrible experience last night,' he called to her.

'Huh?' Sophia said, coming back to the doorway.

'She rang me in an awful state. Seems a taxi driver followed her up to her apartment, hit her and tried to rape her.'

Sophia looked doubtful. 'She must've left out some part of that story.'

'What do you mean?' Joey asked, his brow furrowed. 'She left her bag in the cab, your man dropped it back up and attacked her. She called for me to bring her to hospital.'

'But everything's fine?' Sophia asked, glancing at her watch.

'Yeah, it was a riot. Herself, myself and her new lodger, Skye, hung out in A&E, had a chinwag with the cops and came home. It beats being in bed asleep,' he said tartly.

'Pippa needs to grow up and stop getting herself into trouble. It shouldn't be your problem if she can't behave,' Sophia said. 'I've to go. I'm late.'

She'd already shot off to the living room so Joey just lay there, astounded. How could she act as if Pippa's ordeal was nothing? More to the point, why hadn't she asked if his sister was all right?

'See you later, yeah?' she said, popping her head back into the bedroom. 'Joey, you seriously need to get up. Come on! It's Monday morning!' she said, with obvious exasperation.

'Precisely,' he said. 'It's Monday. It's dark, cold and wintry, and as I just told you, I was out until late last night.'

'Whatever,' she said, not bothering to come over and kiss him.

Sitting up in bed, he called, 'What time are you home this evening?'

'Late. I've a class,' she barked.

'Right. Well, whenever you can fit me in I'd like to chat to you.'

He lay there fuming as he heard the door to the apartment bang. She hadn't even asked what he wanted to talk about! As far as she was concerned, Pippa could be in hospital with a fractured skull and she wouldn't give a damn. Sod this for a game of soldiers, he thought angrily, as he rolled out of bed and turned the main light on. He rummaged in his drawers and cursed, then made his way to the washing machine. The clothes he'd put in the wash the day before had been dumped in a soggy pile on the work surface. Sophia's things were in the washing machine. She had thrown his stuff out and hadn't thought to put them in the dryer.

He'd have to wear a lighter pair of running trousers now and his hi-vis vest was sopping. He dressed quickly, then tied his runners and left the flat. At least his anger might fuel a fast and productive run.

Sophia was just as furious. As she made her way along the frozen paths toward the running track she wanted to yell at the top of her voice. Joey was annoying the crap out of her. She'd no idea what he'd been rabbiting on about just now, but it seemed Princess Pippa had been on the phone causing trouble.

She was always ringing Joey for advice and whingeing about something. Well, Sophia was sick of it. She was going to tell Joey that it was either her or Pippa. She wasn't interested in playing second fiddle to his spoiled little sister.

She worked so damn hard and trained non-stop – the last thing she needed when she got home was hassle. If Joey wasn't prepared to give her the credit she was due, she'd have to reassess her situation. Men were more bloody trouble than they were worth, she thought, as she rounded the corner and the track came into sight. No doubt he'd be on the phone, all hurt and affronted, later on. Well, he could swing. She was going to freeze him out for the rest of the day. She'd flung his wet clothes onto the kitchen work surface earlier. If he thought she was going to become a stay-at-home slave at any point, he was wrong.

'Hey, it's Sophia!' called the boss of the IT company she was doing a session with. 'All hail, mistress!' She knew he was joking but at the same time she felt respected and powerful. This is more like it, she thought, as she high-fived the men and began shouting the stretches to begin their hour.

As soon as he opened the front door to the apartment building, the freezing air snapped at Joey's face. Christ, it was horribly cold. For all her faults, Sophia was tough. She never seemed to flinch heading out in this God-awful weather.

His current route, which meant he'd get in a good ten kilometres, took him along the main road towards Pippa's apartment block and up to the large green belt and parkland. Clicking on his iPod, he began to jog.

Eminem's angry tones weren't going to lift his mood so he pulled the device from his pocket and began to scan through his iTunes list.

Sophia's lack of interest in his family and his life was becoming too much for Joey. He couldn't continue to share his bed with someone who clearly didn't give a toss about him. He wondered whether she'd been quite so selfish when they'd first got together. He'd been so in awe of her drive to succeed that he'd probably missed the underlying harshness.

He'd noticed the roadworks sign and the luminous orange and white tape blocking the area, but that didn't prepare him for the sudden feeling of weightlessness he experienced. It seemed to happen in slow motion but he knew he was falling. His last conscious thought was the intensity of the noise as he hit the bottom of the pit.

The lighting was dim, and unfamiliar voices were zoning in and out of his head. Joey tried to remember what time of day it was and what he was meant to be doing. 'Where am I?' he asked. 'What's going on?'

'You've had an accident. You're in an ambulance. Try not to move,' the man looking down on him said. 'Can you tell me your name?'

'Joey Craig,' he said, as terror shot through him. He was shivering uncontrollably.

'Take it easy, Joey,' the man said kindly. 'I have your mobile phone here. Who would you like me to call? Who lives closest to here, son?'

'Sophia, my girlfriend,' he said, as tears ran down either side of his head.

The man passed Joey's phone to another man and kept talking to him in a calm and hushed tone. 'Fred will call her now. We're nearly at the hospital. You were blessed that a lady was driving past, witnessed your fall and called us. It's damn cold and you could've been in serious trouble if you'd been left lying there.'

'I don't remember what happened,' Joey said. 'My head's thumping.'

'You knocked it and you've broken a few bones, Joey. When we get to the hospital the A&E team will come out and meet us. Things are going to happen very quickly, okay?'

'Okay,' he said. 'Did you get Sophia on the phone?'

'Not yet,' Fred answered from behind.

'We need to get you checked out so we know where you're hurt. Try your best to remain calm, okay, son?' the man said, holding his gaze.

'Okay.'

'We're reversing to the hospital door now.'

Before Joey could utter another syllable, the back doors flew open. The sleet and early-morning light greeted them as hospital staff pulled the trolley he was lying on out of the ambulance. Joey saw the sky momentarily before they entered the building. He felt nauseous. 'Why is my head strapped down?' he shouted.

'We don't know if you have a spinal injury, Joey,' a nurse said, directly above his head. 'We're taking you straight in for a scan and we'll be able to determine if there's any damage.'

'Did anyone speak to Sophia?' he asked again.

'Not yet, but we'll let you know as soon as we have contact with your next of kin,' the nurse said kindly.

'If you can't get her, can you ask them to call Pippa?' he begged. 'She's my sister and she lives on the same road I fell on.' He choked up once more as they rushed him to the scanning room. He'd never been more terrified in all his life. He wished he could be more of a tough guy but, to his shame, tears seeped down either side of his face as the medical team wheeled him onwards.

'We're going to lift you on the count of three, Joey,' a nurse instructed him. 'I want you to keep still. Let us do the manoeuvring, okay?'

'Yup,' he said miserably.

Even though they were impressively co-ordinated and very swift, the jerk as they laid him on the scanning bed made him yelp.

'Sorry about that,' the nurse's face appeared above his once more. 'You're doing really well, playing a blinder. Just bear with us for a few more moments while we get this scan done and we'll be able to make you more comfortable, okay? The worst is almost over.'

His head hurt as the large machine moved back and forth over him. There was another agonising pain too, but he wasn't sure where it was coming from. He desperately wanted to sleep, but every time he closed his eyes the pain hurtled through his body.

'All right, Joey, the scan is done. You're a trouper,' the nurse said. 'Are you allergic to anything?'

'No,' he managed weakly.

'Okay. I'm going to give you an injection now and it'll make you feel a lot more comfortable, I promise.'

'That'll be nice,' he said, closing his eyes and hoping she was telling the truth . . .

'Joey!' He opened his eyes what felt like moments later to see his younger sister standing above him.

'Pippa,' he croaked, and began to cry once more. He couldn't remember the last time he'd cried. 'Jesus, what happened to you?' Her face was battered and bruised.

'I had a bit of an incident last night, remember?' she said, and touched the large plaster on her nose. 'It's nothing compared to what you've managed to do to yourself. I had a scrap with a taxi driver and you brought me in here with Skye,' she reminded him.

'I remember now,' he said. 'I don't think I've ever been in the hospital before and now I'm here twice in twenty-four hours,' he said.

'Pretty good going,' Pippa said, smiling.

'What's happened? Did the nurses tell you anything?

Where's Sophia? Did they call her?' he asked. His body felt like it was made of wet sand.

'It's okay. You're going to be fine,' Pippa said, stroking his forehead. 'You fell twenty feet into a trench. Luckily a woman driver saw you disappear and called 999.'

'We need to take you for surgery now,' a doctor said, arriving into the room. 'Joey, you've swelling in your neck but we don't think that's a serious problem. Your leg's going to require surgery, though. It's broken in several places and so is your arm.'

'What?' Joey said, beginning to shake again.

'You've a nasty cut on the side of your head. Nothing a few stitches won't sort,' the doctor went on. 'You're lucky you were spotted.'

'Funnily enough, I'm not feeling overly lucky right now,' he said bitterly.

'Take it easy and we'll all be here when you come out of the theatre,' Pippa said.

'Where's Sophia?' he asked once more.

'Eh, we haven't been able to get hold of her yet, but I'll keep trying,' Pippa promised. 'Just concentrate on getting through this. I've signed your consent forms for surgery.'

And my live-in girlfriend doesn't give a toss whether I'm dead or alive, he thought.

When Joey was wheeled into the ward after his surgery, his parents had joined Pippa.

'That was some fright you gave us all.' Holly looked exhausted.

Joey scanned the area around his bed for his girlfriend.

'I only caught up with Sophia about half an hour ago,' Pippa said. 'She's on her way.'

'Great,' Joey said, looking from one face to the next. 'I can't remember how I fell. I feel like such a klutz,' he said. 'I could've killed myself.'

'Take it easy there,' Holly instructed. 'You had a nasty fall and it could've been much worse, but by all accounts it wasn't entirely your fault. The hole was meant to be covered over. There were no lights surrounding it either.'

'You just had to take the limelight, didn't you?' Pippa said, with a smirk. 'I thought I was doing well with a smashed-up face, but you, darling brother, have taken the biscuit.'

'Pippa!' Holly glowered at her.

'I'm only joking and Joey knows it,' she said, winking.

'Do I look worse than you?' he asked Pippa. 'Your eyes are manky.'

'I'm like Miss World compared to you.'

'You look very sore, you poor thing,' Paddy said to Joey. 'Half your head is shaved because they had to stitch it. You've a badly broken leg and your arm is fractured too.' He shook his head.

Footsteps made them all turn to the entrance of the ward. Assuming it was Sophia at long last, Joey found it hard to hide his disappointment when he spotted Lainey striding towards him.

'Hi – I came as quickly as I could. It's been so busy in work I couldn't leave,' she explained. 'Jesus, it's like *M.A.S.H.* in here with the two of you.' She was looking from Pippa to Joey.

'Feeling left out?' Pippa grinned. 'I could always whack you with a chair if you want to join the black-and-blue brigade.'

'No, you're all right, thanks, sis. Joey, you poor thing, what on earth happened?'

They all started talking at once, trying to tell Lainey what had gone on, but stopped when the surgical team arrived to speak to Joey.

'We've set your arm. It was a clean break so you didn't require surgery there,' the doctor told him. 'Your leg was in bad shape, though, and we've had to place two pins in the joint at your ankle. You're looking at six weeks of this thigh-high cast, then a further six in a half-cast.'

'What about the spinal damage?' Pippa asked. 'They told me when I arrived earlier on that he'd neck swelling or something?'

'Again, you were lucky,' the doctor said evenly. 'There's severe bruising to the top of your spine but nothing appears broken. We'll scan you again when the swelling's gone down. The cuts to your head look like they were caused by some sharp stones on impact.'

Holly and Paddy looked ten years older as they huddled together at the foot of the bed.

'I'm so sorry about this, everyone,' Joey mumbled.

'Don't be silly,' Paddy said. 'We just want you to get better.'

'Depending on what you and Sophia decide, you'd be more than welcome to come to Huntersbrook when you get out of here,' Holly said.

'You'll need to be looked after. That sounds like a good idea,' Lainey said. 'If Sophia's out at work, you'll be on your own. You'll need help while you can't walk.'

'I'll see,' Joey said, as a nurse came over.

'You should all let Joey have a rest now,' she said. 'He's going to be very tired and sore for the next few days.'

'Would you like one of us to stay?' Holly asked.

'No, thanks. I'm happy to get a bit of sleep,' Joey said weakly.

As he watched them leave, he felt more let down now than he ever had before. Not by his family: they were great. By Sophia. Where was she? He could have been dead by now and she wouldn't have cared either way.

The drugs were causing waves of exhaustion to wash over him. The best thing he could do was give in and sleep. Only a few hours ago he'd been wishing he could spend the day in bed: he ought to be careful what he wished for. It seemed that, sometimes, wishes really did come true.

As the family convened in Reception to discuss visiting rotas, Sophia sauntered through the main door. 'Hi,' she said, as she spotted them. Forcing a smile, she tried not to stare at Pippa. 'Ugh poor you, just look at your face!' she said.

'I don't need any reminders that I look battered thanks, Sophia,' Pippa spat.

Sophia nearly died. She'd never liked Pippa. Lainey was a moany cow but Pippa was a cheeky bitch and she'd just about had enough of her. 'Well, that's nice,' she said. 'Can you tell me where Joey is, then?' She turned to Holly, hoping she'd be less snappy.

'He's in St Matthew's Ward, there on the right,' Holly said, without smiling.

'Great. How's he doing?' Sophia asked.

'He's in cracking form,' Pippa butted in again. Sophia was about to point out that she wasn't actually talking to her, but Pippa continued, 'The smashed leg was a hoot. But he's most delighted with the broken arm and the gash on the head. Sadly he hasn't done irreparable damage to his spine so he can't boast that injury.'

'It – it sounds serious,' Sophia stammered, shocked.

'Yeah, we thought so too,' Pippa said. 'But these things all occurred to us … Oh, let me see, when was it? Yes, I remember now.' She was growing increasingly angry. 'It was first thing this morning when we got the call.'

'Pippa, leave it,' Holly said. 'We're all frazzled, Sophia,' she explained. 'It's been a long day and there's no point in adding any further to the unpleasantness.'

Sophia found Holly patronising at the best of times. She was a real school-teacher type. But at that moment she was glad someone was being less acid towards her.

'You do things your way, Mum, and I'll do them mine.' Pippa spun around to face Sophia again. 'You clearly don't give a toss about anyone but yourself. That's fine by me until you're embroiled with my brother. He needed you today and you weren't there.'

'I was out with a client. I was working. It's not as if I was sitting in a coffee shop ignoring the calls.' Sophia sighed. She'd had enough of Joey's sister. She didn't need to defend herself to this one. 'I'll go and check up on him.'

'Big of you,' Pippa said, as she walked away.

'Pippa, why don't you just get lost?' Sophia said. Who did this one think she was, shouting at her in public? 'It's not my fault your brother had an accident. Stop treating me like some sort of criminal. Is your face really sore?' she asked, hoping to calm Pippa down.

'I've felt better,' Pippa snarled, 'but that didn't stop me being here all day worrying about Joey.'

'Oh, for God's sake, get off the stage, will you?' Sophia

said. 'Clearly you're in the habit of fighting with people.' She pointed at Pippa's black eyes. 'You'd want to learn to keep that temper of yours in check.' She marched towards the ward.

'You're a selfish idiot,' Pippa called after her.

Sophia was furious. She'd have to tell Joey about this. If he didn't give Pippa a serious ticking-off, she'd be really pissed off with him.

He'd told her recently that Pippa had lost her job – again. That girl had no idea of responsibility. She spent her time flitting around being beautiful and useless. The whole family treated her as if she was some sort of china doll. Well, Sophia mused, she didn't impress her. She was a spoiled little madam and she'd no right to try to make her feel guilty for having a career.

Still, Sophia had her priorities right. She wasn't standing here with a punched-up face, no job, no prospects and no sense of worth. Pippa Craig was a loser with a capital L. Joey would explain to his sister that she was never again to address Sophia in that rude manner. She'd done her stint at Huntersbrook, playing country bumpkin, sitting around with all his sad relations and their farmer friends. She was officially *done* with that entire family set-up. If Joey wanted her to stay with him, he'd better realise she wasn't going to be pushed around.

Fair enough, she probably should have listened to her voicemail messages earlier. But in her defence she'd been cross with Joey since this morning. How was she to know he'd hurt himself?

The smell of disgusting hospital food mixed with disinfectant stung her nostrils as Sophia made her way to the ward. This place was a dump. It was probably rife with infection too. She knew Joey'd understand when she explained to him that she couldn't hang out in here for too long. If she contracted one of those hospital super-bugs she'd be out of work and her training would go to pot.

Besides, he'd probably be out by the following day. Fleetingly she thought of her plans for Christmas. This accident might mess them up. Sighing, she strode towards Joey's bed.

17

O Come, All Ye Faithful!

❄❄❄

Holly could barely speak as Paddy drove them back down the N11 towards Wicklow and Huntersbrook House. 'Paddy, what's happening to us?' she asked, as tears trickled down her cheeks. 'Pippa's face is smashed, Joey could've been killed and Lainey is afraid of her own shadow. Where did we go wrong?'

'Don't think like that, love. Pippa got herself into a dicey situation and met a bad egg. It happens. Joey just had an accident. Could've happened to a bishop. You heard what the report showed. The hole the council had dug wasn't sealed off or properly lit up. It was a freak thing,' he said. 'And Lainey's in great form. She's probably been a bit unsure of her direction in life in recent times, but I honestly think she's finding her feet.'

'They say all bad things come in threes,' Holly said, continuing her train of thought. She knew she was sounding dreadfully negative but she couldn't help it. 'What'll befall us next?'

'Don't think like that,' Paddy said. 'It's an old wives' tale.'

'I feel I've let Joey down lately,' Holly went on.

'How?' Paddy asked, clearly puzzled.

'I just float around with my head in the clouds, acting as if everything is wonderful,' she berated herself, 'and the whole family does the same thing. Nobody faces facts. Sophia is a selfish cow. She can't stand us and the feeling is mutual. Why have we pretended all this time?'

'Because she's Joey's girlfriend,' Paddy stated.

'Well, he might consider getting rid of her if he knows we all think she's a horror.'

'She's not my first choice of partner for him. Nobody's arguing with you there, love,' Paddy said. 'But it's up to Joey who he goes out with. He's twenty-five, love. He doesn't live at home. He has to make his own mistakes.'

Holly threw her arms into the air and exhaled noisily. Things needed to change in the family. So much hurt and resentment had been bubbling away for far too long. Her mother had as good as disappeared and none of them really talked about it. But, more than that, things had never been right between herself and Lainey. Maybe it was down to her sense of impending doom, with the family's future at Huntersbrook in the balance, but Holly was tired of hiding her feelings. She didn't want them to turn into people who vented their spleen publicly, like they did on those American chat shows, but there was more than one issue that they needed to address openly.

As they turned off the motorway towards the road leading to Huntersbrook, she decided that the time for burying their feelings was running out. They needed to make some changes – soon.

'Let's have a nice cup of tea and fill Sadie in on what's happened with Joey and Pippa,' she suggested.

As they sipped their tea and ate slices of Sadie's delicious fruitcake, Holly and Paddy brought Sadie up to date on Joey and Pippa's misfortunes.

'My goodness, that's worse than an episode of *EastEnders*,' Sadie exclaimed.

'You couldn't make it up,' Paddy agreed.

'The taxi driver sounds like a right lunatic,' Sadie added.

'Indeed he was. Pippa got a terrible fright. At least her new flatmate Skye was there to help her,' Paddy said.

'Blessed,' Sadie agreed. 'And tell me about poor Joey.'

'He's had an awful fall,' Paddy said, and described Joey's injuries.

'He must've fallen very awkwardly to do all that damage.' Sadie tutted in shock.

'I need to get the smell of hospital off my skin,' Holly said suddenly, scraping her chair back and standing up.

'There should be plenty of hot water. The Aga's been pumping away all morning and I haven't used any water for floors or anything like that,' Sadie said.

'Right . . .' Holly hesitated. 'I won't be too long.'

As she walked from the kitchen the silence was almost palpable. Remembering her outburst in the car with Paddy just now, she braced herself and turned back. 'Sadie, I said to Paddy that I'm fed up of the way we sidestep issues in this family,' she said. 'So, in the spirit of calling a spade a spade, the two of you don't need to sit huddled together wondering if I'm headed for another breakdown.'

'Nobody said you were,' Paddy said, jumping to his and Sadie's defence.

'You didn't have to,' Holly answered, with a slow smile.

'Your face said it all. Just because I'm having a bath doesn't mean I'll be spending most of my time locked in the bathroom from now on. I know I did that once, years ago. But I wasn't well then. I hid away for a reason. Right now, I simply want to stretch out and soak up a more pleasant smell than antiseptic. End of story.'

'All right so, love,' Paddy said, blinking back at her.

As she filled the bath and added a good dollop of bubbles, Holly perched on the edge and pondered.

She spent the rest of the day clearing out one of the downstairs rooms for Joey. Paddy and Scott moved a bed in and Sadie helped her make the place welcoming.

'I'll have to turn the heating on in here for a few hours. It feels a bit damp,' Holly said. They could see their breath in the air, and although Holly wasn't a cold-blooded person, she had to admit it was freezing.

'That might be a good plan,' Sadie said. 'Especially as Joey will be coming from hospital. He'll be used to the heat. Did he say he'd come here for definite, then?'

'Not as such, but I'm assuming he will. Sophia will be working so she won't have time to care for him properly,' Holly said. 'Besides, she's hardly the Florence Nightingale sort, is she?'

'Not that you'd think,' Sadie agreed. 'But you might want to be a little bit careful of how you pitch this to young Joey all the same.'

'There's a bit of a surprise for you in the living room,' Paddy said, poking his head around the door.

'What is it?' Holly asked suspiciously.

'If I tell you, it won't be a surprise, you silly Billy.' He took her hand.

Holly nearly burst into tears when she saw a second Christmas tree in the corner of the room.

'Scott and I did the lights and even put up some decorations,' Paddy said proudly. 'Now, it's probably all wrong and not up to the standard of you ladies, with all your fussing about, but we did our best, didn't we, Scott?'

'It's wonderful,' Holly said, and tried to swallow the lump in her throat. 'Thank you both very much,' she managed.

'I didn't know how to make you feel better,' Paddy added, 'but in the end I figured another glittering mound of coniferous might do the job nicely.'

'How well you know me.'

In spite of the lovely gesture, Holly slept fitfully that night, images of Joey's poor battered body and Pippa's bruised face haunting her.

Early the following morning, before she and Paddy had got up, she called Joey, hoping his mobile phone would be switched on. She sighed with relief when it rang.

'Hi, Mum,' he said wearily.

'How are you feeling today?' she asked.

'Sore,' he said. 'I had a pretty awful night. I can't even tell you which bit hurts the most. I just saw the surgeon and it looks like I'll be here for at least five days.'

'I'm sorry to hear that. But listen to me,' Holly said. 'The main thing is that you'll recover. Don't lose sight of that.'

'It's going to be a long road, though. I'll need lots of physiotherapy and I'm not going to be able to work until the end of January at the earliest. My training's scuppered for next season. Uh . . .' He sounded as if he was going to cry. 'Everything's gone wrong.'

'Poor Joey. Maybe you'll come here when you get out and we can look after you.'

'I'll talk to Sophia about that,' he said. 'Thanks for the offer.'

'Here's Dad,' Holly said, passing Paddy the phone.

'Hi, son,' Paddy said.

They chatted for a bit as Holly got up and pulled on some warm clothes. Then she drew back the curtains, looked out at the heavy frost that blanketed the fields and shuddered. 'I'll go down and make breakfast,' she said to Paddy, who was swinging his legs out of bed.

'It's chilly, isn't it?'

'I'd say it was well below zero last night. Still, nothing some tea, toast and a good thick sweater won't fix,' she said brightly.

'That's true,' Paddy said. Holly watched him wince as he trotted towards the bathroom. He was too old to have to dance around on a freezing floor in the morning.

This wasn't working. If they couldn't afford to stay at Huntersbrook and be comfortable, there was only one thing for it. They were going to have to sell up.

As she made her way down the stairs she could hear Sadie in the kitchen. That was another awful thing she was going to have to face. Sadie would have to be let go. Holly didn't know where they'd end up living, but wherever it was they wouldn't be able to pay a housekeeper, although Sadie was hardly on a king's ransom. And she was more than a housekeeper: she was family. A couple of years ago, Paddy had suggested to Sadie she should retire, which hadn't gone down too well. 'Sure what would I do with myself?' Sadie had asked, hurt and worried. They hadn't mentioned it again.

Holly's thinking had become less clouded of late. She was really beginning to appreciate the amazing, strong-willed people who surrounded her.

'Morning!' Sadie said, bustling around feeding Jess and Millie.

'Morning, Sadie,' Holly said, putting the big kettle on the Aga to boil.

'Any news from Joey? How is he today? I could barely sleep last night worrying about him.'

'Sure I was the same,' Holly admitted. 'We spoke to him just now. He's a bit down in himself, but that's to be expected. Hopefully, he'll come here when they let him out and we can make a fuss of him.'

'Don't bite my head off now, pet,' Sadie said carefully, 'but have you thought of telling Maggie what's happened?'

'No,' Holly stated firmly.

'Don't you think she has a right to know?' Sadie asked.

'Quite honestly, Sadie, I think she waived that right when she flew to the other side of the world without so much as a backward glance.'

'Holly, that's not entirely fair. Maggie —'

' — is *my* mother and I'm dealing with her abandonment the best way I can. Okay?' Holly could count on the fingers of one hand the altercations she and Sadie had had over the years. 'Sorry, Sadie. That was rude of me.' Sadie nodded, but Holly could tell she'd really upset her.

Sadie sat at the kitchen table. She wasn't sure what to do for the best. Then, weighing things up, she came to a decision. She went to the computer and rested her fingers on the keyboard She felt she owed it to their sixty-year friendship to let Maggie know what had happened.

Dear Maggie

I'm sorry to be the bearer of bad news, but a couple of things have happened. I thought you should know. Pippa had a horrible altercation with an aggressive taxi driver. Seems he attacked her and if it wasn't for her new lodger coming to her rescue things would have been a lot worse. As it is, she took a blow to the face and is in shock.

Not taking away from the trauma poor Pippa endured, Joey's situation has some more serious physical implications. He had a bad accident yesterday. Before you panic – he's going to be just fine. He'd a terrible fall. Down into a large hole the council had dug on the side of the road near his apartment. He's broken his arm, his leg, hurt his neck and gashed his poor head. He's been operated on and the doctors say he'll require physiotherapy but he'll be right as rain before long.

Holly is keen to get him back here to Huntersbrook to recover. I think it might be a good plan all right. Sophia isn't the most motherly sort. Pippa is fit to be tied. By all accounts they were phoning Sophia all morning and she only arrived to see Joey late in the afternoon.

Holly went for a bath as soon as they returned from the hospital yesterday. I saw the colour drain from poor Paddy's cheeks when the bathroom door was locked. I know it's a long time since she had that episode but I think Paddy feared she'd slip right back into it all.

She seemed less despondent this morning although she's in

a very dark mood, Maggie. It's not like her. They've gone up the back field to get the tree for the living room. Can you fathom it was Paddy's suggestion? He obviously wants to try and fix at least one member of his family so he knew the thought of another tree would bring joy to Holly's heart. Bless him.

I'll keep you posted. This makes me sound like an informer and believe me, Maggie, that's actually how I feel. But Holly was adamant you weren't to be told about any of this.

If I've overstepped the mark by going behind her back, forgive me. But if I were in your position I'd want to know. Apologies once more for being the bearer of such sad tidings.

Take good care, Maggie, and I'll let you know how Joey and Pippa are doing. Hopefully the next email will be less dark.

All the best for now,

Sadie

18

Rockin' Around the Christmas Tree

It was the day of the office Christmas party so Lainey took a long lunch-hour and visited Joey in the hospital. As she walked towards his bed she spotted her mother and Sophia sitting there already.

'Hi, everyone,' she said. 'I might call back another time.' She bent to kiss Joey. 'It's too difficult for you to talk to us all at the same time.'

'Hello, love.' Holly seemed strained.

'Hi,' Sophia said, without looking at Lainey. 'Don't leave on my account. I'm going now.'

'You only just got here,' Joey protested.

'I'll go, you stay,' Holly said, standing up and gathering her coat from the end of the bed.

'I'll only be here for five minutes – I've to get back to the office. It's the Christmas party tonight,' Lainey put in.

'I'm surrounded by women who are all beating themselves over the head to get away from me,' Joey said, grinning.

'Not at all, love, I just don't want to crowd you,' Holly assured him.

''Bye,' Sophia said, leaning over and kissing him briefly. 'See you both,' she added, without smiling, to Holly and Lainey.

Before anyone could protest, she'd bounced out of the ward.

'Sorry if I caused her to leave,' Lainey said to Joey. She had to admit to feeling more relaxed without her, though: Sophia always set her on edge.

'Don't worry. It's not your fault,' Joey said. 'She's not in good form at the moment. I'll call her later on. What went on between herself and Pippa last night?'

'Nothing much,' Holly said.

'Pippa lost it a bit,' Lainey said evenly. 'I happen to agree with her on this occasion.'

'Well, poor Sophia was in an awful state,' he said. 'She said Pippa yelled abuse at her down the corridor in front of a load of people. Is that true?'

'Steady on now,' Holly said. 'I think maybe Sophia exaggerated the exchange ever so slightly.'

'She was totally talking through her arse, you mean,' Lainey said. 'Pippa just told her a few home truths and madam didn't like it too much.'

'She wants me to speak to Pippa and get her to apologise,' Joey said, rubbing his face with his good hand.

'The best of luck with that one,' Lainey said, pulling a face. 'You know our Pippa when she gets a bee in her bonnet and, believe me, she's got a swarming hive right now where Sophia's concerned.'

Joey sighed deeply.

'This is all just a result of charged emotions,' Holly interjected. 'Pippa is up to high-do over the incident the other night. Then she was in shock seeing you in here. I'm sure it'll all work out for the best.'

'I don't know if I can cope with this right now,' Joey admitted. 'I'll have to phone Sophia in a while and try to calm her down.'

'I'm sure she'll pop back in,' Holly said, trying to sound cheerful. 'Especially seeing as you only live around the corner. At the end of the day we all want you to feel better. That's the most important thing.'

'You're right, Mum,' Lainey agreed. 'How are you feeling today, Joey? Are you still in as much pain or has the medication kicked in?' She didn't want to say as much to her brother but he looked dreadful. The bruising on his head was working its way to the side of his face. He was strung up like a puppet between his leg and arm and he was the colour of putty.

'I'm okay,' he said. 'The surgeon was telling me to keep on top of the pain. He said I'll heal quicker if I take the anti-inflammatories and painkillers so I'm popping away like a junkie here. Tell me about this office party, then.'

'Well, it's tonight in the Regency and I'm staying with Jules, my friend from work. She lives opposite the hotel in those new apartments. It'll save me getting a taxi.'

'Great,' Holly said. 'Do you have the day off tomorrow, then? It's an odd night to have it, isn't it?'

'It's to save money,' Lainey said. 'And to answer your question, a few of us will have to go in tomorrow and I volunteered. I won't drink too much and I should be fine.'

'At least you aren't stuck in hospital like Joey, or with a bruised face like Pippa's. Try to relax and enjoy it,' Holly said. 'You shouldn't always be the one to offer to do the donkey work. You're too soft at times, Lainey.'

Lainey didn't answer. What was the point? No matter what she said it would only start a row. Her mother always had to have a little dig and make her feel like she was doing the wrong thing.

'Your office party sounds pretty desperate,' Joey said, sticking up for her. 'I hate those contrived party nights where you have to cram into a room with people you can't stand and eat crap food followed by dancing to some awful rip-off band.'

'Thank you, Joey,' Lainey said, without glancing in her mother's direction. 'They are hideous nights. But it has to be done. At least I'll have Jules for company this year. She's great fun. You'll meet her at Christmas. She's coming to Huntersbrook.'

'Yeah,' Joey said awkwardly. He still hadn't got around to mentioning Sophia's Lanzarote plan. He wouldn't be able to go now and hoped she wouldn't kick up a fuss at the thought of spending Christmas at Huntersbrook. The row between her and Pippa wasn't exactly going to create an ideal atmosphere over the turkey and ham.

Still, he figured his mum was probably right. It was just Pippa's ordeal and the shock that had caused the upset. He'd get it all sorted over the next couple of days.

Joey knew he needed to address Sophia's behaviour. He wasn't stupid, just sore, tired and feeling sorry for himself. He hadn't the headspace to tackle any major issues. Besides, he was secretly hoping his accident would lead Sophia to realise just how special their relationship was.

'I'd better get back to the office,' Lainey said. She felt like she was saying all the wrong things to her mother and brother. It would be best if she scarpered. 'I'll pop back tomorrow and fill you in on all the gossip from the land of the county council and its employees.'

'I can hardly wait!' Joey grinned. 'Don't forget to take loads of photos. I love nothing better than looking at darkened blurry pictures of drunk people with comb-overs and bulging bellies doing the twist.'

'See you tomorrow, bro,' Lainey said, giggling. ''Bye, Mum.'

''Bye, love,' Holly said, as Joey waved with his good arm.

Lainey started her bike and turned it towards her office. She hadn't imagined her mother being iffy just now. She didn't do it with Joey and Pippa. Not for the first time, she wished her grandmother would come home: life had always been easier with Maggie around to champion her.

The atmosphere in the office was a hell of a lot better than it had been at the hospital. By four o'clock everyone was leaving to get ready for the party.

As Lainey followed Jules to her apartment on her motorbike, the light was already fading and the rain was hammering down. 'That's a dirty evening out there,' she said, as she entered a sea of pink. Although it wasn't exactly to her taste, she couldn't help but like it. 'I've never seen a pink sparkly tree that size,' she said, as Jules plugged in the flashing lights.

'Isn't it divine?' Jules giggled.

'That's one word for it,' Lainey said warmly. 'You're so

good to go to all the bother of decorating. I spend so little time in my place it's hardly worth it.'

'My mum was a real grinch when it came to Christmas, so I go all out.'

'Mine decorates our place to within an inch of its life!'

'There you go!' Jules said. 'We all seem to end up doing the opposite to our mothers. At least you get on well with yours.' A hint of sadness flashed across her face.

'I do and I don't,' Lainey admitted. 'She's always been easier-going with my brother and sister. Grandma and I were closer than Mum and I when I was growing up.'

'Why was that, do you think?' Jules asked.

'I'm not sure. But I've noticed it more since Grandma left. Mum and I get on fine but we don't click massively. There's always a bit of tension there.'

'I win on the tension front,' Jules said, with her hands on her hips. 'Having your mother tell you you've brought shame on the family and that you're not to come home until you've "got over your lezzer phase" is pretty defining.'

'How are you feeling about her now?'

'What can I do?' Jules held up her hands in defeat. 'Before I told her I was gay she used to hit me with the you-ruined-my-life-by-coming-along-when-I-was-so-young routine. At least now she has a fresh reason to shun me.'

'That's awful. But you do have friends and you know that not everyone feels that way about you.'

'Thanks, Lainz,' Jules said. 'Let's get showered and open a bottle of bubbly. This party's going to be fun, even if it kills us!'

By the time they'd drained the Prosecco it was time to get going. Jules pulled out a leopard-print umbrella, slipped into her skyscraper heels and waited for Lainey to appear in her new outfit.

'Okay, this is it, the big reveal,' Lainey said, walking awkwardly out of the bathroom.

'Lainz! You look fantastic! Are you pleased?'

'It might be a bit daring for me.'

'Not at all! Sure it's Christmas! Look at me! I'm probably being a bit daring but I'm not worried.'

Lainey wanted to tell Jules that her outfit was probably illegal in several countries and that she hoped there weren't any men with dickey hearts there. Instead of the black floor-length number that Lainey had insisted she buy on their shopping trip, she was wearing the kelly green glittery tube, which was doing its best to hold her ample bosom in place. Her black stilettos were like something a stilt-walker would use for balance practice. Taking the Christmas theme to an extreme, she'd found a necklace that might have been intended as a dog's choke chain before the Spirit of Christmas had splattered glittery holly leaves all over it.

'My mum would love your necklace,' Lainey said.

'She can borrow it for Christmas Day!'

The hotel had gone all out to make sure the place was the epitome of Christmas cheer. A huge tree greeted them in the reception area. There were more swags and flashing lights than you could shake a stick at. The doorman was dressed in a Santa suit and rang a big brass bell as each person arrived. 'Ho, ho, ho,' he shouted.

'Happy Christmas, Santa.' Jules gave him a hug. 'Isn't it lovely, Lainz?' She waltzed towards the bar.

After they'd got themselves a drink Mr Drake and the others from their office had arrived too. Lainey was thrilled to realise she wasn't half as nervous as usual. In fact she was enjoying herself and even managed a scout around the room for any talent when she put her Kris Kindle gift into the big plastic container marked with their table number.

By the time they were called for dinner, there was a good buzz in the room. 'This is like going to a wedding where you don't know the bride and groom,' Jules chirped, as they made their way into the adjoining dining room.

'Is she ever in a bad mood?' Mike from Accounts asked, as Jules insisted they pull crackers immediately.

'Never!' Lainey grinned.

'You have to wear your party hat too. It's the law of Christmas!' Jules ordered.

'The food is shockingly shite, isn't it?' she murmured to Lainey a few minutes later. 'In a blind tasting I'd say this melon was raw turnip.'

When the turkey was served, the pair were snorting and sniggering like schoolchildren.

'Beware the stuffing,' Lainey said. 'It's like mulched paper.'

As soon as the meal was cleared away the MC, who looked like the love child of an old-fashioned Teddy boy and a roll of tin foil, took to the stage and welcomed them to the party. 'Okey-dokey, folks, it's show time!' he announced.

'Do you think he had to glue on his sideburns?' Jules asked, with her head to the side. 'They're very nylon-looking from here.'

'I think he got the entire outfit from the joke shop,' Lainey mused. 'It's not the most fetching, is it?'

'Well, at least he's made an effort,' Jules said generously. 'Sure God bless him he's only doing his job.' They looked at one another and dissolved into another fit of giggles.

'Folks, put your hands together for the most special guest

of the night! Let's give a warm county council welcome to Mr
Santa Claus!'

A ruptured round of applause welcomed the man in the
big red suit.

'Due to the large number of guests, Santa has brought
some friends along to help distribute the Kris Kindle gifts.
Welcome, if you will, our elves.'

A flurry of mortified men in green tights shuffled through
a side door.

'The barmen from earlier on,' Jules identified.

Their elf seemed decidedly uncomfortable as he dragged
the large plastic bin of gifts to the table.

'He's hardly the Spirit of Christmas, is he?' Lainey said, as
the man scowled and pulled at his felt jacket. He was at least
six feet tall and it was far too small, the sleeves extending
only to his wrists.

Once they'd opened their gifts, which were mostly of the
lurid variety, Santa and his helpers waved and departed.

When Abba-ke-dabra, the Abba tribute band, appeared,
there was a roar of applause as the hammered county council
workers welcomed them warmly.

'I suppose it doesn't matter to most of us that the two lady
singers of the group have lost a few inches in height and
gained several stone in width since they were in Abba full
time,' Lainey murmured to Jules, giggling.

All of the songs were recognisable and the crowd joined
in with each number, helping to drown the band's many
mistakes. Jules had taken command of the dance floor. Soon
she'd arranged a seventies version of line dancing for a large
group of middle-aged men.

'Jules has them eating out of her hand there. We should just
hire her next year and cut back on the cost of a live band,' Drake

said, as he stood beside Lainey to the side of the floor. While she'd got up for 'Dancing Queen' and even joined in with the Mexican wave that shot across the room during 'Fernando', Lainey had been happy to watch for the most part.

At the end, when the house lights went on, everyone squinted and staggered, then went to the cloakrooms to collect their coats. The room emptied rapidly. The staff were already whipping away the tablecloths and tossing the artificial poinsettias into a trough on wheels.

'Jeez,' Lainey said. 'If we stand here too long we'll be shoved into a dishwasher or plastic bucket.'

'What's the plan, Lainz?' Jules asked.

'Will we head home?' Lainey wondered hesitantly.

'No way!' Jules said, linking her arm and frogmarching her towards another bar in the hotel.

'This is for residents only.' A bouncer was blocking their way.

'We're staying the night, we just don't know which room we'll be in yet,' Jules said, without missing a beat.

Roaring laughing, he stood aside and let them in.

'Jules! You're desperate!' Lainey was in shock.

'Ah, sure we'll never see him again and who cares? We're here now. Sometimes you have to think on your feet.' She winked.

Jules wormed her way into the thick of the crowd, Lainey following. A sing-song kicked off fairly smartly, moving from 'Jingle Bells' to the latest Snow Patrol number. Grateful to find a high stool, Lainey perched on it wondering if she'd ever be able to feel her feet again. She'd managed to stay upright in her shoes but her soles were throbbing.

'Sorry,' a guy behind her said, as he moved his pint out of the way.

Lainey swivelled around. 'My fault.'

'I think I've been dumped and I'm meant to be staying the night,' he said, looking mortified.

'Oh, no! Who did you come with?' Lainey was aghast.

'Ah, one of the girls from the Wexford office. I knew her about a hundred years ago. I've just moved back to Ireland from living in the UK. We bumped into one another and she invited me as her plus one tonight. I wasn't expecting too much and we only agreed to share a twin room as the hotel hadn't a spare single room, but I still feel a bit used. It appears she only needed me to smoke out a fella she's had her eye on for a while. Seems her plan worked. She's the one chewing the face off your man in the corner there.'

Lainey glanced at the couple, then turned back. 'Do you have the room key?' she asked.

'As a matter of fact I do,' he said, brightening.

'There you go. If I were you I'd head up, pack her stuff into her bag, dump it in the hallway and lock the door.'

'You're a genius!' he said. 'Thanks. You're obviously staying over too, seeing as you're in the residents' bar. Duh! Sorry, stupid thing to say.'

'Well, actually, it's not. My friend blagged us in here. She lives across the road so I'm staying there. I'm nearly at my limit now, and I've to go into the office tomorrow.'

'Poor you.' He grinned.

'I'd better go and see if I can drag her home,' Lainey said reluctantly.

'I'm going to scarper and clear my date's things out of the room,' he said. 'Thanks for the advice and the chat. You made an awful night slightly less awful.' He hesitated, and Lainey thought he was going to kiss her. He obviously thought better of it and gave her a peck on the cheek.

'Happy Christmas,' she said, as he hurried away.

Lainey wondered why the girl in the corner had been so callous to the poor fella. She'd stopped wearing the face off her beau and they were downing shots of tequila. He was running his hand up her inner thigh as she laughed. Lainey wanted to go over and pour her drink over the girl's face, but while she knew she'd probably gain oodles of street cred with her co-workers, she wasn't ready to take on the role of office cat-fight bitch.

'There you are.' Jules had appeared. 'For a minute I thought you'd gone.'

'Not quite, but I do feel like I've had enough.'

'No worries, let's split,' she said cheerfully. 'I just need the loo. Coming?'

As they walked towards the Ladies, a small girl with short, dull hair got there just ahead of them. She glanced back briefly, saw them and held the door open.

'Thanks,' Lainey said. The girl, who was vaguely familiar to her, scuttled into a cubicle without answering. Lainey didn't need to pee so she went to the mirror to check her makeup. Racking her brains, she tried to work out where she'd seen the girl before.

'It was a fun night, wasn't it, Lainz?' Jules called from inside her cubicle.

'Yeah, not bad.'

As Jules and the other girl emerged from their cubicles simultaneously, Lainey and the stranger locked eyes. Lainey gasped as she recognised her.

'You're Lainey,' the girl stated. 'Seth has a photo of the two of you on his mantelpiece still. I'm his fiancée,' she said proudly.

'Hello,' Lainey said, not wanting her to know she'd seen her picture on Facebook.

'He keeps that photo up to remind him of what he doesn't want in life.'

'Pardon?' Lainey said, just above a whisper.

'It's none of my business and it's all in the past, but you treated him like dirt. You totally destroyed him. Not that you'd care,' she said menacingly. 'But he's happy now. I've made him happy. I let him call the shots. I let him choose where we go and what we do. I've been the reason he's been able to heal.'

This was ridiculous, so far from the truth that Lainey couldn't suppress a smirk. 'What are you on about?'

'I think this one's been misinformed,' Jules said, sidling up to her.

'Seth has never been a victim, let me assure you,' Lainey said.

'Well, you would say that. You lie about everything,' the girl said. 'All I can say is that you missed out. He's mine now and we're really happy.'

'Are you?' Lainey said. 'Is that what he's told you? Believe me, I hope you're right. But make no mistake. He's the liar. He's the one who manipulates, cheats and acts as if every mistake he makes is all someone else's fault.'

The girl opened her mouth and shut it again. Doubt had crept into her face.

'Listen,' Lainey went on. 'I wish you no ill. In fact, I hope you can be happy some day. But, mark my words, Seth will never make you happy. He's like a cancer and I for one am so glad he's out of my life.'

Lainey fled, with Jules in hot pursuit.

'You were dynamite in there!' Jules said.

'I feel ill. That poor girl is so blinkered by him. He's filled her head with a pile of rubbish and she believes him, God love her.'

'Hey,' Jules said, as they walked back towards her apartment. 'It's not your problem.'

'You're right.' Lainey sighed. 'Seth isn't my problem any more. Thank God.'

'Can I let you into a little secret?'

'Sure.' Lainey yawned.

'Anna, the girl in the black catsuit you met at the Bublé gig, is single again and we had a little kiss last night!'

'No way! I can't believe you never said!' Lainey said, pleased for her friend.

'I just wasn't sure how you'd be about it.'

'Jules, you're my friend. You've changed my life so much for the better since you joined our office. Who you go out with is nobody's business but your own,' Lainey said.

'Thanks, that means a lot.'

Soon after that Jules was tucked up in her room and Lainey was on a blow-up mattress in the living room. She listened to the howling wind and lashing rain, and smiled. She'd actually enjoyed the office party this year. Several people had complimented her on her outfit, and now she was glad she'd worn it. She'd wear it on Christmas Day too.

That guy she'd met at the end of the night was really sweet. She'd never have had the confidence to talk to him this time last year. Clicking her phone on, she posted a few lines on her Facebook page.

Just back from a brilliant night out with friends. The Christmas season has kicked off to a fantastic start.

Then she remembered Seth's fiancée, and shuddered. Enough is enough, she thought. With trembling fingers she hit the button that would block Seth from her page. She'd wanted to cut the final tie with him for a while and now that she'd done it she felt fantastic.

I'm Getting Nothing
for Christmas

✳✳✳

Dear Maggie

Thank you for your email. Yes, we're all very shocked by the events over the last few days. As per your request, I'll send you more regular updates on the situation here. No problem. Thank you for not being cross with me. I'm glad you understand I simply want to keep you in the picture. Pippa hasn't been here so I can't tell you first hand how her poor face is looking. Sorry about that. I didn't go up to the hospital with Holly as she said Joey's not in brilliant form. I don't want to impose so please God I'll see him once he gets out.

Holly is teetering on the edge, to answer your question honestly. I could lie to you and say she's coping just fine. But Paddy is being a rock as usual. He's jollying her along and doing a fine job. I hope Joey comes here to convalesce. At least that way Holly will know he's being looked after and she can feel like she's helping to fix him. You know how she loves to fix things.

Pippa will be here for Christmas before we know it so Holly will have them all under her roof. That'll calm her down no end I'd imagine.

Lainey went off out to her Christmas party last tonight. With a bit of luck she survived it and had fun. Holly is convinced bad news comes in threes. So she's almost anticipating something awful happening to Lainey now.

Mind yourself and say hello to Sid for me,

Your old pal,

Sadie

Pippa scrutinised her face in the mirror. That weirdo taxi driver had given her a serious knock. With Vince's help, the police had tracked him down.

'It's up to you if you want to press charges,' the police had explained. Pippa's gut instinct had been to leave it. She didn't want to revisit that night, mainly because she blamed herself for what had happened. A surprise phone call changed her mind.

'Pippa, this is Vince.'

'Oh, hi,' she said. Her heart dropped like a stone.

'I got your number through a friend of Skye's,' he rushed to explain. 'I asked the police but they wouldn't give out your details, which is fair enough. Listen, I wanted to apologise for the other night.' He sounded really tortured.

'Why?' Pippa was stunned. 'You did nothing wrong. Jeez, I'm mortified. I'm the one who owes you an apology.'

'I don't see how,' Vince said. 'I shouldn't have left you with that taxi guy. When I heard he'd assaulted you I was nearly sick.'

'Vince, you're a lovely guy. I'm the one who behaved abominably,' Pippa insisted. 'You were a perfect gentleman. You paid for everything and treated me like a princess.' She didn't want to add that she'd bitched about him to the taxi driver. That the reason he'd boxed her and lost his temper with her was because she was such a horrible little cow. That she deserved to be hit and yelled at.

'I like you and that's why I was happy to treat you,' he said shyly. 'I enjoyed the evening with you and I was kind of hoping we could see each other again. Maybe go for dinner somewhere nice?'

The Pippa of two days ago would've smirked to herself and envisaged euro signs popping up in her mind's eye. She would've gladly gone to dinner a couple of times and strung him along so she could get freebies and be wined and dined. But the attack, although it had terrified the life out of her, had knocked some conscience into her.

'Vince, I really appreciate you asking me out. I think you're a lovely person. I enjoyed your company too, but I don't fancy you,' she said. 'I'm sorry if that's brutally blunt and honest, but I wouldn't feel right leading you on.'

'Oh,' he said, clearly crushed. 'Fair enough, I guess.' He was trying to sound nonchalant. 'At least you're telling me like it is, eh? There's a lot to be said for that.'

'I'm sorry,' she reiterated.

'No hassle. Besides, you'd probably always associate me with one of the worst nights of your life. That's hardly a good place to start a relationship, is it?'

'Please don't think that,' Pippa begged. 'You were nothing to do with the awful incident. You weren't to know, and that crazy man's behaviour is no reflection on the evening we had. You're great fun and I know you'll make the most amazing boyfriend to some lucky girl. But she's just not me. I'm sorry.'

'That's okay. Listen, I'll go,' he said. 'First and foremost I wanted to check that you're okay. I shouldn't have asked you out. But sure there's no harm in trying, is there?' He chuckled.

If Pippa could have made herself feel attracted to him, she would have done just that. He was a sweetheart, but she was finished with sponging and taking advantage of boys. Now she thought of Jay. She'd been a right wench to him. Skye had pointed out on more than one occasion that the rest of the girls were baffled as to why she'd dumped him. 'He's cute, has a brilliant job, makes you laugh like a drain and adores you. What's the problem?' Skye had said, after they'd come back from New York.

Pippa *had* fancied the pants off him before they'd gone to New York. But as usual she'd decided there was a better offer just around the corner. She'd tossed him aside without so much as a second glance.

'Pippa, I would urge you to press charges, though,' Vince said. 'That guy shouldn't be driving young women around. He could do the same thing again.'

'I suppose so,' Pippa said, still unsure. 'I'll think about it. Thanks for calling and maybe I'll see you if you're in Diamonds or about town?' she said.

'Sure. Take care, Pippa,' he said, and hung up.

Pippa wandered into her bedroom. Skye was out meeting a client and she had the apartment to herself. She'd planned to go to the hospital and spend a bit of time with Joey. He seemed really pissed off and she didn't blame him. Sophia wasn't exactly in line for Girlfriend of the Year.

It suddenly dawned on her that Joey had found a partner not too unlike herself. The two of them had always been close and now he'd landed himself a girl who was as heartless as she could be.

Tears burned her eyes as she dialled the number the policewoman had given her on the night of the assault. 'If you feel like going ahead and pressing charges, call this number,' she'd said.

The man who answered was kind and helpful and asked her to call by to sign some forms and file an official complaint.

'Good for you for doing this,' he encouraged her. 'As you rightly say, this man could attack another innocent girl. We promise to make the whole process as painless as possible. Ask for me, Officer Thomas Grey, when you come down to the station and I'll ensure you're looked after.'

'Thanks,' Pippa said. As she hung up, she still harboured serious doubt. She believed she'd deserved that punch. But the voice of reason was driving her forward, telling her she had a duty to other, perhaps nicer, girls to stop that man driving a taxi.

Feeling a bit lost, she padded into the living room where she spotted the holiday tickets she still hadn't returned to Jay. Dialling his number she bit her lip, wondering, now that the line had connected, what she was going to say. Any time she'd called him before he'd answered on the first ring – second, at worst. This time it went to voicemail.

'Hi, Jay,' she said, feeling like a small child standing in front of an angry teacher. 'It's me, Pippa. I was wondering if you would possibly meet me for a drink. Or a coffee, even. Or just for a chat really ...' she said, as sweat beaded on her forehead. 'If you could give me a call I'd really appreciate it. Thanks a million.'

She put the phone down and exhaled loudly. Her nose

hurt. Her head thudded and she wanted to curl up in a ball on her bed and stay there for ever.

Skye had been amazing since she'd moved in. Pippa had used the accident to hand over the running of the apartment to her. She knew it was a bit of a cop-out but it also meant she'd have to keep up with her payments from here on.

'Here's the bank details and the dates the rent needs to be in by,' Pippa had said.

'I'll make sure I keep abreast of it and transfer the money as required,' Skye had agreed.

There was still a massive problem that Pippa needed to address. Lainey had given her the money to pay off her bank and credit card debts, which she'd lodged. She was in the clear, thankfully, but she'd no way of paying Lainey back. She couldn't work in Boutique Belle with a smashed-up face. 'I'm sorry to be so callous, Pippa, but I need immediate help over Christmas,' Sue had said when Pippa called to tell her what had happened. 'I'll have to hire someone else.'

'I understand,' Pippa said. 'It wouldn't really sell your new Chanel range or any of your other gorgeous stuff if your assistant is looking like she's been in a scrap with Katie Taylor.'

So Pippa was stuck in the apartment, wondering how on earth she was going to make ends meet. The cash Sue had given her for working last Sunday would tide her over for the next few days. She'd a couple of hundred left from Lainey's loan so she could at least pay her share of the money to Skye for that week. But after that she was snookered.

She hadn't the energy to search out a cool outfit to visit Joey, so she pulled on her tracksuit, a puffa jacket and a woolly hat and set off for the police station, first, then the hospital. The complaint was swiftly filed and Pippa left feeling rotten. She'd nearly told the police officer it had been her own fault, but focused on the fact that violence against women was wrong.

The crisp yet sunny December weather was just what she needed. As she walked the short distance to the hospital she pulled her shades from her pocket and placed them tentatively on her battered face, wincing at the pain.

Moments later, she was in the hospital and walking towards Joey's bed. 'Hey, big brother.'

'Hi,' he said, sounding disappointed.

'Don't look so thrilled to see me,' she said, perching on the end of his bed.

'Sorry, Pippa. I'm not myself at the moment for obvious reasons,' he said. 'I'm like something from *Carry On Nurse* here. If I wasn't so sore and fed up I'd find this almost funny.'

'No sign of Sophia, then?' Pippa raised an eyebrow.

'No.' He looked at the door to the ward. 'I rang her earlier and she was busy. I assume she's coming in this evening but I actually don't think I'm going to call her again.'

'Joey, don't you think you should talk to her properly?' Pippa suggested. 'She's hardly the most thoughtful person you've ever encountered. I've behaved like a serious idiot in the past so I'm not casting any aspersions here, and as you can see from my face I'm hardly the best person to give advice right now, but Sophia doesn't seem to give a toss about you.'

'She's busy, that's all,' Joey said defensively. 'She's a really great person.'

'Yeah, well, that's a matter of opinion.' Pippa sighed. 'But the fact of the matter here and now is that you're vulnerable and need her support for the next while. If she's not there for you, why are you with her?'

'I know I should reassess things a bit,' Joey said, 'but I need to get through the next couple of days first. Then I'll sort it. Anyway, why are you looking like you've the worries of the world on your shoulders? And why are you being so self-deprecating?' he asked. 'It's not like Princess Pippa to put herself down. Are you still freaked by what that taxi guy did?'

'It was really scary,' she said, 'but that's not it. I'm going to press charges and I hope that'll put a stop to his gallop. It's forced me into a real reality check. I need to get my act together, Joey.' She explained about the money she'd borrowed from Lainey and that she'd no idea how she'd pay it back.

'You'll think of something. You're a jammy cow,' he said. 'You're like the cat with nine lives.'

Suddenly tears were streaming down Pippa's cheeks.

'Hey!' Joey struggled to move. 'Shit, I'm stuck here. I can't even lean forward to give you a hug. Don't cry, Pip. I was only trying to cheer you up.'

'I know,' she sobbed. 'But I've messed up big-time, Joey. I push people too far. I take, take, take and never give back. Mum and Dad must hate me. All I do is tap them for cash. I sponge from everyone and I deserved the punch I got the other night.'

'Wait a second!' Joey hissed. 'You take that back! Nobody *deserves* to be hit, Pippa. Especially a young girl on her own late at night by a man she's paid to take her home safely.'

'I didn't pay,' Pippa said, with dead eyes.

'What? Did you do a legger and he chased you? Was that why he was so angry? Not that it's an excuse,' Joey reiterated.

'Nothing like that. The fella I met at the bar paid. But that's just it …' Pippa poured her heart out. 'You're such a good listener,' she said with a shuddering sigh when she reached the end of the dismal tale a few minutes later.

'Well, in all fairness, I can hardly walk away.' He grinned. 'But I'm glad you told me all this, Pippa. You already know that sponging and letting others take the financial heat isn't cool, but please get it out of your head that it's okay for anyone to hit you. Don't you see? So many women, and even men, who are victims of abuse feel the same way.'

'But I feel guilty, Joey. I should've been nicer. I shouldn't have been so spoilt and mean. It's my own fault.'

'It's not your fault that a man twice your size chose to punch you in the face. There is no excuse for that. End of.' Joey's eyes flashed with anger as he spoke. 'Promise me you're listening to what I'm saying.'

'Yeah, I hear ya.' She sighed. 'I guess you're right. I was behaving badly but two wrongs don't make a right, do they?'

'No!'

'Well, seeing as it's doling-out-advice hour,' Pippa said, turning to face him, 'what are you doing with Sophia?'

'We love each other,' he said.

'Ah, come off it,' she said. 'I don't think you even convinced yourself then.'

'It's complicated,' he said, ruffling his hair. 'Ugh, my head is like a chip pan.'

'Nice,' she said. 'Sophia's a selfish little mare. It takes one to know one.' Pippa raised an eyebrow. 'Honestly, she reminds me of myself at times. Except she has zero redeeming features.' She grinned.

'I'm a bit head-wrecked just now, Pip. I'll deal with it when I have to, yeah?' he said, glancing towards the door again. 'Let's stick to your messed-up life for today. I'm better at dealing with your problems than my own.'

'Fair enough,' she said. 'I know I'll have to go job hunting as soon as my face heals. But I've come to the conclusion I don't want to float from one thing to another any more. A couple of years ago I had a good job. But since I did that foundation course last year I've been messing around,' she admitted.

'The most important thing is that you can see you need to sort yourself out,' Joey said.

'I was going to ask Mum and Dad for another loan but they already bailed me out at the end of the summer. Even I know I shouldn't ask them again.'

'You need to work out what you're good at and start there,' Joey said, lying back and trying to get comfortable.

'I love art, but that doesn't pay much. I'm brilliant at shopping but tend to lose money at it rather than making it. I'd adore to own a shop. After the short stint I did at Boutique Belle I know I'd be good at it. But paying rent and buying stock and all those things would cost a small fortune. Right now, I haven't a pot to piss in, let alone the equity to open a shop.'

'Why don't you set up a shopping website so other crazy people like you can indulge?' he joked.

'That's it!' Pippa said, leaping from her chair. 'I'll set up a personal shopping service online. I did it with Lainey recently and it worked.'

'What?' Joey looked intrigued.

'She needed an outfit for the Michael Bublé concert so I dropped into her office and directed her to a whole pile of stores and we chose the perfect thing,' Pippa explained. 'If I can set up my own version with links to specific stores I could help others too. I'll charge a signing-up fee and sketch some funky designs to front each section. If I put outfit ideas together and show people finished looks that they can just click on and purchase it would save them time and effort.'

'That sounds good, but how will you launch it?' Joey asked, caught up in her enthusiasm.

'I'll ask Skye for help. She designs websites and works from the apartment. I'll ask if I can pay her when I make some money back.'

'Well, if you think Skye would help you, it's worth a try.'

'You're brilliant. Thank you!' Pippa stood up and kissed his forehead.

'Is that it? Are you leaving me already?'

'Sorry! I have to go and ask Skye this second. Christmas is around the corner and I haven't a minute to lose.'

As Pippa grabbed her coat and bag, she waved and blew kisses to Joey.

'You're a mental patient, do you know that, Pip?' he called as she rushed away.

It was seriously cold when she dashed outside from the heat of the hospital, ignoring the strange glances she attracted from everyone she passed. She hoped Skye would agree to help. She knew it was a long shot but she had such a good feeling about her website idea. It was something she knew she could build on over time.

When she got home, she boiled the kettle and made Skye a cup of tea before knocking on her bedroom door.

'Come in,' Skye said.

'Sorry to disturb you,' she began. 'I've got an idea and wondered if there's any way you could help me with it?' She proceeded to outline it. 'I have some sketches in my portfolio from my art course last year. I thought I could scan some of those and use the images to front the different pages the clients can click on,' she said, and dashed into her room to find her work. 'It might make it all stand out a bit more and add a professional touch.'

Skye's expression changed as she began to flick through the charcoal and watercolour drawings of swishy women's clothing. 'These are really good, Pippa,' she said. 'The vague brushstrokes creating the arms and legs and faces are fabulous. The movement you've injected into it all is amazing. You're on to something here. They'll be perfect on screen to mark each page.'

'To get it on track quickly I'll concentrate on Christmas party wear. I need to go live as soon as possible,' Pippa admitted. 'You see I borrowed some money from my sister and I have to pay her back.'

'I'm directly connected to thousands of email accounts, not to mention Facebook and Twitter,' Skye said. 'I can spread the word.'

'Wow! Thank you. One of my sister's schoolfriends works for a Dublin PR firm. I'm guessing they have a massive database too.' Pippa was getting more excited by the second. 'I'll see if Lainey will ask her to send a mail around as well.'

'Once we're ready to go live, you can think of who else might be good. It's often surprising how many people can be helpful when it comes to this sort of thing. Social media is massive, so you can tap into a ready-made market fairly quickly these days.'

'So does that mean you'll help me?' Pippa asked.

'Of course I will,' Skye said. 'I reckon if we download lots of sketches and use them as the big draw for your site it'll serve two purposes.'

'How do you mean?' Pippa asked.

'If you really want to make some money, why not sell the sketches as well as the membership to your site?'

'You're a genius! The only problem is that my portfolio will be gone if I sell them all. If I decide to try for art college in the future I won't have anything left.'

'You don't have to sell the originals. Echo works for a printer. I can easily get him to make copies. He'd do it after hours. I reckon we could encourage him to omit telling his boss until you have enough cash to pay him.'

'That's hardly very hippie and tree-hugging of him.'

'Nope, but his boss is a git.'

Skye was so quick and capable it blew Pippa away. She'd grown up drinking herbal infusions, so when Pippa made her a double espresso, she became turbo-charged. They worked until four that morning, and when Pippa woke at just after seven Skye was at the computer again. 'It's almost ready to go live. Come and see,' she said.

Pippa was blown away by how well her drawings looked. The site was really simple to use, and although they hadn't had time for much flash-player action, it was perfectly functional.

Pippa had chosen fifty different looks, which could be mixed and matched, all suitable for Christmas. She'd included some 'at home' outfits with soft knits and cosy leggings right up to full-length evening gowns with matching stoles. She'd put a little image of an apple or pear, triangle or square shape beside each one to show which body shape it would suit best.

'All you need to do now is tell people you're out there,' Skye said, stretching. 'My eyes are literally crossing. I need to go out for a bit of fresh air. I've emailed my list of clients and put a link on Twitter and Facebook,' she added, as an afterthought.

'Thanks, Skye.' Pippa hugged her. 'I'll pay you as soon as I can.'

'No need, it's my Christmas present to you.'

'I can't let you do that,' Pippa protested.

'You can. We're friends and you're in a pickle. Besides, you've had a terrible week so let's just hope this marks the start of a whole new beginning for you.'

'You're a star. Thank you,' Pippa said.

'Okay, Pippa! This is it!' Skye cried. 'You're officially live!'

'Thank you so much,' she said again as she hugged Skye. 'All I can hope is that there are some people out there with a bit of money for Christmas clothes. I'm going to email everyone I know and tweet about it. I've my own Facebook page too, so that'll get the ball rolling.'

An email pinged through on Pippa's laptop less than ten minutes later. 'Oh, my God! It's my first customer,' she squealed. 'There are three people asking questions now! One wants to buy the main-page sketch! How many people did you send the link to?'

'Eh, with Facebook, Twitter and my own contacts around twenty thousand,' Skye said easily.

'*Whaaat?*'

'I've been doing this on and off for quite a while so I know a few people.' She shrugged.

'Oh, my God!' Pippa shrieked. 'I'm going to call Lainey right now and ask her to call her friend in that PR place about putting a link on her work website for me too.'

Lainey agreed straight away.

'No problem at all, sis. I know Joanna has done stuff like this for other people before. I can't see it being a problem.'

'Cool, I've sent the link through so you can have a look and forward it to her.'

'I'm just opening it this second,' Lainey said. 'Pippa, these sketches are brillliant. I love the whole feel of the site and I'm sending the link straight through to Joanna now.'

When Pippa hung up, Skye suggested they go to see Echo about copies of the sketches. 'I think they'll sell brilliantly.'

Pippa thanked her lucky stars that Skye had come to live with her when she had. Then she answered her emails. All five of them! For the first time in her life Pippa knew she was doing the right thing. Her family would approve. She was determined to make it work. She wanted everyone to be proud of her for once.

20
Lonely this Christmas
❄❄❄

Joey was growing increasingly frustrated as he lay in his hospital bed waiting to have it out with Sophia. It was lucky he wasn't holding his breath: she'd only been in to see him for the odd moment over the last few days.

He knew she was busy but it was plain to him that she had room in her life for just one person – and it wasn't him. His conversation with Pippa the day before resounded in his head. He'd had an inkling his family didn't like her, but Pippa had left him in no doubt as to her feelings towards Sophia.

Later, when she arrived, looking gorgeous in skinny jeans, high black boots and a cropped jacket, he wondered if he had judged her too harshly. She was stunning.

'Hi,' she said, shuddering as she sat on the horrible brown plastic seat beside his bed. 'This place gives me the heebie-jeebies. I don't know why it has to be *so* disgusting.'

'Hi,' he said, a bit crestfallen that she hadn't kissed him.

'How are you today?' she said, crossing her legs and jigging her foot. Her eyes darted around the ward.

'I'm okay,' he said. 'I've felt better, though.'

'What's the story with the stubble?' she asked, finally looking his way. 'It doesn't really suit you. I *hate* beards so you'd better get rid of it ASAP.'

'In case it's skipped your notice, I'm kind of incapacitated here,' he said. 'I've only been able to have bed baths over the last few days. The nurse said I can try an assisted shower tomorrow. They'll fit me for some rubber coverings for the arm and leg casts this afternoon so I can—'

'Okay, I get the picture,' she interrupted. 'Spare me the depressing details.'

'Sophia,' he began. 'Clearly you're very annoyed with me for having this accident.' He expected her to jump in and tell him that wasn't true.

'Stop whining, Joey, please,' she said, picking at her nails. 'What do you want me to do? Come in here looking ecstatic? This isn't really how I had it planned, you know.'

'Well, it isn't exactly fun for me either, believe it or not,' he said, growing angrier by the second.

'Right,' she said. 'So the thing is … I need to know what to do about Lanzarote. Have you spoken to the doctors about when they're letting you out of here?'

'Pardon?'

'When are you getting out?'

'Sophia, there's no way I can go to Lanzarote for Christmas. End of. I can't move, let alone get myself to the Canaries.'

'Oh, so the world has to stop now, does it?'

'Sophia,' Joey began, 'you've made it crystal clear that all of this is totally outside your plans. But accidents happen and this is the way I've been left. I didn't do it on purpose and, believe me, there are a million places I'd rather be than here. But I have to stay where I am until at least the day after tomorrow. After that I'll need to convalesce for quite a while. I'll need physiotherapy and plenty of time to get back on my feet.'

'Um, yeah. Why don't you go and stay with your family? They like clucking around you. I'll go to Lanzarote and we'll see each other when I get back,' Sophia said. 'That way you're looked after and I can get on with my training.'

Joey didn't speak or move for quite a while. Sophia rooted in her bag. 'I'm trying to find the information on the Canaries,' she explained. 'I need to read the terms and conditions. With a bit of luck you'll get your money back if we can prove you were too ill to travel.'

'Is that it?' he asked.

'Mm?' she said, looking up from the document.

'Is that it?' he said, louder. 'You have no concern for me or how I'll be? I can be offloaded to my parents and you can fly off for two weeks without so much as a second thought for me or us?'

'What are you getting so excited about? Joey, you didn't seriously expect me to sit around because you had an accident, did you? What do you want? That we both lose out on the racing season?'

'Don't you care about me at all?' Joey asked, and wished he hadn't. 'Actually, you don't need to answer that. Can you leave your keys on the kitchen counter when you move your stuff out of my apartment?'

'What? Why am I being punished now?'

'I've tried to make excuses for your behaviour for months now. You're rude to my family. You suit yourself all the time. You're about as much fun to live with as a kick in the crotch.'

'That knock to your head's really confused you,' she said. 'But I'm not about sitting around to be insulted. By the time you come to your senses, it'll be too late.'

'Whatever you say,' Joey said calmly.

'Are you seriously telling me to move out?' Sophia flared angrily. 'I won't come back, Joey. I don't play games. If you do this now you won't get me back.'

'Is that a promise?' Joey asked. 'Just go away.'

'You're making a big mistake,' she said.

'No, I'm not,' Joey shot back. 'For the first time in a long time I'm finally making sense. You are without doubt the most selfish person I've ever come across.'

'I don't have to listen to this,' she hissed, as Pippa walked into the ward and headed for Joey's bed.

'Is everything okay here?' She looked from Joey to Sophia.

'Your sap of a brother has just finished with me. You're welcome to him. He's a total dweeb, lying there feeling sorry for himself. Enjoy Christmas in your tumbledown old house,' she snarled, and stalked away.

'Screw you, Sophia,' Pippa said.

'Leave it, Pippa,' Joey barked. The other people in his ward were staring at them, but that wasn't what was bothering him: it was the realisation that Sophia could be so cold.

'Hey,' Pippa said. 'She's not worth it.'

'I know, but it's an awful kick in the balls to realise that your girlfriend doesn't give a toss about you.' Wiping the dampness from his eyes, Joey sighed. 'Do me a favour and don't say, "I told you so."'

Pippa sat on the chair beside his bed and grasped his hand.

'It's not like you to be so quiet,' he said, turning his head to look at her.

'You said not to say, "I told you so."'

'Was she that bad?'

'Ah, no,' Pippa said gently. 'She was much worse than that.'

Joey did his best to smile but he was feeling too awful.

'Crap day, huh?'

'Pretty much, but I'm getting good at those.'

'Any news on when you're breaking out of here?' she asked.

'Maybe the day after tomorrow. I think I'll take Mum and Dad up on their offer of going to Huntersbrook. I can't face being in the flat on my own.'

'You won't be able to look after yourself either,' Pippa reasoned. 'Go home and they can all make a big fuss of you. Besides, it's nearly Christmas so Lainey and I will be around too. She's bringing her friend Jules. I'm bringing Skye and maybe her cousin Echo.'

'His name isn't really Echo, is it?' Joey asked.

'Yeah, God love him. The parents are pretty out there by all accounts.'

'I'll call Huntersbrook in a while and tell Mum I'll be home,' he said. 'If I've any chance at all of having a fun Christmas, it'll be there.'

'That's the spirit,' Pippa said. 'Listen, I don't want to do a Sophia on you now but I have to leave.'

Joey had to laugh. 'Jesus, Pippa, you drop some serious clangers at times.'

'Sorry.' She wrinkled her nose. 'I didn't mean it to sound like that.'

'No, you never do,' he said. 'Catch you later.'

She leaned over and kissed him. 'I'm kind of digging the beard thing. You look very rugged. I'd say you might pick up a hot-looking nurse if you play your cards right.'

'See ya,' he said, waving.

So that was that, Joey thought.

His phone buzzed and he looked at the screen: Clive.

'How's it going?' his boss asked.

'Pretty shit,' Joey said. 'How are things in the office?'

'Busy, but we'll get there. I intended dropping in today but it's not looking good. I didn't want you to think we're not bothering,' he said.

'I don't, Clive!' Joey said, putting on his invincible workman voice. 'I got the plant and the fruit hamper. Thanks a million.'

'That was the ladies. I must admit it wouldn't have entered my head to send you a pot plant or a basket of fruit, but I'm glad you got it.'

'The plant is good for blocking the view to the poor old fella with no teeth in the bed opposite. And I've eaten a couple of the apples, so I'm putting it all to good use.'

'Good man,' Clive said. 'I'll fly here but give me a call if you need anything. When are you getting out?'

'Next day or so with a bit of luck,' Joey said. 'I'm going to shift myself down to Wicklow and stay with the folks for Christmas. I'd get stuck in the hallway in the apartment and left for dead otherwise,' he joked.

'Will Sophia join you?' he asked.

'Nah. We've decided to part company,' Joey said, trying to sound as if it wasn't important.

'Sorry to hear that. I don't think this'll go down as one of the best weeks of your life, eh?'

'No, I don't suppose it will,' Joey said. He looked at the yucca plant and the fruit, which had arrived that morning. All the staff at the company had signed the card, which meant Jemima had taken the trouble to go around to everyone and get them to do it. He was chuffed they'd made the effort but it highlighted how little Sophia had cared.

'I would've preferred to tell you this in writing, but I think you need a bit of a boost right now,' Clive said. 'We only sent you the plant and healthy stuff to make sure you come out of there safely. We have to look after our new manager.'

'What?' Joey said. 'Ouch. Sorry, Clive. I've just jerked my leg in the excitement.'

'I've come from a partners' meeting and as we won't be seeing you for a few weeks I asked them to take a final vote on it so you should expect the paperwork in the next couple of days.'

'Gosh, I'm made up!' Joey said. 'Thanks, Clive. That really is something worth celebrating once I can hold up a pint.'

'I'll keep you to that. And, as I said, lift the phone if I can do anything. I'll chat to you over the next few days.'

'Cheers, Clive. Talk to you soon.'

The nurse came around and asked him if he needed any pain relief. As it made him kind of drowsy and stoned, he took some. Feck Sophia, he thought. She thought she was so amazing and such a catch. He almost wanted to phone her and tell her she'd picked the wrong time to be such a selfish bitch. He was about to move up the food chain at work. He'd find a much less cold and irritating girlfriend next time.

As the drug flooded his system, Joey closed his eyes and settled in for a sleep.

21

Mistletoe and Wine

It was six days before Christmas, and although she desperately wanted to feel jovial and lighthearted, Holly was dragging herself around. News of the local Christmas market had spread and she felt that a visit would be the perfect pick-me-up. She seemed to be stuck in one of those days where everything took ages and nothing was achieved.

The phone rang. 'Hello,' she said, sounding a lot more cheerful than she felt.

'Hi, Mum,' Joey said.

Holly heard sadness in his voice. 'Hi, love. How are you today?' she asked.

'Mixed. I've just split up with Sophia.'

'Oh, no!' she said, because she felt she ought to. Inwardly she was doing a little dance. That girl had been a right madam, and although she wasn't sure anyone would ever be good enough for her son, Sophia wasn't even in the running.

'These things happen. She wasn't right for me and often it takes a bit of a crisis to bring it all to a head,' he said. 'I know you weren't mad about her, Mum, but I'm pretty gutted, I have to say.'

'I'm sorry you're hurting, pet,' she said.

'On the more positive side of things, Clive called and I've been promoted in work.'

'That's fantastic,' she said. 'Half the world is being made redundant and you're being promoted – you must be doing something right.'

'I suppose when you put it that way I'm not a total lamer. Anyway, if everything goes to plan I can escape from here tomorrow. If the offer still stands, I'd love to come home.'

'Of course it does,' she said. 'Sadie and I have your room all ready. Dad and Scott moved a bed into the front room downstairs so you'll be able to get in and out. Let us know what time and we'll be there to pick you up.'

'Thanks, Mum. I really appreciate that. At least someone loves me!'

'We all love you. Don't mind that Sophia pup. She'll rue the day she let you go. She'll never find another man like you.'

'And you're not a bit biased, of course,' Joey said, sounding a lot more like himself.

'I'll see you tomorrow, please God,' she said, and hung up.

Paddy was beside himself. He loved a bit of male company, and the fact that Joey was going to be fairly immobile meant he'd have the perfect fireside companion.

Recently Holly had turned off as many radiators as she could, but when she inspected the room she and Sadie had set up for Joey it was like standing outside in the garden. She fetched a pair of pliers and turned the reluctant old nut at the side of the radiator until she heard the clunking of the pipes followed by water gurgling in to let her know it was working.

Determined to find her Christmas spirit, she readied herself for the market. She didn't have to spend much and it would be lovely to get out and see some of the locals. She fetched her good coat from the wardrobe. It was cashmere with a fur collar and she'd owned it for as long as she could recall. She always felt transformed when she wore it. The luxury of the soft material, so beautifully cut, gave her an instant pep in her step. She pulled on the matching fur hat, then added a bit of lipstick and decided she'd do nicely.

'I'm going to the Christmas market,' she called to Paddy as she trundled down the stairs towards the front door. 'Do you want to come?'

'No, thanks,' he shouted back. 'I've things to do here. Enjoy it.'

She was secretly glad he wasn't interested. He'd only get bored after ten minutes and badger her to leave. Sadie had been the day before and told her it was marvellous. 'They're all the rage on the continent and this one is a roaring success,' Sadie said. 'I know a couple of the women who've set up stalls. You'll love it, Holly. You can buy baked goods or lots of good-quality ingredients if you prefer to do your own.'

Holly had phoned Sadie early that morning to say she was going to pop down for a look. 'Will you meet me there? Maybe we could potter about together.'

'I'd love that,' Sadie said. 'According to Maeve Dempsey, there'll be a tent with cookery demonstrations today so I'd every intention of going back to see them. We might learn something new.'

They'd agreed to meet at eleven o'clock at the gate.

Holly arrived in plenty of time to be directed to the adjoining field where there was free parking. 'Will I be clamped in here?' she called out the window to Tommy Green, who was looking very officious in a hi-vis vest.

'Indeed you will not. But some young boyo might go mad drinking the brandy-laced hot chocolate and go joyriding up that back field.' He grinned.

As she walked towards the market Holly felt as if she'd just stepped off an Aer Lingus flight to Vienna. All the stalls were linked by strings of glowing lights, and the local choir and Garda band were serenading the milling crowd. A round of applause at the far end announced Santa's arrival. Holly stood to watch, her face aglow, as Jimmy O'Shea from Arklow, in a wonderfully convincing Santa suit, waved at the squealing children. That Santa appeared to have travelled from the North Pole in a trailer of hay pulled by a twenty-year-old Massey Ferguson tractor didn't seem odd to anyone.

There were live reindeer too, but instead of pulling a sleigh, they were grazing in a little sectioned-off area where the children and adults could admire them. 'They're feeding themselves up to get ready for Christmas Eve,' Jimmy said loudly.

Holly had never studied reindeer at such close range before. They were much smaller than she'd imagined and far cuter.

'Don't their thick coats and fuzzy brown antlers make you want to reach out and stroke them?' a voice said behind her.

'Sadie!' Holly said, turning and smiling. 'Aren't they pretty?'

'Indeed they are,' she said. 'Not great to eat, though. I'd venison stew not so long ago and the meat was like leather.'

'Maybe we shouldn't discuss recipes in front of them. It might ruin their snack.' Holly felt better already.

Wafts of gingerbread and mulled wine filled the crisp, cool air. Pulling her list from her pocket, Holly set about buying the ingredients for her Christmas cake. A stall selling organic dried fruit was her first port of call. The stallholder, who looked frozen to the bone, was so helpful and enthusiastic Holly ended up buying enough to make two cakes. 'I'd no idea raisins even came in that golden colour. They taste like sweets,' Holly exclaimed.

'Have you tried my special crystallised ginger?' The woman offered her a slice.

The tangy lemony flavour was like a fresher, more delicious version of sherbet.

'Chop it finely into your cake mixture. It's also gorgeous for making homemade gingerbread. I'm doing a little baking demonstration shortly at the main tent, if you've time to come,' she said.

'Will we be able to taste what you bake?' Sadie asked, always eager for a freebie.

'You will. I'll be sure to give you the nod when it's time,' the woman said.

'Will we go on in and get a good seat?' Holly asked.

'Why not?' Sadie said. 'It's so cold out here, and I think snow is on the way,' she said, sniffing the air.

They went into the marquee and shuddered. It was colder inside than it was out.

'It'll improve in here once the little stove is turned on and people flock in to see what's happening,' Sadie said stoutly, but she looked unsure.

Holly would gladly have turned and left if they hadn't been ushered to the front row and made to sit beside a woman who smelled as if she'd just crawled out from under a cowpat.

'Hello, Cynthia,' Holly said, shocked. The bad-smelling woman was her next-door neighbour.

'Hiya, Cynthia.' Sadie leaned over to pat her hand.

'I hate Christmas,' Cynthia said, showing more gum than Holly had ever longed to see in one mouth.

'Poor you,' Holly said.

'It's a waste of time, energy and money. I don't believe in any of the Jesus, Mary and Joseph nonsense, and the rest was invented by greedy bastards who want to make a quick few quid at the expense of fools who have nothing better to do but squander their year's savings on crap other folk don't want.'

'I'm sorry you feel that way about it,' Holly said.

'How are you?' Sadie asked, having chosen to ignore the rant. 'We haven't seen yourself and Jacob for a while. I believe your boy Matt is home from England.'

'He's a useless string of piss, that boy,' Cynthia snarled.

Holly was alarmed. Cynthia had always been quiet and reserved.

'Her dementia has changed her personality,' Sadie whispered. 'Bless her.'

'He took everything he could get. I breastfed and nurtured him his whole life. He never wanted for a thing,' Cynthia said. 'How did he repay me? He buggered off to live in Zambezi.' She tutted.

'Wasn't he in England, Cynthia?' Holly ventured.

'Don't you think I know my own husband?' Cynthia said, blinking. 'As soon as the war broke out he was gone.'

'She's totally mixed up,' Holly whispered to Sadie.

'Two fellas have taken over my house,' she continued. 'They tell everyone they're there to look after me. Truth of the matter is that they're German soldiers. They steal my things, you know,' she said.

'Really?' Holly caught Sadie's eye: how should they answer her?

'I had fine clothing and jewels once upon a time and they took the lot. Sold them to the pirates.'

'Mum!' Holly and Sadie turned to see a well-built, better-looking version of Jacob walking towards them.

'Hello, Holly and Sadie. It's Matt. You haven't changed but I know I have. It's been a long time,' he said, shaking their hands.

'Hello, son,' Sadie said. 'We've been having a great chat with your mother here.'

'She's pretty confused, isn't she?' Holly mouthed to him.

'It's been a nightmare, to be honest,' he said, looking strained. 'I brought her here thinking she'd enjoy the outing. I was paying for a coffee outside, turned around and she was gone.'

'She's fine here with us if you want to have a wander,' Holly said.

'You're very kind but I'll probably take her home. She'll get cold sitting and I can't imagine she'll stay too long. She gets very agitated, poor love.'

'Did you meet my Matthew?' Cynthia asked, in a moment of lucidity.

'We did, Cynthia. He's looking great. We're delighted to see him.' Holly smiled.

'I think we'll head away now, Mum,' he said, taking her arm. 'Oh, no, you've stepped in some cow dung.'

'It's time to get ready for school,' she said, drifting off again. 'He never wants to go but he has to. That's the fact of the matter, isn't it, ladies?'

'Take care of yourself,' Sadie said, as Matt led her away.

'Bye-bye, Cynthia,' Holly called after her. 'Come over some time, Matt,' she said. 'We'd love to see you. Bring your mum and dad for a bit of dinner one of these evenings.'

'Thanks so much, Holly. I appreciate that. Sure I might see you soon,' he said, as his mother babbled beside him.

'It's so sad, isn't it?' Sadie said, with tears in her eyes. 'And it could be you or me.'

'Sure is,' Holly agreed. Cynthia was only a little older than she was, and Matt was much the same age as Lainey. Jacob had said they were having an awful time with Cynthia and she'd sympathised but hadn't really understood what he'd meant until now.

'That boy of theirs is good to come back and look after her,' Sadie said.

Holly didn't answer. It hit her once more that Maggie had gone. She'd known things were on a knife edge with Huntersbrook House and she'd gone anyway. What kind of family were they?

By the time the baking demonstration was about to get going lots of chilly spectators had come into the marquee, making it cosier.

A very nervous squeaky-voiced girl took to the makeshift stage. 'I'm going to show you all a traditional fruitcake,' she said shakily.

'We can't hear you at the back, lovey,' someone shouted.

The girl did her best to project her voice.

'She's no Nigella, is she?' Sadie said. 'Wouldn't she make you want to cry she's so nervous?'

'God help her,' Holly said in sympathy. 'Still, isn't she great to do it all the same?'

Once the painfully awkward demonstration was over,

and the plate of tasting slices from a cake she'd made earlier was passed around, the atmosphere relaxed. A much more confident older woman took over. 'I'm going to show you two ways of icing your cake,' she said, clearly well used to speaking to groups. 'One involves covering the cake in almond paste and toasting it and the other is the more traditional white icing.'

Holly and Sadie watched in awe as she showed them how to make dainty little red rosebuds with fondant icing.

'I'm going to set up a little workshop at my stall outside. Anyone who'd like to come and either buy some ready-made decorations or have a one-to-one demonstration is most welcome. In addition I have bags of fondant icing in all colours for the more adventurous of you.'

'I'll definitely visit her,' Holly said to Sadie.

'Let's get some red and green and we'll do roses and leaves. The family will think we're great altogether.' Sadie smiled.

Holly's favourite item in the demonstration was the stained-glass-window biscuits, which involved cutting stars from the dough, placing them on a baking tray and popping a boiled sweet in the centre of each. As the biscuits baked, the sweets melted and bubbled.

'Once they're out and cooled they do this,' the woman said, rooting in a box for the finished product and holding it aloft.

'It really does look like a stained-glass window,' Holly said. 'Very impressive.'

Next up at the demonstration table was a man with a crippling speech impediment. He did his best to show them how to make Christmas crackers but he was too much for Holly and Sadie, who had to retreat outside.

'Let's get a hot chocolate and pick up a few bits and pieces,' Sadie suggested. 'Then I'm going home. I've a meeting with Do Gooder Gloria about the old folks' knitting challenge.'

'What's that?' Holly asked, as they went to order their drinks.

'It's part of the initiative to get the elderly involved in some local activities. They all love the knitting, but we're low on supplies,' Sadie said.

'What do you need?' Holly asked, as she paid for the hot chocolate. She sipped hers. 'This'll put hairs on your chest. It's laced with brandy. Once they've poured the hot chocolate into the cup they produce a bottle of cognac and glug it in! In no other place would you see the Garda band playing while they sell lethal hot drinks and wave you off to drive into a hedge on the way home.'

'We need wool. We have some but not enough.'

'I'll tell you what,' Holly said. 'We're not doing big presents this year as you know. Why don't I buy the wool for a sweater for each person, the old folk can knit them and I'll give them as my gifts?'

'Well, if you're sure?' Sadie said, as she finished her hot chocolate. 'That stuff is pretty potent all right.'

Holly drove home slowly. She wasn't in the habit of drinking and driving and was glad when she pulled to a halt at the front door.

She set to work baking her cake. With a Christmas CD playing, she allowed herself the odd skip as she weighed the ingredients. 'Boys! There you are!' she shouted over the music.

'What on earth is going on in here?' Scott asked, grinning at Paddy. 'Looks like Holly's finally lost the plot.'

'Drunken baking! I'd heartily recommend it,' she said. 'I had a hot chocolate at the Christmas market and I'm flying now!'

'A hot chocolate? What did they put in it?' he asked.

'Well, look what we got you,' Paddy said, appearing with another tree.

'Isn't she a beauty?' Scott said. 'We spotted it while we were fixing a part of the fence over near the front and figured it might cheer you up. Little did we know you were here having a Christmas party for one!'

'We'll shove it in a stand, if I can find another, and you'll be set to decorate it,' Paddy said.

'Thanks, love. I'm being spoilt this year! Three trees! Didn't I say all things come in threes?' she said. As she turned the music down, the mood in the room settled.

'How was the market?' Paddy asked.

'Lovely. I met Sadie and we had a great time. Cynthia was there too,' she said. 'She's getting pretty bad.'

'Yeah,' Scott said. 'She can't be left now. Matt's a good bloke and he's really patient with her, but he'll have to get some work after Christmas. They might have to put Cynthia in a home.'

'How awful for them,' Holly said. Once more she thought of Maggie. She wouldn't wish her mother ill, especially not like Cynthia.

'Are you all right, love?' Paddy asked.

'Fine,' she said. 'Thanks for getting the tree.'

The smell of nutmeg and cinnamon was divine as the cake began to bake. She rang Do Gooder Gloria and agreed to drop off some wool the next day at the community centre for the old folks.

'Sure you're a dote,' Gloria said, patronising as ever. 'You're great altogether.' Holly was glad they were on the phone. She knew the other woman did fantastic work but she was very annoying all the same. 'You can sleep easy now tonight, knowing you've been such a great girl.'

Holly, Paddy and Scott set to work decorating the tree. 'The house is getting really Christmassy now,' Holly said. The shot of alcohol and quick dance around the kitchen had done her the world of good. 'I'm going to ask Cynthia, Jacob and Matt to join us for Christmas dinner,' she whispered to Paddy. 'Otherwise they'll have a miserable time.'

'Ah, you do that,' Paddy agreed readily.

'Will you ask the others to join us with your good self for Christmas dinner?' she said to Scott, as he put the lights on the tree in the kitchen.

'That sounds great, Holly, cheers!' Scott said, smiling. As he burst out laughing they both looked at him.

'What?' Holly said.

'I think Do Gooder Gloria's rubbing off on you, my girl. I'm going to rename you Saint Holly.'

'Oh, shut up, you!' Holly said, swatting him with a string of tinsel.

Next morning Sadie arrived first thing, saying she'd get started on covering the cake with marzipan and white icing.

'I'd love to give those flowers a shot, so wait for me for that part, will you?' Holly asked. 'I'm going to grab that wool and drop it in to the community centre for the oldies to get going.'

Paddy was on his way to Dublin to collect Joey from

hospital. Scott was accompanying him in case they needed to lift him into the car.

'I'll be back and ready to take care of him once I drop my wool off,' Holly promised.

Going into the wool shop was like stepping back in time. The smell evoked vivid memories from Holly's childhood. The proprietor was delighted to chat to Holly, commended her for her charitable donation and offered to throw in a few extra balls for free.

'Those Christmas sweaters can be quite tricky and detailed though,' she said.

'I'm sure they can, but Gloria's in charge. I'm just delivering what I was asked for and leaving it at that.'

'Quite right. The less said to that woman the better. She'll only lecture you on everything from washing clothes to wrapping presents. She thinks she knows it all.'

Holly got into her car with several bags of wool and drove to the community centre. She went inside where she found Gloria, who was very busy so hadn't time to talk much.

'Just wait until your family see what these ladies are going to produce,' she said. 'You'll be amazed.'

'Will they have enough time? It's less than a week to go,' Holly wondered.

'There are so many who want to do a bit that we let them do a section each and sew them together,' Gloria explained. 'Some are more interested in sleeves, while others love the patterned fronts. Don't worry, I'll have a good few sweaters ready for you to give as gifts next week.'

'Well, if you're sure . . .'

'I heard about your Joey by the way. Let me know if I can help when he gets out of hospital. It must be very difficult for you since your mother eloped with that wine man,' Gloria said. 'I believe your daughter was stabbed by her boyfriend too. Awful for you and Paddy.'

'Joey will be fine and Pippa wasn't stabbed,' Holly said, trying not to sound snappy. She didn't like the way Gloria was painting them as a dysfunctional family to be pitied.

As she made her way home, Holly tried to focus on the positive. Her neighbours had happily accepted her invitation to Christmas dinner. All the children would be there, with friends thrown into the mix. She'd more beautifully decorated trees than she could shake a fairy at. All in all it was shaping up to be a fun and festive day.

Holly hoped against hope it wouldn't be their last at Huntersbrook House. She was a firm believer in the power of positive thinking, and until now she'd tried to believe that something would turn up so that they could hold on to the house. But the walls were closing in on her. Her latest idea was to ask a Dublin estate agent if they knew of a developer who would buy the land for building.

It might be an option, but Holly wasn't sure that she could bear the reality of machines crashing in and building apartment blocks on the beautiful landscape. Either way, she supposed, investors with money to spend had disappeared along with the extinct Celtic Tiger.

As was now the norm, she was shrouded in sadness as a terrible sense of finality settled on her.

22

The Power of Love

The Dublin office drinks party had evolved quite by chance on Friday 20 December. Mr Drake had decided they should have a quick drink in the pub after work since it was their last day before Christmas.

'I know we were all at the big party but it'd be nice to have a quick one together, just us lot. What do you say? Put it this way, I'd have no objection to any of you buying me a Christmas drink.'

'Jesus, for a terrifying moment there I thought he'd come over all Christmassy.' Jules rolled her eyes.

All the same, the majority of the staff liked and respected each other so they decided to go along with Drake-ula's suggestion. They all dropped their cars home and Lainey parked her bike at the flat. It was beginning to snow quite heavily so she took a taxi. The driver was full of Christmas cheer – not. 'This is a terrible time of year if you're not loaded,' he said, as soon as she sat into the car. 'It's awful pressure for people. There's not a sniff of the real meaning of Christmas any longer.'

'I'm really looking forward to it,' Lainey said. 'My family are all getting together. Apart from Grandma. She's in Australia.'

'Your *granny* is in Australia?' he said. 'It's usually the young ones who go down there. Your family sounds weird,' he said, as she hopped out and shoved her money at him.

'They probably are,' Lainey said. 'But I think they're pretty cool.' She didn't bother wishing him a happy Christmas, deciding it would be a waste of breath.

She went into the pub and up to the bar. 'What can I get you?' the barman said, in just as cheerful a voice as her taxi driver had used.

'One glass of white wine for my friend, who's on her way,' Lainey said. 'I don't know what I feel like.'

'Well, you'd want to make up your mind because this place isn't exactly empty,' he said, tapping a twenty-cent coin off the bar like an irate woodpecker.

'I'll have a hot port,' she said. 'It is Christmas,' she added, with a sweet smile as she batted her eyelashes.

He didn't smile or answer, so when he banged the drink down in front of her she tried again: 'You looked like you wanted to stab me there, but if it helps at all I'm really looking forward to this. I've just finished up at work for Christmas.'

'I'm delighted for you,' he growled. 'Some of us are miles away from any sign of a break.' He held out his hand for the money.

Figuring she wasn't going to find any Christmas cheer with this string of misery, Lainey grabbed the drinks and found a round table near the crackling open fire.

'Hiya!' Jules said, as she ran in.

'Hello!' Lainey said. 'I'm delighted to see you. I've come across several members of the I Hate Christmas Club over the last half-hour. There are some seriously grumpy people about.'

'Well,' Jules said, as she raised her glass, 'feck the lot of them. Happy Christmas and cheers! No sign of the others yet?'

'They'll be here any second, I'd say. Sit yourself down and relax,' Lainey instructed.

The warm port was so delicious that Lainey lost count of how many she downed.

'I was fine a few minutes ago,' she slurred at Drake, who was also looking the worse for wear after several pints of cider mixed with shots of sambuca. 'I mean, it's not even like a real drink. It's sort of like that stuff you get for a cold. Yet when I tried to stand up just now my legs weren't working so well.'

'I always know I'm going to end up feeling messy when I have shots,' Drake said.

'Well, you're obviously more sensible than me,' she said. 'When it comes to drink anyhow.'

'Why don't you have a shot yourself?' he asked. 'I'll even buy you one. I'm proud to say I haven't put my hand in my pocket since I got here.'

'Thanks, but I'm fine with the port,' she said, giggling.

'I didn't think you'd say yes. I was only being polite.'

'Why didn't you think I'd let you buy me a drink?' Lainey asked, smiling.

'Sure all the lads think you're a lesbo,' he said. 'You're kind of manly, although lately you've made a bit of an effort and look less like a dyke. He obviously thought he was being complimentary. 'I've always liked you because there's none of the girly shit with you. No tittering and whispering, and you never stand with doe eyes looking like you've been mortally wounded if I bark an order. Not like some I could mention,' he said, jerking his head sideways towards Jules. 'That one, if you so much as glance at her crooked, she looks at you like you've stabbed a barrel of kittens with a knitting needle. In fairness to you, Lainey, you're consistent and a good worker. What you do in your spare time is none of my concern. I'm open-minded, me.'

Lainey opened her mouth to retaliate and realised she'd no idea where to begin. So much of what he'd said had shocked her. 'Have a good Christmas, Mr Drake,' she said, hoping to God her eyes weren't showing the hurt that was bubbling inside her.

So, they all thought she was gay. That she dressed, worked and thought like a man. On the up-side, her boss seemed to have some respect for her.

The irony was almost too much: three men were swarming around Jules.

The thought of more port made her feel ill. Knowing she needed to get the hell out of there, she went to Jules and whispered that she was going home.

'I'll come with you, Lainz.'

'Are we not good enough for you, girls?' Drake asked, laughing.

'I'm in a bit of a hurry,' Lainey said, sounding strangled.

Jules must have realised she was upset. 'You're the best, Mr Drake,' she said, hugging him. 'I have a date, that's all.'

'Anyone we know?' he asked.

'Definitely not,' Jules said, winking at Lainey.

Lainey had advised her not to come out to Drake or the rest of the crew in work. 'I'd wait until you're more confident. In light of the way your mum reacted, give yourself a bit of time. People like Drake aren't what I'd consider the most open-minded. He's horrible to you anyway. I think he'd hold it against you.'

'You're probably right,' Jules said, chewing the inside of her cheek. 'The only thing is, Lainz, I'm not ashamed of who I am.'

'Nor should you be, but I wouldn't tell them too much about yourself full stop. They know nothing about me and that's the way I like to keep it. Before you came along, I never had much to do with any of the work crew. I've been there eight years and I'm glad I've kept my nose clean.'

'You're right, Lainz, as usual,' Jules said. 'I don't know what I'd do without you! I trust everyone and think the world is my friend. That's really stupid, isn't it?'

'No, Jules. You're open and lovely and I'd hate you to change, but a little self-preservation can go a long way in work, that's all.'

As they said their goodbyes and wished the crew a happy Christmas, Lainey was glad she'd advised Jules to keep schtum. As they linked arms and made their way out into the freezing air, she couldn't hold back her tears a moment longer and pulled Jules around the side of the building.

'What happened?' Jules was horrified.

'Oh, Drake was drunk and shooting his mouth off.' She was trying to breathe deeply and stop making a show of herself.

'I'll kill him,' Jules said, about to march back inside.

'No! Please leave it. He didn't mean any harm. He was just being … honest. I've had too much port and I need to go home and sleep it off.'

'I'll come back with you,' Jules said, and hailed a taxi.

'You're going on your date,' Lainey said.

'Not now I'm not,' Jules said, as she stuck her head through the window and gave the driver Lainey's address.

Lainey hugged her friend. 'I can't believe you'd pass up a date for me. I really appreciate it, but I wouldn't hear of it. Now go, and tell me all about it in the morning,' she ordered. 'I'm fine now. I was just being silly. I'll blame the stress of the build up to Christmas.'

Jules hesitated. 'I've no problem coming with you.'

'I know, and thank you. I'll talk to you in the morning.' Lainey waved to her friend, climbed in and the taxi drove away. The snow was still falling in big fat flakes and this time Lainey had Mr Personality, who told her all about his children and how excited they were about Santa coming. 'They've been counting the sleeps that are left,' he said. 'They're the best reason in the world to go out to work on a cold and snowy night.'

When they pulled up outside her building, Lainey gave him a decent tip. 'To put another little thing in their stockings.'

'Thanks a million. Happy Christmas to you!' he called, as she ran inside.

The room was spinning as she climbed into bed. She managed to rid herself of her boots but couldn't bring herself to take off her clothes and makeup.

Her hand rested on her phone. Normally when she was inebriated she'd look at Seth's Facebook page. Now she turned over and snuggled deep into the duvet. That was when she remembered she'd blocked him anyway.

A new feeling crept through her. In her drunken stupor she reckoned it might be relief. Relief that she was no longer controlled by Seth. That she was totally free of him and out of his life in every way. She felt a twinge of sadness for the poor girl he was currently destroying, but hoped she might come to her senses before it was too late.

Next morning Lainey realised there was nothing quite like a port hangover. She'd never actually been hit by the 45A bus or beaten with a lump hammer, but she knew that this feeling would probably prepare her quite adequately should either eventuality ever come to pass.

It was minus three outside, according to the weather forecaster on the radio, so she chose Dundrum Town Centre as her final gifts destination. The large indoor shopping area offered a great selection of all the most popular stores. These were the times when her bike was a godsend. Although the roads were pretty treacherous, she'd take it handy and zip past the traffic. She strapped her panniers to the back of the bike and set off. The crisp freshness eased her thumping head. She could almost feel the sub-zero temperatures cutting through the dull fug of last night's booze.

She left the bike in the car park and went into Primark, grabbing a basket at the entrance. She didn't know what she was looking for until she spotted them: onesies. All-in-one zip-up fleece suits with feet. Just like they'd all worn as babies. The designs ranged from pink with snowflakes to full-on penguin-style with a hood. The leopard-print one even had a tail. She felt as if she was going to expire with excitement as she stuffed them into her basket.

She could just see the scene on Christmas morning when she produced one for everybody. They'd be the most perfect lounging-about attire and would encourage the silly streak in all of them. The thought of her dad in the dog one with ears and a tail made her giggle. She could just imagine the photographs they'd end up with.

The girl at the cash desk was obviously over the humorous aspect of the onesies: Lainey was rather disappointed with her lack of chat as she scanned them.

Her phone rang in her handbag: 'Jules', the screen read.

'Good morning!' Lainey said.

'Hey, Lainz, you sound chirpy. What are you up to?'

'I'm in Dundrum, shopping.'

'No way! You've got the bug!'

'I think it's more necessity, but I'm doing well so far. How was the rest of your night?'

'It was good.' She sounded a little unsure.

'Go on.'

'Well, I met Anna and we got on really well, but nothing happened. Neither of us made a move and by four o'clock we'd called it a night. I was at the turning point where I could have ended up messy drunk or go home with my dignity intact.'

'Fair enough. Maybe you both need time to adjust to your new-found feelings before you make any big leaps?'

'That's true,' Jules agreed. 'But I can't help thinking that if she really was interested she'd be wanting to rip my clothes off. Does true love wait for the right moment?'

'Probably not in the movies, but this is real life. Maybe it's worth taking it slowly. You've been friends for a while so the next step probably needs to be nurtured a little.'

'Lainz, you're the best.' They said goodbye and hung up.

Lainey couldn't get Drake's comments out of her head. She knew she needed help on the fashion front but she'd never realised quite how androgynous she appeared to men.

She didn't want to spend Christmas moping, and the post-drinking fear had set in, so she went into Starbucks and treated herself to a hot drink. As she nibbled her brownie and dived into her gingerbread latte, complete with gingerbread-flavoured syrup, whipped cream and nutmeg, she knew things must be all right with the world.

Ten minutes later, she gathered up her bag of onesies and walked back out to the shops. She glanced up and saw that a whole floor seemed dedicated to hairdressing. An invisible force beckoned her towards it. She went to the lift and pressed the button. When the doors opened, she got in and rode up.

She went into the first salon she came to. 'I don't have an appointment, but is there any way you could fit me in now?' she asked a girl with bubble-gum pink hair.

'What did you want done?' she asked, chewing her pen as she consulted the computer screen with the schedules.

'I don't know.'

'Oh.' The girl looked up at her. 'Maggie's free. She's one of our top stylists and her next appointment just cancelled. Do you want to have a chat with her?'

She had Grandma's name, which Lainey took as a sign. 'I'd love to.'

The girl led her to a chair, and a moment later Maggie was with her. 'What do you have in mind?' she asked.

'If I tell you something, do you promise not to laugh at me?' Lainey asked.

'Sure.'

'I was out at drinks with some colleagues last night. One of them told me in a drunken moment that the entire office had assumed I was gay. They also think I'm manly. I know you're not a magician, and there's only so much you can do with a pair of scissors and curling tongs, but could you help me to look more like the person I know I am inside?'

'First off,' Maggie said, 'your man sounds like a prick. Second, you have the most amazing features and I know exactly what to do. Would you let my colleague shape your eyebrows too?'

'Go for it,' Lainey said. 'I'm all yours.'

It was a bit weird. One minute she'd been drinking a latte and the next she was giving her verdict on Maggie's handiwork.

'What do you think?'

'Wow,' Lainey whispered.

'You look stunning!' Maggie seemed thrilled by the transformation.

'That's gorgeous.' Pink Hair had sidled over. 'Isn't Maggie the business? She does my hair too.'

Lainey didn't say she was glad she hadn't known that before because if she had she wouldn't have let Maggie within an ass's roar of her head. Instead she agreed that she loved her new look. Her hair was curving onto the sides of her face in sharp, spiky points – almost elfin. The dark colour remained, but Maggie had put a deep purple rinse through it. 'It's so funky,' Maggie said now. 'This is soft wax, which I'd recommend you buy. It just keeps the pixie look happening throughout the day. Cara did a great job with your brows too. Are you pleased?'

'I really am,' Lainey said, awed. 'I had no idea I could look like this.' She had never envisaged herself as a funky pixie, but now that she'd become one, she couldn't help but like it. As she pulled on her leather biker jacket, Maggie wished her a happy Christmas.

She left the shopping centre, still clutching the onesies,

returned to her bike and roared towards her flat. She'd changed so much since this time last year, she marvelled. The timid and unsure girl who'd relied on Grandma for everything had gone. She was probably what the world would class as a late developer, but Lainey was starting to feel ready to make her mark on the world. Drake had actually done her a favour last night, she decided. He'd given her the final push she'd needed to kick-start the rest of her life.

Seth had undoubtedly left her a little tarnished, but now was her time to shine.

23

Step into Christmas

❄❄❄

Pippa was exhausted but happy. The police had been so kind to her since her ordeal with the taxi driver. They had reassured her that he was in no doubt that he must keep away from her and her apartment.

'I'm just terrified he'll turn up and really show me who's boss next time,' she'd said to the policeman.

'If he knows what's good for him he'll keep his temper and his fists to himself in future,' he'd told Pippa. 'He's a typical bully. Now that he's been taken to task for what he's done, he's changed his tune. If you'd seen the shock on his face when we cautioned him you'd understand. If you catch so much as a sniff of him coming near you, just call me.'

Now Pippa and Skye were having a cup of coffee at the kitchen table.

'I can't believe I'm almost addicted to coffee.' Skye giggled. 'I'd barely tasted it before you made me that espresso when we were putting the website together. It's like rocket fuel!'

Pippa grinned. 'I get the shakes if I drink too much of it. Look at this.' She slid a form towards Skye.

'Are you getting a new phone?' she asked.

'Yeah. I looked at my phone bill last night and I'm paying stupid money each month. If I switch to this, I'll get all sorts of benefits, like free texts.'

'Well done, Pippa. You're really getting yourself together.'

'For the first time ever, I'm living to a set budget.'

'Are you finding it awful?' Skye asked.

'Surprisingly not. Before, I just drifted from one thing to the next and flew by the seat of my pants. Now I know exactly what I have to spend and, more to the point, I'm fully aware of my outgoings. No more surprise phone calls from the bank, I hope.'

She couldn't believe the response she'd had to her website. Not only had she people clicking on it constantly but she'd sold fifteen of her framed sketches in less than a week.

'I can do you a deal if you buy fifty frames,' Echo had said when she'd gone to buy a few more after the initial purchase.

Knowing she might be getting herself into more debt, Pippa had gone for it anyway. And she had already made back half of the money she owed Lainey.

There was one person Pippa knew she needed to talk to.

'Hello.' The phone was answered on the third ring.

'Hi, Jay, it's me,' she said. She'd tried to sound chilled out and relaxed but failed.

'How's it going?' he asked, in a businesslike manner.

'I'd really appreciate it if you could meet me for a coffee,' she said, cutting to the chase.

'There's no point in dragging this out, Pippa. Why don't you just post the tickets to my office? That way I won't take up any of your time.'

'Jay, I'm really sorry about the way I behaved.' There. She'd said it. 'I'm not proud of myself and I know I was a complete bitch to you. I'd love to see you, if you can spare me the time.'

The silence that followed seemed to go on for ever.

'Jay, are you there?' she asked.

'Yup.' His voice still sounded tight but not quite as harsh as it had a few minutes before.

'Please?' she begged.

'I don't know, Pippa . . . It might be best to let sleeping dogs lie.'

'Tell you what,' she said, 'I'll be at the Tower pub at seven thirty this evening. If you feel like coming, I'd love to see you. If not, I'll post you the tickets and leave you alone.'

'Pippa ...'

'Just see how you feel later on. 'Bye.' She might have set herself up for a fall, but Pippa didn't care. She hoped Jay would come, but she would understand if he didn't want anything more to do with her.

The emails were coming through to her site steadily. Sadly, due to the recession most of the people were only buying small gifts or single pieces, meaning Pippa wasn't exactly in danger of becoming an overnight millionaire.

Still, Pippa knew she would need to put a lot more time and energy into her new venture before she could really reap the benefits. Most of her customers were Skye's contacts, so she had decided to draw her a special picture to say thank you, using the Chanel jacket from Boutique Belle as inspiration. Her strokes were deft yet confident as the image took shape. It was as if her fingers were actually creating the garment from scratch.

'Wow, Pippa,' Skye said, coming up behind her. 'I'll be

your first customer for one of those. I love it. Even the most alternative of us still harbour a longing for Chanel.'

'I'm glad you like it,' Pippa said. 'It's for you.'

'No way! Thanks a million! I love it – but other people will too, so you have to make some copies.'

'You're seriously business-minded for a hippie child,' Pippa said.

'Just because I don't care if my hair is perfect doesn't mean I expect money to fall out of the sky via carrier pigeon.'

'So it appears. I learn more from you every day.' Surveying the sketch, Pippa wondered if she should add more to it. Then, deciding its simplicity spoke volumes, she tore the page from the pad.

'I'm meeting Echo later for a bite to eat, so I'll take the picture and get some copies if you like,' Skye offered. 'Will we photograph it and put it up online right now?'

'Brilliant on all counts.'

Working together, they posted the picture on the site.

Once Skye had gone, Pippa went through her emails and came across one from a luxury department store. 'Holy God in the sky above!' A member of their PR team had investigated her site and, more to the point, her sketches. Could she call Briana at her leisure on this mobile-phone number?

'Hello – Briana? This is Pippa Craig.'

'That was quick! This is the type of enthusiasm we like to see.'

'I know I should probably pretend I'm too busy to see or speak to anyone and that my diary is full until June twelve months but I was stoked to see an email with House of Fashion attached to it!'

'I'm glad you know of us.'

'I'd love to be locked in there overnight some time so I could try everything on!'

Briana laughed. 'Would you like to come into the office on the top floor of our Grafton Street store for a chat?'

'Does the Pope wear a funny-shaped hat? I can be there in an hour.'

'No time like the present! See you then.'

Putting the phone down, Pippa dashed around the apartment and ended up back in the living room out of breath and wondering what the hell she needed to do next. She couldn't wait to tell someone her news, and Joey was a captive audience. 'Hey, dude, guess what's happened?' She blurted out the latest bulletin.

'That's so cool, Pippa,' he said. 'It sounds as if you're on the cusp of really exciting stuff.'

'I seriously hope so,' she said. 'For the first time in my life I feel like I could actually be heading down the right road. Scary monsters!'

'Good luck today and don't sign anything until you let me have a look first,' he said.

'I won't. One other thing – I called Jay and asked him to meet me this evening for a drink.'

'I thought you were so over him and he was a sap and you'd moved on and he was . . . How did you put it last week? I remember! "He's a complete lamer."'

'Ugh!' She cringed in shame. 'I know he probably hates my guts but I asked him to meet me tonight so I can give him his tickets back.'

'What tickets?'

'I don't want to tell you.'

'Pippa, what have you done now?' he said.

'Jay bought us tickets to the Seychelles and I threw them

back in his face. Well, not literally, because I still have them here. But he invited me and presented me with the holiday and I broke up with him.'

'Jesus, Pippa. What were you thinking?'

'It's really bad, isn't it?'

'Well, all I can say is, you've no right to slag Sophia off. I thought she was in the clear for Bitch of the Year, but you're a strong contender now.'

'Thanks,' she whispered.

'Sorry, that was mean. And I can hear that you've had second thoughts. But don't meet Jay and do the nicey-nicey thing now just to ease your conscience,' he warned. 'If you're really not interested, be honest.'

'I'm not even sure he's going to show up. Quite honestly, I wouldn't blame him if he didn't.'

'Me neither,' Joey agreed.

'Cheers. Thanks for the family support and all that.'

'Pippa, I've just been on the receiving end of having a girl I thought loved me do a drop-kick with my heart so I'm fresh out of sympathy for bitches right now.'

'And I'm starting to think Sophia should be made a saint,' Pippa snapped.

'Touchy!'

'I can *hear* you smiling, you horrible shit.'

'I'm bored! Give me a break!' Joey said. 'But all jokes aside, remember Grandma saying it's nice to be nice? It honestly is.'

'I know,' she admitted. 'I'll talk to you later.'

'Fair enough. Good luck with the interview and I hope Jay turns up. If he liked the uppity-cow version of you, he'll probably love the new improved Pippa.'

'Piss off,' she said good-naturedly as she hung up.

Going for a sleek all-black look, Pippa pulled on a pair

of no-fuss black cigarette trousers, teamed with a fine-knit Karen Millen sweater. The little bit of black and white spotty chiffon at the neck and sleeves gave it a lift without killing the corporate look. She added a well-fitting black blazer and felt presentable enough to face Briana. She really believed in her new business venture, but Pippa was under no illusions that it could take a long time to build up and make serious money – if ever.

She drove the short distance to the city centre, parked the car, then went into House of Fashion and up the escalators to the office floor. She forced herself not to look at the racks of exquisite, blingy, Christmas clothing as she pressed on up – she'd save that for later, when she could enjoy it.

She found Briana's door, took a deep breath, stood tall and knocked firmly.

A blonde, pencil-thin woman, with an elegant side-split bob and beautifully cut navy suit, answered the door.

'Briana?' Pippa asked.

'Yes, and you must be Pippa. You look like a Pippa.'

'At least you're polite enough not to say I look like I should be called Mike Tyson!'

'That does look sore. Poor you,' Briana said, wincing.

'I don't make a habit of getting myself involved in fights, for the record,' Pippa assured her. 'I was caught up in an unfortunate incident which wasn't my fault.'

'I hope you'll be okay.'

'I'll be fine, thank you. It was just a case of being in the wrong place at the wrong time,' Pippa said, brushing it off.

'Anyway, we're not here to discuss bruises,' Briana said brightly. 'We've much more pleasant things to talk about.'

'Fantastic,' Pippa said, relaxing visibly.'

'Come in. I'm delighted to meet you! I love what you're

doing with the online personal shopping, but the real reason I wanted to talk to you is this,' Briana said, swivelling her screen towards Pippa.

'That's my sketch!' she said.

'Yes, and as you can see, I've done a quick mock-up of the type of things we'd like you to produce in the future. We don't actually stock Chanel but I used your sketch as an example to show you what I would like to do with our own labels.'

'Seriously?'

'Totally.'

'Where do we go from here, then?' Pippa couldn't take her eyes off the image on screen, which showed her sketch of the Chanel jacket with the words 'Chanel collection' in black scrolling letters written across it.

'We'd like to commission you to do all our in-store and online signage. You'd have to see the collections so you could sketch an image of, say, a Louboutin shoe to front that section, or a Tiffany necklace, and so on.'

'OMG, this is amazing!' Pippa squealed. 'I know I'm meant to be all laidback and cool, and I should probably say that I need to consult my design team and talk to my lawyers and attempt to fit you in, but the team is me, I've never met a lawyer for so much as a cup of tea and I love-love-love the sound of this.'

'Do you know what? I believe you!' Briana joked. 'Obviously you're going to need a bit of advice now. You'll want to work out some figures so we can do a proper deal with you.'

'Sure.' She'd call Joey and pick his brains. Lainey was really good with the fine detail of business matters too.

'We have one immediate request,' Briana said. 'We work a year ahead of schedule and we want to invest in you to work on our store image for winter next year.'

'Right.'

'So we'd like to purchase the sketches you have left in order to keep our brand from being used by anyone else and also to keep it fresh.'

'I see,' Pippa said, thinking of Skye and Echo who were making copies right now of the Chanel drawing.

'I can see that the idea is putting a kybosh on your current business plan, and I appreciate that asking a person to stop selling a lucrative product a few days before Christmas is a tall order. So we'd be prepared to buy all the rest of your stock at the recommended retail price and give you an extra thousand euro on top.'

The voice in Pippa's head wanted her to leap across the desk, hug Briana and run around the office shaking her head like a rocker and wiggling her bum while clenching her fists and pretending to drive an imaginary wheel around in circles and shouting, 'Oh yeah, oh yeah, Pippa rules, oh yeah.'

Instead she remembered what Joey had said and nodded, wearing an expression she hoped was appropriate to a canny businesswoman.

'Do you want to think it over?' Briana asked.

'Yes. How about we meet again in a couple of days?'

'That's fine by me, Pippa. I'll be here until the doors shut late on Christmas Eve,' Briana said. 'You have a think, and I'll get a contract drawn up for you to look at. Here, I jotted a few notes on the kind of things we'll be covering. Cool? Thanks for coming and I look forward to speaking to you soon.'

It wasn't until Pippa was back in the underground car park, belted into her seat with the engine running, that she remembered she hadn't walked round the fashion floors.

No matter – she'd do it another day. She couldn't have concentrated on what she was looking at anyway. Her mind was whirling, and she could hardly breathe for excitement.

'Yee-haw!' She stamped her feet so much the brakelights came on and off at a rate of noughts. She hugged herself with delight. Then she pulled out her phone and called Joey. 'Who's with you?' she asked, hearing voices in the background.

'Mum and Dad, with yummy cake from Sadie. Hang on, and I'll put you on speakerphone,' he said.

'Hi, everyone!' Pippa shrilled.

'Hi, Pippa,' they chorused.

'Are you there to take Joey home?' she asked.

'Unfortunately not,' Joey said. 'I've to stay another night. The surgeon said my blood pressure is still a bit wonky so they want me to give it another twenty-four hours.'

'Sorry to hear that.'

'Yeah, it sucks,' he said, trying to be positive. 'Anyway, enough of that. Tell us what happened at the meeting.'

'It was so exciting!' she said. 'I feel like I'm going to explode.' She took a couple of deep breaths.

'Were they positive about your stuff?' Holly asked.

'They loved it, Mum!' Pippa said. 'I can't believe this is happening. I wanted to take stock of it all so I'm going back to see them in a couple of days, hopefully to sign a contract.'

'Well, first things first,' Joey instructed. 'Get Skye to fly straight to Echo's workplace and run off a few hundred copies of each picture.'

'If I'd zero conscience I would,' Pippa giggled, 'but I'm too worried that Fate would step in and I'd end up broke and destitute. I want to make a go of this. Joey, she had my drawing on her computer screen! It was just brilliant.'

'Good for you, sis.'

'Yes, well done, love, we're very proud of you,' Paddy added.

'Good girl yourself,' Holly said.

'I've to go back in and let them know if I'd like to work with them,' Pippa said. 'What do you think? I'd love to have this sewn up so I can relax over Christmas.'

'It sounds like a wonderful opportunity for you. As long as it's all contracted and above board,' Joey advised. 'Can you come in here for a few minutes and I'll go through some stuff with you? It'd be good to have an idea of what to look out for in the contract.'

'Are you sure you feel up to that?' she asked.

'Of course,' he said. 'I've nothing else to do, have I?'

'I'll come straight over. Will you still be there, Mum and Dad?'

'Sadly not, love,' Paddy said. 'We've to head back down to Wicklow. I've a guy coming to see about putting his horse in livery and we need to take all the opportunities we can get.'

'Sure I'll see you for Christmas anyway.'

'Off you go now, and concentrate on the road,' Holly instructed. 'And well done again, love. You're great.'

Pippa hung up and turned on the radio full blast, tapping the steering wheel in time to Katy Perry belting out 'Firework'. The sky was grey and gloomy, but Pippa didn't care. She was buzzing.

Her heart skipped as she thought of Jay. She hoped he wouldn't stand her up this evening. It would be the icing on the cake if he came, but right now she wanted to enjoy her success.

It was a full hour later by the time she made it into the hospital ward.

'Did you come via China?' Joey asked.

'It's mental out there. The weather's brutal so everyone's driving. The festive season is well and truly under way,' she said, helping herself to a corner of cake from the Tupperware box at Joey's bedside.

'Oi! That's mine,' he said.

'It's divine! I can't wait to get back to Huntersbrook and spend a few days gorging on Mum and Sadie's delights!'

'I'm really looking forward to it,' Joey agreed. 'I was dreading Christmas when I thought I'd have to go to the Canaries.'

'I can't think of anything I'd hate more than spending Christmas in a hotel in the heat.'

'It wasn't even a hotel. It was some hostel with a training camp attached.' He changed the subject, clearly wanting to avoid talking about anything that reminded him of Sophia. 'Show me the stuff Briana gave you.'

'Well there's not a massive amount to go on until I see the proposed contract but this is what they're thinking,' Pippa explained, as they read through the points Briana had typed up. 'I didn't give her much time to prepare anything. It all happened so quickly.'

'It's a whirlwind all right,' Joey said. 'But they've such a reputable name it'll be pretty cut and dried in many ways. Your drawings are your property, though, so it's just a question of negotiating the rest.'

'Maybe I sound like a complete lamer here, but I really liked Briana,' Pippa said.

'That's not lame. It's important you have a good gut feeling about her, and that the two of you hit it off. It's not easy to work with people you can't stand.'

'I love the whole concept and I'll be working with all the new clothing, footwear and jewellery collections. I want to puke when I think about it. It's so exciting.'

'It sounds like a job that was tailor-made for you,' he said, laughing.

At that point Joey's doctor appeared so Pippa had to calm down and sit quietly.

'If your blood pressure is still stable by mid-morning tomorrow, I'll be happy to let you out of here,' he said. 'Have you someone to mind you? Is this your girlfriend?' he asked, looking at Pippa.

'No, I'm his sister. But I'll gladly pour him glasses of wine and cut him pieces of cake over Christmas,' she said, flashing him a cheeky smile.

'That sounds very helpful.' The doctor chuckled.

He was very good-looking, Pippa thought, distinguished too. He'd be a fantastic husband, probably loaded. She'd never considered a medic. Maybe she should. As he left them, Pippa scraped her chair back to Joey's side. 'He's a bit of a dish, isn't he?' she said.

'I wasn't sizing him up, to be honest,' Joey said. 'I'm just grateful he was able to fix my leg.'

'What about the nurses? Any of them tickle your fancy? Now that you've rid yourself of the miserable stick insect, maybe you could date a few.'

'I'm not really on form right now,' Joey said, shaking his head. 'Pippa, you are something else.'

His dinner arrived.

'What's that supposed to be?' Pippa said, peering at it.

'Some sort of pie, I think,' Joey said. 'The cake'll do me. It's safer.'

'Yeah, and Sophia won't be telling you how many calories

per bite you're consuming. See? There are advantages to not having her breathing down your neck.'

'She really was very difficult in a lot of ways.'

'You'll be fine,' Pippa said. 'And now I have to go and see if I can sort out the mess I've made of my relationship. I'll be down to Huntersbrook in a couple of days. Skye's coming with me and Lainey's bringing Jules. She's very Barbie doll to look at. So, all in all, you're going to be surrounded by gorgeous women for the season of goodwill.'

'Lucky me!' Joey said, trying to inject cheer into his voice.

'I know you must be really pissed off at the moment. But you won't be crippled for ever and you'll find a much better woman in no time.'

'Pippa, you're a tonic,' he said, cracking a smile. 'You really believe in moving things along swiftly, don't you?'

'No point in wallowing like an old rhino in mud! You need to keep your sunny side up. Just think of yourself as evolving from a rhino to a unicorn.'

'A what?' he asked.

'I've always thought rhinos look like sad old shrunken unicorns. The ones that ate too many burgers and drank pints of Jameson whiskey, ruining their complexion and ending up in a dodgy mud slick instead of all shiny and gorgeous at the end of the rainbow.'

'Pippa!' Joey held up his good arm. 'You're gone in the head! Try not to say anything like this to Jay if you want him back.'

'Fair enough,' she said, as she kissed him on the cheek and skipped out.

24

Pipes of Peace

✳✳✳

Pippa was bricking it as she found a table. She was ten minutes early, a miracle in itself, and the pub was busy with groups of rowdy revellers practising their drinking skills. She ordered some sparkling water. Right at that moment she'd have preferred a large gin and tonic to steady her nerves, but the new improved Pippa felt it was better that she conducted this possible meeting sober. In any case, she'd gone off the idea of drinking herself under the table since the attack.

'Hi,' Jay's voice said above her, as she rooted in her handbag for her phone.

'Jay!' she said, overwhelmed with relief that he was there. 'Thanks for coming.' As she stood up to greet him and inhaled his familiar musky scent, she felt an urge to kiss him.

'Drink?' he asked, keeping his hands in his suit pockets.

'I've ordered one. And here it is.' A waitress had brought it over from the bar. 'Let me get you one,' she insisted. 'What'll you have?'

'Just another sparkling water,' he said to the waitress, and smiled.

Not knowing where to put herself, Pippa sat down and sipped her drink. 'How have you been?' she asked.

'Better than you, by the look of it,' he said, staring at her nose.

'Oh, yeah. That,' she said, suddenly embarrassed. 'I forgot you didn't know about it.'

'What happened?' he asked, full of concern.

As Pippa explained, Jay sat with his hands clasped, only moving when his drink was placed in front of him. Pippa paid the waitress before he could put his hand into his pocket for his wallet. 'It was my own fault,' she concluded. 'I deserved to be boxed really.'

Jay sat in silence for a moment, which felt like an hour. 'I can't work you out, Pippa,' he said finally. 'One minute you were lovely and fun and seemed really into me. Then it was like you'd had a lobotomy and your entire personality changed. Now you're back to being the girl I fell in love with,' he said. 'I know we were only together a few months but I honestly thought I'd hit the jackpot with you. Then you clearly wanted nothing more to do with me. Why the change of heart now?'

Pippa dropped her head into her hands. 'I'm such an idiot,' she said. 'I think I lost the run of myself. I went to New York and came back thinking I was some sort of superstar and that the world owed me a living. You were so lovely and I got overly cocky.'

'I just don't understand,' Jay said. 'You were great. If a little impulsive. But you suddenly became—'

'—a total bitch,' she finished for him. 'I know. I'm really sorry.'

As she looked up at Jay she felt butterflies in her tummy. She'd taken his returned love and affection for granted. She'd misused his care for her and somehow twisted it in her mind, deciding it was dull. 'I wish I could take back the horrible things I said to you,' she said. 'I thought I could do better than *us*. But I was wrong.'

Jay's eyes softened.

'I did what the proverb tells us not to.' She wrinkled her nose. 'I looked a gift horse in the mouth.'

In spite of himself, Jay burst out laughing. As she stood up and handed him the envelope with the tickets inside it, he put his hand on her arm.

'Neigh,' he said.

Raising an eyebrow, she walked around the low table that was separating them and into his arms. She wondered how she could have thought he wasn't worth having.

'Keep the tickets for the moment,' he said, after he had kissed her gently on the lips. 'Let's just rewind the story a little.'

'Okay?' she said.

'I didn't think I'd ever want to sit in the same room as you again, let alone kiss you,' he admitted. 'I was so angry and hurt. But you have a way of wriggling under my skin, Pippa.'

'Good.' She grinned.

'Eh, not so quick,' he said, placing his finger on her lips. 'I need to think this through. I don't know that I can trust you.'

'I'll wait. I'm getting good at doing stuff I never did before,' she said. 'I have Skye living with me now. I have a spending budget and I keep to it. I've even started a new company.'

Laughing, Jay shook his head in disbelief. 'I haven't seen you for a couple of weeks and more has happened to you in that time than it would to most people in a year.'

'I'm going to call a spade a spade here, Jay,' she said, taking a deep breath. 'I want you back. I know I've messed up big-time so the ball is in your court. I'll understand if you tell me to take a hike. But there you go.' She made a wide, sweeping gesture with her arms. 'My cards are on the table.'

'I hear you,' Jay said, smiling.

'Oh, and Joey fell down a hole and skulled himself,' she added.

'*What?*'

'He's properly gonzoed, poor fecker,' she said. 'He's made a total mess of himself.'

They chatted for another few minutes, then walked outside.

'Just give me a bit of time.' He tucked a strand of her hair behind her ear.

'You got it,' she said, stroking his cheek.

The drive home was surreal. Pippa glanced at the Christmas trees inside people's homes. The world was preparing to share magical moments with loved ones. She hoped so much that Jay would forgive her. She knew she was asking a lot, but time would tell if she'd get her wish.

Echo was at the apartment with Skye when Pippa got home.

'Hello there,' she said, surprised.

'Why are you looking at me like that?' he asked, smiling.

'Sorry. I guess I expected you to have dreadlocks, a woolly beard, and to dress in old flour sacks because of your name.'

'Apologies, but I'm more into dance music and shopping at TopMan,' Echo said.

'Please tell me you at least smoke weed and drink home-brewed beer from a chipped dirty mug,' she teased.

'Sorry,' he said.

'Ah, you're crap,' said Pippa, good-naturedly. 'Guess who I just saw?' she said to Skye.

'Santa Claus?'

'Almost. Jay.'

'Ooh.' Skye whistled. 'How did it go?'

'Good, I think. He's lovely, Skye,' Pippa moaned. 'He's gorgeous and cute and I just wanted to kiss him.'

'Sounds like a lucky fella,' Echo said.

'He's a dote, and genius here dumped him a few weeks back, figuring he was superfluous to requirements,' Skye told him.

'Urgh! Stop!' she said, yanking at her hair. 'I'm such a gobshite. But I grovelled and told him I want him back.'

'Fair play to you.' Skye looked pleasantly surprised. 'What did he say?'

'He's going to think it over. He'll have to go home and remove the pins from the voodoo Pippa doll and rethink his feelings towards me,' she said. 'He said I get under his skin, though.'

'Like scabies or in a good way?' Echo laughed.

'In a can't-live-without-me way, I hope.'

'I love the drawings you've made. They're seriously cool. Skye was telling me all about the website. Sounds like it's going pretty well already,' Echo said.

'Certainly is, thanks to both your help,' Pippa said. 'Skye, you won't believe what Briana's offered me.' She filled them in.

'Well, the good news is that I made twenty copies of the Chanel sketch. They're all framed and you've another twenty varied ones framed behind the sofa,' Skye said. 'So you can bring them in to Briana and change them into cash.'

'Fantastic!' Pippa said, clapping. 'This is like the grown-up version of bringing back the glass bottles to the local shop. Did you guys do that when you were kids?'

'We used to root through people's bins in the hope of finding a Lucozade bottle,' Skye said.

'Lainey, Joey and I would get the money and cash it in straight away for penny sweets,' Pippa said. 'Hopefully this version will generate a good bit more cash.'

'And you won't be spending it on sweets, I'm guessing,' Echo said.

'Did Skye tell you that you're both invited to my family home for Christmas dinner?' Pippa asked.

'We were just talking about it before you came back, and thanks for inviting me,' Echo said, 'but I'm going to stay put in my place with the lads.'

'If you change your mind, just come along, yeah?' She flung herself onto the sofa.

'Skye told me you were very laidback,' he said.

'That's me,' she replied. 'I'm in the chrysalis state at the moment.'

'You're what?' Skye laughed.

'You know the way a caterpillar goes into a chrysalis and evolves into a butterfly?' They nodded. 'Well, I'm going to emerge as a top businesswoman.'

She meant it. Pippa felt she was changing for the better. She was taking control and moving forward in making something of her life.

25

Walking in the Air

✳✳✳

It was 22 December. Each year on this date she and Paddy went to Dublin for a day of Christmas shopping. When the children were young it was traditionally on the eighth, which was a holy day. The schools were closed and the day off was the perfect opportunity to go to Grafton Street to look at the shops and see Santa Claus in Brown Thomas.

Since they'd grown up and moved out, though, Paddy and Holly had changed the date. 'If we leave it until nearer Christmas Day, we can pick up all the last-minute gifts and really get into the spirit of things,' Paddy had suggested.

This year Holly would have skipped the day out. They had more important things to spend their limited budget on. But Paddy had surprised her with his insistence that they honour the tradition.

'I know things are tight this year, love,' he said, 'but we don't have to spend a fortune. A day out, soaking up the Christmas atmosphere, will do us both the world of good.'

So Holly had reluctantly agreed.

'I'll run you guys to the city in the truck. Then you can have a nice meal with a few bevvies and really spoil yourselves,' Scott offered.

He dropped them at the top of Grafton Street, which was decorated with flashing lights at roof level. Each store was prettier than the last. With every theme exploited, from goblins to traditional fairytale characters, the pedestrian shopping street was a sea of glitter and Yuletide cheer.

'Isn't it lovely?' Holly said, clasping Paddy's hand. After all the years they'd been together, they still held hands when they walked out.

'It certainly is, love,' he said, kissing her. 'So many people tear off to New York to go shopping at this time of year but I never understood why.'

'Nor me,' Holly said. 'All that travelling and the time difference, not to mention the expense, when we have a wonderful setting right here. Thank you for insisting we come and do this today.'

'It would have been a terrible shame to miss out,' Paddy agreed.

The windows at Brown Thomas, the street's department store, didn't disappoint. The theme was *Alice in Wonderland*. 'Oh, Paddy, look! It's the Cheshire cat! Isn't it so clever how they've dressed him in men's designer clothing?'

'And Alice is looking rather more stylish than I've ever seen her before,' Paddy pointed out. 'I think she's sporting about a hundred grand's worth of Tiffany jewels, let alone the amazing dress.'

The next window depicted the Mad Hatter's Tea Party.

'Isn't this just incredible?' Holly said, almost pressing her face against the window so she could drink in every magical detail. 'The Dormouse is just beautiful with his soft fur, glittery little waistcoat and matching suit. He's even wearing Jimmy Choo shoes!'

'The March Hare appears to have stopped off at Ralph Lauren by the look of him.' Paddy grinned.

'And the lucky Mad Hatter has obviously got an in with Philip Treacy!' Holly said, in awe.

'If you say so, love. I thought I was doing well recognising Ralph Lauren but I don't know that Tracey girl.'

'Philip Treacy is one of the most famous living milliners. He's known for his outlandish and lavish designs,' Holly explained. 'He's Irish, too, which is fantastic. He clearly made the headpiece Alice is wearing too. That's called a fascinator. Isn't it divine? Look at the tiny feathers and the twinkly detail. It's just out of this world.'

Paddy smiled and made all the right noises as Holly took in every detail of the five large windows.

'Can you guess how many Swarovski crystals have been used to make up the midnight sky on that dark blue velvet?' Holly gasped at the final display.

'I couldn't even begin to try, my dear,' Paddy said. 'Will we venture inside and have a cup of something?'

'Yes, please.'

The traditionally dressed doorman greeted them politely, and a whoosh of warm air, mixed with exotic fragrances, welcomed them inside. A brass band, the musicians dressed in red, trimmed with fur, as old-fashioned toy soldiers, played festive music in a corner. Paddy and Holly made for the café where Holly ordered coffee and a slice of chocolate torte.

'I'll have a cappuccino and a taste of your cake,' Paddy said. 'Is there anything you really want to buy, or do you just want to soak up the atmosphere?' he asked.

'I've nothing I desperately need, actually,' she said. 'Why?'

'*Weeell,*' he looked delighted, 'I've a surprise for you.' He took an envelope from his inside pocket and handed it to her.

She opened it, and her eyes filled with tears. '*The Nutcracker*! Oh, how wonderful! But how can we afford treats like this?'

'I got a present of them from Mrs Nichols. Remember I rescued her little girl from the back field during the first hunt of the season? Well, she dropped these over to the house last week as a thank-you gift.'

As Paddy put his arm around her and hugged her, Holly knew again how lucky she was to have him. She'd been difficult to live with since her mum had left but Paddy hadn't complained.

'We have an hour to wander and then we can head down to the O₂,' he said.

Later, they sat enraptured by the Russian State Ballet. As the dancers, dressed as toys and mice in twinkling costumes, spun in front of her, Holly forgot her worries and was spellbound.

'That was one of the most beautiful things I've ever seen,' she said to Paddy as they made their way towards the exit. 'I'll have to call Mrs Nichols tomorrow and tell her what a wonderful time we had. People are very kind and generous, aren't they?'

Darkness had fallen, along with a soft blanket of snow. 'Paddy! How are we going to get home?'

'G'day!' Scott had appeared from nowhere. 'How was the dancing?'

'Wondrous,' Holly said. 'Enchanting.'

His jeep would cope easily with the snow on the way back to Huntersbrook House.

'It turns out Joey's been discharged,' Scott said. 'He called Huntersbrook and Sadie spoke to him.'

'Oh, shoot!' Holly said. 'We had our phones off for the performance. He must've been trying to call.'

'Sadie told him where you were, and we're going to pick him up now,' Scott said.

'Perfect,' Paddy said. 'You can give me a hand helping him into the jeep, Scott.'

By the time they reached the hospital Joey was dressed and waiting for them in a wheelchair.

'Hi, love,' Holly said, rushing to him and grabbing his bag. 'Have you packed everything?'

'It's cool, Mum,' he said. 'The nurses did it for me. I'm more than ready to get the hell out of here.' Scott and Joey chatted as Paddy pushed the wheelchair and Holly led the way, clucking and chatting away

When they were in the jeep, Paddy announced that he was starving. They'd had snacks at the theatre but nothing that Paddy would consider proper food.

'Would you like something, Joey? Or do you not eat takeaways any more?' Holly asked.

'Ooh, it's ages since I've had a Chinese. It borders on illegal in Sophia's books,' he quipped. 'I'm going to have the unhealthiest option of all – sweet and sour chicken balls with fried rice, please.'

'Coming right up!' Holly said. It must have been hard on Joey to split up with his girlfriend so close to Christmas, but she couldn't help thinking it had been the right move.

Paddy ran into the Chinese restaurant while Holly, Joey and Scott waited in the warmth of the jeep.

'Sadie has the fire lit so the house will be warm when you get home,' Scott assured them.

'I can't wait to have a proper night's sleep away from the noise of the hospital,' Joey said. 'The staff were amazing and they do their best, but it's like sleeping in a railway station.'

'Hopefully you'll start to feel more like your old self after a couple of days at home,' Holly said.

'I might ask you to run me up to Dublin to the apartment tomorrow, Scott,' Joey said. 'I need to make sure the gas is turned off and that kind of thing.'

'Sure, mate. Just give me a holler and we'll go any time.'

'Has Sophia moved out?' Holly asked.

'I'm not sure,' Joey said. 'That's the other reason I want to stick my head around the door.'

'Haven't you heard from her, then?' Holly asked.

'Not a dickie bird,' Joey said.

'Silly cow,' Scott said. 'I'll never get the way sheilas think. Sorry, Holly, you're a great girl, but in general women are a bloody mystery to me.'

Joey burst out laughing and for once Holly was silenced.

'Here we are,' Paddy said, as he hauled himself back into the jeep with the bags of food.

'There's a sight for sore eyes,' Joey said a short time later as they pulled up at Huntersbrook House.

'The twinkling lights and familiarity of home are always a good combination,' Holly said, smiling. 'Let's get you inside and we'll see if the fire is still going.'

When they went into the living room, they saw that Sadie had banked up the grate before she'd left. A flickering tangerine glow lit and warmed the space.

Holly grabbed plates and cutlery as Paddy opened the foil containers. Scott fetched bottles of beer for the men and a glass of white wine for Holly.

'Cheers,' Holly said with a smile. 'Welcome home, Joey love. You'll be right as rain again soon.'

'Cheers!' he said. 'It's great to be here, even though I can barely move.'

'Is it very frustrating?' Paddy asked, as they helped themselves to the food.

'I'm so doped up with painkillers that I haven't been as fed up as I might have been,' Joey said. 'And there's nothing wrong with my appetite. I'm not going to spend the next couple of months getting fat, but once in a while there's nothing wrong with a good feed like this.'

'Speaking of which,' Holly said, as she delved into the chicken in black bean sauce, 'we need to work out what food we'll need to tide us over the Christmas break.'

'Well, the turkey, ham and spiced beef are being delivered by local farmers tomorrow and on Christmas Eve. All that remains is the general grocery shop,' Paddy reminded her.

'I wouldn't mind getting that out of the way tomorrow,' Holly mused. 'The girls will be here on Christmas Eve with their guests and I want to be around then.'

'We'll go first thing in the morning,' Paddy promised.

As they chatted, the snow continued to fall.

'I hope everyone makes it home for Christmas,' Holly said worriedly, as she went to the window to look out.

'They will,' Paddy assured her. 'When has this house ever been quiet at Christmas?'

He was right. Huntersbrook House was *the* place to be at Christmas time.

Later Holly perched on the edge of the stool at her dressing-table. 'What are we going to do, Paddy?' She hadn't wanted to raise the subject, but she couldn't put it off any longer.

'I don't know, love. I've tried everything. None of the farmers are looking for extra land right now and the estate agents say nobody is buying it. The main problem in Wicklow, though, is that it's nearly impossible to get planning permission.'

'Unless we can think of some drastic way to raise some money we'll have to put Huntersbrook on the market in the new year,' Holly said. She had been praying for a miracle to dig them out of the debt that was swamping them. But now she was being forced to realise that Huntersbrook would have to be sold.

The wonderful day they'd shared, walking hand in hand down Grafton Street, followed by the magic of the ballet, seemed like a bittersweet dream. She wanted to curl into a ball and hide from the world.

Blue Christmas

❅❅❅

Dear Maggie

I'm worried about you. You didn't respond to my last email, which is very unlike you. I tried phoning that number you gave me when you left at first, but it doesn't seem to connect. Please send me a quick line or two to let me know you're okay.

Your faithful friend,

Sadie

As he lay back against his pillows Joey wondered how he'd reached such a low point in his life. He was delighted to be home but he missed Sophia. She was difficult, certainly, and his family had no time for her, but he'd really thought she loved him. It was an awful kick in the teeth to realise she could toss him aside so easily.

He was looking forward to seeing Pippa and Lainey and spending Christmas here at Huntersbrook but he couldn't shake the sadness he felt at losing Sophia. She hadn't so much as texted him since she'd stormed out of the hospital. Today was the day they had been due to fly out to the Canaries. Looking at his watch he figured she'd be boarding the plane to Lanzarote around now. He'd stupidly thought she might call him before she left. When his mobile phone pinged with a text his heart leaped. He glanced at the screen and was disappointed to see it was from Clive.

He threw the phone onto the bedside table without reading the message and tried to get comfortable. It was lovely to have a soft duvet rather than the scratchy hospital blankets, and the Wicklow silence engulfed him as he fell into a deep sleep.

The following morning the smell of bacon wafting from the kitchen woke him. As he struggled into the wheelchair, which was beside his bed, and made his way to the door, he cursed. Wheeling with one arm meant he did a lot of circling. It was exhausting.

His hair was already growing back where he'd been shaved for the stitches on his head but the plastered arm and leg, with the impressive black eye, made him look pretty scary.

'Oh, sweet Jesus, you have been in the wars,' Sadie said, blessing herself. 'How are you feeling today, pet?'

'I've been better, Sadie, but it's good to be home,' he said.

'Will I take you somewhere?' she asked.

'Not unless you want to accompany me to the toilet.'

'I'll leave you to it and see you for your breakfast,' she said, scuttling back to the safety of the kitchen.

By the time he'd had a makeshift shower in the small downstairs bathroom and dressed himself, he was starving.

'Good morning!' Holly greeted him. 'Just in time.' She

banged a plate of scrambled eggs, bacon and toast in front of him.

'Thanks, Mum,' he said. 'It's so good to be home. I can't imagine a time when I'll be too old to enjoy Huntersbrook. We're so lucky to have it.'

'Yes, indeed . . .'

Once breakfast was over Joey was wrecked again. Everything he did was tiring. It was beyond annoying. 'I'm such a useless git but I need to go and lie down again.'

'You just take it easy,' Holly fussed. 'It'll take time and patience to get yourself back on track, Joey.'

As he lay in the living room, studying the tree and its decorations, he admitted to himself that he'd been living on a knife edge for some time now. Sophia wasn't easy to be around. He knew he probably had tons of quirks and habits that bothered her but now he was away from her he felt as if he'd let go of a breath he'd been holding for ages. He hadn't been allowed to bring friends home after training because she cycled on her turbo-trainer in the living room. Burgers were as bad as heroin. And there was the constant questioning: how many kilometres had he cycled that day? How fast had he swum in his trials? There was no time for relaxing or, he suddenly realised, having fun. Sophia was always in competition mode.

'Dad and I are off to the supermarket,' Holly said, appearing in the living room. 'Scott has just arrived to take you to the flat now if you're up to it.'

'Great. Catch you later, Mum.' The sooner he got this out of the way the better. At least Scott was a bloke and wouldn't be asking him how he felt every five seconds, like his mother or one of his sisters. He'd go in, grab some stuff and get the hell out of there.

Scott helped him into the jeep and they zoomed back towards the city centre.

'Are you single?' Joey asked him.

'Yup. Had a girl back home but she couldn't decide whether or not she loved me so I made the decision for her,' he said matter-of-factly. 'I told her if she needed to think about it that deeply she couldn't care.'

'Right,' Joey said, impressed. 'No regrets?'

'Nah, mate. I reckon I'm better off on my own than with someone who sees me as a conundrum.'

Joey laughed. Scott had a point.

As Scott rolled him into the apartment, Joey could hardly believe his eyes. 'She's stripped the place bare!'

'It's looking pretty minimalist, all right,' Scott said, wandering into the bedroom. 'Did you have a mattress in here?'

'She's taken my pans,' Joey shouted from the kitchen. 'She doesn't even cook!'

'Lucky escape, mate. Better to pay in bedclothes and stuff and know where you stand, eh?'

At Joey's direction, Scott stuffed clothes and a few other things into a bag.

'Let's get the hell out of here,' Joey said, sighing deeply.

'You'll be good, mate,' Scott said, putting his hand on Joey's shoulder for a moment. 'You've got the best family back at Huntersbrook. That's what really matters. Anything or anyone else you pick up on the way is a bonus. But you've got some decent folk in your life.'

Scott flung the bag over his shoulder and pushed Joey to

the lift. By the time they were back in the car and driving towards Huntersbrook Joey felt a lot happier. Scott was right. He had so much to be thankful for. Sophia was welcome to all that stuff. No matter what she'd stolen, none of it would make her happy until she took a long, hard look at herself. He wasn't going to let her spoil his Christmas.

27

Have Yourself a Merry Little Christmas

✻✻✻

Even though she knew there was going to be a positive outcome from their meeting, Pippa's heart was pounding as she knocked on Briana's door.

'Pippa, come on in,' Briana said, looking hassled. 'Sorry it's so busy. I've been in the office less than an hour and I already want to go home. Please tell me you're here to cheer me up.'

'I hope so!' Pippa said. 'I'd like to think we could do some great business together.'

'Judging by the look on your face, you're as excited about this as I am.'

They arranged for a couple of the floor staff to help move the framed pictures from Pippa's car, and Briana paid for them as promised. 'I just love these,' she said, as she stacked them in her office. 'You have a great eye, Pippa, and I reckon this is the start of a very lucrative career for you.'

'I sincerely hope so,' Pippa said. Not only could she return Lainey's money but, more than that, she felt in control. 'Once I can see the key pieces from each collection and get a feel for the look and vibe each designer is aiming for I can start sketching.'

'We can give you an office here or you can work in your own space.'

'If I use my own space the money would need to reflect that,' Pippa said. Her heart was thumping and she felt rather ill, but Joey had insisted she charge for her services properly.

'If you don't demand respect from the word go you're on the slippery slope,' he'd explained. 'Don't be a pushover.'

Briana didn't seem fazed by what she'd said and agreed they'd have the contract drawn up and ready for approval straight after the Christmas break.

With the cash in her hand for the sketches, Pippa found it incredibly difficult to walk directly to her car and drive away without treating herself to a little something. A couple of months ago she'd have blown the whole lot on an evening dress or gorgeous pair of boots.

Hesitating for a moment, she remembered the ads she'd seen on television advertising the latest must-have high-end lip glosses. They came in several shades, but there was a special Christmas one with a shimmer through it. An invisible force attempted to drag her towards the escalator and the beauty hall section. She could buy one for Mum and Lainey. She reckoned Sadie had never owned anything like that either. She'd appreciate it if Pippa bought her one, surely.

She went as far as the counter. The huddle of excited

shoppers spurred her on. They were all chatting animatedly about what a wonderful product the lip gloss was.

'It's our best seller *ever*,' the über-glamorous woman behind the counter was saying.

'I'll take one of each colour,' a girl around Pippa's own age said, and pulled her wallet out of her Jimmy Choo handbag.

'Next, please,' another assistant called. Her and Pippa's eyes met. 'Yes? Can I help you?' she asked.

'I'd like some of the lip gloss, please,' Pippa said firmly.

'Sure, how many would you like? They come in five colours. Of course, the *pièce de résistance* is this one.' She held out a sampler of Christmas Bauble. 'It's the most divine red and contains real gold, providing a flattering and wonderful glow to the complexion,' she parroted.

'I'll have two of those and three others,' Pippa said, her voice shaky. 'This one, this one and that one.' She pointed to her chosen colours.

'Would you like me to gift-wrap them for you?' the woman asked.

'That'd be super,' Pippa said, feeling the familiar buzz that shopping gave her.

'I'll bind them in the cream and black House of Fashion logo paper, and would you like our traditional black ribbon or red for Christmas?'

'I can't decide,' Pippa said, getting flustered. 'Maybe some in red and some in black.'

'Perfect! I'll just take for those before I start wrapping. That'll be one hundred and seventy-five euro, please, madam.'

'Pardon?' Pippa said, as terror shot down her spine. 'How much?'

'One hundred and seventy five euro,' the woman said, without blinking. 'They're thirty-five euro each, madam.'

The Pippa of old would have justified the cost by thinking all sorts of things. It's Christmas, it's designer, it's worth it, I'm worth it, we're all worth it ... But the money she'd just earned and the pit she'd just dug herself out of had awoken in her the voice of reason.

'I'm terribly sorry to mess you about,' she said, with her heart thumping, 'but I didn't realise they were so dear. I can't actually afford them.'

'No problem,' the woman said politely. 'Would you like to take just one Christmas Bauble?'

Although she really, really wanted it, Pippa knew she didn't need it. She'd bought bright red lipstick in Duty Free on the way back from New York. 'I'd better not,' she said regretfully. As she walked away from the counter, stood on the escalator and headed towards her car, Pippa felt something she wasn't used to. She realised it was pride.

Smiling, she got into the car and started the engine. As well as the makeup adverts on television, she'd also seen one by a large supermarket chain. They had all sorts of offers on gifts. She knew the rule was to keep the presents small this year at home, but she still wanted to bring something fun.

A few minutes later she drove into the car park, grabbed a trolley and skipped inside the shop. Fair enough, the experience didn't match that of the House of Fashion – there were no assistants offering her squirts of expensive fragrances – but the music was certainly seasonal and her shopping wasn't going to cost her an arm and a leg.

She started the present-buying in the chocolate aisle. Selection boxes were practically free, so she tossed fifteen into her trolley. Then she made for the bathroom essentials area, thinking that hand cream or shower gel might go down well. Perhaps it was the contrast with the beauty counter, but none of the bottles looked great and they weren't that cheap either, so she stuck to the kiddie theme. To go with the selection boxes, she picked out her favourite family games: Twister, Buckaroo, Scrabble, Monopoly, Jenga, Operation, Ker-plunk and Guess Who? Two of each would cover everyone, including any extra visitors.

Done. That had been easy enough. Some clever person must've known she was coming because the shelf-stackers had thoughtfully left packets containing three rolls of festive paper, matching ribbon and Sellotape beside the till. She scooped up two and flung everything onto the conveyor belt.

Fantastic. She'd no idea why anyone got in a flap over gift shopping. She paid, packed her shopping back into the trolley, went to the car park and put it into the boot. It was sleeting quite heavily so she felt it wasn't worth schlepping across the car park to return the trolley for the sake of a euro coin.

'Merry Christmas to someone who's more diligent than I am,' she announced, as she fitted the trolley neatly between two neighbouring cars. For a brief moment she felt a stab of guilt. That was a whole euro she'd just wasted. Then she shrugged her shoulders. She didn't want to become *too* perfect.

The snow from the night before had melted slightly and the rapidly falling sleet made for treacherous driving conditions, but she was glad to be in her car and not at a bus stop.

Hailstones took over from the sleet as she turned into the car park at her apartment complex. She reversed as close to the main door as she could, propped the lift open with the piled-up games and proceeded to fire in the goodies.

Skye was out so she had the place to herself. She put on some music and set to work wrapping the things. She'd come up with a plan to wrap the games individually, then put them all into a black sack. The family and whoever turned up on Christmas morning could play lucky dip. That way she didn't need to label them or spend unnecessary time wondering who'd prefer Twister to Guess Who?

Then she turned on the gas fire and poured herself a glass of wine, kicked off her shoes and turned on the television.

The Wizard of Oz was just starting! Could today get any better? Drenched in nostalgia and red wine, she curled up and enjoyed every moment of the movie. Their tiny Christmas tree winked festively at her. The heart-warming tones of the Munchkins singing made her sigh in delight.

She hadn't intended to fall asleep, but the next thing she knew Skye was calling to her from the hallway.

'Hi, honey, I'm home!' Skye called, as she slammed the front door. 'God, it's seriously Baltic out there.'

'Well, it's warm and cosy in here,' Pippa said, stretching. 'I've had the best day,' she said, and told Skye all about Briana.

'That's amazing, Pippa,' said Skye. 'I'm delighted for you.'

The phone rang and Pippa answered chirpily. 'Hello, Santa's workshop!'

'Hello there!' Holly said, with a giggle. 'You sound like you're full of Christmas cheer, darling!'

'Oh, I am, Mum! I've had such a good day! I've seen Briana at House of Fashion . . .' She filled in her mother on the deal. 'So, new year, new start. I'm ready to make things work.'

'I'm so proud of you, love,' Holly said. 'I always knew you'd sort yourself out when you were ready. While I have you there, who are you bringing and when are you coming?'

'Definitely Skye and possibly Jay,' she said. She hadn't heard from him yet and was worried that he'd decided he didn't want to get back with her. She was trying not to think about it too much.

'Jay?' Holly said. 'Well, we'd all be thrilled to see him. But I thought you and he were finished?'

'We were. But that was then and this is now.' She sighed. 'I've asked him to think about getting back with me. I'll let you know when I know, okay?'

'All right, love,' Holly said, with a degree of resignation. 'I can't keep up with you kids and your love lives,' she said. 'I'm glad I'm old and married and your father's still here. I wouldn't have the energy for all this.'

''Bye, Mum.' Pippa rolled her eyes.

Pippa and Skye spent the rest of the evening playing Who Am I?, in which they each stuck a famous person's name to their forehead and asked questions to elicit information that would help them work out who they were. 'You can only answer yes or no to the questions!' Pippa instructed Skye, who had forgotten this rule.

When they went to bed, the snow was falling again.

'I'm really looking forward to Christmas now. It's going to be lovely to have a traditional day. It'll be a first for me,' Skye admitted. 'I usually end up at my parents' where they refuse to "conform" to the whole Christmas thing. Instead of being alternative, they're just killjoys,' she said.

'It'll be great craic,' Pippa assured her. 'If you enjoy it, maybe it'll be the first of many you'll spend at Huntersbrook.'

Pippa's phone lit up with a text. 'Oh, my God!' she said. 'It's Jay.'

28

Driving Home
for Christmas

❅❅❅

Lainey knew she wouldn't be able to fit much on the motorbike so she'd arranged for Jules to meet her at her apartment. It was Christmas Eve and not yet nine a.m. 'Try to make it to my place early so we can get there in good time,' she'd told her friend.

As Lainey's flat was slightly out of the way this was the first time Jules had been there. 'It's really nice, Lainz,' she said. She paused in front of a large photo on the wall. 'Is that Huntersbrook?'

'Yeah, Grandma gave it to me when I moved.' Her eyes misted. Grandma had called this area a real no man's land.

'The developers bought a field in the middle of nowhere and built on it without a thought about any community living,' Maggie had complained.

'It's on the motorway, Grandma,' Lainey had attempted to defend her choice.

'Precisely,' Grandma had snapped.

Recently Lainey had understood why her grandmother had been so against her living there. For years it had suited her to be within equal commuting distance of Huntersbrook and work, but since she'd started going out with Jules, she'd found her apartment a bit lonely. Maggie had been right: there was no community. It was anonymous. 'I'm having second thoughts about living here,' Lainey admitted now.

'Why?'

'It's soulless. I'd like to either move into the city or back towards the country. I need a proper identity, if that makes any sense?'

'Totally,' Jules said. 'It must get a bit lonely out here night after night.'

'It's probably the worst time to move, with a global recession when property's taken a nose dive, but maybe I could rent for a while.'

'Why don't you look into it after Christmas? New year, fresh start?'

Lainey picked up her bags and took them to Jules's car. The snow was falling steadily so they had decided it wasn't safe to take the motorbike. 'It'll be more fun to travel together anyway,' Jules said. 'Besides,' she laughed, 'I've no sense of direction so I'd probably end up in Belfast and miss Christmas altogether.'

As they set off along the motorway, Lainey asked, 'Have you spoken to your mum?'

'I called her before I collected you. She made it clear that her feelings towards me haven't changed.'

'I'm sorry.'

'Yeah, well, I've come to terms with it now,' Jules said. 'I can't make her accept me and I can't change to suit her. If she insists on being the way she is, then it's better that we stay apart.'

'That's harsh of her.'

'I have great friends and lots of people in my life who make me feel good. People who accept me for who I am. I don't need a negative influence pecking away at me all the time. It's like having a cancer eating away inside when she's around. Some times it's better to just leave people be. Keep away. Then we both have a chance to be happy.'

Lainey felt sad for Jules. Her mother should be protecting her and offering support when she was feeling vulnerable, not shunning her. She hoped her friend would enjoy Christmas at Huntersbrook. Her own relationship with Holly was sometimes fraught but she hoped that her mother would never push her away to the extent that Jules's mum had her daughter.

Soon they arrived at Huntersbrook and turned into the driveway. When the house came into view Jules stopped the car.

'Oh, my! What a gorgeous place. No wonder you're not happy living where you do. If I lived here I'd never want to go anywhere else.'

'I do love it,' Lainey said, 'but there comes a time when we all have to move on and do our own thing. I think they call it growing up.'

'That notion is highly overrated,' Jules said, moving off again.

As they parked at the front of the house the door opened and Paddy came out to greet them, followed by Jess and Millie, barking and wagging their tails.

'Hello there!' Paddy raised a hand.

'He's no idea who we are,' Lainey said. 'The older he gets, the more short-sighted he is. And he isn't wearing his glasses. Hi, Dad! It's me and Jules.'

'Ah, hello, love. I didn't recognise the car. I'm glad you're here now. The snow is coming down in sheets. I was a bit worried about you driving on the motorbike.'

'That's why we came together in Jules's car,' she explained.

'Well, it's very nice to meet you, love,' Paddy said, moving around to the driver's side of the car and holding out his arms. If Jules had thought of shaking his hand formally, he quickly dispelled that idea. 'I'm Paddy! Merry Christmas, and you're very welcome, pet.'

Welcome to Huntersbrook and a family who will accept you, Lainey thought.

'Come on in and meet Holly, Lainey's mum.' Paddy was clearly enjoying himself. 'We're delighted you're joining us for Christmas.'

'Thank you, Paddy. I'm a bit in awe here. You've such a gorgeous home,' Jules said. 'It's like visiting a Christmas card!'

Paddy roared laughing as he took the girls' bags and shepherded them inside. 'Oh, dear Lord, it's freezing out there. Come in and see the fantastic fire I have blazing in the living room. Holly, Lainey and Jules are here!' he shouted.

It was Sadie who appeared from the kitchen, clutching a dishcloth. 'Hello, pet,' she said to Lainey. 'Hello, and delighted to meet you.' She pumped Jules's hand.

'This,' Lainey said, with a grin, 'is Sadie. Huntersbrook would simply fall apart without her.' She flung her arms round Sadie and hugged her.

'Ah, I don't know about that . . .'

'Isn't all this beautiful?' Jules was taking in the decorations and twinkling lights.

'Holly loves Christmas and all the décor,' Paddy explained.

'What were you saying about me?' Holly asked, as she came down the stairs.

'Mum!' Lainey said. 'You look great!' Now that she knew about Jules's mother, Lainey had a strong urge to improve relations with her own.

'Thanks, Lainey. Hello, Jules,' Holly said. 'I'm Holly, and we're delighted to have you here with us.'

'Thank you.'

'Hello?' Joey's voice floated to them from the living room.

'Hi, Joey,' Lainey called, and ran in to see him, pulling Jules with her. 'How are you doing? This is Jules,' she said.

'Excuse the state of me,' he said.

'Lainey told me about your accident. How are you feeling?'

'Better than I did yesterday,' he said. 'I got back here last night. I'll soon be on the mend now, with Sadie's cooking and Mum and Dad spoiling me.'

'Sounds about right,' Lainey said, smiling.

'Well, if you have to be broken, I reckon you're in the right spot to get fixed,' Jules said.

'Never a truer word was spoken,' Joey said.

'Let's all have a cup of tea,' Sadie said. 'Have you girls had breakfast?'

'Yes, thanks,' Lainey said. 'I'll just show Jules her room.'

'I thought we'd put her in the pink back room. Is that okay?' Holly asked, as they went towards the stairs.

'Perfect.'

Upstairs in her room, Lainey felt like she was back in school with her best friend coming for a sleepover. It was a long time since she'd felt so excited about having someone to stay. There was a knock on her door and Jules appeared. 'Hiya,' she said. 'Can I come in?'

'Of course! Do you have everything you need?'

'Sure do. Your family are so lovely. Thanks for bringing me here.'

They went downstairs to sit by the fire with Joey and have a cup of tea. 'It's great to be here. Now we can just relax and kick back,' Lainey said. 'That was a long week. Work was just crazy. I know things close for a few days over Christmas but it's not as if we'll never open again.'

'I reckon it was one of the longest weeks I've ever had,' Joey said.

As they looked at him, wincing with pain, Lainey felt sorry for him. 'You win,' she said, grinning. 'Any news from Sophia?'

'Nah.'

'We don't have to talk about her if you don't want to,' Lainey said, 'but I didn't want you to think I don't care.'

'Always striving to do the right thing,' Joey teased her. 'Thanks for asking. I haven't had so much as a text from her.'

'Well, I've only recently come to this conclusion, but people who don't make us feel good about ourselves are usually not worth having in our lives,' Lainey said.

'Does that include Seth?' Joey asked, with a raised eyebrow.

'Especially Seth,' Lainey said. 'Did you ever like him, as a matter of interest?'

'No. I thought he was a dick,' Joey said. 'But I wasn't shagging him so I figured it was none of my concern.'

'Well, apply a similar logic to Sophia.'

'Except you might want to use a different epithet, seeing as she's a girl.' Jules grinned.

By ten o'clock Pippa was falling out of bed to find out why there was so much noise in the apartment. As she staggered out of her room she was met by Skye. She had Christmas music pumping from the iPod docking station and was hopping from one foot to the other.

'I was just about to wake you. The snow is starting to really lash down. I'm worried we mightn't make it if we don't get on the road soon.'

Pippa was yawning and stretching. 'I'll get my arse in gear. Are you moving to Wicklow for ever?' she asked, looking at the pile of bags.

'Have I too much stuff?' Skye looked momentarily nervous.

'Nah,' Pippa said, flicking the kettle on. 'We'll be grand. Oh, by the way,' she grinned wickedly, 'we need to stop off at Jay's to pick him up.'

'He's coming too?'

'He texted last night to say he was finished torturing me and that he wants us to get back together.'

'I'm so happy for you, Pippa. I always said he was a great guy.'

'Lucky you didn't tell me you thought he was a total shit and you were thrilled we'd split. It might have made things a little awkward in the car now!'

Knowing she was holding everyone up, Pippa threw some clothes into a bag, showered and dressed hurriedly. In the bathroom she pretty much swept her arm across her shelf and tipped all her stuff into a supermarket bag.

Moments later they were in the lift. 'I can't believe today is Christmas Eve!' Pippa said, doing a little jog on the spot as they rode down towards the car.

She stuffed all their bags and presents into the boot. 'It's lucky I drive an estate car, isn't it?' she remarked, as they rammed the door shut. 'It's going to be so nice to have space for the next while. You'll love the grounds at Huntersbrook, Skye,' she said, as they drove out of the car park and onto the snowy roads. 'Would you call Jay for me? I don't want to mess with my phone. The road's really slippery. Tell him we'll be outside in less than a minute and he's to come on out. Oh, I'm so excited!'

Seconds later Pippa was in his arms. As they stood kissing on the side of the road, she thanked her lucky stars she'd seen sense and begged for his forgiveness before it was too late.

'Hi, Skye,' he said, ruffling her hair as he slid into the back seat.

'Hi, Jay,' she said, smiling. 'Good to see you again.'

'I'm only really with her so I can have another Christmas at Huntersbrook,' he joked. 'Last year was amazing. Prepare to eat, drink and be very merry.'

They were soon at the start of the N11, hurtling along. 'Look at that!' Pippa said, as they travelled down the motorway. 'Welcome to Wicklow, folks, the garden of Ireland!'

The blizzard only added to the beauty of the scene as the Sugar Loaf Mountain and surrounding patchwork of fields came into view.

'Look at the huddles of sheep dotting the landscape!' Skye said. 'It's like a picture on a linen tea towel in Dublin airport!'

'You have the most left-of-centre way of looking at things.' Pippa chuckled.

It wasn't long before they were pulling in at the gate. The tree-lined avenue was serenely beautiful as the fat snowflakes fluttered down. As Huntersbrook House emerged through the trees, they all gasped.

'Mum's made an amazing job of the front door!' Pippa

squealed. Holly's wreath, complete with thick red velvet ribbon, was glistening with frost.

'Charles Dickens, eat your heart out,' Jay said.

The box hedges at the front of the house twinkled with tiny white lights, but the show-stopper was the holly-studded swag of ivy, with more twinkling lights and tiny red bows, that had been attached to the doorframe. The Georgian house looked enchanting.

Beeping the horn, Pippa pulled up and ran to embrace her parents, who had appeared on the steps.

Holly pulled her younger daughter into her arms and ushered them all, with their bags, into the warmth. 'I'll show you to your room, Skye. Come and have lunch, and after that we'll leave you to your own devices. For the record, the rules of this house are that there are no rules. Our home is your home and we're thrilled to have you all here.'

'Hello, Holly.' Jay bent down to kiss her.

'It's great to see you, Jay. I'm glad you two have sorted out your differences. It wouldn't have been the same without you this Christmas.'

'Thanks.'

'We need to keep up the male population in this place,' Paddy said. 'I'm delighted to have another able-bodied man on site!'

Skye tried not to do open-mouthed staring, but Huntersbrook House was quite simply magnificent. She couldn't stop herself exclaiming, 'Look at the tree!'

'I think I have a fellow Christmas enthusiast on my hands here,' Holly said.

'You bet!' Skye said.

'Do you want to see the other trees before I bring you to your room?'

'Others?'

Holly giggled. 'I feel like a teenager again, being able to show you my decorations.'

As they opened the dining-room door, Skye gasped. 'It's like a fairyland – look at the tiny birds! Even better than that, I think I must've arrived in heaven!'

'Now I'd better show you your room. It overlooks the front of the house,' Holly explained. 'Hope you like it!'

They went upstairs, and along a corridor. Holly opened a door and Skye rushed in, dropping her bags. Yellow and gold damask wallpaper was complemented by the golden carpet. A sleigh bed, with a toning patchwork quilt, made the room inviting and cosy. 'This is like a luxury hotel. Thanks a million for having me,' she said, turning to Pippa, Jay, Holly and Paddy, who were huddled at the doorway.

'Pleasure,' Holly said sincerely. 'There's tons of space in the big old wardrobe so do use it.'

'We'll let you get settled,' Paddy said.

'Sure!' Skye said. 'I'm warning you, though, you might never get rid of me. This is like a fairytale castle!'

'See you whenever. We're going to throw our stuff into my room. Come and visit!' Pippa said. 'I'm just across the landing. Mum and Dad are at the top of the house.'

'Should we wait until later when your parents are asleep?' Jay asked, as he pulled Pippa into his arms.

'God, no!' She giggled. 'They're off downstairs playing host. They won't miss us for a few minutes,' she said, and began to peel off his clothes. As they made love, she tried again to remember why she'd nearly let Jay go.

29

Santa Claus Is Coming to Town

❄❄❄

Holly wanted to press pause on the moment. This was what she'd waited for all year. Her entire family, except Maggie, were under one roof. Her children all enjoyed coming home so much that they'd even brought friends. She was flattered by that, but didn't take it for granted.

'Once they hit their teens they don't want to know you,' Mrs Lambert had told her many years ago. 'I thought we were close, but as soon as they could get away they did.'

Holly could still recall the panic that had flooded her at that moment. Her own children had been small, but the comment had stuck with her. Now here she was, many years later, still surrounded by her children.

There was a knock on the door.

'Hello, all. Hope I'm not disturbing you?' Scott said, taken aback by the group of women confronting him. They were sitting at the kitchen table, gossiping. The men had taken drinks to the living room and were probably involved in a conversation about rugby.

'Not at all,' Holly said, and introduced him to Skye and Jules.

'It's getting a bit messy out there. Snow must be hitting four feet by now,' he said. 'Pretty awesome, mind you. Back home Christmas means sun and barbies on the beach, so I'm really digging this version.'

'I can't imagine Christmas in the heat,' Pippa said.

'Me neither,' Lainey agreed. 'If our Joey hadn't fallen down that hole he might have been in the Canary Islands now with Sophia.'

'He'd a narrow escape,' Pippa said.

'Are there any men around this place at all?' Scott asked hopefully.

'They're in the living room,' Holly said. Looking relieved, Scott dashed out of the kitchen.

'God, he's good-looking, isn't he?' Jules said. 'Not my type, mind you,' she winked at Lainey, 'but he's very beautiful.'

'He's a nice fella too,' Holly said. When neither of her daughters commented she said it again, louder, 'He's a nice fella too.' Staring at Lainey, she waited for a reaction.

'No, thanks, Mum,' Lainey said. 'He's too lumberjack for me.'

'Oh,' Holly said. 'I'm not sure I know what that means but far be it from me to tell you what to do. You can pick your own men, I'm sure,' she said. 'Not that the last one was any great shakes.'

'Thanks,' Lainey said, crushed.

'Right, ladies,' Sadie said, moving towards them with a

large pot. 'Sorry to break up the party but I need the Aga to do a bit of cooking. The Christmas dinner won't make itself.'

'Many hands make light work,' Skye said. 'Why don't we all take a job and it'll be sorted in jig time? Besides, it'll make us feel like we're not just sponging.'

'Well, we have quite a bit to do before tomorrow so it would be lovely to have some help,' Holly admitted.

Lainey set to work chopping onions to soften in butter for the stuffing. 'Panda eyes!' Pippa shouted, as Lainey's mascara ran down her cheeks.

'Those onions are damn strong,' she said, dabbing her eyes. 'I'd better be careful or I'll chop my finger off while I'm doing the herbs. I know makeup's meant to enhance me and Jules has encouraged me to wear it more often, but it's a right pain when it streams down your face.'

'Would you two girls like to get the huge pot from the larder and we'll put the ham on to boil?' Sadie asked Pippa and Jules.

'Are we using cola?' Pippa asked.

'Sure are!' Holly laughed. 'That was the only way I could get Joey and Pippa to eat ham as little ones,' she explained to the group. 'They'd see me pouring in bottles of Coke and decide it simply had to be all right.'

'The spiced beef is ready to go, so we can put that on the other ring of the Aga,' Sadie instructed. 'I made pickled red cabbage last week and that's in the freezer along with the carrot and parsnip purée. I'll get it out now so it's thawed in time.'

'Can we skip the sprouts this year?' Lainey asked hopefully.

'No!' Paddy said, as he walked through the kitchen. 'I happen to love sprouts. Jay is giving me a hand stocking up the firewood and turf.'

'It's like Santa's workshop in here,' Holly told him. 'The girls are being amazing. I'll be ready for tomorrow in no time.'

'Good work, everyone!' Paddy said, as he and Jay headed out into the elements.

'Will I make some bread sauce?' Jules offered. 'It looks like porridge but it tastes delicious.'

'Thank you, love,' Holly said. 'Take one of my aprons off the back of the door. I don't want you ruining your outfit.'

Pippa switched the radio on and Christmas music added to the wonderful atmosphere.

Holly leaned against the worktop to watch Paddy and Jay chopping wood outside. The girls were joking behind her, and Sadie was clucking like a mother hen. Would this be their last time preparing Christmas dinner in this kitchen?

As tears threatened to trickle down her cheeks, Holly saw clearly for the first time that the gathering she was a part of was about the people, not the house. She would do anything in her power to hold on to Huntersbrook, but either way she'd still have her family.

When Paddy returned with Jay, both laden with logs and kindling, they were buzzing. 'We took the liberty of going up the back field in the tractor and it's absolutely calling for people to come and slide down it. There's enough snow for a good session. I've found the three toboggans in the shed,' Paddy said. 'Any takers?'

'Great idea,' Holly enthused. 'We'll be finished here in a few minutes. You might as well make the most of the snow while we have it.'

'But bags have the old oven tray,' Lainey called. 'It's by far the fastest.'

'I'll go in and get the men,' Paddy said. He returned moments later, with an ecstatic Scott and a pissed-off Joey. Holly's heart went out to her son.

'I'll have to sit it out.' Joey sighed.

'I'll stay with you,' Skye offered. 'I'm an awful scaredy-cat when it comes to toboggans.'

'You don't have to miss out on my account,' Joey said.

'I really don't mind.' She held his gaze.

'That's all sorted so,' Holly said. She hadn't missed the look that had passed between the pair. Skye was a lovely girl and fitted in with the family beautifully. Not wanting to be an interfering old woman, she decided to do her level best to keep her nose out of the situation.

The tobogganing party left in their outdoor gear, complete with pairs of Marigold rubber gloves at Holly's insistence. 'You'll thank me when your hands are dry – there's nothing better for snowball fights and tobogganing. Wear them over your usual gloves!'

'I had my day planned around the cooking and now it's all been done!' Holly said to Skye, Joey and Sadie as she came back into the kitchen. 'All that's left to do is set the table in the dining room.'

'We'll get that done in a jiffy,' Sadie said.

'I could make you a nice centrepiece, if you like,' Skye offered. 'One thing I learned from my hippie mother was how to arrange bits of bushes.'

'Thank you, Skye!' Holly was genuinely thrilled. 'I've two

stubby red pillar candles I was going to do something with. Maybe you could work them in.'

'Perfect,' Skye said. 'I'll go and pick some holly with berries.'

'I'll keep you company,' Joey said. 'I'm not much use to anyone, seeing as all I'm good for is sitting. But I'd love a breath of fresh air. Do you think you'd manage to push me? There's a decent holly bush just to the right of the back door.'

'You can show me where to go so I don't get lost.'

Holly wrapped Joey in a blanket, then helped Skye to push him out the back. 'Do you want to come into the dining room first and see the candles and their holders?' she asked Skye.

'She can see them later on,' Sadie interrupted, grabbing Holly's elbow and shoving her into the kitchen.

'Okay,' Holly gasped. 'What was all that about?' she asked Sadie, when Joey and Skye were out of earshot.

'Take the hint, for goodness' sake, woman!' Sadie hissed. 'Don't you feel the electricity between the two of them?'

Holly burst out laughing. 'For an old bird you're very intuitive when it comes to young love! And for your information I had noticed a little bit of a frisson there.'

'Then do the decent thing and make yourself scarce while the others are out of the way,' Sadie said.

They gathered the things they needed to set the table and went into the dining room.

'I can't believe it's Christmas Eve and I'm not running around like a blue-arsed fly, yet we've a house full of guests!' Holly mused.

'They're a lovely bunch of kids,' Sadie said. 'I'm glad that Sophia isn't here. Skye's a much nicer young one.'

The two women pulled the huge white linen cloth into place on the table, then found the good china and silverware.

'The crackers are pretty, Holly.' Sadie removed them, gold and red, from their boxes.

'I'm very pleased with them,' Holly agreed.

Taking advantage of the quiet, Sadie and Holly sat on the sofa and put their feet up for a while.

'Isn't this the life?' Sadie said. 'How many years have we prepared Christmas in this house?'

'I've never had Christmas anywhere else,' Holly said sadly.

'Isn't that a lucky thing to be able to say?' Sadie nodded to herself.

'I've never taken it for granted,' Holly said.

'I know you haven't. You love this place with all your heart, don't you?'

Holly jumped to her feet. 'If you'll excuse me for a minute, I'm going to root in those boxes upstairs. I bought Mrs Claus in the sales last year and she'd be lovely on the sideboard.'

'You do that, dear,' Sadie said, looking at her in mild surprise.

She was still worried by Maggie's silence. As Holly went upstairs, she walked to the kitchen and turned on the laptop. There was still no email from her old friend. She wondered whether or not she should say something to Holly but at that moment the tobogganing party reappeared and in the flurry she forgot about it.

'You should've seen Lainey,' Jules said. 'Talk about fearless.'

'Leave all that wet stuff at the door, please,' Sadie instructed. They did as they were told, then went upstairs to change into dry clothes. 'Where's Scott?'

'He was soaked so he's gone next door for a shower. Why?' Paddy asked.

'I was going to ask him to bring over the eggs from Jacob. He knows I'm sending someone over today so he should have them gathered for me.'

Lainey pulled her boots back on. 'I'll go.'

'Would you, love? That'd be great.'

'No bother,' Lainey said. 'I won't be long.' As she trudged across the field to the fence, Lainey felt relaxed and happy. The snow had stopped falling and the low winter sun was casting a bright glow over the pristine whiteness. Climbing the fence, she looked around. It was years since she'd been here. 'Hello?' she called. There was no response and no sign of Scott. She turned to go back when she heard footsteps.

'Hello?' said the man.

As he came into view, Lainey flushed. 'Hello, it's Lainey from next door.'

'Hi,' he said. 'Of all the people I thought I'd meet today you weren't one of them.'

'Ditto!' Lainey giggled. 'How are you doing?'

'A lot better than the last time we met,' he said. 'I'm Matt, by the way. Although I'm sure you know that.'

'I do now, but I didn't work it out in the bar that night after my office party,' Lainey said.

'Well, in fairness it must be twenty years since we've seen one another, and I wasn't in the best form considering the situation I was in,' Matt said.

'What happened with the awful wagon you were with?'

'I did as you suggested, left her bags outside the room. When I woke the next morning her stuff was gone and there was no sign of her.'

'Didn't she call you afterwards to apologise?'

'Nope,' he said. 'It was a fairly quick way to find out what sort of person she was. Really embarrassing, but that's about it.'

'Well, hopefully tomorrow will be a lot more fun. Yourself and your folks are coming to Huntersbrook for dinner, aren't you?' Lainey asked.

'So I heard,' he said, looking hesitant.

'Listen.' Lainey held her hands up. 'I promise I won't mention our first encounter. At least we've met properly now so the awkward moment is done with and we can move on to how-time-flies.'

'Thanks, Lainey,' he said, relaxing visibly. 'Your family are so kind to invite us. Dad's really glad to have a plan for tomorrow. Things have been awful with Mum. She's deteriorating so fast and it's really hard on him.'

'I can only begin to imagine. I'm so pleased you're coming over. I've a pal called Jules staying and my sister Pippa's brought her boyfriend and flatmate so we'll be a lively bunch.'

'Sounds great.'

'Oh, I almost forgot. I was sent for eggs,' she said.

'Hiya, Lainey,' Scott said, appearing from the house. 'What yah doing?'

'I'm here for the eggs for Sadie. The tobogganing was fun, wasn't it?'

'Brilliant!' Scott turned to Matt. 'You'll have to join us next time, mate.'

'I'd love to, but I'm a bit grounded with Mum. It must be ten years since I did anything like that. And now I'd better make sure she's all right. She's not having a great day.'

'Great to catch up,' Lainey said. 'Can you give me a hand with the eggs, Scott?'

'Sure. See you later, Matt.' Scott scaled the fence.

'Around two tomorrow, if that suits?' Lainey called to Matt.

'I'll look forward to it,' he said.

As they trudged through the snow Scott chatted, and although Lainey replied, she wasn't really listening. Her mind was on Matt and how her pulse had quickened at the sight of him. Now more than ever she couldn't wait for Christmas Day.

30

'Twas the Night Before Christmas ...

✳✳✳

Joey and Skye had picked plenty of holly and were in the shed putting the finishing touches to the table centrepiece. 'This is great,' Skye said, as she shoved the wheelchair towards the back door.

'Are you being sarcastic?' Joey asked. 'Sorry for making you push me around.'

'I'm glad to do it,' she said. 'I love being back in the country. I grew up with very few comforts and I don't miss that side of it. But I do love clear air.'

'Where exactly did you live?' Joey asked, as they reached the kitchen door.

'We were in a couple of places, but for the most part we were outside Kildare. Three families lived in a house the size of your kitchen, pretty much. Echo, he's my cousin, and I

335

were the only ones who wanted to get out. As soon as we finished school we came to Dublin.'

'Wow.'

'We were the only two who weren't home-schooled,' she said. 'We were allowed to attend an educate-together school where the rules were less stringent than they were in the usual religious-run institutions.'

'And how on earth did you end up in computers of all things?' Joey was intrigued.

'I guess it was the easiest way to rebel against what my parents wanted me to do,' she said.

'I wouldn't say you're the most confrontational person I've ever met, but you obviously knew your own mind from an early age and how to use it.'

'Yeah, and luckily my family were okay with it. My aunt Sue was my saviour, really. She understood that I needed to choose my own direction and supported me for a while.'

'Do you still have contact with your folks?' Joey asked.

'We see one another from time to time, but they live in their own little cocoon.'

'Fair enough.'

'They just do their thing and I do mine,' she said, shrugging.

'I can't imagine not being close to my family. We drive each other to distraction at times and, believe me, we used to kill each other as kids, but we're pretty tight.'

'Your family's amazing. I'd give anything to have what you guys share.'

'My accident really brought home to me what I have here,' Joey admitted. 'My ex-girlfriend Sophia hated coming here.'

'Why?' Skye was incredulous.

'I don't know,' Joey said. 'I never asked her. It was just

an awful unspoken tension between us. She avoided coming down here at all costs.'

'Didn't she get along with your parents?'

'I think everything from the actual house to the way my family do things was alien to her. She's a suburban girl who only likes triathlon and going out the odd time to poser-type bars.'

'She sounds like hard work,' Skye said. 'Sorry.' She blushed as she realised she was pulling a face.

'Don't sweat it.' Joey grinned. 'I'm sure Pippa's been giving out yards about her behind my back. She couldn't stand her!'

'No comment.' Skye winked and smiled.

By the time they bumped the wheelchair into the living room and everyone was in clean dry clothes, a sense of calm came over them all. The Craigs and their guests spent the rest of the afternoon together beside the fire, reading magazines, watching old movies and playing team Scrabble, which turned into a highly competitive loud version of the supposedly civilised game.

'"ZUKS" isn't a word, you two,' Skye said to team Lainey and Scott.

'Yes, it is,' Scott said seriously. 'It's an Aboriginal tribal name from the far outback of Australia.'

'You made that up because it's worth twenty-four points,' Jay remonstrated.

'Prove it,' Lainey said, staring him down.

'There's a children's mass in the village at five thirty,' Holly said, stretching. 'I was thinking of going, then buying fish and chips for supper. I thought we could eat them out of the packets at the fire.'

'God, that sounds good!' Joey said. 'I'll be the size of a space hopper by the time I get back to work, though.'

'It's Christmas,' Holly reminded him.

'Does anyone fancy going to mass, then? No pressure, but it might be nice. I'm going to tip along with Holly,' said Paddy.

'I'll come,' Lainey said. 'I feel like I'm going to take root here if I don't move.'

'Me too,' Jules said.

'Do you think you can fit me onto the trailer safely?' Joey worried.

'We'll pile up some bales to make you a snug seat. You'll be grand,' Paddy said.

In the end they all piled into the back of the tractor-trailer around Joey to keep him steady.

The local church was small, with a traditional crib at the top, complete with straw and live animals, in the shape of a cow chewing hay, two sheep and a donkey. A woman stood beside the donkey, holding his noseband, while he shook his head to show his distaste at being on display.

All the local children were gathered at the other side of the altar, eyes shining with anticipation. The highlight for the entire congregation had to be the donkey peeing. The children giggled and even the most pious adults cracked a smile.

'I've never been to church like that before,' Skye said, as they filed out.

'It's not usually that exciting,' Pippa told her. 'Usually you're sitting there, bored out of your mind, with a numb bottom and a crick in your neck.'

'Pippa, behave!' Paddy said. 'No danger of you running off to join the nuns, then?'

'That was seen as a fabulous thing to do when I was young,' Holly said, as they headed into the chipper. 'If you'd a boy going into the priesthood you were asked to tea and treated like a celebrity.'

'Sorry about that, Mum,' Joey said.

'Nine rounds of fish and chips, please,' Paddy ordered.

The usual row ensued where everyone insisted they were paying. 'You can all put your money away because it's paid for,' Holly said, accepting her change.

'Ah, Mum,' Lainey said. 'That was very sneaky, zipping in behind us while we were all busy arguing.'

The money discussion continued all the way home as they left a trail of steam and a whiff of vinegar in their wake.

When they got back to the house, the fire was smouldering in the living room so Paddy built it up with a few briquettes and some coal.

'Gather around, everyone, your plate is your lap,' Holly announced, as she came in with the food.

'And your leg is your napkin,' Joey added.

'No, we'll stretch to a festive napkin each, but only because I bought so many packets in Lidl we could cover every wall in the house with them,' Holly said. 'We're not getting all upmarket, mind you. You see, we have a tradition in this house,' she explained to the visitors. 'There's no washing up on Christmas Eve!'

In line with Holly's stipulation, Paddy produced bottles of beer and passed them round. 'We like a bit of style around here,' he said. 'Cheers, everyone! Happy Christmas Eve and thank you all for coming and cluttering up our living room.'

'Cheers!' They got to their feet, gathered around Joey and clinked bottles.

31

Merry Christmas, Everyone!

❄❄❄

As she pulled her case from the conveyor belt in Dublin airport, Maggie wondered how the family would react when they saw her. It was almost a year to the day since she'd left them. Dear Sadie had kept her in the picture. Most eloquently, too. But it wasn't the same as speaking to or seeing them.

She hoped they'd understand now why she'd had to go.

As she pulled her case into the arrivals area the row of taxis outside the door beckoned. She knew she could have asked Paddy to come, but it had seemed the wrong thing to do. She needed to arrive unannounced and hope for the best.

'Wicklow, please,' she said to the driver.

'Wicklow? In this snow?' He looked at her as if she were crazy.

The freezing temperature was shocking after Australia. So was the awful attitude. She moved to the next car and bent down to speak to the driver.

'You can't do that. I'm first in line so you have to talk to me,' said the rude man.

'I don't *have* to do anything,' Maggie shot back. 'You were obnoxious. This journey is going to cost me a lot. As you pointed out so helpfully, it's snowing so it's probably going to take a while too. I'd rather sit in a car with someone less cranky.'

The next man was delighted with the fare. 'I live fairly close to Wicklow myself so I'll drop you home and knock off for Christmas,' he said, taking her bag. 'I've the heating turned up in the cab so it'll keep you nice and warm.'

Maggie sank into the back seat and closed her eyes. In the next hour she'd be back at Huntersbrook. For the last few months she'd woken in the depths of the night and thought she was at home. She'd even put her feet on the floor several times expecting to make her way to the big old kitchen only to realise she was thousands of miles from her Aga and familiar things.

The emails from Sadie had kept her going. At least she knew they were all fine, if still cross with her.

When she'd heard about the farmers having to pull their sheep from the land, then about the dropping numbers at hunts and horses in the livery yard, she had been worried. But she had been sure that Holly and Paddy would find a way to keep things going.

When she'd heard that Pippa had been attacked by some maniac and Joey was lying smashed in a hospital bed, though, that had been it.

The taxi driver must've assumed she was suffering with

jetlag and thankfully left her alone. He flicked on the radio and hummed along as one Christmas song after another flooded the car.

When Chris Rea's gravelly voice began to croon 'Driving Home For Christmas', Maggie had to fight back tears: the song told the story of someone making their way back to the warmth of their loved ones.

She couldn't wait to see their faces.

As Huntersbrook came into view, her heart skipped a beat. There had been so many times over the past year when she'd wondered if she'd ever see this vista again.

Now that she was here she was overwhelmed with gratitude.

'Are you all right, love?' the driver asked, as he stood in the inky night air holding the door open.

'I'll be just fine now,' she said, with a shaky smile. 'Thank you.' She handed him a wad of cash, including a generous tip.

'Will I leave your bag on the doorstep?' he asked.

'Yes, please, and merry Christmas,' she said. She'd wait for him to leave before she went inside, she thought.

The red brake-lights had disappeared before she'd plucked up enough courage to go inside. She'd spent all her life here, except the past eleven and a half months. Yet she was wondering what the right thing to do might be. Should she ring the bell or turn the large brass knob and walk in? Unless Paddy had pulled across the top and bottom bolts inside, the door should be unlocked. Seeing the lights twinkling from the hall tree through the small glass panes on either side of the door, she realised they were all in the living room, gathered around the fire.

In the end her longing to see the faces she loved spurred

her on. She turned the handle and the door opened. The muffled sound of chatter and laughter hit her, along with the pine scent of the tree.

Leaving her suitcase against the wall, she walked stealthily towards the living room and opened the door.

'Merry Christmas, one and all,' she said, with as much conviction as she could muster.

32

O Holy Night!

❄❄❄

The silence in the room was deafening.

'Now I know how John Wayne must've felt every time he walked into the wrong saloon.'

'Mum!' Holly was on her feet and rushing to embrace her.

'Maggie.' Paddy had joined them.

Lainey, Joey and Pippa had frozen where they were. The guests looked from one face to another, not sure what to say or do.

'It's good to be home,' Maggie said simply. As she dabbed her eyes, she allowed Paddy to lead her to the chair he'd just vacated.

'There's a million things I want to ask you,' Holly whispered, as she dropped to the floor in front of Maggie's chair.

'I know, love,' she said, stroking her daughter's hair. 'It's wonderful to see you again, my darling girl.' Her smile was warm and lit up her thin features. 'Joey, you poor darling. What on earth have you done to yourself?' He was covered with plaster of Paris and sitting in a wheelchair.

'I could ask you the same thing,' Joey said, as tears slid down his cheeks. 'You look terrible.'

'Now I'm being insulted I know for sure that I'm home,' she said.

'Grandma, why didn't you tell us?' Lainey asked. Still unable to move from her spot on the sofa, she peered across the room at Maggie and the unquestionable side effects of rigorous chemotherapy.

Maggie was bald, pale and half the woman she'd been just a year previously.

'Why on earth didn't you tell us?' Lainey repeated, as she burst out crying.

'I had my reasons.'

'Mum, I can't believe you did this,' Holly said, sobbing now. 'Why did you keep us all in the dark? What made you think you needed to do it alone?'

'I did what felt right at the time,' Maggie said.

'But where have you been?' Pippa asked. 'Did you actually go to Australia or not?'

'Yes, I did. Sid was and still is a very welcome addition to my life.'

'Did you know you were ill when you left?' Holly asked.

'Yes, love. I found out just before Christmas last year. It was secondary stage ovarian cancer.' She sighed. 'The doctors were fairly positive about my prognosis.'

'So why didn't you let us know?' Holly asked again.

'I'd met Sid by then. I told him.' She smiled at the memory. 'He lost his wife to cancer many years ago and has been doing amazing fundraising work ever since. He knew of a wonderful hospital close to his vineyard and told me he'd arrange everything for my care.'

'But we would've done anything to help if you'd told us,' Holly whispered.

'I know, Holly. I know.'

'But you felt more comfortable about going through this with Sid?' Paddy threw her a lifeline.

'Yes,' she said. 'He was unfazed by the diagnosis. He understood what the doctors were saying with regard to the surgery and treatment. He made me feel safe.'

'Where is he now?' Pippa asked.

'In Oz. He'll come over at the end of January to see how I am.'

'Are you planning on going back?' Holly asked.

'I'll see,' Maggie said.

'Skye, Jay and Scott, we should all go and get some beers for everyone,' Jules said. 'I'm Lainey's friend, Jules,' she said, holding her hand out to Maggie. 'It's lovely to meet you but I reckon you all need some privacy for a while. We'll be in the kitchen,' she said.

'Mum, this is Skye, and this is Scott,' Holly introduced them. 'You remember Pippa's boyfriend Jay, don't you?'

'Of course I do,' Maggie said. 'Hello, everyone. I'm sorry for barging in and upsetting your lovely evening like this. It's not usually so dramatic at Huntersbrook on Christmas Eve,' she said, giggling through her tears.

'I think we might all need something a bit stronger than beer,' Paddy said. 'If we're really not allowed to do any washing up, I'll swig directly from the brandy bottle.'

'Beer would be good, I reckon,' Scott clambered to his feet.

'I recognise that accent,' Maggie said.

'Yeah. Sadie mentioned to me where you were and

I'm from down the road,' he said shyly. 'Well, a couple of thousand miles down the road. Anyway, come on, you two.' He, Skye, Jules and Jay left the room to get the drinks.

'What's the story with your chemotherapy now?' Lainey asked, unable to stop staring at her grandmother's bald head.

'I'm finished. It was a long haul. I did six months of chemo initially, followed by surgery.' She laughed. 'You'd think eighty-year-old ovaries would just lie there and be quiet, wouldn't you?' She rolled her eyes. 'Well, mine didn't so out they came. More chemo, followed by four months of radiation.'

'Oh, Mum,' Holly choked back fresh tears, 'I can't believe you've had such a hideous time. And I had the cheek to be here, seething over the notion that you'd left us all in the lurch.'

'What else were you expected to think?' she said evenly. 'I knew you'd be angry. I knew you'd all be hurt and cursing me. But I thought that was better than having you worrying.'

'Maggie, let me get you a drink,' Paddy said, suddenly realising she must be parched and starving after her journey.

'Do you know what I'd love?' she asked, as her eyes creased up at the corners. 'A lovely cup of Barry's tea and a Tayto-crisp sandwich.'

'Coming right up,' he said, and bent to kiss her cheek. 'It's so good to see you.'

'And you, my pet.'

As Paddy left the room, the others fired more questions her way.

Ten minutes later Maggie was exhausted. 'I feel like I'm on *Mastermind*,' she said. At that moment, Paddy came back into the room with a tray. 'Let me have my cup of tea – oh, Paddy, you diamond.' He passed her a plate with the Tayto sandwich. 'While I'm being fed and watered, tell me what's been going on. Starting with Mr Bashed-Up.' She gestured at Joey. 'It's like a soap opera around here.'

They did a little news round-up, then explained who the visitors were.

'We've the neighbours coming along tomorrow as well,' Holly said. 'So we'll have a full house.' Suddenly she was riven with sobs.

'What is it?' Maggie almost choked on her tea.

'This could well be our last Christmas at Huntersbrook.' She pulled a tissue out of her sleeve, wiped her eyes and blew her nose.

'*What?*' everyone said in unison, horror written across each face.

'This is a nightmare,' Joey said.

'What is it with this family?' Lainey had stood up, furious. 'Why have you all felt the need to keep secrets? Isn't love meant to be built on trust?'

'Lainey!' Holly was angry now too. 'Grandma deserves a little more respect and so do I.'

'Really, Mum?' Lainey was blazing. 'Respect has to be earned. I'm devastated Grandma didn't choose to share her illness with us.' She turned to Maggie. 'I know I'd never be Mum's first port of call for a confidante. I've learned to live with that. But I thought you and I were close.'

'We were. We are,' Maggie said, and began to cry. 'I didn't want to hurt you, love.'

'Well, you've made a complete bags of that,' Lainey said. 'Sorry, Grandma, but you have. Mum, you're worse. At least Grandma has the excuse of being on the other side of the world. You've been here and hiding the truth about our home from us all. We're adults! We had a right to know.'

'We all need to take a chill pill,' Pippa said. 'What's done is done. Grandma, I get why you went away.' She paced up and down. 'It was your way of coping and, hey, who are we to shoot you for that? Mum and Dad, we need to put our heads together as a family and try to figure out what we can do to save Huntersbrook.'

'There's not a lot we can do,' Paddy said. 'We own this place but the running costs are crippling us. The revenue from the farms and horses is dwindling – it just isn't enough to sustain us any longer. We thought we had another person coming with a horse for livery the other day, but it turns out we're too expensive. There just isn't the money around right now.'

'How much would you need?' Lainey asked.

'More than any of us has,' Paddy said.

'Not necessarily,' Joey said. 'In true Grandma logic, there's usually a reason why things happen. Now I know why I fell down that hole and smashed myself to bits!' He grinned. 'So I could earn the money to keep Huntersbrook.'

'What are you on about?' Pippa asked.

'I got a message from my boss the other night. A text I stupidly ignored. I was too busy wallowing in the fact that my ex-girlfriend is a heartless cow.'

'True, but what's that got to do with money?' Pippa asked.

'Clive's done a bit of delving on my behalf and now I have an amazing personal-injuries lawyer at my disposal. Clive took the liberty of contacting him on my behalf.'

'Go on,' Paddy said.

'They reckon I'm in line for a massive pay-out. It seems the council are wholly liable for what happened. They should've covered up the hole I fell into.'

'We couldn't take your money,' Holly said immediately. 'That kind of cash would set you up for life.'

'Maybe you won't need all of it,' Joey said. 'Besides, I could work something out. Perhaps I could buy part of this place or something,' he suggested.

'I need to sit down,' Holly said faintly.

There was so much to take in. Less than an hour ago they had been eating fish and chips with nothing but a fire to contemplate. Now they were trying to solve the problems of the world according to the Craig family in five minutes flat.

'I agree with your mother,' Paddy said gruffly. 'We're not taking your money.'

'Don't be so bloody stupid!' Pippa said. 'If Joey has a bag of cash and you need some to keep this place, then it's a no-brainer.'

'Precisely!' Lainey agreed. 'None of us would ever allow Huntersbrook to be sold unless there was no way of saving it.'

'It's not your problem,' Holly said, through gritted teeth.

'It's not just your problem any more either, Mum,' Joey said firmly. 'We Craigs stick together. You think you're stubborn? Well, I've got the stubborn streak coursing through my veins too, you know.'

'I've had it,' Maggie conceded. 'I'm going to have to hit the sack. Tomorrow is another day. A very special one at that. We can't fix everything this minute so I'd like to suggest we all try to enjoy tomorrow and take it from there.'

'I know it's easier said than done, but I agree with Maggie,' Paddy said. 'We have guests huddled like refugees in the kitchen, and the woes of the Craig family aren't going to be solved this evening. We should make the most of Christmas – especially now we're all together.'

'I agree,' Lainey said. 'If this is our last at Huntersbrook, so be it. None of us wants that, but seeing Grandma and looking around the room right now, the only thing we should be concentrating on is us.'

'I'll go with that,' Pippa said, standing up and hugging Maggie. 'I'll go and get our friends, if they haven't all fled back to Dublin!'

Maggie kissed her family and allowed Holly to bring her to her room.

'Sleep well, Mum. I'm so glad you're home,' Holly said. 'I won't bleat on at you, but I wish you'd told me.'

'I did what I thought was right,' Maggie answered.

'I know you did, Mum.'

'I need to sleep now, darling. I'm still low in energy and the journey has taken its toll on me.'

'All right,' Holly said. 'I'll just go and get your favourite hot-water bottle.'

Holly felt like she was dreaming as she found Maggie's cream hot-water bottle with the sheepskin cover and filled it. By the time she got back to her room Maggie had changed into her flannel nightdress and pulled on some bed socks. 'It's seriously cold in here,' she said, shivering.

'Sorry,' Holly apologised. 'I would've turned on the heating in here if I'd known.'

Maggie put her hand on her daughter's arm. 'It doesn't matter. Thank you for this,' she said, taking the bottle. 'Forgive me for going to bed but I need to.'

'Night, Mum.'

'Night, Holly.'

As she went downstairs, Holly was reeling. She could hardly believe everything that had just happened. How could she have been so selfish? She might've known Mum would never leave Huntersbrook without good reason. She'd been so caught up in her own anger and self-pity she'd forgotten to see the bigger picture.

As she walked into the living room Lainey was giving their guests some background to the evening's dramatic events. 'And she met Sid and suddenly she was gone ...'

'That's pretty heavy stuff, Lainz,' Jules said. 'It's really special for you all that she's back for Christmas.'

'Holly,' Skye began, 'we were just saying in the kitchen, things have changed for you guys. We have no problem with heading back to Dublin. Jules is welcome to join me.'

'Absolutely not!' Holly squawked. 'I'd die if you all left. You're so thoughtful to say that but we're delighted to have you here with us.'

'I still think we could do with a stiff drink,' Paddy said, and went to the old-fashioned drinks trolley. 'Who's for a whiskey or brandy – a Bailey's, even?' Looking at Holly, he winked. 'I'll go Greek and smash all the glasses when we're finished so you don't have any washing-up.'

'I'll have one or all of the above,' Joey said. 'What a crazy Christmas this has turned out to be.'

'I'll grab some ice from the freezer,' Lainey offered. As she left the room, Holly followed her.

In the kitchen, putting tumblers on a tray she wondered what she could say to her elder daughter. 'Lainey,' she began.

'What?'

'I know you're angry with me and Grandma. You explained that you hate secrets and I understand why you're so cross. But you said something earlier that really upset me,' Holly ventured.

'What was it?'

'You said you don't expect me to confide in you. I didn't realise you felt so disconnected from me.'

'Didn't you, Mum?' Lainey's eyes were flashing. 'I don't believe that for one second and neither do you. Face it, you've never acted the same way around me as you do with Joey and Pippa.'

There was a deathly silence as Holly squeezed her eyes shut in an effort not to cry. She cleared her throat. 'I was very unwell for a long time after you were born,' she began. 'I couldn't eat or sleep. I couldn't bond with you. I wanted to desperately. I loved you but I wasn't able to be your mother.'

'Why?' Lainey whispered. 'What did I do that was so awful?'

'Oh, honey, you didn't do anything,' Holly said. 'It was me. I had crippling post-natal depression. It wasn't spoken about back then. I thought I was evil. I felt I was being punished for some dreadful unknown crime I'd committed. It was the worst time of my life. Grandma took you under her wing. Don't get me wrong, I was so grateful that she was here and able to care for you, but as a result I lost you.'

'But you were fine after Joey and Pippa's births,' Lainey said doubtfully.

'It was five years before I could face the thought of another child. But when I was pregnant with your brother, my doctor realised what had happened and I received treatment.'

'I see,' Lainey said.

'I know this might be too little too late, but I'm sorry, Lainey. I'm sorry I never told you. I'm sorry I stood aside and wasn't there the way I should have been. I'm sorry you still feel different from the others. I'm sorry.'

As Holly dropped her head into her hands and cried, Lainey did something she couldn't ever remember doing before. She walked over to her mother, put her arms around her and held her tightly.

'This isn't exactly the way I'd planned on spending Christmas,' Holly said eventually.

'No, but isn't it good to get it all out?' Lainey asked.

'I suppose,' Holly managed.

'Mum, let's try to move on now. The barrier between us isn't made of stone.'

Holly felt a rush of love for her eldest child. Many would have deemed it thirty years late, but Holly vowed she was going to make up for the lost years.

33

Grandma Got Run Over by a Reindeer

❄❄❄

Maggie crawled into her old bed as Holly shut the door. Now that she was alone she allowed herself to wallow in the emotion she'd fought so hard to hold back. Tears flowed over the hot-water bottle in her arms. The familiarity of home was so comforting.

She sat up in bed and knew there was one person she needed to speak to. Reaching for the phone on her bedside table, she dialled the number.

'Sadie?' she said quietly.

'Maggie! Where are you, girl?'

'I'm home, Sadie.'

'Since when?' Sadie asked, and offered to come over to Huntersbrook there and then. When Maggie had convinced her not to risk it in the dark, Sadie proceeded to bombard her with questions.

Eventually Maggie said, 'Will we see you here tomorrow?'

'Of course.'

'That's good. But there's something you should know.' Maggie told her friend about her illness. 'I want to thank you, Sadie. You were the only one who accepted my decision and kept in touch regardless. Not for one second did you judge me or push me away.'

'Of course I wouldn't. Haven't we known one another too long for that?'

'That's not the point,' she continued. 'You didn't know why I left. All you knew was that I was trying to be happy. Not only were you pleased for me but you supported me and kept me in the loop.'

'Well, I was glad to do it, my friend, and now that I know what a time of it you were having, I'm all the more pleased.'

'Holly and the children are stunned by my surprise return,' Maggie explained. 'They're shattered about the cancer. But I know we'll get over it. I've no regrets about the way I did things. I'd do the same again if I'd the year over.'

'Why? They'd all have wanted to help. They'd have been on the phone every day and sending you more emails than you could reply to. You know that's true, don't you?'

'I do,' Maggie said softly. 'But I also know that if I'd told them I'd never have gone at all.'

'And you're glad you went,' Sadie said.

'Oh, yes. It was a hard year, but it was made as painless as possible by the warmth of the breeze, fine wine, and the love of a good man.'

'Will Sid come here to you or do you plan on heading back down under?'

'We haven't decided. Once you told me about Joey's accident, and I read between the lines that finances had become more strained for Holly and Paddy, I knew I needed to come back. Even for a while.'

They chatted for a little longer, then said goodnight.

Maggie sank down into the enveloping softness of her duvet. The last time she'd lain in this bed she'd wondered if she'd ever see it again. When she'd gone to Australia, she'd tried to convince herself that she would survive and return feeling well and rested. But there'd been no guarantee.

As she drifted into sleep, she had never felt so glad to be alive.

34

We Wish You
a Merry Christmas
✳✳✳

Pippa didn't care that she wasn't meant to be up at six in the morning. The fact that they were all adults didn't mean they had to be sensible, did it? If she'd learned anything from last night it was that time was precious.

'It's Christmas!' Pippa shouted, jumping on poor Jay. 'Get your lazy arse out of bed. Let's go!' She ran round the house, flinging open all the bedroom doors to make sure everyone was awake. 'There's not a minute to waste!'

Paddy and Holly emerged from their room on the top floor, tying the belts of their dressing-gowns.

'Bedheads, ahoy!' Pippa said, hugging them. Then she was hurtling down the stairs.

'How do you stick her?' Paddy chuckled to a bedraggled Jay.

'Come on, you,' Pippa said, bursting into Joey's room and tugging at him to get up. 'Into your chair and let's be having you.'

'This is crazy madness. Why have you woken us all at this hour?'

'It's Christmas!' she screeched into his face.

'I'll ease you all into the day with some coffee,' Holly announced to the bleary-eyed procession.

'I'll help,' Skye said, padding into the kitchen while the others gravitated towards the living room.

Pippa plugged in the tree lights and Paddy gave the fire a poke – it was still salvageable from the night before.

'Let's get some fresh logs on,' Jay said. 'I'm very into this cosy fire thing you have going on here, Paddy.'

'Morning, all! Merry Christmas!' Maggie had appeared. 'I'm glad to see that Pippa is still bossing everyone around.' She beamed at her granddaughter.

'Good morning, Mum!' Holly called, as she and Skye appeared with trays of coffee and bacon sandwiches.

'Morning, love. Merry Christmas.'

'Okay, you've to open my pressies first,' Lainey insisted.

'This is intriguing,' Holly said, feeling hers to try to guess what it was.

As each person opened a onesie the atmosphere lifted from half asleep to frenzied.

'Dad, you look gorgeous dressed as a Dalmatian!' Lainey laughed. 'Turn around and put your hood up!'

Jules was like a marshmallow in her pink snowflake version, while Holly and Skye made spontaneous miaows and moos as a marmalade cat and a Friesian cow respectively.

'I'm at a bit of a loss here,' Pippa said, looking mildly confused.

'Why?' Lainey wondered.

'What noise does a reindeer make?' she asked, as her furry antlers swung down and whacked her on the chin.

'You've got us there!' Jay said.

Joey's was a brown bear, which he couldn't model, so he passed it to Maggie. 'Grandma, do the honours, if you will,' he said.

'Gladly,' she said, pulling on the suit amid giggles.

Lainey had bought Jay a Santa suit, correctly guessing he and Pippa might be back together for Christmas. He decided to act out his role responsibly, scooping up a pile of presents from under the tree and sitting himself on an armchair.

Pippa's games and selection boxes went down a treat.

'We'll have a marathon after lunch!' Holly exclaimed. 'Once we've drunk too much they'll be great craic.'

Twenty minutes later there was a four-foot pile of wrapping paper and a sea of smiling faces.

'Just before you all get dressed,' Holly said, looking devious, 'I've a special pressie for each of you.' She produced a parcel for everyone in the room. She was dying to see how each member of the family would receive her gift.

'More clothes!' Pippa said. 'Fantastic.'

'Open it first,' Holly advised.

'Oh, my God, I've seen it all now!' Pippa giggled. 'What happened to his head? Is he melting?'

'They all look deranged!' Holly said, weak with laughter.

'Where on earth did you get them?' Lainey asked.

'Don't tell me! It was one of those crazy websites selling nostalgic stuff from the seventies, wasn't it?' Joey asked.

'No!' Holly said.

'I think you'd better explain!' Paddy said, laughing.

'I got into a conversation with Do Gooder Gloria. I had a bit of a defining moment and realised that I wanted to help with the local elderly people.'

'Don't try and blame this on Gloria,' Pippa said, wagging a finger at her mother.

'She said they wanted to knit and needed wool so I gave them enough to make each of you a sweater and more. Gloria told me she already had patterns. I thought I was helping and that I had the answer to my Christmas-gift quandary. They made me twenty,' Holly said.

'Twenty?' Pippa yelled.

'There were lots of elderly folk involved and most of them practically knit in their sleep, they love it so much. The idea was a roaring success so they made loads.'

'So there are more?' Joey asked.

''Fraid so,' Holly said, still shaking with laughter, 'and each one is worse than the last.'

'Well, it's good wool,' Maggie said, stifling a giggle. 'I could easily unravel them and re-knit them into something we could actually wear in public.'

'Great minds think alike, Mum,' Holly said.

Lainey had to lie on the rug she laughed so much when she opened hers. It was fire-engine red with what should have been Santa Claus on the front but he had three eyes and no beard.

'Do we have to wear these?' Pippa asked, once she could speak again.

'Yes, you do!' Holly said, trying to look fierce.

'I'm *so* glad I broke my arm now,' Joey chortled.

'Tell you what, if you all put them on for a group photo I'll allow you to take them off afterwards,' Holly said, compromising. 'And you don't get away with it that easily,' she told Joey. 'I'll pull one over your head and you can improvise for the duration of the picture.'

'Deal,' they all agreed.

At this point Sadie arrived and made a dash for Maggie.

'Give me a look at you . . . Holy God, you look shocking,' she said, tutting.

'Thanks, Sadie,' Maggie said. 'You're looking older too.'

'Ah, go on out of that,' she said, swiping Maggie's arm. 'Would you not wear a wig or something until you've more hair? I'd say you're frozen back here in the snow with nothing but a few wisps dusted around your head.'

'The wig was so itchy in the heat I gave up,' Maggie explained. 'But I must say I'm freezing now.'

'This was meant for Holly but I'm sure she won't mind you using it for a while,' Sadie said, as she handed a wrapped gift to Maggie.

They all giggled when she opened a tea-cosy in the shape of a Christmas pudding.

'It actually looks like a pudding too,' Lainey pointed out. 'It's really good. Fabulous stitchwork and detail.'

'It's great the way the person managed such definition between colours,' Joey said.

'Have you all gone mad?' Sadie expostulated. 'When have any of you lot had the least bit of interest in knitting?'

'We hadn't,' Joey started to laugh. 'Until we got our presents from Mum this morning.'

As they held up their sweaters, Sadie had to grip the sideboard for fear she'd fall over, she was laughing so hard. 'They're priceless,' she managed finally, dabbing at her eyes.

'Here is yours,' Holly said, presenting Sadie with a parcel. It was meant to be a pudding too.

'Who gave the poor old dear blue wool to knit a pudding? It looks mouldy.' Sadie giggled. She pulled it on and stood beside Maggie, who was now wearing the tea-cosy.

'Take a photo!' Maggie commanded.

Four of the group produced iPhones and snapped.

Operation Christmas lunch took effect. With all hands on deck, things happened quickly. Sadie was in control, issuing instructions. 'Lainey, stuff the turkey, baste it and put it in the oven. Pippa, peel the sprouts and put them in the pot. Holly, you and I can do the spuds and leave them in water ready to boil. Paddy, can you carve the cooked ham and spiced beef onto platters?'

There was a knock at the back door and Scott came in.

'Hey, Scott,' they all chorused. 'Merry Christmas.'

'Many happy returns, folks. I've a few pressies here for you,' he said. 'Ah, hi there, Mrs Pudding,' he said to Maggie, who still had on the tea-cosy.

'What did I tell you?' Sadie whispered. 'Gorgeous or what?'

'You weren't lying,' Maggie agreed. 'Nothing wrong with him.'

'We thought you might like this,' Paddy said, handing him an Irish rugby jersey.

'Cool! Thanks, guys,' he said, pulling off his top and tugging the jersey over his head.

'And here's a special gift I got for you,' Holly said.

'Aw, cheers, Holly, I'm made up. Thanks so much. All you guys have been so good to me. I'm having the best time in Ireland,' he said.

'I'm glad, and you're so welcome,' Holly said, struggling to keep a straight face.

When he opened his sweater, they all shrieked with laughter again. It was supposed to be a reindeer but the resemblance was slight.

'Eh, thanks, Holly,' he said, biting his lip. He snorted, and burst out laughing.

Pippa pulled hers out from behind her back and the others showed him theirs.

'I reckon you could put those on your website next year, Pippa, and make a fortune.' Scott lapsed into more helpless laughter.

'Good plan,' she said. 'Jumpers you wish your gran had never made but were too polite not to wear!'

Feeling underdressed, Scott put on his army-patterned onesie.

'Now I feel like I fit in.'

'I'm waiting for the men in white coats to come and put me out of my misery,' Paddy said.

By the time they'd all dragged themselves upstairs, had showers, dressed in normal clothing and reconvened, it was after midday.

'Where does the time go?' Holly said. 'I want to make today last for ever.'

'I don't think I could cope every day with the madness that takes over this family at Christmas,' Paddy said, feigning alarm.

'Isn't it great?' Holly giggled. 'Now, the turkey went into the oven just after eight, so we should be ready to sit down to eat at three.'

'Well, I've just had half my selection box,' Joey said.

'That's not very triathlon man of you,' Pippa teased.

'I'll get back to the training once my body heals,' he vowed. 'But for now I'm having everything that's put in front of me.'

Cynthia, Jacob and Matt arrived at two, laden with bottles of wine and champagne.

'Come on in,' Holly and Paddy greeted them at the front door. 'We're delighted to see you all.'

The rest of the household joined them around the blazing fire in the hall.

Maggie was delighted to see her neighbours and made no apologies for wearing a smart dress with a tea-cosy on her head. If they thought it was odd they did a good job of hiding the fact.

🎄🎄🎄

'Happy Christmas,' Matt said, handing Lainey a small gift discreetly.

'Thank you, Matt,' she said, blushing furiously. 'I didn't get you anything. Now I'm mortified.'

'It's only a tiny thing,' he said, smiling.

Lainey opened the red box and found a little silver charm bracelet.

'You were so friendly to me on that awful night, and when we met yesterday, you still didn't make me feel like a fool. So I wanted to get you a small gift,' he said. 'I found it in the chemist in the village so if you hate it you can always change it for some Sudocrem or a packet of plasters.'

'No, I think I prefer this.' As she leaned up to kiss his cheek she noticed the musky freshness of his cologne. 'You smell nice,' she said, without thinking.

'Thanks. I bought it while I was in the chemist. I did all my Christmas shopping in there. It took almost twenty minutes.'

'Well, mine took even less. I bought everyone the same thing. I'm not the best shopper you've ever met.'

'Are you delighted to have your grandma home?' he asked, looking at Maggie, who was chatting to his mother. 'I didn't realise she'd been sick.'

'None of us did. She didn't tell us. Then she surprised us by arriving home unexpectedly last night.'

'Will she be okay?'

'So she says. I wish she'd told me. I thought we were close. I can't help feeling she shut me out. It hurts.'

'I can understand where you're coming from, of course,' Matt said, 'but the other side of the coin is that she probably kept quiet because she loves you so much.'

'That's what she said.'

'Well, I've never been close to my parents. When my father phoned, told me Mum was getting worse and more or less summoned me home, I can't say I was delighted. In fact, I was pretty angry at first.' Matt looked at the floor and took a swig of his bottle of beer.

'How do you feel now?' she asked.

'I'm beginning to settle in. But it's not my choice to be here, Lainey. I had a life in the UK. But I knew I'd never forgive myself if I didn't come home when Dad asked me to. What could I do?' He shrugged his shoulders. 'I should shut up. We've barely seen one another over the last twenty years and now it seems every time I meet you I pour my heart out to you. You must think I'm a right weirdo.'

'Not at all. I'm doing the same thing to you,' she pointed out. 'Maybe it's a good thing that we can chat.'

Lainey considered what Matt had told her. She'd been so busy being angry with Grandma that it was hard to change her perspective. She gazed at Cynthia, perched uncomfortably on the arm of a chair, rocking back and forth, unable to join in with much conversation, and her heart went out to her. Jacob looked older and thinner, and she suspected there was very little joy to be had in their home.

Then she looked at Maggie, with the knitted pudding on her head. She was animated, chatting to Mum.

Lainey knew there and then that her grandmother hadn't let her down. She hadn't shunned her or tried to run away. She'd done the least selfish thing of all. She'd spared them the grief of the past year.

'I don't blame my father for asking me to come home,' Matt said, interrupting her thoughts. 'There was no way he could've coped alone. But the time is coming when Mum will have to go into a home. Then I'll decide whether or not to stick around here.'

'Do you think you might?' Lainey said, sounding substantially more hopeful than she'd intended. 'Eh, I mean, it would be great if you did. I'm always around at weekends. I'm actually thinking of moving back in this direction. I hate my apartment.'

'I'll see how things go for the next couple of months.' He held her gaze.

'Can I get you another beer?' she asked.

'That'd be lovely.'

Holly and Sadie ushered them into the dining room, Cynthia shadowed by Jess; she seemed to have found solace in stroking her coat.

'Is the dog allowed in the dining room?' Jacob asked.

'Not usually, but we'll make an exception,' Paddy said.

When they had sat down, Paddy stood up and pinged his glass with a teaspoon to command silence. 'Welcome to family and friends, new and old,' he began. 'We're so delighted to have our beloved Maggie back in our midst.

It's great to have our children too, even if Joey is about as much use as an ashtray on a motorbike.' They all laughed. 'Thankfully, Pippa's boyfriend Jay came along again this year – I'd never have got the wood chopped without him,' he said. 'Jules is a delightful addition to our table and most welcome. As for Skye, you've encouraged my other daughter to stop shopping and make other people pay her for the privilege, so you're most welcome too!' He coughed. 'Jacob, Cynthia, Scott and Matt, we're thrilled to have you with us. Last, and by no means least, Sadie. She's kept our family together in more ways than one this past year and we'd be lost without her. Please raise your glasses and join me in a toast! Merry Christmas, all!'

'Merry Christmas, all!' they chorused in response.

'Let's do a tag-team effort so,' Pippa said. 'All cross your arms at chest height and hold your cracker to the right! With both hands, we all pull on the count of three,' she said.

'What about me?' Joey said. 'That's discrimination!'

'I'll help you,' Skye said, and leaned across him.

'One … two … three!'

They pulled their crackers and the popping and banging was mighty as they tried not to fall off their chairs. Then they put on their paper hats and read out the jokes.

By the time they'd cleared the soup bowls and put the platters of meat into the middle of the table, with the bowls of vegetables, Holly's sides ached with laughing. 'I'm letting you all help yourselves,' she said. 'Don't be shy or you'll starve! Dig in, folks!'

Skye picked up Joey's plate. 'Shall I do yours?'

'Thanks a million,' he said gratefully.

'No problem. Will I cut it up for you?'

'Would you mind?' he said.

'Not at all. This should help too.' She stood up and tied his napkin around his neck. 'Seeing as I've no bib it'll have to do.'

Joey wondered why he'd only just noticed how pretty Skye was.

The eating and drinking lasted well into the early evening as they shared stories of Christmases past. Holly and Paddy, at opposite ends of the big table, caught each other's eye from time to time and shared unspoken delight in having their family around them.

Skye topped up Joey's glass from time to time, exchanging with him secret smiles.

'My mother wasn't big on Christmas so I was never that excited about it,' Jules said matter-of-factly. 'As it stands, we're not speaking.'

'I'm sorry to hear that, sweetheart,' Holly said, taking her hand. 'You're welcome here any time, isn't she, Paddy?'

'She certainly is,' he agreed readily. 'We know how lucky we are to have all our children here today. The fact that you still want to be with us is amazing and wonderful.'

'Not only do we want to come but we've brought extras,' Lainey said. 'We're the lucky ones, Dad.'

Maggie and Sadie had snuck off into the kitchen together and now reappeared with the pudding. 'Jay and Scott are in charge of setting it alight,' Maggie said.

'Take it easy, guys. It's Christmas, not Hallowe'en,' Joey teased, as the brandy burst into purple flames.

'You're just jealous because you can't move your arm,' Lainey told him.

'I'm so full but I'm going to stuff a massive helping of that down my gullet,' Joey said. 'It's a good thing Sophia isn't here.'

'I agree,' Skye whispered.

They spent the evening playing Twister, then Buckaroo, which Holly claimed was going to give her heart failure if they didn't stop. 'I know it's meant to be fun, but when that plastic horse bucks the things off, it frightens the living daylights out of me. Not to mention the fact that he looks like a hinny.'

'A what?' Lainey asked.

'A hinny is the offspring of a stallion and donkey,' Holly explained.

By ten o'clock Jacob said he'd better take Cynthia home. Reluctantly they pulled on their coats for the trek across the field in the snow.

'I could drive us in the tractor,' Scott offered. 'But I might take out the fence and the hen-house on the way. I'm a bit pissed.'

'The air will do us good,' Matt assured him.

The family waved them off, then went back into the house. Lainey hovered at the door, praying Matt would turn around. He did better than that: he ran back and kissed her. 'Merry Christmas, Lainey. Can I call over to see you tomorrow?'

'I'd love that.'

She found everyone in the kitchen putting the last of the glasses into the dishwasher.

'I'm going to stay in the spare room,' Sadie said. 'I'll see you all in the morning.'

Before she could move, though, Joey wheeled himself in and made an announcement: 'The money I get from this accident is going towards keeping Huntersbrook House in the family. My accident has made me realise that nothing is more important than having people who really care,' he said. 'I know this place is only bricks and mortar and we'd all make any place a home, given time, but we love Huntersbrook, and I know I won't be wasting my money by holding on to it.'

'Let's talk about this another time,' Holly said.

'We can and will,' Joey answered. 'But none of us wants this place to go so we'll work it out together. If the email I received the other day, with the estimated figure of what I stand to gain in compensation, is anything to go by, Huntersbrook House will stay in the Craig family for many years to come.'

'I'll go for that,' Lainey said. 'I could sell my apartment and put some money into the place too.'

'I haven't a bean but I'll gladly do all I can to help,' Pippa added.

'Let's discuss it over the next few days,' Paddy conceded. 'And now it's bedtime for us old fogeys at least,' he said, and put his arm around Holly.

'Night, everyone,' Holly said, as they moved en masse towards the stairs.

'Night, Skye, merry Christmas,' Joey said, hovering momentarily at his bedroom door.

Pippa picked up on his words from halfway up the stairs. 'Goodnight, Mary Ellen, goodnight, Jim-Bob,' she said, amid giggles.

'Shut up, Pippa, you hinny,' he shouted.

'I heard that!' Holly yelled, from the top of the house.

'Will you be able to manage?' Skye asked, as Joey manoeuvred his wheelchair through the door. 'I can help if you like.'

'I'd love that.'

They went in together and closed the door. When they kissed, Joey felt happier than he had for a long time.

On the top floor Holly and Paddy clung together as they mulled over the events of the day.

'That was the best Christmas ever,' she said, yawning.

'You say that every year. This time, though, I have to agree. We're blessed with the people we have in our lives.'

'I'm sorry I've been so awful lately,' Holly said. 'I've been terrified that everything we hold dear would go along with the house.'

'No matter where we end up, we've created a strong team, you and I.'

'I know that now.' Holly pulled him closer.

On the next floor down Lainey skipped around her bedroom reliving the kiss she and Matt had shared as they said goodnight on the doorstep.

There was a knock on her door. 'Can I come in?' Jules asked.

'Of course.'

'I was watching you today with Matt. You're smitten, aren't you?' Jules grinned.

'Was it that obvious?' Lainey was blushing.

'Maybe not, but I could tell . . .'

Pippa and Jay were planning their holiday.

'I can't believe we're going to the Seychelles,' she whispered. 'I'll have to start a holiday clothing page on my website.'

Epilogue

✳✳✳

St Stephen's Day dawned silently, and fresh snow blanketed the landscape.

'It looks like the largest Christmas cake in the world out there,' Holly said, propping her elbows on the windowsill. 'There won't be a hunt today. It'd be far too dangerous.'

'That mightn't be a bad thing,' Paddy said, stretching. 'We can relax and eat more!'

'You're a good man, Paddy, do you know that?' Holly turned to face him.

'If you say so. What brought that on?'

'You always look for the positive side of things. You try to bring the best out of every situation,' Holly mused. 'Even after Lainey was born and I had that awful post-natal depression you just stayed by my side.'

'Of course I did,' he said simply. 'I love you. Always have. Always will.'

'I know the past year hasn't been easy, with Mum gone and the financial problems. You never buckled, though. You're one in a million, Paddy.'

'You're not so bad yourself,' he said. 'Can you believe we're over thirty years married? That's a long time by any watch, but I reckon it's nearly a miracle by today's standards.'

When Holly got downstairs, her family and their friends were crowded around the open front door, whooping and shouting. 'What's up?' she asked.

'It's like a crazy blizzard out there!' Pippa called back.

'It's serious stuck-inside-for-a-week type snow,' Lainey added.

They pulled coats and boots over their pyjamas and ran outside.

'Snowman!' Paddy announced, as he joined them.

Hearing the commotion, Maggie came out of her room.

'Can you help me gather the accessories for the snowman?' Joey asked, as they met in the hall.

'Well, we need coal for the eyes and a carrot,' Maggie said. She pushed him in his chair to the kitchen.

'I think he should be well dressed,' Joey said, and picked up a forgotten party hat and a scarf.

None of them knew what the year ahead would bring. Life had a way of being unpredictable. But as long as they had one another, they were pretty certain they'd survive.